"JUST ADMIT YOU WERE WRONG. SURELY YOU'RE MAN ENOUGH TO DO THAT," PARIS SAID SOFTLY.

"I hardly think the respective length of our reproductive organs is relevant to this discussion," Cambridge replied directly into Paris's transceiver.

Paris rose from his bunk at the sound of approaching footsteps. The entrance to his cell was composed of a single metal door with a large transparent window—a sturdy one, Paris had already determined—set within a thick stone wall. Two guards appeared.

"Move to the corner and face the wall," one of them ordered.

Paris lifted his hands in a universal sign of compliance and did as he had been ordered. The prospect of allowing a pair of armed men into the cell and offering them his back to shoot was disquieting, but he really didn't have a choice in the matter.

"Are your prisoners offered legal counsel?" Paris asked as he moved toward the corner, sneaking one last look at his captors.

The voice that responded was cold enough to send ice pouring down his spine, but its familiarity had the opposite effect.

"I don't think that's going to be necessary."

STAR TREK VOYAGER®

A POCKET FULL OF LIES

KIRSTEN BEYER

Based on *Star Trek*®
created by Gene Roddenberry
and
Star Trek: Voyager
created by
Rick Berman & Michael Piller & Jeri Taylor

POCKET BOOKS
New York   London   Toronto   Sydney   New Delhi

Pocket Books
An Imprint of Simon & Schuster, Inc.
1230 Avenue of the Americas
New York, NY 10020

This book is a work of fiction. Any references to historical events, real people, or real places are used fictitiously. Other names, characters, places, and events are products of the author's imagination, and any resemblance to actual events or places or persons, living or dead, is entirely coincidental.

™, ®, and © 2016 by CBS Studios Inc. STAR TREK and related marks and logos are trademarks of CBS Studios Inc. All Rights Reserved.

This book is published by Pocket Books, an imprint of Simon & Schuster, Inc., under exclusive license from CBS Studios Inc.

All rights reserved, including the right to reproduce this book or portions thereof in any form whatsoever. For information, address Pocket Books Subsidiary Rights Department, 1230 Avenue of the Americas, New York, NY 10020.

First Pocket Books paperback edition February 2016

POCKET and colophon are registered trademarks of Simon & Schuster, Inc.

For information about special discounts for bulk purchases, please contact Simon & Schuster Special Sales at 1-866-506-1949 or business@simonandschuster.com.

The Simon & Schuster Speakers Bureau can bring authors to your live event. For more information or to book an event, contact the Simon & Schuster Speakers Bureau at 1-866-248-3049 or visit our website at www.simonspeakers.com.

Manufactured in the United States of America

10 9 8 7 6 5 4 3

ISBN 978-1-4767-9084-8
ISBN 978-1-4767-9085-5 (ebook)

"*Everything we see is a perspective, not the truth.*"

—Marcus Aurelius

"*The truth will set you free, but first it will make you miserable.*"

—Unknown

HISTORIAN'S NOTE

Admiral Kathryn Janeway leads the Full Circle fleet—*Voyager, Vesta, Galen,* and *Demeter*—on a mission of exploration in the Delta Quadrant. The landscape is quite different since a lone, lost *Starship Voyager* was trying to find her way home. The fleet is charged with discovering what has changed in the Delta Quadrant since *Voyager* was last here and the ultimate power in the quadrant, the Borg, departed.

This story begins in June and continues through July of 2382.

Prologue

And how is the most recent addition to our crew this morning?" Admiral Kathryn Janeway asked as she settled herself on the side of Commander B'Elanna Torres's bed and stared lovingly at the tiny face of the newborn boy sleeping soundly in his mother's arms.

"He's perfect," Commander Tom Paris replied from the other side of the bed. He stood beside Captain Chakotay, who had accompanied the fleet admiral to the Parises' quarters.

Torres glanced up at her husband. Tom had worn the same sleepy grin for the first thirty-six hours of his son's life. Their daughter, Miral, who was about to turn four in a few weeks, was curled up beside her mother, studying her brother's face and stealing shy peeks at those who had intruded into her family's sanctuary.

"He certainly looks that way," Janeway agreed.

"Would you like to hold him?" Torres asked.

"Absolutely," the admiral replied, smiling. Torres gently transferred the baby to Janeway's arms. He yawned as he settled himself in unfamiliar territory. "Hello, little one," she greeted him softly.

"Does he have a name yet?" Chakotay asked.

"Michael," Miral replied before Paris or his wife had a chance.

"Michael Owen," Torres added.

Janeway smiled broadly. "Named for his grandfather and great-grandfather. Those are some large boots to fill, young man. But don't worry. You've got plenty of time."

"What was great about my grandfather?" Miral asked.

Paris moved to sit across from Janeway and pulled his daughter onto his lap. "Your grandfather was Owen. You met him when you were too little to remember. *Owen's* father was Michael. Your grandfather's father is *your* great-grandfather."

The small ridges on Miral's forehead, testament to her Klingon heritage on B'Elanna's side, grew more pronounced as her eyebrows scrunched together. "But what was so great about him?"

Paris chuckled. "A lot. I'll tell you the whole story when we head to the park later this afternoon."

"Can we go now, Daddy?"

"Not yet, sweetie. We have company."

"Did I have this much company when I was born?" Miral asked.

"No, you had more," Torres replied.

"You were born on a very important day for all of us," Janeway said. This pleased Miral, who favored the admiral with a smile.

"The day we came home," Miral said.

"That's right."

"But why did we go home if we were just going to come back to the Delta Quadrant?" Miral asked.

"We came back so we could learn more about this part of our galaxy," Chakotay offered.

"You should have learned enough the first time," Miral suggested. All four of the adults laughed knowingly in response.

Janeway spared another long look at Michael before handing him back to Torres. "He's beautiful, B'Elanna. Congratulations, to all of you."

"Thank you, Admiral," Torres said.

"Seconded," Chakotay added. "I'm formally ordering you both to take as much time as you need before returning to duty. Harry's had plenty of practice filling in for Tom and I understand from Counselor Cambridge that Lieutenant Conlon will be officially reinstated this morning."

"How's Icheb doing?" Torres asked.

"As well as can be expected," Chakotay replied.

Torres wondered what that meant, but chose to let it pass. Michael was stirring and would no doubt require another meal momentarily.

"We'll let you get your rest," Janeway said, rising.

"Feel free to stop by whenever you like, Admiral," Torres said.

"You seem to be a natural at this. He screams his head off when Tom holds him."

"Already wise beyond his years," Chakotay teased.

"Clearly," Paris agreed.

"When are you going to have a baby?" Miral asked of Janeway.

A sudden, awkward hush descended. Torres broke it. "Miral, it's not polite to ask such personal questions."

"It's all right," Janeway assured her. "Babies are a wonderful gift, Miral, but not everybody chooses to have one. This is one challenge I intend to enjoy vicariously."

"What's vicar . . . vicarus . . . ?" Miral asked.

"I'll let your parents explain that one," Janeway replied with a wink at Paris.

Torres looked toward Chakotay and noted a brief flash of something . . . disappointment, perhaps, in his eyes. She hadn't slept more than two hours at a time in the last three days, so she might have imagined it. The captain moved quickly to join the admiral, stepping aside to allow her to leave the room before him.

When their visitors had gone Paris scooched Miral over and settled himself beside his daughter on the bed. He stared contentedly at his family. "Do you think . . . ?" Torres began. Tom's eyes were closing before she could finish her question.

Returning her gaze to her son's face, Torres said softly, "She doesn't know what she's missing, does she?"

1

STARSHIP GALEN

What were his exact words?" Seven demanded of Ensign Icheb.

The newly minted young officer paled, highlighting the irregular red blotches burning his cheeks. "Commander

O'Donnell said that I should not set foot in Lieutenant Elkins's engine room again without a direct order from Commander Torres or Admiral Janeway."

The Doctor lowered his head to hide his amusement.

"And did you report this to Commander Torres?" Seven continued, simultaneously shooting the Doctor a warning glance.

"Not yet," Icheb admitted.

"You should do so at once," Seven suggested.

"I was assigned to assist the commander. I do not believe she will find this evidence of my obvious inadequacy helpful," Icheb countered.

"Commander Torres is fine, Icheb," the Doctor interjected. "I was with her a few hours ago. She is understandably exhausted, but not yet buckling under the stress of the inevitable sleep-deprivation the next several days will bring."

"And she *did* order you to evaluate and rate the current operational efficiency of each fleet vessel's engineering department," Seven added. "She should know how those under her command are responding to your input."

"*They're* not the problem, Seven," Icheb insisted.

Seven took the padd that rested on the table next to Icheb's untouched breakfast plate and read silently for a few moments. When the Doctor had joined Seven and Icheb in *Galen*'s small mess hall for an early breakfast they'd had the room to themselves. The entrance of Lieutenants Benoit and Velth signaled that alpha shift was about to begin.

Icheb glanced toward *Galen*'s chief engineer, Benoit, who nodded in greeting toward the ensign.

Seven sighed, returning the padd to the table. "While it is true that Lieutenant Elkins might find strict adherence to Starfleet protocols tiresome, the inefficiencies you have highlighted here are all accurate." As she continued, the Doctor reached for the padd and began to peruse it. "Regulations apply to everyone, whether they believe they know better or not. Lieutenant Elkins's compliance is mandatory, not optional. And Commander O'Donnell should not prioritize placating the egos of those he supervises above requiring them to perform their duties appropriately."

"Six hundred nineteen?" the Doctor gasped.

Icheb's and Seven's heads instantly turned in unison toward the *Galen*'s holographic chief medical officer.

"You cited Elkins for six hundred nineteen violations?" the Doctor asked.

"Each violation contains a citation to the applicable regulation," Icheb noted.

"I see that," the Doctor said. "But Icheb, surely the years you just spent at Starfleet Academy acquainted you with the chasm that exists between humans and perfection. Did it not occur to you to prioritize your findings and perhaps present Chief Elkins with a series of more manageable recommendations?"

"While onerous, the requirements Starfleet places on engineers to constantly monitor every system under their purview are both necessary and attainable," Icheb replied. "Your Chief Benoit is proof of that. I found only twenty-six violations in his department and he accepted his review without question."

"*Galen* is even smaller than *Demeter*," the Doctor reminded the ensign, "and she hasn't seen near the action in recent months that Commander O'Donnell's ship has. Never mind the fact that Chief Benoit has access to dozens of highly specialized holographic engineers who are programmed to perform their duties to regulation specs and to do so without the need for rest or the inclination to complain when a task is mind-numbingly boring."

"Be that as it may," Seven said, "Icheb is performing an essential duty, and he should not be reprimanded for the failings of others."

"Seven, do you want Icheb to succeed at his first assignment with the fleet?" the Doctor asked.

Seven appeared momentarily stricken. "Of course I do."

"And have you heard him refer obliquely and directly to his perceived failures up to this point? He didn't ask us to meet him this morning to lie to him, or worse, to shift the blame for the challenges he is now facing onto others. He *knows* he is not living up to his or B'Elanna's expectations. *Our job* is to help him find a way to do that."

Seven sat back. "What do you suggest?"

"For Icheb to be able to perform his duties effectively, he must gain the confidence of those he will interact with on a daily basis. Otherwise, his ability to function as Commander Torres's personal aide will be severely limited." Turning toward Icheb with sincere compassion, the Doctor continued, "I know it is difficult. We could talk continuously for days and barely scratch the surface of the challenges I have faced over the years in establishing realistic expectations of our fellow officers and developing mutually respectful and productive relationships. But you don't have time for that. Commander Torres has just given birth. She needs you to function as her eyes and ears for the next several weeks as she recovers and sees to the needs of her family. Your job is to make her life easier and worry-free, not to nit-pick her subordinates into defiance."

"But—" Seven began.

"And *you,*" the Doctor continued, "do our young friend here no favors in suggesting that he is not, at least in part, responsible for creating discord. Being right is important. But that's not the only thing being asked of him anymore. He also needs to be sensitive to the feelings of his compatriots and to the reality that none of them are going to be willing to submit to the overly officious will of a green ensign. Learning does not end when one graduates, Icheb. The coursework changes, but the process continues."

"You are suggesting that I lower my expectations?" Icheb asked. "They are no more than I demand of myself."

"I am suggesting that you not use your abilities, or Seven's, as the only means of measuring performance. You were both *raised* by the Borg, a species that believed perfection was attainable. Those you are now supervising in Commander Torres's stead were not." After giving this a moment to sink in the Doctor asked, "How many of the violations you presented to Lieutenant Elkins would you consider critical to ship operations?"

Icheb looked to Seven before replying, "Twenty-three."

"The magnetic constrictor retuning . . ." Seven suggested.

"Twenty-two," Icheb allowed.

"Take a revised evaluation directly to Commander O'Donnell as soon as possible, highlighting only critical suggestions for improvement. Apologize for wasting Chief Elkins's valuable time and ask that the commander pass along your recommendations."

"And if Commander O'Donnell refuses?" Seven asked.

"He won't," the Doctor replied. "He's not questioning your position or authority, nor is he blindly defending his officer. He's testing you. This is how you pass that test."

"Is it your intention to give Icheb the same series of instructions in social skills you provided to me when I first came to *Voyager*?" Seven asked.

The Doctor's program paused momentarily as it attempted to access memories that no longer existed. The immediate chagrin on Seven's face indicated that this lapse had not gone unnoticed.

"Forgive me," Seven said quickly. "I was referring to a series of interactions that began on stardate 51652.3. You were attempting to assist me—"

"It's all right, Seven," the Doctor interrupted. Much as he was growing to treasure Seven's attempts to provide him with the data about their early years together that had been purged from his matrix in order to simultaneously rid it of a Seriareen consciousness determined to steal his holomatrix, this was not the time. "Icheb needs to get to work, and you have a meeting aboard the *Vesta* to attend, don't you?"

"I do."

"I believe the Doctor's suggestions are valid," Icheb said as he rose from his seat and collected his full dish of fresh fruit and utensils. "Thank you both."

"You are always welcome," Seven said. "Report back to me when you have spoken to Commander O'Donnell."

"I will," Icheb promised.

Seven followed Icheb with her eyes as he hurried toward the replicator to recycle his breakfast.

"He's going to be fine, Seven. It will take him some time to adjust. But he'll get the hang of it. You did."

"It is still difficult to watch someone for whom you care deeply struggle."

"Don't try to take it away from him," the Doctor suggested.

Seven turned back to face him. "I won't."

As they rose to begin their duties, the Doctor asked, "Did the social lessons you referred to actually help you become better acclimated to your life aboard *Voyager*?"

"They were extremely tiresome," Seven replied honestly. "And yes, they did."

The Doctor smiled. He could not help but believe that no matter how much data he had lost when Xolani had attacked his program, nothing essential had been taken from him.

VOYAGER

Lieutenant Nancy Conlon was impatient for this meeting to end. Counselor Hugh Cambridge was the last officer required to sign off on her complete recovery from the incident of a few weeks prior that had left her briefly dead and temporarily comatose. Cambridge and the Doctor had done exemplary work. She was more than ready to return to engineering and get on with the rest of her life.

Cambridge sat opposite her in a deep black chair, his long legs crossed at the knee with one swinging idly as he perused her updated medical records. He spoke without lifting his eyes from the padd. "I see you have already resumed your normal exercise regimen."

"The Doctor was concerned about some early motor weakness, but it has improved in the last several days," Conlon reported.

"And the headaches?"

"Gone. And I don't miss them."

Cambridge nodded as he continued to read.

"What's this about bananas?"

"Banana pancakes. B'Elanna introduced me to them a few months back and ever since I woke up I've been craving them. I was begging for them long before the Doctor rescinded my dietary restrictions. Even increasing my potassium supplements didn't help. Lieutenant Neol took pity on me and snuck me a serving. The Doctor was not pleased."

Cambridge chuckled. "I bet he wasn't." Finally setting the padd aside, the counselor looked up at his patient and said, "Which just leaves the most important question."

"Nothing," Conlon said simply.

"Still?"

Conlon shrugged. "I don't know what to tell you. The last thing I remember, I was in the main holodeck, reviewing the most recent access logs. The next thing I knew, Harry and B'Elanna were arguing over my bed."

Cambridge shook his head. "Obviously we have no baseline for a case like this. You are the only person on record who has ever survived Seriareen possession and the expulsion of that essence."

"All I had to do was die."

"And that doesn't bother you?"

"Given the alternative, no. Besides, I'm in good company: Lieutenant Kim, Admiral Janeway. The dead don't often stay that way on this ship, do they?"

"Some do," Cambridge replied. Conlon detected a faint note of genuine regret from him. "Of course *your* death took place under medical supervision. You were revived the moment the Doctor could confirm that Xolani had left your body."

"Isn't it a good thing that I don't remember? Yes, the *idea* of it is traumatic to think about, but it's almost like it happened to somebody else."

"Except that it didn't. You and I have talked at some length about how your refusal to fully process some of your past experiences left you nearly paralyzed in the face of overwhelming tragedy."

"And I agreed with you and decided to do that work here."

"I would have thought this incident might have set you back a bit, perhaps created a certain amount of anxiety at the reality of your own vulnerability."

"I know how lucky I am, Counselor. I've come to really love my life here on *Voyager* and the people I serve with. I'm trying to stay focused on the positive things that fall within my control."

"A good strategy," Cambridge agreed. "*But*, and this is a big *but*, I would not be the least bit surprised if in the future your subconscious finds ways to force this trauma into your conscious mind. I want to see you on a weekly basis, just to check in. I want to hear about any unusual dreams, anxiety, anything at all that just feels off. It's possible you may live the rest of your life without the memory of a few days that anyone would be glad to forget. It's just too early for me to believe that will happen."

"Works for me," Conlon agreed.

"Very well, Lieutenant," Cambridge said, rising from his chair. "It's time for you to get back to work."

Conlon smiled in genuine relief. "Yes, it is, sir."

STARSHIP VESTA

Captain Regina Farkas stared across the table at Commander Liam O'Donnell, *Demeter*'s captain and one of the Federation's most accomplished botanical geneticists. His hair had begun its retreat from his forehead years earlier and the dark brown tufts left above his ears and circling the back of his head were generously flecked with gray. His eyes, however, danced merrily when they met hers. He seemed to be in a good mood. This was rare in Farkas's experience, but enjoyable. It lent an air of youth and vitality to O'Donnell.

"Commander, you asked for this meeting," Admiral Janeway reminded him from her place at the head of the table. Captain Chakotay was seated at the admiral's right hand, the *Galen*'s Commander Clarissa Glenn at her left.

"I did," O'Donnell agreed. "I was hoping Seven would join us before we began."

On cue, the doors to the *Vesta*'s large briefing room slid open and Seven entered.

"I apologize for my tardiness," the statuesque mission specialist said, moving briskly to the empty chair beside O'Donnell.

"It's all right," Janeway assured Seven. "We're just getting started."

"If you would turn your attention to the data now appearing on your personal screens," O'Donnell began as the small interfaces imbedded in front of each seat at the conference table were activated—a design standard to the *Vesta*-class ships—"you will find a list of several species that were added to our database during our most recent visit to New Talax."

"Ambassador Neelix has been busy," Farkas noted.

"Thankfully for us, he takes his role as the Federation's ambassador to the Delta Quadrant quite seriously," the admiral said.

"And Neelix has no qualms about seeking far and wide for new trading partners," Chakotay added. "His latest report offers intelligence on several species tens of thousands of light years from New Talax."

"Has he made contact with these species?" Seven asked.

"Not so far. But he offers his trademark hospitality to everyone who comes in range of New Talax and as a result, he hears all sorts of fascinating rumors."

"I'm intrigued by several entries here," O'Donnell said, refocusing their attention, "but the one I'm most curious about are the Nihydron. They're referenced in *Voyager*'s database, although apparently you never made contact with them during your first visit."

Admiral Janeway was already cross-referencing the entry on her personal screen. "They were grouped with a few other species, including the Rilnar, Zahl, Krenim and the Mawasi whose territory fell within an area of disputed space."

"It's almost hard to believe we managed to avoid getting ourselves into the middle of that," Chakotay quipped.

Admiral Janeway shot him a good-natured smirk as O'Donnell asked, "Did the Borg ever run across them?"

"Species 1184," Seven replied. "The Nihydron are humanoids with well-developed frontal lobes. They did not make particularly good drones."

"I like them already," Glenn said.

"According to Neelix's report, they don't have a homeworld, but operate from a number of small, well-hidden bases. The reputation they have gained for possessing critical data that covers vast swaths of the Delta Quadrant suggests that they have developed some form of propulsion similar to our slipstream drives."

"It's also possible that they, like some of their neighbors, have discovered ways to effectively utilize the Seriareen's subspace tunnels," Chakotay suggested.

"Either way, they are extensive data collectors," O'Donnell continued. "Neelix suggested that they would likely have the best information available on any new developments in the several sectors they explore."

"Those sectors fall very near the borders of the next area of former Borg space we're scheduled to investigate," Janeway observed.

"It is doubtful the Nihydron will freely share any intelligence they have gained," Seven said.

"Why?" Farkas asked.

"Like many collectors, they prize the accumulation of data for their own purposes. They are excellent at evading detection when it suits them, one of many reasons their entire species was not completely assimilated."

"Perhaps," Farkas agreed, "but our fleet just spent months exploring the Confederacy of the Worlds of the First Quadrant and making inroads with the Devore, the Turei, the Vaadwaur, and the Voth, *collecting* a great deal of useful intelligence of our own." She caught an approving glance from O'Donnell. Clearly, they were already thinking along similar lines.

"They also might be curious to know what became of the Borg," Chakotay interjected. "Now that the Confederacy and the former *Kinara* allies have learned the fate of the Collective and of the Caeliar, some of them are likely sharing that information. We'd be offering the Nihydron direct access to the original source."

"I'm inclined to agree," Janeway said. "But this is a first contact with which we will need to proceed very carefully."

"How so?" Farkas asked.

"If four fleet vessels enter their territory at once, we could be perceived as a threat," Janeway replied. "Depending upon their capabilities, the Nihydron could make it very difficult for us to find them. I don't want to waste a lot of time on this."

"What do you suggest, Admiral?" Chakotay asked.

Janeway locked eyes with O'Donnell. "This was your idea, Commander. The entire fleet will accompany you to the borders of Nihydron territory, but I think I'll send *Demeter* in first to attempt to draw them out."

Uncertainty flashed briefly across O'Donnell's face. He quickly squared his shoulders, obviously accepting the admiral's challenge.

"How best might we do that?" O'Donnell asked.

"I'm sure you'll think of something, Commander," Janeway replied. "With Captain Chakotay's permission, I'd like Counselor Cambridge to join you as a first-contact specialist."

"I think we can spare him for a bit," Chakotay agreed.

"Training wheels, Admiral?" O'Donnell asked pointedly.

"Additional resources," Janeway clarified.

Farkas sat back in her chair, crossing her arms and grinning at O'Donnell's discomfort. Traditionally, a mission like this would be handled by one of the fleet's larger ships: the *Vesta* or *Voyager. Demeter*'s function with the exploratory group was to collect samples of unique botanical life-forms, to consult with species requiring their expertise, and to provide "home-grown" food when possible to supplement the fleet's replicated fare. O'Donnell had already expanded on those parameters, as when the fleet had encountered the Children of the Storm, and occasionally because it suited the commander's personal whims. Farkas knew O'Donnell was astute, but nursed a propensity toward rashness. He was also the last man anyone would call a "people person." It obviously hadn't taken Admiral Janeway long to realize this. Clearly, she intended to push the commander to hone his diplomatic skills to match his technical abilities.

"Very well, Admiral," O'Donnell said, "I'll need two hours to confer with Commander Fife before we depart."

Janeway nodded, signaling that the briefing had ended. "You should treat the Nihydron with the same delicacy you reserve for your most temperamental botanical specimens," she suggested.

"Don't worry," O'Donnell said. "I'm not planning on kidnapping their commanding officer, at least not right away."

"This should be interesting," Chakotay offered.

"I assume we'll be monitoring *Demeter*'s communications," Farkas asked of Janeway.

The admiral nodded. "Just in case. Commander O'Donnell will do us all proud." With a sharp nod she departed, leaving the rest of the fleet's commanding officers to their own devices. O'Donnell started to follow her out, but paused as Farkas said, "The earliest *Demeter* might make contact would be nineteen hundred hours. Psilakis will have *Vesta*'s bridge."

"Lieutenant Kim has *Voyager*'s third watch tonight," Chakotay noted.

"I was planning to turn in a little early, but in this case . . ." Glenn began, smiling broadly at Commander O'Donnell.

"My ready room, eighteen forty-five," Farkas offered, winking at *Demeter*'s captain, "And bring your own popcorn."

O'Donnell considered his fellow captains, sighed deeply, and shook his head, leaving the briefing room without further comment.

The moment the doors to the briefing room slid open, Ensign Icheb straightened his posture, shifting his weight from the bulkhead where it had rested while he waited.

Admiral Janeway's face shifted from concern to surprise the moment she saw him. "Ensign," she said warmly.

"Good morning, Admiral," Icheb greeted her, keeping his eyes forward.

Janeway paused momentarily. "At ease, Icheb."

He complied, widening his stance while still refusing to meet her eyes.

"What brings you to the *Vesta* this morning?" Janeway inquired.

"I have a report to present to Commander O'Donnell before I begin my efficiency evaluation of Lieutenant Bryce and *Vesta*'s engineering department."

"Excellent," Janeway said. "I know Commander Torres was pleased when you were assigned to assist her. I am too. It's wonderful to have you with us again."

"Thank you, Admiral."

Janeway started to say more, but turned as O'Donnell stormed out of the briefing room. He barely took note of either of them as he passed until Icheb called out, "A moment, please, Commander."

O'Donnell halted and turning back only slightly, nodded to Icheb.

"Carry on," Janeway said, and departed down the hall in the opposite direction.

Icheb moved toward O'Donnell, who resumed walking, forcing the ensign to quicken his steps to keep pace.

"I have revised my efficiency report for Lieutenant Elkins, Commander, and with your permission would like to present it to him," Icheb said.

O'Donnell did not reply, nor did he look at Icheb, but he did extend a hand and accept the padd Icheb offered. As both stopped to wait for the turbolift, he perused the new report quickly.

The doors to the lift slid open. O'Donnell stepped in, handing the padd back to Icheb.

"May I—" Icheb began.

"Try again," O'Donnell said as the doors slid shut.

Deflated, but not defeated, Icheb allowed his shoulders to sag.

Try again? Icheb had been so certain that the Doctor's advice would prove helpful in resolving this situation. After serious consideration he had actually shortened the list to include only nineteen areas of concern. *Where had he gone wrong?*

As no immediate answer was forthcoming, Icheb lifted his chin, swallowed his embarrassment, and made his way to *Vesta*'s engine room.

VOYAGER

Lieutenant Harry Kim, *Voyager*'s chief of security, caught up with Lieutenant Conlon just before she reached the doors to main engineering. "Lieutenant," he greeted her crisply.

"Lieutenant," she snapped back.

"Back on duty?"

"Good as new," she replied with a smile.

Kim quickly checked the hall and as they were alone, stepped into her personal space. Conlon held her ground, gazing mischievously into his eyes. Their lips had almost touched when Conlon said, "Why aren't you on the bridge, Lieutenant?"

"I got a call from Neol," Kim replied hungrily. "It sounded urgent."

"Why?" Conlon demanded, stepping back and immediately shifting gears. "What's the problem?"

The doors to engineering slid open and two of Conlon's ensigns stepped through them, their uniforms covered in a thick, viscous fluid. Looking past them, Conlon noted that the engine room was a flurry of tense activity.

"Lieutenant Conlon," Ensign Mirk said with relief. "Please tell me you're back on duty."

"I am. Why are you two covered in lubricant?" Conlon asked.

"Ensign Icheb," Ensign Worlin replied through gritted teeth.

"Get cleaned up and back here as soon as possible," Conlon ordered. "And try not to track too much of that down the hall. That's freshly replicated floor covering you're walking on."

"Yes, sir," they replied in miserable unison.

Conlon spared a knowing glance toward Kim. "Whatever this is, I'll handle it," she assured him.

"I think you're going to have your hands full today."

"Shall we pick up where we left off a little later?" she asked.

"I have Tom's watch for the first half of beta shift," Kim replied. "I get four whole hours to myself before taking command during gamma shift."

Conlon nodded, obviously disappointed. "Oh, well in that case . . ."

"Go," Kim ordered. He watched her return to her engine room with a frustrated sigh.

The number of bodies present suggested to Conlon that most of gamma shift had stayed on after hours. Two panels of deck plating lay near the entrance, along with several large coils of conduit. A variety of standard tools were scattered on every work surface. A large case of new isolinear chips lay open and within reach of Ensign Amiri, whose head was buried beneath the main diagnostic terminal. The air was thick with sweat and a faint tinge of plasma. Ensign Charvet stood on a portable lift taking readings from the magnetic constrictors near the top of the warp core. Lieutenant Saracen was analyzing a set of benamite crystals, newly removed from the slipstream portion of the assembly.

It looked like half of engineering was in the process of being repaired or replaced.

Conlon found Lieutenant Neol, one of her slipstream specialists, on his hands and knees about to enter an access port behind the secondary data terminals.

"Neol," Conlon said, bending down and keeping her voice low.

The officer jerked his head back. It impacted the edge of the portal with a soft thud.

"Ow," Neol said.

"Careful," Conlon ordered as she helped to guide him safely back. When he was seated before her, gingerly rubbing his pale blue scalp, Conlon said, "I appreciate you assuming command in my absence, but there's a difference between taking initiative and destroying engineering."

"It's not my fault," Neol pleaded. Grabbing a padd from a nearby stack he called up a file and handed the device to Conlon. "Four days ago Ensign Icheb presented us with his efficiency evaluation. He found three hundred sixty-six protocol violations and ordered us to begin rectifying them immediately."

"On whose authority?" Conlon demanded.

"Commander Torres's, I presumed," Neol admitted.

Conlon reviewed the padd quickly, noting that more than half of the issues Icheb had cited could only be safely addressed when a ship was docked at a space station or port. A handful related to standard repairs and maintenance Conlon already had on her to-do list. The rest were, at best, minor infractions.

Shaking her head, Conlon extended a hand to help Neol to his feet. Lifting her voice she called out, "Engineers, attention."

The room quickly fell silent.

"Finish your scans, note your readings, and then put this room back in working order immediately. No one, I repeat, *no one* is to continue on any projects designed to improve our efficiency rating. I'm back, and effective immediately, you will take orders only from me. Understood?"

Conlon's ears stung from the loud whoops and cheers that greeted her announcement.

2

STARSHIP DEMETER

Counselor Hugh Cambridge had been standing beside the seat positioned in the center of *Demeter*'s claustrophobic bridge for what felt like his entire life. It was unseemly for a senior officer to yawn while on duty. It was growing more challenging by the minute for Cambridge to stifle that impulse.

For the better part of the last six hours he had watched as Ensign Vincent and Lieutenant Url, the ship's operations and tactical officers, respectively, searched for any sign of the Nihydron. This system was the one that Neelix said held one of their larger bases. It featured four planets orbiting a young G-type star, none of which were suitable for habitation. The single gas giant farthest from the sun had an unusual atmospheric composition. A crewman named Brill had joined Commander Fife at the rear science station. The two were discussing their readings in hushed tones.

At least they appeared to be enjoying themselves. Cambridge felt he had been banished to one of the lower levels of Dante's hell. Commander O'Donnell did not seem to share his frustration.

"Any response to our friendship greetings?" O'Donnell asked.

"No, sir," Vincent replied. "I have expanded the transmission to include several frequencies in the outer bands and increased the signal's power to the broadest possible range."

"And still, they ignore us," O'Donnell said.

"Assuming they're out there at all," Cambridge noted.

"They are."

"You can't possibly know that."

"Unless Mister Neelix's intelligence was in error, they're here. We've already ruled out the terrestrial planets. I'm guessing they're hiding inside that gas giant's outer atmosphere."

"Why?"

"Because that's where I would hide if I were them."

"Do you have any actual data to support this guess?"

"Atlee?" O'Donnell asked.

"We are picking up faint, highly localized tachyons. They could be residue, but more likely they are evidence of phase variance," *Demeter*'s XO, Lieutenant Commander Atlee Fife, replied.

Cambridge turned a blank face to O'Donnell.

"A gas giant can offer some natural camouflage," O'Donnell translated. "The deeper you go into the atmosphere, the easier it is to flummox sensors. It's also harder to survive for any length of time, as the atmospheric composition will degrade most alloys common to hull plating fairly rapidly. But if the Nihydron live here, or spend most of their time here, they've solved that, probably with some version of multi-phasic shielding. Calibrated properly, shields like that would render them virtually invisible and bleed highly localized tachyons."

"How do we flush them out?"

O'Donnell shrugged. "It's a tough call. I don't want to force their hand."

"Because despite all previous evidence to the contrary, you have the patience of a saint?" Cambridge asked.

"Because it is an act of unwarranted aggression," O'Donnell corrected him. "It's rude to strip someone of their defenses when they haven't demonstrated any hostile tendencies toward you. I'd rather not get off on the wrong foot with these people, especially since we hope to enter into a meaningful dialogue with them."

"Instead of transmitting our standard friendship greetings, why don't we sweeten the pot?" Cambridge suggested.

O'Donnell smiled. "That's my instinct as well. Atlee, are you ready to do the thing?"

"Aye, sir," Fife replied cheerily. "Ensign Vincent, launch the probe."

After a few silent moments Vincent confirmed the launch.

"The *thing*?" Cambridge finally asked. "Is that the technical term?"

A fleeting smile graced O'Donnell's lips. "We've loaded that probe with data on some of our most recent contacts in the Delta Quadrant. Not the whole story, mind you, and nothing that would compromise our security, just enough to pique their curiosity. It will transmit that data on a number of likely bands from within the gas giant's atmosphere to guarantee the best possible signal strength. If the Nihydron take the bait, we should be in contact with them in the next few minutes."

Cambridge considered this. Finally he said, "You've had that probe ready to launch since when?"

"A few hours before we entered the system."

"And you've been waiting all this time to launch it because . . . ?"

"We've taken some truly spectacular readings of this area over the last few hours and added a great deal of valuable information about this sector to our astrometrics databases," O'Donnell said, feigning innocence.

"You did this on purpose," Cambridge realized. "You were waiting for your fellow captains to lose interest in observing the proceedings, weren't you?"

"That's possible."

Had he not been so exhausted, Cambridge would have laughed. When Chakotay had briefed him on this away mission he had noted that most of the fleet's captains intended to watch O'Donnell's contact attempt from the *Vesta*. By now, no doubt all of them had retired for the evening.

"You're that shy?" Cambridge asked.

"Not really. At some point, I'm going to have to develop the self-confidence to initiate diplomatic relations with new species all by myself. No time like the present, right?" When Cambridge did not reply immediately, he added, "You look weary, Counselor. Can we get you a chair?"

"No, thank you, sir."

Vincent interrupted, "Captain, we are receiving a response to the probe's transmission. A Nihydron shuttle will clear the atmosphere and make orbit within the next two hours."

"Imagine that," O'Donnell said. "Good work, everyone."

Cambridge sighed. "With your permission, sir, I think I'll retire to that supply closet Mister Fife assigned me for a short nap. I'd appreciate it if you'd wake me when the Nihydron make contact."

"You don't want to stick around? After all, I could still screw this up between now and then."

Cambridge chuckled. "I should live so long."

"Sleep well, Counselor."

VOYAGER

Doctor Sharak, *Voyager's* CMO and the first Tamarian to ever serve in Starfleet, had returned to the Delta Quadrant only a few weeks earlier. To his surprise, it had felt like coming home. He had left the planet of his birth, his family, and his friends for Earth to learn Standard and help further relations between the Children of Tama and the Federation. He had served with the Full Circle Fleet for a year. His heart would long for the golden plains and bright constellations burning above Sigma Tama IV to the end of his days. But, he had built new relationships, particularly with Miss Seven and Commander Paris, that felt as essential and significant as those he enjoyed with his Tamarian kin.

After dispatching a letter to Lieutenant Commander Samantha Wildman and her family on Ktaria, Sharak had begun his review of the crew's medical issues that had arisen during his absence. He had taken special care with the file of Lieutenant Conlon. She had just endured a serious physical trauma involving alien possession of her body. Initially she had been treated by the *Galen's* CMO, the Doctor, formally an emergency medical hologram on *Voyager*. Nancy Conlon was once again Sharak's responsibility, and while he marveled at the speed of her recovery, there were a number of recent test results that concerned him.

He had contacted the Doctor before coming on duty this morning. Sharak was having some difficulty re-acclimating to starship time after his lengthy stay on Earth and often woke well before the start of alpha shift. The Doctor did not require sleep and had been happy to discuss Sharak's concerns about Conlon.

"You don't consider the slight elevation in AFP levels cause for alarm?" Sharak asked.

"They would be, were she still a child," the Doctor replied.

"They might indicate any number of potential immunological disorders. But the lieutenant has enjoyed excellent physical health her entire life."

"There is nothing in your treatment regimen that might have caused the elevation. And some of her immunoglobulins and lymphocytes remain low."

"They have almost returned to normal levels," the Doctor countered, *"and no doubt will in the next several weeks. I can't explain yet why the transfer of Xolani's essence into Lieutenant Conlon prompted such a severe immunological response, but it's not really surprising. Her body appears to have marshaled every available defense against the invading consciousness. I intend to study this further. But I do not believe it is cause for concern at this time."*

Sharak nodded. "I will, of course, continue to monitor her and advise you of any further issues."

"I would appreciate that," the Doctor said. *"Galen out."*

Sharak terminated the contact and immediately sent out another transmission to the *Vesta*. Within a few minutes, the face of Doctor El'nor Sal, a human woman in her eighties, appeared on the screen.

"Good morning, Doctor Sal," Sharak greeted her.

"If you say so," Sal replied.

"There is a notation in our database about a contagion first encountered by Starfleet on Stardate 26484."

"Is this a quiz, Doctor?" Sal asked.

"No," Sharak replied. "I would not trouble you except that the virus was first identified by you when you served aboard the *Thetis*."

Sal's face hardened visibly. For the briefest of moments, her eyes betrayed her, allowing Sharak to glimpse an old wound that had clearly never properly healed.

"You're talking about Vega Nine?"

"The virus in question is listed as Vegarus Axilataria—"

"Vega Nine for short."

"It attacked multiple systems, but began by damaging the patient's DNA, did it not?" Sharak asked.

"Vega Nine is the most complex DNA damage repair syndrome I've ever seen, and the only one like it transmitted virally rather than inherited. It was caused by an insect bite. Its effects were horrific. Patients lost mobility, vision, their immune response. It opened the door to a variety of secondary infections. Twenty-three officers died before we cured the damn thing." Sal paused, shaking off the memories. *"Why?"*

"Would it be possible for you to forward me all of your records on Vega Nine?"

"Yes. But why?"

"Research."

"For whom?"

"For my own edification."

"Doctor, we eradicated every known source of Vega Nine thirty years ago."

"I know. I am not suggesting that we have encountered a new strain. I am interested in learning more about your methodology."

"Very well," Sal said. *"I'll get you those records right away. Do yourself a favor. Read them on an empty stomach."*

"I will," Sharak said.

VESTA

Ensign Icheb had spent most of the previous afternoon observing Lieutenant Phinnegan Bryce at work. His second meeting with Commander O'Donnell had shaken him, and he had not yet devised a new approach to the problem. He hoped that observing Lieutenant Bryce might prove helpful.

Thus far it had been interesting. Bryce was one of the youngest chief engineers Icheb had ever encountered. His manner was so relaxed it belied the vigorous intellect at work. Bryce was regularly several steps ahead of those he commanded, but he never flaunted his intellectual capacity. He listened attentively to his engineers' suggestions, possessed enviable amounts of patience, and accepted bad news with grace and good cheer. His crew seemed to genuinely enjoy serving with him.

Bryce was running engineering for a vessel only recently refitted that had yet to take any serious damage during combat. Like Lieutenants Conlon and Elkins, *Vesta*'s chief clearly did not take to heart many of Starfleet's regulations regarding routine maintenance. Icheb had found over a hundred efficiency citations in just a few hours. By this day's end, he would likely have noted twice that many. The thought of presenting these flaws to Bryce turned Icheb's stomach.

Which was ridiculous.

Icheb had a duty to perform. He did Bryce no favors by ignoring his lapses. Commander Torres was counting on him.

But a small voice buried deep in Icheb's subconscious insisted strenuously every time the ensign noted another transgression that he tread lightly with Bryce. Icheb could not precisely name the hesitation, or the odd and intense emotional responses observing Bryce conjured within him. He only knew that even after a few hours, he liked Bryce very much. Here was a fellow officer not that much older than himself, one whose manner quickly gained the confidence and respect of those around him. While Icheb doubted his ability to emulate Bryce, he certainly hoped to eventually share a similar rapport with those he supervised.

Icheb knew it was wrong for him to worry about offending or injuring Bryce. Still, his failure to make any progress with Commander O'Donnell coupled with his growing admiration for Bryce immobilized the ensign.

VOYAGER

Lieutenant Harry Kim was exhausted by the time he stumbled into his quarters an hour before gamma shift ended. Commander Paris, who was not going to be sleeping regular hours for several days to come, had relieved him two hours before his watch was to end, and after managing only a short nap during beta shift, Kim was happy to accept Tom's offer to turn in early.

Kim didn't even bother to raise the lighting in his cabin. Instead, he moved directly to the 'fresher, took the briefest sonic shower in history, and quickly donned his preferred nightwear, shorts and a tank top, before slipping into his rack. He reached automatically for the sleeping mask he wore to eliminate any ambient starlight that might disturb his rest. He had barely settled it into place and released a deep sigh when he was startled by a faint motion to his left.

"What the . . . ?" he began as a warm hand grazed his cheek.

"Shhh," a soft, feminine voice ordered.

Kim might have argued were it not for the fact that his nose quickly identified his companion. This unique combination of wildflowers and spice belonged to Nancy Conlon.

He immediately lifted a hand to remove the mask, but Nancy simultaneously kissed his cheek softly while taking that hand and placing it somewhere infinitely more pleasant.

"Leave it," she whispered.

Harry Kim had imagined this moment, or one like it, for a long time. He and Nancy had engaged in their fair share of explorations, but theirs had been a slow dance, interrupted by duty and limited by their mutual desire to proceed slowly.

Apparently that part of their relationship was now over. Kim didn't mind, but part of him would have enjoyed seeing her face. That imperative vanished in an overwhelming rush of sensations too intoxicating to ignore as Nancy's hands and lips began to move over his body.

"Don't you want to . . . ?" Kim began.

The moment he spoke, Nancy paused. Kim cursed himself silently for his obvious error.

"Harry," she finally said. "I have to be on duty in two hours. You want to spend that time talking?"

It wasn't a difficult question.

"No."

VESTA

Kathryn Janeway stood in the *Vesta*'s briefing room with Captains Farkas and Chakotay, Commander Glenn, and Seven.

Her personal aide, Lieutenant Decan, was already seated at the large table. The admiral approved of Farkas's choice to remove two of the three smaller conference tables the room usually held. The third had been pushed to the far wall and generously heaped with several plates of appetizers Doctor Sal had confirmed would be compatible with the Nihydron's digestive systems.

Janeway had opted to forgo the formality of full dress uniforms for this combined reception and negotiation. In addition to transmitting all of the sensor logs *Demeter* had already compiled about the Nihydron during their initial encounter, Commander O'Donnell and Counselor Cambridge had assured the admiral that their guests did not prefer ceremony.

Chakotay came to her side and faced her with a knowing smile. "Nervous?"

"Excited," she replied.

"If the Nihydron know as much about local politics as Neelix's report suggested, this could be a long day."

"I'm just glad we managed to contact them."

"Did you ever find out why it took O'Donnell so long to draw them out?"

"He followed all of our standard protocols," Janeway replied, then added, "But according to Counselor Cambridge, the commander might have extended the process a bit for the benefit of his fellow captains."

"Admiral?"

A long look into the admiral's steel blue eyes brought a touch of chagrin to Chakotay's face.

"We were just curious," he finally offered.

"You, Farkas, and Glenn?"

Chakotay nodded.

"Why wasn't *I* invited to that party?" Janeway asked with mock disappointment.

Before Chakotay could answer, the doors to the briefing room opened. O'Donnell and Cambridge led a delegation of three humanoid aliens inside, each wearing variations of the Nihydron uniform: deep brown suits with long overcoats and wide, bright-orange belts. Clusters of small colored stones covered the long sleeves of each. According to Cambridge, the number and arrangement of the stones indicated rank.

Seven had reported that the Nihydron possessed well-developed frontal lobes. She had not exaggerated. Their waxy flesh was a deep rouge color, and their small translucent eyes, wide noses, and thin-lipped mouths were overshadowed by two large, rounded protrusions where a human's forehead would be. Their skulls likely held more than twice the gray matter of anyone else present. They stood at least half a meter shorter than an average human. For once, Janeway and Farkas would not be the shortest people in the room.

The group ambled toward the fleet commander. Cambridge and O'Donnell continued whatever conversation had likely begun in the transporter room. The brief moment she'd had to observe them as they entered suggested that the Nihydron were already quite comfortable with O'Donnell and Cambridge. They listened attentively to Cambridge until the leader of the three aliens caught sight of the admiral and stopped short. This created a slight traffic jam for those behind him, but they quickly adjusted.

"Admiral Kathryn Janeway, it is my honor to introduce you to *Adatoir* Tesh, and his diplomatic advisors, *Bedtens* Yil and Gral," Commander O'Donnell said warmly.

"It is my pleasure to meet all of you and to welcome you aboard the Federation *Starship Vesta*," Janeway said, matching O'Donnell's tone. When the three Nihydron continued to stare, almost rudely, at Janeway, the admiral attempted to cover. "Permit me to introduce the other commanders of our exploratory fleet, Captain Regina Farkas of the *Vesta,* Captain Chakotay of *Voyager,* and Commander Glenn of the *Galen.* Seven is one of the fleet's mission specialists, and Lieutenant Decan is my diplomatic aide."

Tesh turned sharply toward O'Donnell, who stood at his left hand. "Is this meant to be a form of amusement?" he asked without moving his lips. Janeway was startled by the distant, tinny sound of Tesh's voice.

When Yil spoke from behind his leader, the admiral realized that their "voices" were reverberating through some sort of voder, a distinct small set of silver stones set in the base of the Nihydron's necks that Janeway had initially assumed were merely decorative. "A joke, perhaps, *Adatoir*?"

O'Donnell and Cambridge shared a brief glance of consternation.

"Begging your pardon, *Adatoir*," Janeway said quickly, "no insult or attempt to humiliate your delegation is intended."

"We have, of course, collected limited data about you and your Federation, Admiral," Tesh said sternly, "travelers from a distant quadrant who say they come in peace to explore space."

Gral spoke for the first time, the slightly higher pitch of his "voice" communicating fear. "It has been reported that the Federation travelers recruit natives of this quadrant as guides."

"And make them their leaders?" Tesh asked dubiously.

Finally Janeway stepped in. "You have us at a disadvantage, sirs," she said kindly. "Several years ago, the ship I commanded, the Federation *Starship Voyager*, was brought to the Delta Quadrant by a Nacene we came to know as the Caretaker. Over the course of seven years, we encountered many local species on our way home. We were joined, from time to time, by a few natives of this quadrant. Seven is one such individual."

"Is she not human?" Yil asked.

"She is, but when we first met her, she was a member of the Borg Collective," Janeway clarified.

All three Nihydron looked in unison toward Seven, who inclined her head in greeting. "*Voyager*'s crew freed me from the Borg, allowing me to reclaim my humanity," she said, radically simplifying the story.

"It has been theorized that the *denzit* was captured. Her heritage was never established, but she is clearly not Rilnar," Gral offered.

"The *denzit*?" Chakotay asked.

Tesh returned his cold gaze to Janeway. "You have abandoned the Rilnar, then?"

Janeway swallowed her growing frustration. "Forgive me, *Adatoir* Tesh. Neither I, nor my crew, understand what you are suggesting. We have never met the Rilnar, although we have heard of them. All of the individuals present here today, including Seven, were born in Federation space and all have served with Starfleet for several years."

"An illusion?" Yil asked of Gral.

"The resemblance is too striking," Gral replied.

"*Adatoir*," O'Donnell interjected, "as I told you, we sought out the Nihydron to help us better understand the Delta Quadrant. Can you assist us by explaining your obvious surprise and discomfort in meeting our fleet commander?"

"Do you possess multidimensional visual rendering technology?" Tesh asked.

O'Donnell turned to Decan.

"We do, sir," the lieutenant replied. "The controls are embedded in this surface," he added, gesturing to the conference table.

"May I?" Tesh asked.

"Of course," Janeway replied.

Tesh moved almost furtively to stand beside Decan, pausing briefly to stare at the lieutenant's pointed ears, a gift of his Vulcan heritage. Tesh then inhaled deeply and placed both of his hands flat on the table. For a moment they moved randomly, as if searching for something. Finally they settled over one of the inactive displays and the *adatoir*'s eyes blackened. A few moments later, a grainy holographic image appeared in the center of the table, that of a woman's head and shoulders. What could be seen of her uniform was unidentifiable.

Her face, however, was eerily familiar.

Yil stepped forward to explain. "Since long before the Nihydron entered the void between stars, the Rilnar and the Zahl have fought to control Sormana."

"What is Sormana?" Cambridge asked.

"Not what, *where*," Yil replied.

Behind the image of the woman, an orange starscape appeared. One system was enlarged and a single planet magnified again.

Yil continued. "Sormana is the third planet of six orbiting a sub-novan yellow star aged approximately five billion years. Eighty percent of its surface is composed of water. Its topography and resources are consistent with several similar terrestrial worlds and its atmospheric parameters make it suitable for habitation by series-eight carbon-based life-forms. There is nothing exceptional about Sormana apart from the fact that both the Rilnar and the Zahl originated there. They have waged sustained conflict for thousands of years without either side achieving its goal of driving the other from the planet.

"Many suspected that a Zahl victory was inevitable and imminent. That changed three rotations ago when *this* alien female was elevated to the position of *denzit*, or supreme Rilnar commander. Since her ascension, the Rilnar have gained significant ground against the Zahl. She is credited with reversing Rilnar fortunes and is known for her decisiveness, cunning, and tactical brilliance."

The image floating above the table flared slightly as Tesh's eyes again became translucent and met Admiral Janeway's. "You now understand the source of our confusion?" he asked.

Janeway did. As Yil had related the history of Sormana, she had listened as attentively as possible, despite the fact that her focus had been entirely captivated by the image of the face Tesh had projected for them.

Her face.

The admiral's first thought was that this must be an unsettling coincidence. In a galaxy populated by countless beings, it was reasonable that several might share many physical characteristics. As she instinctively stepped forward to examine the display more carefully, her stomach turned and her heart began to run a thready, uneven race.

This was more than resemblance. This was duplication. The woman before her, *whoever she might be,* was identical in almost every perceivable way to Kathryn Janeway.

"*Adatoir* Tesh, how long ago was this image taken?" Janeway asked softly.

"It was collected less than one solar cycle ago, from a Zahl infiltration team," Tesh replied.

"Do you have any more recent intelligence about this woman's actions?" Chakotay asked, clearly sensing the significance of this line of questioning.

"Our last tactical update regarding Sormana and the surrounding system were collected within the last two lunar cycles."

"Two months?" Chakotay asked softly of Janeway, who nodded in response.

A faint ray of hope presented itself. The Nihydron had entered the room and immediately accused Janeway of duplicity. Was it possible that they had manufactured this image from their own scans of *Demeter*'s logs and were now engaging in some sort of ruse to further their own agenda?

Regardless, this meeting was over.

"*Adatoir* Tesh," Janeway said. "I appreciate very much your sharing this intelligence with us. While we remain anxious to begin a broader exchange of data between our peoples, at this time I must ask that we postpone our discussions until my fleet investigates this truly perplexing situation."

Tesh lifted his hands from the table and the holographic images vanished. He moved to stand in front of Janeway again and nodded to her. "We sincerely hope that the next time we meet, you are able to illuminate this odd circumstance."

Chakotay stepped closer to Janeway, saying, "You can count on it."

As the Nihydron were escorted from the room by Decan, the rest of the fleet officers collected themselves around the briefing table. Farkas was the first to speak.

"If memory serves, Admiral, you do have a sister, don't you?"

"Yes," Janeway replied. "Phoebe."

"She's not your twin?"

"No. Nor does she possess any tactical training. She's never left the Alpha Quadrant."

"Then I've got nothing," Farkas said.

"The most probable explanation is a superficial resemblance, Admiral," Seven suggested. "It is true that this *denzit* shares many physical attributes with you, but that could simply be a coincidence."

Janeway's eyes briefly met Seven's and then slipped past them to stare into the distance as she brought her clasped hands to cover her mouth, resting her chin on them.

"We still have to confirm that one way or the other, don't we?" O'Donnell asked.

"Yes," Chakotay replied. "Although, for the record, I agree with Seven. The resemblance is alarming, but she *can't* be any version of Kathryn Janeway."

"Why not?" Glenn asked. "We've encountered stranger things. There are many reports on record of Starfleet officers encountering versions of themselves from some alternate universe."

"Improbable," Seven said.

"It might be simpler than that," Cambridge offered. "We could be looking at an alien who has altered its appearance intentionally to look like the admiral."

"Why would anyone do that?" Glenn asked.

"*Voyager*'s reputation," Farkas suggested. "The Nihydron have heard of you. Perhaps the Rilnar have as well and decided that Kathryn Janeway might be one leader that would strike fear into the hearts of the Zahl."

Janeway turned to stare at Farkas. "I don't know whether to be flattered or offended."

"I'd go with flattered," Farkas suggested.

"Is it possible we are looking at a version of Kathryn Janeway from another timeline?" O'Donnell asked.

"Also improbable," Seven said, "but technically possible."

"No," Janeway corrected her.

"Admiral?" Seven asked.

"Whoever this woman is, she *can't be* me, even a temporally displaced version of me."

"Why not?" Farkas asked.

Janeway sighed deeply.

"Because the admiral's death was a fixed point in time," Chakotay replied for her.

Farkas narrowed her eyes. "That's what the Q said, right?"

Janeway shook her head. "It's more than that. When I was in the Q Continuum, I experienced the deaths of every single Kathryn Janeway that has ever existed. This woman cannot be any version of me because all of them died, under a variety of circumstances, at the exact same moment almost two years ago. The Nihydron told us that their data is more recent than that. Even if this was me, temporally displaced or from an alternate universe, she still would not have survived this long."

"Are you sure?" Farkas asked. "Not to diminish anything you experienced, Admiral, but are we clear on the rules in play during the Omega Continuum crisis? I mean, if there were somehow two versions of you existing in a single timeline, would the multiverse have destroyed them both?"

"Yes," Janeway assured her in a pained, low voice.

The somber pause was broken by Counselor Cambridge. "Didn't I read once in our logs about some biomimetic alien life-form your crew encountered that duplicated every one of you?"

"Yes," Chakotay said. Turning to Janeway, he said, "*That* might be a possibility, Admiral."

"I don't see how," Janeway countered. "The duplicates created by the Silver Blood couldn't survive outside the Demon planet's atmosphere."

"Perhaps they adapted," Seven suggested.

"Perhaps," Janeway acknowledged, "but I don't think even a cloned version of me would have been given a pass by whatever forces were trying to restore the balance between Omega and the Q."

"What about Species 8472?" Seven asked. "We know they are capable of impersonating any individual they have scanned."

"The last time we spoke, they were very clear about their intentions to remain in fluidic space," Chakotay noted. "I suppose it could be another stray spy, but even then, I have a hard time understanding why they would intentionally insert themselves into someone else's war."

"Do we let it go?" O'Donnell asked.

"No," Janeway replied. "We're going to locate Sormana and set course. When we are within range, Captain Chakotay will take *Voyager* to make contact with the Rilnar and as discreetly as possible determine who the hell that woman is."

3

VOYAGER

Wow," Lieutenant Nancy Conlon said as Commander B'Elanna Torres entered her family's living room holding her newborn son swaddled in her arms.

Torres smiled. "He is pretty darn cute. I think we're going to keep him."

"Agreed, but I was referring to you," Conlon said. "You look great."

"Thanks," Torres said sincerely. She had bounced back fairly quickly after Miral's birth, but had largely credited that to the number of friends and family members who happened to be on hand to offer their assistance. This time, there was less help to be had, but Torres felt good; much better than anyone running on so little sleep probably should.

"You don't look half-bad yourself," she continued.

Conlon smiled. "Work agrees with me."

"How's it going down there?"

Conlon paused, clearly searching for the best way to frame her response.

"What?" Torres asked.

"I know Icheb is a friend of yours," Conlon began.

Torres sighed. She had already reviewed a blistering report on her new aide from Commander O'Donnell. "He is, but you still need to speak freely."

"I've served with my fair share of tight-asses. The next time we have dinner I'll tell you about Lieutenant Commander Mor glasch Tev. But Ensign Icheb is treating the Starfleet Engineering Manual like it's holy writ. He's bright as the day is long, but he has no practical awareness of the realities of everyday life aboard a starship."

"Yes, he does," Torres countered. "He was on *Voyager* for the last several years of our journey home. He was young, but he paid attention to everything we did. And there were times when he was genuinely helpful."

"Do you think the Academy wrecked him?"

"No." Torres shook her head. "I think the last few months might have."

"How so?"

"Tom and Seven leaned on him pretty heavily during their time on Earth. They asked him to break some rules. He had already bent a few others trying to get in touch with Seven. By all rights, he should have been separated for cause from the Academy. Tom said he was called on the carpet by Admiral Akaar before his posting to the fleet was approved."

"Oh," Conlon said, "that would do it."

"Yeah," Torres agreed. "I intended these efficiency evaluations to serve as an opportunity for him to get to know each of the fleet's chiefs and their engine rooms."

"He's treating them like final exams. And we're all failing."

Torres grinned knowingly. "Benoit did okay."

"Really? Give me a year of peace and a staff of holograms and I might do the same. Keep ripping my ship to pieces . . ."

"I'll talk to him," Torres assured her.

"Thank you." Offering the fleet chief engineer a padd, Conlon added, "And in your copious spare time, would you mind reviewing this? I would have given it to Icheb to pass along but I really didn't want to see the poor kid's head explode."

Torres started to accept it awkwardly.

"Trade you," Conlon offered.

Transferring Michael to Nancy's arms, Torres took the padd and perched on the arm of a sofa to scan it. It didn't take long for her stomach to sink. The padd contained a proposal for a radical overhaul of the ship's bioneural processors and a dizzying array of enhancements to the security protocols of the main computer. "What is this?" she asked.

"Just my thoughts. I had a lot of time to analyze our standard procedures while I was recuperating. The only reason we survived the Seriareen's attempt to take over this ship was because Meegan happened to be a hologram and Xolani transferred all of our command subroutines to her."

"The root code corruption I created was also critical."

"Yes, but it was installed on the fly and never tested. It could just as easily have destroyed us. We need to be prepared. Starfleet's regs don't begin to cover what the Delta Quadrant throws at us every damn day. Your instinct to create that modification was right, even though it goes against all of our security protocols. What I am proposing would maximize the potential of and simultaneously secure our bioneural gel packs. While we're at it, we need to add another essential layer of security between our main computer and anyone who might attempt to corrupt it."

"I agree, in theory. But this isn't an experimental vessel. *Voyager* is leading this fleet and we're too far from home to risk modifications like this."

Conlon seemed to struggle for a moment to maintain her composure. The fact that she was holding a sleeping child in her arms helped. "The Seriareen's actions demonstrated a number of vulnerabilities with our current security. I'm not blaming anyone. We did what we've been trained to do. But we still missed Xolani's infiltration of our systems, and he succeeded, however briefly, in taking our ship away from us. Had the synthetic amebocyte I'm proposing already been integrated into the gel packs, he couldn't have done that. His presence would have been detected and contained. If the main computer had the ability to request multiple command clearances based upon the nature of the alterations being made prior to Xolani, or Admiral Batiste's lock-outs, we would also have been better off. What good are experiences like this if we don't learn from them?"

Torres considered Conlon carefully. During her first seven years in the Delta Quadrant B'Elanna had suffered her fair share of odd alien encounters and been driven by them to craft safeguards like the one that had recently saved *Voyager*. But Admiral Janeway had taken her to task for it, and rightly so. Harry's attempt to do the same, creating a personal back door into the holographic systems, had initially given Xolani the access he required and exploited. No matter how well-intentioned, untested modifications like these, meant to counter specific situations, could do as much harm as good. But Conlon wasn't going to be able to see that objectively for some time.

"Let me review these more carefully," Torres finally said. "I understand what you're saying and I'm open to suggestions. But don't do anything until I have a chance to consider all of the potential consequences."

"Of course," Conlon agreed.

Torres set the padd aside and retrieved her son from Conlon.

"I've got to get back," the lieutenant said.

"I'll try and join you during his next nap," Torres said. "I'd like to review Icheb's recommendations personally."

Conlon nodded. "Feel free, but if you ask me to degauss anything with a micro-filament you're going to have a mutiny on your hands."

Torres smiled for Colon's benefit. As soon as the chief engineer had departed, she asked Icheb to join her and revised one of his standing orders.

"You're awfully quiet tonight," Counselor Cambridge observed.

His dinner companion, Seven, looked up briefly from her

plate. She'd been moving her sautéed vegetables from place to place with her fork without eating any of them. "Apologies."

Cambridge sat back in his chair and emptied the last of the merlot he had chosen to accompany his replicated pasta. Placing the empty glass back on the table he said, "I wasn't offended, just concerned."

Seven lowered her fork and crossed her arms at her chest. "Did you see her eyes?"

A dozen flatteries came to mind and were immediately rejected. Seven had entered his quarters a half hour earlier but had not really been present. There was no redirection of moods like this, not with this particular woman. "The admiral's?" he asked, assuming this was a thought process that had been festering since their meeting with the Nihydron.

"The holographic projection."

"I can't say I noticed them. It wasn't the best image. It was an extraordinary thing to see Tesh utilize our technology to project so much detail from his mind."

"They were *her* eyes," Seven said flatly.

"You have known Kathryn Janeway longer and better than I," Cambridge conceded. "I'm willing to defer to your judgment."

"Since the meeting I have considered and rejected five hundred and ninety-three possible circumstances by which another version of Admiral Janeway could exist at this time on that planet. Many of the required parameters are not known to Federation science but would have been part of any calculation undertaken by the Borg in analyzing this situation."

"And you have rejected them because . . . ?"

"Their projected probability falls between a thousandth and a hundredth of one percent when you include the assumption that Admiral Janeway's death was a fixed point in time," Seven replied. "My initial instinct was that the image had to be some sort of fabrication. I still believe that must be so. *But her eyes . . .*"

"Cognitive dissonance isn't for sissies. You must either abandon one of your instinctive responses, or accept that both are true."

"But they can't be."

"I don't know about that."

"Explain," Seven challenged him.

"In a moment. Tell me first, what did you see in those eyes that convinced you that woman is Kathryn Janeway?"

"A very specific and unsettling combination of defiance and pain."

"I know that look," Cambridge allowed. "The problem then becomes determining a means by which a version of Kathryn Janeway, other than the one returned to us eight months ago, could still exist."

"No such woman could."

"And yet she does. How could that have happened?"

"The only high-probability response is through the interference of another being with power that surpasses what we experience as ordinary reality, with some vested interest in saving another Kathryn Janeway's life."

"Q?"

Seven nodded warily.

"And is there some reason you did not suggest this as a possibility when the matter was open for discussion?" Cambridge asked.

"I had not yet had sufficient time to consider all of the possible alternatives," Seven replied, then shook her head. "After the loss of his son to Omega, Q departed this plane of existence in a rage."

"And you feared to speak the devil's name?"

Seven stared at him quizzically. "I do not fear him. I do, however, respect his capabilities and his intemperance."

"Both are limitless," Cambridge agreed. "But I seriously doubt that's what we're seeing."

"Why?"

"Q was wrong to lay the blame for his son's death at the feet of Admiral Janeway. It probably took him a few minutes to realize it, but our continued existence suggests that he figured it out. Had his initial rage warranted vengeance, he would have taken it by now. Whatever this is, it's too subtle for an angry Q."

"I cannot think of any other species with the capabilities required to counter the actions of the multiverse."

"Nor can I," Cambridge agreed. "But that doesn't mean they're not out there. If you are right, and that is another Kathryn Janeway, we should probably gird our loins in preparation for encountering such a species."

"That potential doesn't trouble you?"

"I'm glad I finished my dinner before we broached the topic, but honestly, all things considered, that's a fairly typical day around here."

VESTA

Captain Chakotay didn't know what had abruptly awakened him. He reached instinctively to his left and found cold rumpled bedding where Kathryn should have been. He scanned her darkened bedroom. She was not there, nor was any ambient light bleeding in from her living quarters where she retreated to work when sleep proved elusive.

The next sound that met his ears brought him upright in an instant. *Breaking glass?* Throwing his feet over the side of the bed he moved toward the 'fresher. He heard nothing through the door and knocked softly.

Kathryn's muffled voice met his ears in response.

Chakotay continued to listen for sounds of distress. None came. Finally the door slid open and Kathryn emerged, her hand wrapped in a small towel. "What happened?" he asked.

"You missed it," she replied, brushing past him.

Poking his head inside the small room, Chakotay saw that the mirror that hung above the sink was broken. Stepping inside for a better look he noted that a single point in the lower left quadrant had been impacted and the surface of the mirror shattered. He stared for a moment wondering how this had happened as dozens of partial images of his face looked back at him.

"Kathryn?" he called.

Chakotay awoke, calling Kathryn's name. Momentarily disoriented, he fought for his bearings. Kathryn was not asleep beside him, as she should have been. The door separating the bedroom from the rest of her suite was closed. It hadn't been when they'd retired for the evening.

He rose quickly and peeked inside the 'fresher. The mirror above the sink was in one piece. Chakotay availed himself of a robe hung on the back of the door and moved hastily to the admiral's living quarters.

She was seated at her desk wearing a uniform tank and long, soft trousers. A steaming mug sat at her right hand. Her left held a padd.

"Trouble sleeping?" he asked.

"What gave it away?"

Chakotay crossed to stand behind her and gaze over her shoulder at the padd. Reaching for her coffee with one hand, she used the other to offer him the material she had been reviewing.

"When did this come in?" Chakotay asked.

"A couple of hours ago. I asked O'Donnell to contact the Nihydron before they were out of range and request any data they were willing to share with us about Sormana. This was waiting in my queue when I gave up trying to sleep."

The captain quickly reviewed the padd. It was dense reading, including lists of settlements and major military engagements on Sormana going back hundreds of years. Biographical data was provided on several notable leaders on both sides of the conflict. Information on the *denzit* who shared Kathryn's face was limited to her title and a handful of recent battles. Nothing shed any light on who she might be or how she had come to lead the Rilnar on Sormana.

Chakotay moved to the other side of the desk and pulled a chair close, sitting. "Did anything in particular catch your eye?"

"This planet. It has no tactical value. Both the Rilnar and Zahl are advanced civilizations. Both developed interstellar flight hundreds of years ago and have colonized other worlds since then. Any of them could easily absorb the population of Sormana."

"The Nihydron said they originated there," Chakotay reminded her. "Clearly this conflict began among their ancient ancestors."

"So? Given all they have conquered and held within much safer territories, what difference does one planet make now?"

"It's their Earth, Kathryn."

"This report suggests that both possess formidable starships and considerable arsenals of advanced weapons. Assuming they harbor enough ill will between them to allow this conflict to continue, why hasn't it expanded to include a wider field of battle? Nothing here indicates that there are regular engagements between these ancient enemies beyond Sormana."

"I guess we'll find out more in a few hours," Chakotay replied.

Kathryn shrugged and lifted her hands to massage her shoulders. Chakotay stood and moved to stand behind her, assuming the task of relaxing the tense knots that had formed in her muscles.

"Whoever that woman is, Kathryn, she's not you," he assured her softly.

She inhaled deeply and released the breath slowly. "I know."

"Why is there a *but* at the end of that statement?"

"I can't un-see what Junior showed me," Kathryn said softly. "I can't tell you how many of them there were. But each one had a life she valued as much as I do mine. And each of those lives was snuffed out in an instant. What if resetting the balance between Omega and the Q had some unforeseen effects? What if we somehow reversed what the multiverse did to bring those deaths about?"

Kneeling beside her, Chakotay took her hands in his, noting that they had turned to ice. "We didn't alter time, Kathryn. Everything that had happened up to the point where Junior and Afsarah sacrificed themselves to save us was left untouched. But let's say it wasn't. Let's say all of them were somehow restored to life. Would that bother you?"

Kathryn paused, staring into his eyes. "I don't know," she finally whispered. "Twice now I have encountered alternate versions of myself. Both of those encounters ended with their untimely deaths to ensure my salvation. Confronting my own mortality is difficult, but it doesn't bother me nearly as much as watching them die. I worry about finding myself in a situation where the temptation will be to save this woman at all costs."

"From whom?"

"Herself."

"She's not you, Kathryn," he insisted. "At most she is some version of you whose life diverged from yours at some point in your past. Whatever she has experienced since then has redefined her and made her a unique being. You are *not* responsible for her choices any more than you were those of the Admiral Janeway who helped us destroy that transwarp hub."

"I know."

As Chakotay stared into her troubled eyes, his thoughts turned back to the strange dream that had awakened him.

"Come back to bed," he suggested.

Nodding faintly she rose and once she had settled herself in his arms soon slipped into a deep sleep. Chakotay found no such solace.

4

VOYAGER

What have we got, Lieutenant Lasren?" Commander Paris asked. After a week spent beside his wife through labor, delivery, and the first days of his son's life, bridge duty felt like a reprieve. He might have pushed it one more day, but B'Elanna was doing great, as were his children, and

Paris felt he had already asked too much of his best friend. Kim had been covering many of Paris's duty shifts on top of his own.

At his right hand, Chakotay sat reviewing the latest sensor reports on the data panel in the arm of his chair.

"We are holding position approximately three light-years from Sormana," the ops officer replied. "Several ships have been detected on long-range sensors. They appear to be patrolling a perimeter that begins roughly twenty million kilometers from the planet."

"What's between them and the planet?" Paris asked.

"Nothing, so far as we can tell from this distance."

"Huh," Paris said.

"Helm, set course to intercept the nearest Rilnar vessel and engage at warp two," Chakotay ordered.

"Aye, sir," Ensign Aytar Gwyn replied.

"Why so slow?" Paris asked.

"Give them a look at us," Chakotay replied.

Voyager had maintained their course for only a few minutes when Lieutenant Aubrey reported from tactical, "Captain, one of the Zahl vessels has broken formation and is moving to intercept us."

"That will work too," Chakotay said. "Slow to one-quarter impulse when we are within five thousand kilometers, identify us, and begin transmitting standard friendship greetings."

Shortly thereafter the face of the commanding officer of the Zahl vessel appeared on the viewscreen. She was humanoid with light-brown flesh and slight brow ridges that were broken by a bony spine that ran from her hairline to the top of her nose. Both sides of her face were riddled with darker, pitted flesh that suggested battle scars, but were too regular in their placement for that to be likely.

"*Captain Chakotay, I am Shipmaster Pilusch of the Zahl space vessel* Tascara. *I must ask that you alter your course to avoid breaching the no-fly-zone currently in effect around the planet Sormana.*"

"We've come here hoping to learn more about this planet and its history," Chakotay said.

"Permit me to transmit coordinates of our capital world, Zahlna II, where our diplomatic envoys will provide you with any information you require," Pilusch replied courteously, but with a hint of steel in her voice.

"I appreciate that, Shipmaster. Is anyone allowed to approach the planet or send researchers to its surface?" Chakotay asked, just as reasonably.

"Not at this time. It is a precaution put in place for your own security, Captain. As you may be aware, this planet is in dispute. While neither the Rilnar nor the Zahl born beyond Sormana's shores condone the continued bloodshed this conflict produces, we also recognize the sovereignty of the planet's people and their right to resolve this situation without our interference. A large field of subspace mines has been placed around the planet, ensuring that neither side's space fleets will engage or assist those on the surface. Exceptions are made for a limited number of relief vessels that provide humanitarian aid. It is our sincere hope that someday the people of Sormana will choose peace and learn to live with one another as we have learned to respect the borders of our interstellar territories. Until then, no outsiders can safely access the planet."

"I assure you—" Chakotay began.

"Reverse your course, Captain, lest I be forced to conclude that your intentions here are to offer aid to the Rilnar. You will receive no further warnings. Tascara out."

The image of Pilusch's face was replaced by one of her ship, a patrol vessel half *Voyager's* size but armed with enough hull-mounted cannons to deter engagement.

"She was downright pleasant up until the end," Paris noted.

Chakotay sighed. "Reverse course and take us out of the system," he ordered. "Once we're out of sensor range we'll plot a return course from the other side and see if we can get the Rilnar's attention this time."

"You think they'll be any more helpful?"

"No, but it can't hurt to ask."

VESTA

"*Ornzitar Rileez, the commanding officer of the Rilnar vessel Golant, told a similar story,*" Captain Chakotay reported. "*His concern was that we had come to aid the Zahl. Voyager's specs were transmitted to every ship monitoring the perimeter of their no-fly zone on both sides the minute we made contact with the Zahl. We were met with courtesy, respect, and absolute defiance while being assured that this was for our protection.*"

"They've been playing this game for a long time, Captain," Farkas pointed out. Admiral Janeway sat to her right on *Vesta*'s bridge listening to Chakotay's report without comment. "It's likely that every local spacefaring species is well aware of Sormana's status and simply avoids the area. Any newcomers are bound to be met with suspicion."

"*We did detect several small vessels that appeared to be utilizing some sort of Rilnar checkpoint,*" Chakotay continued. "*Probably the humanitarian aid the Zahl shipmaster mentioned. Three were granted passage to the planet. Their courses were erratic, but all of them made orbit safely, so it can be done, Admiral.*"

"Both sides must possess the capability to bring resources to the planet. The Zahl probably have a similar site somewhere along the perimeter."

"*None that we detected,*" Chakotay said, "*but that doesn't mean it's not there.*"

"Can we breach this perimeter without attracting the attention of the patrol vessels?" Janeway finally asked.

"You want to run the blockade?" Farkas asked, clearly surprised.

"Not with that minefield intact. But I want an away team on the surface of that planet before we grow old waiting to see who ultimately wins this war," the admiral replied tersely.

"*The Rilnar and Zahl appear to be quite civilized,*" Chakotay noted. "*They also seemed, I don't know, embarrassed might be too strong a word, by this whole situation. But it's clear that the Rilnar and Zahl not living on Sormana have agreed to a strict noninterference policy.*"

"At least there's one thing we have in common," Farkas noted.

"But why?" Janeway demanded. "If those living beyond this system's borders have learned to live and let live, what the hell is wrong with the people of Sormana? And if neither side's government is feeding military supplies to the natives or providing more than humanitarian aid, how have they managed to continue this war for so long? Where are their resources coming from? What kind of weapons are they using down there that the entire planet hasn't been destroyed by now?"

"All good questions," Chakotay said, *"but not ones we are necessarily entitled to have answered."*

"Would the Rilnar tell you anything about this *denzit*?" the admiral asked.

"No. They referenced her only by title. They don't answer to her. I'm not sure how much the crews of these patrol vessels even know about her."

"If you still want to find out, we're going to have to do this the hard way," Farkas said.

"I know," the admiral replied dismally.

VOYAGER

Commander B'Elanna Torres had kept her word to Lieutenant Conlon. She had thoroughly reviewed the proposal to enhance the security of their computer systems and while they were brilliant and testimony to the Starfleet Corps of Engineers' fabled reputation for outside-the-box thinking, Torres was standing by her initial assessment. Modifications like this didn't happen in the middle of a long-term deep-space mission. They happened in Starfleet labs and were tested to death before they saw the inside of a starship.

Breaking this to Conlon was going to be a difficult conversation. Torres set this aside when Ensign Icheb entered her quarters for his daily report. He stood at attention until she had greeted him and asked him to take a seat beside her workstation.

"I've completed my review of your evaluation of the *Vesta*," Torres began. "You can't take this to Bryce."

"I know," Icheb replied. "But I wanted the evaluation to exist in its proper form before I revised it."

"You're learning," Torres said approvingly.

"Perhaps," Icheb allowed.

"How do you intend to approach the *Vesta*'s chief engineer?"

"I have observed his interactions with his crew for two days now. He usually begins by praising the efforts of his subordinates prior to pointing out their shortcomings."

"You cited him for over two hundred violations. Did you also take note of areas in which he excels?"

"Yes. Most of the violations are a result of rushing to completion. Small but sometimes critical steps are ignored that may have no discernable immediate effect but they could result in system disruptions or failures. The speed with which he evaluates problems and addresses them, however, were critical to *Vesta*'s survival at the time."

"So he's on the right track, but he needs to cut fewer corners?"

"A fair assessment."

"And a better approach," Torres pointed out. "Report back to me after his review."

"Yes, Commander."

"What else?" Torres asked.

"As you requested, I have reviewed all of the duty logs of each member of Lieutenant Conlon's staff over the last few days. She pulled Ensign Mirk from magnetic constrictor realignment and ordered him to synthesize a dozen separate molecular compounds and to introduce them into test samples of our bioneural fluid."

"What were the results?" Torres asked.

"Mirk's station logs show that he has only completed his analysis of the first three. All destabilized the medium and showed probable adverse effects to the bioneural filaments."

Torres nodded. The addition of the amebocyte Conlon had proposed—a cell-like structure capable of encasing any unknown infiltrate in an impenetrable solid shell and preventing further transfer or corruption to the ship's bioneural gel packs— was an intriguing one, and something Starfleet should definitely explore. But it was not a task *Voyager*'s engineers should undertake. The fleet chief engineer had ordered Conlon to refrain from pursuing her theories but Torres believed Conlon might choose to intentionally limit her *understanding* of that order to *installing* the modifications she had proposed. Experimenting with their component parts was harmless enough and avoided the appearance of flouting a direct order.

Torres had ordered Icheb to study the engineering logs in order to see the depths of Conlon's devotion to her pet project. Torres's initial skepticism had not derailed Conlon. If anything, it seemed to be driving her to prove her theories.

Which was a problem.

"It might also be noted that Ensign Mirk's assignment was not recorded in Lieutenant Conlon's official duty log. Shall I continue my observations?" Icheb asked.

"Yes," Torres replied. "And please advise me of any further similar requests."

"Aye, Commander."

"Where do you stand with *Demeter*? Have you submitted your revised report to Commander O'Donnell?"

"I have. He glanced at it and told me to 'try again.'"

"Try again?"

"Yes, Commander."

Torres considered this development. Finally she said, "I want you to let it go. I've reviewed the violations and while it's clear that Elkins has less regard for Starfleet protocols than I do, which is something I wasn't sure was possible, nothing he is doing is endangering his ship or the crew."

"But shouldn't he be made aware—"

"What's critical to me is that you are able to function as my representative on all fleet ships for the next few months. I'll deal with O'Donnell and Elkins. They're no longer your concern."

Icheb appeared ready to argue further when a man, roughly

Paris's height and build, with light-brown skin, shoulder-length black hair, a single cranial ridge, and a small growth at the bridge of his nose, entered her suite. The sides of his head and temples were mottled in a way that suggested scarring, similar to but not exactly the same as the Zahl's. He wore a nondescript green uniform and scuffed black boots.

"Hi honey, I'm home," this stranger greeted her cheerily.

Torres rose from her desk, crossed to him, and searched for any sign of her husband behind the newly blackened irises and alien visage. It was faint, but present. Tom had just completed the surgical reconstruction required for his upcoming mission to Sormana.

"Amazing," Torres declared.

"What do you think, Icheb?" Paris asked.

Icheb rose from his chair, his discomfort clear.

"It's not that bad, is it?"

"No, sir," Icheb replied quickly. "The Doctor has done his typical exemplary job. It's just . . ."

"What?" Paris demanded.

"It is unsettling, sir. I would prefer making contact with these aliens openly rather than by using subterfuge."

"So would I," Paris agreed. "But the direct approach isn't always best."

"Good luck, Commander Paris," Icheb said, extending his right hand.

Paris took it, grinning gamely. Even with the prosthetics, there was no mistaking his smile. "Thanks, Icheb. Don't worry. We're going to be fine."

"I know, sir."

The ensign looked to Torres, who dismissed him with a nod, saying, "Let me know how things go with Bryce."

When Icheb left, Paris took his wife firmly in his arms. "Come back to me in one piece," she ordered when their embrace ended.

"I promise," he said.

"And let me say good-bye to the kids for you."

"Aw, come on. Miral will love it."

"I don't think so, honey."

"You'll see." Stepping into the hall between his son's and daughter's bedrooms, Paris said, "Miral, come say goodbye to your daddy."

He stepped back as the child came rushing into the living room, her face alight. The moment she saw him she stopped so abruptly she nearly tripped over her feet. Her mouth opened in a perfect oval and a shriek of terror flew toward Tom. Miral darted back into her bedroom and ordered the door closed as her brother began to cry in alarm from the opposite room.

Paris looked back to his wife, who shrugged. "You broke it, you fix it," she ordered before hurrying to Michael's room to comfort him.

SHUTTLECRAFT *TUCCIA*

"Stop scratching, Counselor," the Doctor ordered Hugh Cambridge.

"It itches," Cambridge replied petulantly, continuing to rub his new nasal ridge.

"You will only further irritate the surrounding epidermal cells."

"Can you give me something for the pain?" Cambridge pleaded.

"No."

"Do you two want to keep it down back there?" Commander Paris asked from the cockpit. "We're almost to the front of line."

The Doctor glowered at Cambridge, hoping to shame him into silence.

"This shuttle is stocked with medical supplies," Cambridge whispered vehemently.

"Actually, Counselor, that is inaccurate," said Ensign Ti'Ana from the seat beside Commander Paris. She was one of the *Vesta*'s science officers who had been added to the away team given her telepathic and empathic abilities, inherited from her Vulcan father and Betazoid mother. Like the counselor and commander, she had been surgically altered to pass for Rilnar. The Doctor's appearance had been altered by less radical means, a simple modification to his matrix.

"The vast majority of those cases marked *supplies* are empty," Ti'Ana continued.

"There's nothing in the others to help you," the Doctor added. "At the admiral's request, they contain only the most basic first-aid items. She was concerned that should the shuttle be captured and our cargo confiscated, we will not be accused of providing significant material aid to either side of this conflict."

"A wise precaution," Ti'Ana agreed. "Despite Lieutenant Bryce's belief that the holographic projectors installed on the exterior of the shuttle to project the image of a Rilnar medical supply transport will fool any advanced sensors, I rate this mission's odds of success at no more than thirty percent."

"Thanks for the vote of confidence, Ensign," Paris commented wryly.

"Ow!" Counselor Cambridge shouted, grabbing his right ear in pain.

"Oh, what now?" the Doctor demanded, exasperated.

Paris turned his seat back to cast a disparaging eye on his away team. "You both understand this is a covert mission, right?"

"My apologies, Commander," Cambridge replied. "Captain Chakotay just made contact with me through the subaural transceiver the Doctor implanted in my auditory canal and the signal was only a few decibels shy of shattering my ear drum."

"What did he say?" Paris asked.

"That we should continue this conversation after we have passed through the Rilnar checkpoint."

"Motion seconded and carried," Paris said.

VOYAGER

Most of the time, Captain Chakotay thanked the unknown gods of his father profusely for the crew that he led. They were dedicated, experienced, and brave.

Then there were moments like this one when he wished fervently that he were free to abandon Starfleet disciplinary regulations momentarily and apprise them of his displeasure in the *Maquis* way: a swift punch.

The captain had monitored the camouflaged shuttle's progress since they had entered the line of ships approaching the Rilnar checkpoint from an open channel on *Voyager's* bridge. When the bickering between the Doctor and Cambridge had begun to make his bridge crew struggle to hold back their laughter, he had ordered Lasren to open a channel to Counselor Cambridge's transceiver to put an end to the unproductive exchange. What he'd actually said to Cambridge was, *"Stifle it, Counselor. That's an order. I don't care how much your prosthetics itch. Suffer in silence, or so help me I'll have Lasren patch the first act of* Gav'ot toH'va *directly into your transceiver and run it on a loop until you land on the surface."*

Cambridge's report of his comments had been accurate in substance, so Chakotay had let it pass. He assumed all of them were blowing off a little steam. Ti'Ana's estimate of their probable success rate was likely accurate and they all knew it. It was also not what they needed to be focused on at this moment.

The turbolift doors opened and Chakotay turned to see Commander Torres enter. She wore a soft cloth sling wrapped over a shoulder and around her waist that held her infant son.

Torres nodded to Kim as she passed him and paused before the open chair to Chakotay's right. "Got a minute?" she asked softly.

Chakotay nodded.

"Mister Kim, the bridge is yours. Advise me the moment the shuttle reaches the second position in line."

"Aye, sir," Kim replied.

Chakotay gestured for Torres to precede him into his ready room and as soon as the door was shut, crossed his arms. "Problem, Commander?"

"Conlon," Torres replied.

"I thought she was doing fine. Our engineers seem happier than they've been in weeks."

"She is," Torres conceded. "She *seems* to be. She came to me with a request to consider major modifications to our gel packs and computer security protocols. Her ideas are innovative. I like them. But they are too labor-intensive considering our mission profile and too dangerous to risk installing in the middle of the Delta Quadrant."

"I assume you told her as much."

"I ordered her to set them aside until I had completed my evaluation. I had a feeling she wouldn't. Icheb confirmed that. She's already started working on one of them."

"Sit her down and make sure she understands that she was given a direct order, not a suggestion."

"I would . . . I will. But I wonder if she might *need* this right now."

"Need?"

"She just recovered from a serious trauma. I know Counselor Cambridge signed off on her return to duty, but I have a feeling that's what's driving this. She doesn't want what happened to her ever happening again. I understand that."

"And you understand what happens, even to the most dedicated officers, when they attempt to solve complex emotional issues alone, rather than asking for the assistance they really need," Chakotay added, grasping intuitively why Torres would be sensitive to a situation like this. A very different trauma had once led Torres to incredibly self-destructive choices. Chakotay had ultimately been able to reach her and force her to confront the source of her behavior. The injuries she had done to herself along the way were still painful to remember. If Torres believed there was more to Conlon's actions than devotion to her duty, Chakotay wasn't going to second-guess that.

"Yes," Torres agreed. "So what do I do?"

"Nothing that will endanger her or the ship."

"I'm not sure I see a solution that can guarantee both."

"If she wants to run a few experiments on her own time, would there really be any harm?"

"Depending on how far she gets, ultimately refusing to allow her to implement the modifications might be more troubling than if I shut her down immediately. For now, she's at least directing her energy toward something productive. Is that such a bad thing?"

"B'Elanna, you know her better than I do. If your gut says she is using this project as a means to work through some emotional issues, I'd give her some space. If you think her issues will cloud her perspective and allow her to unintentionally put the ship at risk, you have to put an end to it."

"What if I'm wrong? I've been kicking myself pretty hard the last few weeks for some glaring personal oversights that might have prevented our last mission from devolving into chaos. I'm no counselor. Maybe I'm seeing connections that aren't there because I'm afraid to miss anything."

Chakotay nodded thoughtfully. Finally he said, "When our instincts try to tell us something, we rarely regret acting on them. It's the ones we ignore that usually end up biting us in the ass. The counselor should be back in a few days at most. Why don't you run this by him before making a decision? But keep your eye on her, obviously."

"Okay. Thanks."

Chakotay was about to return to the bridge when he caught his distorted reflection in the ports that lined his ready room. For a second, he flashed back to the image of the shattered mirror, hearing Kathryn's voice in his head. "*You missed it.*"

"Chakotay?" Torres asked.

Returning his attention to her, he shook his head. "Sorry. I had a really weird dream last night."

"You want to talk about it?"

Chakotay did, but before he could reply, his combadge chirped. "*Bridge to Captain Chakotay. The* Tuccia *has almost reached the checkpoint,*" Kim reported.

"Acknowledged."

TUCCIA

This is taking too long, Tom Paris thought. He didn't say it. He didn't have to. The tense silence of his away team indicated clearly that they shared his misgivings.

When he had hailed the vessel monitoring the checkpoint, the Rilnar Colonial Force officer had demanded his identification, cargo manifest, and clearance codes. *Voyager* had been monitoring comm traffic at the checkpoint for almost two days and had acquired what they believed to be the most current codes available. The intelligence they had gained had been used to modify the shuttle's appearance, falsify its registration, and concoct its manifest.

Worst-case scenario, he could turn and run. He'd already plotted an escape vector that would be risky, given that they were in-system, but not nearly as dangerous as engaging any of the Rilnar ships patrolling the blockade.

What Paris didn't know was how long he should wait before pulling the trigger on Plan B.

Voyager was observing comm silence until the shuttle reached orbit and the first sensor scans were taken. Paris wondered what Chakotay would do. It didn't really matter. The captain wasn't leading this mission, Commander Thomas Paris was. *His* was the only opinion that counted right now.

Paris inhaled deeply. If he received no response by the end of a slow exhalation, he was going to abort. His lungs had begun to tighten when the voice of the Rilnar officer blared over the comm. *"Transport T-199, you are clear to proceed. Transmitting course now. Do not deviate under any circumstances."*

"Confirmed," Paris replied. In his relief, he almost offered the officer a cheery, "Have a good day," but refrained. No reason to press his luck.

Paris entered the course he had just received into the shuttle's navigation system and engaged at low impulse. When the ship was a few thousand kilometers closer to the planet Paris said, "See, no problem."

"Yes, these last twelve minutes have been incredibly relaxing, Commander," Cambridge quipped.

"Did you get anything while we were waiting?" Paris asked the science officer.

"No, sir," Ti'Ana replied. "It took seven minutes and thirty-eight seconds longer for them to clear us than ninety-two percent of the ships that have passed this checkpoint while under our surveillance, but I cannot tell you what prompted the additional scrutiny."

"Doesn't matter now," Paris said. "They cleared us and gave us our course."

"Is there any chance this course leads directly into a mine?" Cambridge asked. "Watching us blow up is certainly less labor intensive than engaging us, on the off-chance they saw through our disguise."

"Are you this cheery on all of your away missions, Counselor?" Paris asked.

"In my experience he's usually much worse," the Doctor offered.

"Ti'Ana, initiate another sensor sweep. Maybe we can detect something from inside this field we couldn't get from *Voyager*."

"Aye, sir."

For the next several silent minutes, the shuttle continued forward on its erratic course. Each correction turned Paris's stomach, but he kept his fears to himself.

"Sensors show nothing new, Commander," Ti'Ana finally reported.

"That's all right, just a few minutes more . . ." Paris said, the thought trailing off as he realized that their current course was going to bring them in range of one of the largest orbital platforms and its array of phase cannons.

"Ti'Ana, pull up a display of all of the other courses followed by the Rilnar vessels that have passed that checkpoint."

"Why?"

"Now, Ensign."

"Sorry. Of course, sir."

When the display appeared, Paris took note of two patterns that intersected with their current course but ultimately broke off in slightly different directions. One of them would take the shuttle quite a bit farther from the platform. Paris didn't honestly believe the Rilnar were intentionally sending them to their deaths, but he couldn't ignore the possibility. His instincts told him avoiding that platform was important enough to risk a course alteration. With less than thirty seconds to spare, Paris manually overrode their current course and set the shuttle on a new trajectory, following the path traveled by another Rilnar transport vessel.

Ten seconds became twenty, then thirty. When a full two minutes had elapsed, Paris decided he had chosen wisely.

"We're going to make orbit in six minutes," Paris advised his team. "We'll initiate a sensor sweep and once we have the location of the Rilnar command center, the Doctor, the counselor, and I will transport down. The data the Nihydron shared with us suggests that the command center will be shielded. We'll be taking pattern enhancers down with us. Our subaural transceivers will replace our combadges for the duration and all of our communications will be monitored by *Voyager*. Our first goal will be to find a way through the shielded perimeter. Double-check your packs to make sure you have rations for . . ."

Paris couldn't say what triggered his internal alarm. It might have been the sudden faint sluggishness of the helm. Most people wouldn't have noticed the shift but Paris flew more by feel than data. As there was no way to know what a safe direction might be, the commander simply reversed course, intending to take the shuttle back along the same path it had safely followed thus far.

"Commander—" Ti'Ana began.

A clap of thunder and blinding light that sent the shuttle spiraling down into the atmosphere of Sormana told Paris that his course correction had come too late for the shuttle to avoid the subspace mine it had just triggered.

5

VESTA

Janeway sat in Captain Farkas's ready room reviewing the grim spectacle of the shuttle's uncontrolled fall toward the surface of Sormana. Their sensors couldn't penetrate the atmosphere at this distance, so they had no way to determine the away team's fate. Farkas stood behind the admiral, and Chakotay's face stared back at her from half of the data panel.

"Do we know why Commander Paris altered his course?" Farkas asked.

"Not yet. But I trust Tom's instincts. He must have had a good reason," Chakotay replied.

"Have you been able to raise them on their personal transceivers?" Janeway asked.

"Negative. Something on the surface is jamming our signal," Chakotay advised bitterly. *"How do you wish to proceed, Admiral?"*

Janeway placed both hands on her forehead and aggressively massaged her temples with her thumbs. A direct assault would bring both the Rilnar and the Zahl ships in the area down upon the *Vesta*. She might be able to hold out long enough to give *Voyager* enough cover to run the blockade. From orbit they could locate the shuttlecraft—or its debris—quickly enough to transport out any survivors.

Only the estimated yield of those subspace mines kept her from giving the order. *Vesta*'s shields might protect them from two or three direct mine impacts. *Voyager*'s smaller mass could sustain one or two at the most. The number of course corrections taken by every ship that had safely traversed the field suggested there would be more than a dozen along any path taken to orbit and back.

"We come clean," Janeway said. "Initiate contact with the

Rilnar checkpoint and advise them that we have lost a ship and intend to mount a rescue operation."

"And if they say no?" Chakotay asked.

"I can see them refusing us," Farkas said, "but what about the *denzit?"*

"Beg pardon?" Janeway asked.

"We throw one of their uniform jackets on you and *you* make the contact. You pretend to be her and you order them to allow us through the minefield," Farkas clarified.

Janeway considered the possibility. Depending on the Rilnar security protocols, it might work. *Then again . . .*

"Let's see what they do with Captain Chakotay's request first," Janeway decided.

"How many shots do you think we're going to get at this?" Farkas asked.

"If they refuse," Janeway said, "I'm not going to bother trying to fool their perimeter guard. I'm just going to demand an audience with the *denzit*. I have a funny feeling she'll take my call."

SORMANA

A good pilot might have been able to pull the shuttle out of its free fall. Only one like Thomas Eugene Paris, who had made a habit in his younger days of courting destruction during the most hazardous emergency situations imaginable, could have landed the shuttle in one piece.

Paris remained conscious after the mine exploded. As Ti'Ana reported their damage, including a small hull breach where the port impulse engine had been lost, the commander had busied himself rerouting power to emergency forcefields and stabilizing their remaining engine. The next priority was scanning the area the shuttle was about to impact. Fortunately, they were headed for the desert twenty kilometers from a large installation Paris hoped belonged to the Rilnar.

Sheer nerve carried Paris through the roughest landing sequence he'd endured in years. When the *Tuccia* was once again on solid ground, she was no longer space worthy, and much worse for the wear, but her passengers were alive.

Once everyone had confirmed they were okay, apart from Cambridge, who'd commenced retching as they'd landed, Paris initiated scans of the area.

Sensors showed that two small surface vessels were already approaching their position from opposite directions. Paris had no idea if they were Rilnar or Zahl, but those en route from south-southwest were going to arrive a few minutes before their counterparts.

"Perhaps they will be so busy fighting one another that we will be able to escape undetected," Ti'Ana suggested as she studied the scans Paris was seeing.

"We don't have enough power left to raise our shields and we're in the middle of desert," Paris replied. "Not to mention the fact that we didn't come down here to add to the body count. Unless they kill one another to the last man, we surrender to whoever gets here first."

"It will be the Zahl," Cambridge said as he wiped his mouth and sealed the cloth in one of the few medical supplies that was handy—a biohazard bag.

"You can't know that," the Doctor insisted.

"Of course, I can," Cambridge retorted. "Anything else would be a lucky break for us, and I'm afraid that's just not the kind of day we're having, Doctor."

VOYAGER

"Captain Chakotay, to what do we owe the pleasure of this contact?" Ornzitar Rileez was every bit as cordial now as he had been the first time Chakotay spoke to him a few days prior.

"I'll make this quick," Chakotay replied. "I dispatched a team to the surface of Sormana a few hours ago. Their shuttle impacted a subspace mine and as best we can tell, crashed on the surface. We intend to mount a rescue operation and hope you will be willing to assist us."

"That's quite a tale, Captain. A moment, please." Rileez abruptly closed the channel but did not leave Chakotay in suspense for long. Less than a minute later his face, pasty white apart from the Rilnar's characteristic ridges and mottled flesh running from his hairline to his cheeks, once again filled *Voyager's* main viewscreen. *"I have checked our logs and confirmed them with the rest of the Colonial forces. We have no record of a Federation ship entering the minefield and our surface scans reveal no debris. I apologize, Captain, but we cannot permit you to pass beyond the perimeter to rescue this non-existent vessel. High marks, however, for creativity. It is clear you intend to reach the surface of Sormana. I wish we could accommodate you. However, for your safety, and ours, I must refuse."*

"I see," Chakotay said, keeping his face and voice neutral despite the taste of acid in the back of his throat and the raw state of every nerve ending in his body. "Is there any chance you could put me in touch with the Rilnar leader on Sormana, the *denzit*?"

Rileez appeared taken aback. *"It is doubtful she would trouble herself to speak with you,"* he replied. *"I will certainly convey the substance of this conversation to my superior, Tilzitar Deet, in my next status report. If he finds cause to question my actions or reaches a different conclusion, we will contact you at once."*

"Let me be clear," Chakotay said. "I'm going to determine the status of my crew with or without your permission. There is no reason for this to devolve into aggression between us. We have no fight with you, nor any desire to interfere with the engagement on Sormana. Starfleet's first general order, the Prime Directive, restricts us from doing so. But I will not abandon my people. Is this really how you want to do this?"

Chakotay was surprised to see Rileez's face soften. *"I will speak with the* tilzitar *as soon as possible, Captain. That is the best I can do. What you choose to do in the interim is entirely your call. Any action you take to breach the perimeter, however, will force my hand. Do you understand?"*

"I do," Chakotay replied.

"End transmission."

SORMANA

"Just admit you were wrong. Surely you're man enough to do that," Paris said softly.

"I hardly think the respective length of our reproductive organs is relevant to this discussion," Cambridge replied directly into Paris's transceiver.

After a brief skirmish, in which the Rilnar had emerged victorious, the away team had been brought to the installation Paris had detected. The settlement was, despite Cambridge's pessimism, a Rilnar outpost. The team had been immediately separated, locked in private cells located within a warren of tunnels beneath the base. Finally left alone, they had checked in with one another through their transceivers. For some reason, their transceiver signals were strong enough to allow them to communicate with each other but no longer able to reach beyond the planet's surface.

A few hours had passed by Paris's internal calculations. None of them had been interrogated yet. Their captors had confiscated their gear and had probably already brought the shuttle in for analysis. Its holographic projectors had failed even before it landed. But it seemed that their Rilnar disguises and faked identities had earned them reasonable treatment: cells with bunks, blankets, and a small supply of fresh water. Paris wondered idly what kind of reception captured Zahl prisoners received.

Paris had considered ordering the team to observe comm silence. Their transceivers had been adjusted to allow a constant open connection between all four of them. It was likely that everything they said was being monitored and an observer might realize quickly that they were in communication with each other. The team had limited their words and their few "conversations" had been brief. This contact had been essential in maintaining morale as the minutes ticked by. It was good to know that they were all well and accounted for.

Paris rose from his bunk at the sound of approaching footsteps. The entrance to his cell was composed of a single metal door with a large transparent window—a sturdy one, Paris had already determined—set within a thick stone wall. Two guards appeared.

"Move to the corner and face the wall," one of them ordered.

Paris lifted his hands in a universal sign of compliance and did as he had been told. The prospect of allowing a pair of armed men into the cell and offering them his back to shoot was disquieting, but he really didn't have a choice in the matter.

"Are your prisoners offered legal counsel?" Paris asked as he moved toward the corner, sneaking one last look at his captors.

The voice that responded was cold enough to send ice pouring down his spine, but its familiarity had the opposite effect.

"I don't think that's going to be necessary," the deep, rich voice of Kathryn Janeway replied.

Paris turned automatically as she stepped past the guards into the cell. He hadn't seen her face during the Nihydron meeting, but Chakotay had prepared him for it. Apart from the Rilnar uniform—a long forest-green jacket belted at the waist by wide taupe bands and matching pants that were tucked into knee-high brown boots—she was Kathryn Janeway's doppelganger. Her eyes were the same clear blue. Her hair was cut shorter than Paris had ever seen it in a straight bob that barely reached her chin. The flesh of her neck had been scarred, burned perhaps, though it was hard to tell in the faint light cast by two small rectangular sconces embedded in the rear wall of the cell.

The sight of her was disconcerting and oddly comforting at the same time.

Her next gesture confirmed for Paris that however impossible, this woman *was* Kathryn Janeway. Crossing her arms over her chest and lifting her chin slightly, she said, "Mister Paris, we really have to stop meeting like this."

VOYAGER

Lieutenant Harry Kim refused to remain seated at the conference table. He had first risen to examine the viewscreen embedded in the wall displaying the minefield. The closest he had come to a chair was to squeeze the headrest of his assigned seat in frustration between fitful paces.

Captain Chakotay understood and let him be. Had the current briefing consisted of a larger group, he might have taken issue, but allowing Kim to pace was better than having Kim calculate firing solutions on the Rilnar vessels standing between him and the away team.

"I can try to use the data we have already collected by observing the routes of the other ships that have entered the field to extrapolate a course for us," said Ensign Aytar Gwyn, *Voyager*'s alpha shift conn officer and best pilot, short of Tom Paris. She had recently begun exploring different hues of hair color. In the past she'd moved through a dozen shades of blue. Today, Gwyn's short, spiked locks were a violent shade of chartreuse.

"The Rilnar will follow us in," Chakotay retorted. "And they undoubtedly possess a detailed map of the subspace mines. Their firing solutions might force us into course corrections that would lead us directly into the path of a mine we don't know is there."

"Are we close to being able to detect them?" Kim asked.

"Seven is working on it," Chakotay replied.

"And we don't have an answer?" Kim asked.

Chakotay shrugged.

"I say we take our chances," Gwyn said. "I'll get us around those mines. If the Rilnar follow us in and suffer for it, that's their problem."

"The Rilnar are not our enemy," Chakotay reminded her. "This is their territory. Yes, they are being obstructive to a degree I find unwise, but let's be careful how we frame their position."

"She's right, though," Kim said. "We could—"

"Bridge to Captain Chakotay. Ornzitar Rileez is hailing you."

"Keep at it," Chakotay ordered, rising from the table.

Rileez's face was already on the viewscreen when Chakotay entered the bridge.

"Have you spoken with your *tilzitar*?" Chakotay asked by way of greeting.

"I have, Captain. And much to my surprise, this matter has already come to the attention of the denzit. She has requested that you, and you alone, transport to the surface of Sormana immediately."

Chakotay released a sigh of relief. "I'd be happy to do so," he acknowledged. "But the planet's surface is a little beyond our transporter's range from this point. If you can provide us with a course that will take us into orbit—"

"The denzit has authorized us to send you down using our transport system," Rileez advised. "It is an extremely rare protocol, established only for the use of our diplomatic envoys."

"You have transporters that can safely cover twenty million kilometers?" Chakotay asked dubiously.

"I can personally attest to our system's accuracy and safety, Captain," Rileez replied. "And I can assure you that none of us would willingly risk the denzit's displeasure by failing to bring you safely to her presence."

Chakotay believed him, but remained skeptical. "How do we do this?"

"I will provide coordinates for rendezvous with my vessel. You will transport aboard the Golant and be sent to the surface from here."

"Send them now," Chakotay said, "and we'll be under way as soon as we can lay in our course."

"Very good, Captain. End transmission."

6

RILNAR COMMAND CENTER—SORMANA

The denzit stood at ease, awaiting the completion of the transport reintegration sequence. It seemed to be taking longer than usual, but that was probably just her impatience talking.

Once she had dreamed, day and night, of a moment like this. As she stood, waiting for the appearance of Captain Chakotay of the Federation *Starship Voyager*, she wondered if she could make him understand. She wondered why it suddenly meant so much to her that he *should* understand.

She owed him nothing.

The high-pitched screech of the transporter built to a crescendo as a man whose face she barely remembered materialized before her. She tried to keep her countenance neutral as their eyes met, but couldn't help a brittle smile as the memories of their brief shared past returned with stunning clarity.

She thought she had left regret behind long ago. The disquieting heat rising suddenly in her chest suggested that her feelings were more powerful than she dared admit.

"Denzit," he greeted her.

"Welcome to Sormana, Captain Chakotay," she said, willing her voice to calmness.

He stepped down from the transporter pad hesitantly. She waited for him to move closer, but he held his ground.

"I accepted a long time ago that we would never meet again," she said. "But I must admit, part of me always hoped we would."

"You and I have met before?" he asked.

"The last time I saw you, you were a commander, *Voyager's* first officer."

"I served in that capacity for seven years. I'm afraid that doesn't narrow it down enough . . ."

"And I had just become *Voyager's* captain," the *denzit* added.

Chakotay's eyes narrowed as he seemed to struggle to arrange the pieces of this puzzle in his mind. Quite suddenly, she saw comprehension mingled with disbelief.

"The shattered mirror. The shattered ship. But that's not possible," he said.

"It seems we have some catching up to do."

"We do," he agreed. "But . . ."

"Your four officers are fine," she assured him, wondering

how it had taken him this long to inquire. Had their positions been reversed, that would have been her first question. "They were initially detained in our secured cells but after confirming Mister Paris's identity to my satisfaction, I had them taken to more appropriate and comfortable quarters. Your chief medical officer is more skilled than I would have believed possible of a hologram. Their Rilnar physiology fooled everyone but me, and he couldn't have had much information at his disposal when he performed their cosmetic alteration."

"Why do you assume that?" Chakotay asked.

"Had any Starfleet vessel made contact with the Rilnar prior to a few days ago, I would have been advised immediately. The Rilnar Colonial Force doesn't have as many general orders as Starfleet, but I added that one to their books the moment I took command on Sormana."

Chakotay tore his eyes away from her face to glance at the transporter officer.

"I will reunite you with your people shortly," the *denzit* said, "unless you'd prefer to see them now."

"If you say they are safe, I have no reason to doubt you."

"Really?"

"You're Kathryn Janeway, aren't you?"

"*Denzit* Janeway."

"Kathryn Janeway wouldn't lie to me about something that important. She would know how deeply a betrayal like that would be felt and how badly it would damage our relationship. You brought me here because you want me to understand what you're doing here. You had the capability to send my away team back using this transporter. If all you wanted was to return them, you'd have done it. You kept them here so I would come. Here I am."

He had said once that they had become the closest of friends. She'd glimpsed some of the crucible in which that relationship had been forged without ever experiencing it in depth, but she had never doubted his sincerity and every word he spoke now confirmed it.

"We'll talk in my office," she said.

"Lead the way."

Chakotay's head was spinning as *Denzit* Janeway led him through a series of well-lit but nondescript stone hallways toward her office. He remembered well the incident he believed she referred to. He was the only individual in existence in this timeline who *could* have remembered it.

When *Voyager* had encountered what he believed was a temporal anomaly and been broken into thirty-seven different time periods, the one Kathryn Janeway had occupied was set before *Voyager* had entered the Badlands and been pulled by the Caretaker to the Delta Quadrant. After the Doctor had injected Chakotay with a chroniton serum that had allowed him to safely travel between time periods, he had found her on the bridge and had been forced to take her prisoner in order to inject her with the same serum and earn her trust. Together they had journeyed through *Voyager*'s past and potential future trying to resolve the crisis. When they had parted, Chakotay had believed that neither she nor any of the other alternate versions of the friends and enemies he had encountered that day would remember the incident. For them, it would never have happened.

How she had survived with her memories intact was one of many mysteries requiring an answer in order for him to accept her claim.

They passed several closed metal doors. Those with windows revealed other uniformed officers at work over desks and conference tables. Every intersection was guarded by a single armed security guard.

The installation hummed with palpable energy. The light fixtures emitted a faint buzzing chorus and every officer they passed offered crisp salutes to the *denzit* before continuing on with long, purposeful strides. The air was recycled and a distinct smell of burned coolant was everywhere.

The office she ushered him into was twice the size of any of the others he'd glimpsed, but still smaller than his ready room aboard *Voyager*. A single metal frame chair rested in a corner and the *denzit* placed it before her desk and gestured for him to sit.

"I can offer you water or coffee," she said as she moved to take the seat behind the desk, a larger metal chair that looked even less comfortable than the one she'd given him.

"No, thank you," he replied, smiling, then asked, "Did the Rilnar always have coffee or was that something you brought them?"

She almost laughed. The brief smile softened her face somewhat but was closer to a grimace than a genuine expression of delight. There were dark memories that still haunted *his* Kathryn's eyes from time to time. *This* Kathryn Janeway's eyes were storm filled. He wondered how long it had been since they had been clear.

"The Rilnar are civilized people, but the weak water they called *saffa* was worse than nothing. A friend found me a suitable replacement off-world and it has since become a profitable commodity on the black market. It is the only luxury I permit myself."

After a short silence she continued. "I assume from your presence here, along with Mister Paris's, that you successfully restored the temporal field that shattered *Voyager* into all those disparate time periods."

"I did. The ship was returned, as we expected, to my time frame and no one on board but myself was left with any memory of the events we experienced."

She nodded thoughtfully. "I questioned Mister Paris delicately about it. His obliviousness seemed real."

"But something went wrong, or you wouldn't be here."

"You believed *Voyager* encountered a temporal anomaly that day," she went on.

"We both saw the rupture and the chroniton readings."

"But you never determined the cause?"

"There was nothing left to investigate after we restored the timeline."

"Not for you, perhaps. What I know now, and you apparently never suspected, was that the rupture was caused by the detonation of a chroniton torpedo."

"Someone fired a chroniton torpedo at *Voyager* and we never detected the ship or the weapon?" Chakotay asked dubiously.

"The ship was Zahl. The torpedo was designed to disrupt the time continuum, to force *Voyager* back to an earlier time frame, prior to the actions you took that caused the Zahl to target you. To target *me*, actually."

Chakotay shook his head in confusion and disbelief. "We never encountered the Zahl on our journey home," he corrected her. "We passed through an area of disputed space that contained their territory, along with that of several other local species, but no contact was made."

The *dénzit* leaned forward, resting her chin in her left hand, and searched his face for deception. "Captain," she finally said, "I realize that finding me here has created questions in your mind as to my identity and my loyalty. But you must not lie to me. You have no cause to do so. I am not now, nor will I ever be your enemy. If the Zahl contacts were classified, just say so."

"*There were no contacts,*" Chakotay insisted. "I know you aren't my enemy. You are clearly the victim of some terrible misunderstanding and I am prepared to do anything and everything in my power to make this situation right."

"Misunderstanding?" she asked in a tone suggesting he'd fallen woefully short of the mark. "The Zahl fired on *Voyager* in an attempt to revise history. When their torpedo failed to do that, they chose the next best option. They captured me. They succeeded in transporting me off the bridge just before you activated your lightning rod and restored the timeline. They imprisoned me. They tortured me. They presented me with evidence of *your* Captain Janeway's actions over almost an entire year that clearly indicate *Voyager* was involved in a lengthy military campaign that radically altered the balance of powers in this sector. They blamed *me* for the loss of a significant amount of what they considered to be *their* territory. It took them the better part of two years of repeated interrogations to accept the fact that *I* was not the Kathryn Janeway who had wronged them. At least not yet . . ."

Chakotay's head was swimming. He did not doubt her and he was completely unprepared for the riot of emotions her words provoked in him. Intellectually, he understood that this woman was not the same one he'd spent seven years standing beside during their first journey through the Delta Quadrant; the one he had loved, grieved, and recovered; and the one to whom he had since entrusted his heart and his soul.

But that did not change the *denzit's* unique claim on him.

It had been a strange and intriguing experience to meet Kathryn before she'd become his captain, his confidant, and dearest friend. Her skepticism had been alarming, as had her willingness to bend the Temporal Prime Directive to learn more about the choices she would eventually make and how they would affect her crew. Their shared experience of that day had helped him see how good the journey had been for her, despite the tragedy of its origin and the painful losses they suffered along the way. The Kathryn he had spent that day with had been tempted to restore the timeline to her period, to avoid the mission altogether. There had been a hardness in her then, something she had gradually shed over the years they worked together to survive and explore the Delta Quadrant on their way home. She'd never lost the capacity to call on her inner strength, to stand and fight when it was warranted. But she had committed herself to finding what joy there was to be had along the way and had allowed herself to form deep and powerful personal relationships with those she led.

This Kathryn Janeway had never had those experiences. Her reality had been quite different. She had moved directly from that strange day into captivity and torment. Somehow she had ended up here, fighting the people who had attacked *Voyager* and taken her prisoner. Chakotay had always assumed that like everyone else on board, she had been restored to her proper timeline with no memory of those events. It enraged him now to think of what she had suffered, what *might have been averted* had he thought to question the source of that temporal anomaly.

"*You missed it,*" Kathryn's voice said again in his mind.

But equally frustrating was this story she told of a year of combat he could never have forgotten had it occurred. This made no sense.

"Kathryn," he began.

"*Denzit,*" she corrected him sharply.

"No," he shot back. "*Kathryn*, I swear to you, my *Voyager* never encountered the Zahl. The only protracted conflict we knew during the seven years it took us to return to Earth was with the Borg. Whatever evidence the Zahl showed you must have been fabricated."

The *denzit* sat back in her chair, dropping her arms to her sides. She seemed deflated by his insistence. She had clearly brought him here looking for as many answers as he'd hoped to find and was every bit as puzzled by his words as he was by hers.

"If the Zahl used a chroniton torpedo, that suggests they have some advanced facility with temporal mechanics. Is it possible *they* got their facts wrong and even they didn't realize it?"

"I don't know," she admitted. "I heard her voice, more times than I care to remember. *My voice.* I don't see how. . ."

"You've been fighting the Zahl for how many years now? You must know their capabilities."

"I've been coordinating the war effort of the Rilnar natives on Sormana," she corrected him. "The Zahl Regnancy wants as little to do with this planet as the Rilnar Colonial Command. But all Rilnar, here and beyond, have long feared that the Zahl had access to temporal technology. Tantalizing rumors and fragments of half-remembered myths were all they had to go on. They've never been able to confirm it. My capture was as close as they've come to concrete evidence of the Zahl's dabbling.

"I can't give you detailed information on the technological capabilities of the Regnancy or the Colonials. Before I volunteered to serve on Sormana, I was either a prisoner or an honored guest. My sense is that both sides have advanced tactical systems, likely on par with Starfleet's. Both possess transporter technology. But as you must know by now, the colonists on both sides and their leaders have moved on. Colonial Command has refused to aid the natives of this planet in their quest to rid themselves of the scourge that is the Zahl. I could tell you everything about the Rilnar and Zahl capabilities here, but it bears little resemblance to those of either side's spacefaring fleets. I'm afraid we're fighting a conventional ground-based campaign."

"Go back," Chakotay requested. "How did you escape the Zahl?"

"I was rescued by the Rilnar. Their intelligence operatives had somehow learned of my capture and were investigating any evidence of Zahl temporal research. They freed me during a raid on the Zahl ship where I was being held. When I told them my story, they were intrigued. They knew nothing of me, or *Voyager*, but they were able to verify that I was not some Zahl counteragent. One of their lower ranking but very experienced officers made me his personal project. We spent more than a year traveling to nearby sectors, searching for any evidence of *Voyager*'s fate. We learned little. There were rumors of an alien vessel from a distant quadrant, enough to keep us going long after we should have abandoned the search. But they came to nothing. When we reached the outskirts of Borg space we were forced to turn back."

"We're only a few light-years from the heart of Zahl territory," Chakotay said. "They launched that chroniton torpedo at us tens of thousands of light-years from here. Are their propulsion capabilities that advanced?"

"To this day I cannot tell you how the Zahl found *Voyager* when and where they did. I only know that when I was brought to their vessel to be imprisoned we were in Zahl space. I have not seen evidence of technology that would allow them to cover that distance, but obviously they must have it."

Chakotay shook his head. This didn't add up. "What happened after you gave up your search?"

Janeway sighed wistfully. "By then, a great deal had changed. The Rilnar officer I spoke of, Dayne," she said, her voice suddenly thick, "became more than my ally and friend." Her jaw tensed as she continued, "Those lines you once said you and I never crossed—Dayne and I did. He is a remarkable man. He reminds me of you, in some ways. He was born on Sormana but left when he was young to study in the colonies, hoping to use what he learned to aid those he left behind. He convinced me that we could do more good here than by risking assimilation. The Rilnar Colonial Command would have put me to work, but *here,* I could actually make a difference.

"On stardate 56863, I sent a transmission to Starfleet using the Rilnar's longest range arrays, advising them of my resignation. I then accepted Rilnar citizenship, and a commission with the Sormana Liberation Force. I came here, where I served for four months under the previous *denzit,* Kal Uthar. When he lost his life in battle, I was promoted and have led our forces here for almost three years now."

"But your quarrel is with the Zahl Rengnancy. They were the ones who captured and tortured you. You can't learn anything about their true motivations from here, can you?"

"The Zahl are all the same," she replied. "When we liberate Sormana, Zahl everywhere will know that *I* was the one who beat them."

"I see," Chakotay said. It made a certain amount of sense. Part of him couldn't imagine any version of Kathryn Janeway abandoning her quest to return home, but given the extenuating circumstances, the entrance into her life of this *Dayne,* anything was possible. He couldn't blame her for choosing a little personal happiness after so many years of pain and frustration. He admired the courage it must have taken her to risk it. But to lose herself, her identity as a Starfleet officer, was still a leap he had a hard time reconciling. It would have been one thing had she simply built a life with Dayne, settled on some peaceful planet, and committed herself to living the rest of her life there. Instead, she had taken up arms, used her training and considerable abilities to help her adopted species perpetuate an ancient grudge, and turned her back on any future she might have had with her own people.

There were still so many questions, but only one would absolutely confirm the truth of her words.

"I know this is going to sound like an odd question," Chakotay continued. "But on or around Stardate 57445, did you experience anything unusual?"

He expected to see her search her memory. Instead, she started visibly, as if she had been slapped. Her eyes flashed as the demons there she barely held at bay struggled for release. She seemed briefly on the verge of tears, but some defense solidified around her, transforming her from cold to stone.

"What significance does that stardate hold for you?" she demanded slowly.

"Please, just tell me."

She obviously wanted to refuse. She looked away, collected her thoughts, and turned to face him again.

"I was seriously injured," she began, her voice utterly devoid of emotion. "The doctors tell me I died while they were attempting to repair what damage they could. The base from which I was coordinating our defenses at that time had come under attack. We lost many good men and women that day. A specialist had come in, an off-world physician sent to reinforce our dwindling supply of doctors. He saved me. He brought me back."

Chakotay released a deep breath he had not realized he was holding. He wanted to apologize for all she had suffered, all she had endured, all she had been forced to risk. The life of the woman he loved had been excruciating enough. He had never imagined that anyone's could have been worse. But *hers* came damned close.

He didn't expect this part of the truth to make any sense to her and he wished to spare her the additional suffering but he knew she deserved as much of it as he could share.

"The Kathryn Janeway I serve with died on that day," he finally said. "She had gone to investigate an unusual Borg cube. It absorbed her and transformed her into its queen. It was ultimately destroyed."

"I'm so sorry," the *denzit* offered, truly meeting his eyes for the first time among the ruins of shared grief. "And you now command *Voyager* in her place?"

Chakotay shook his head. "We made it home about six months after you and I met. We continued to serve in the Alpha Quadrant until a year ago. Kathryn's death happened there. Starfleet assembled a fleet of vessels to continue our explorations of the Delta Quadrant after her death."

"And you were the obvious choice to lead that fleet?"

"Not at first. A lot has happened in the last year, including the resurrection of our *Admiral* Janeway."

"I beg your pardon."

"To make an incredibly long story short, the Q took exception to Kathryn's death. They returned her to us to correct an imbalance created in the multiverse by the actions of an ancient species."

"The Q? I vaguely remember—"

"*Voyager* didn't encounter them until about a year and a half into our journey."

"Are you saying we both died at the same moment in time more than two years ago, and *both* of us are still alive?"

"It looks that way. Admiral Janeway leads our fleet."

The *denzit* took a deep breath. "I see."

"There's so much more to tell you. Obviously, Starfleet had no idea that you existed. If we had, we would have moved heaven and earth to find you. But we're here now. You can come back with me. We can return you to the Alpha Quadrant, you can see your mother and sister again; whatever you wish."

"I apologize, Captain, if anything I have said or done here has misled you. Your Admiral Janeway is living the life of which

I once dreamed. But that life is *hers*. When I resigned from Starfleet, I did not intend it as a temporary solution. I have accepted my new life here. My presence is critical to the Rilnar efforts to free Sormana from the Zahl. I won't abandon them now or ever." Rising from her chair, she said, "If you will come with me, I will take you to your crew. You will all be returned to your ship. At that point you should set your course away from Sormana and never look back."

VESTA

The conference room was filled with expectant faces when Captain Chakotay entered. In addition to the other fleet captains—Farkas, Glenn, and O'Donnell—Admiral Janeway had ordered Paris, the Doctor, Seven, and Counselor Cambridge to join the briefing. There had not been time yet for the Doctor to return Paris and Cambridge to their human appearance, but he had restored his matrix's customary display. Lieutenant Decan stood behind her chair making notations on a padd.

Chakotay took the seat to Janeway's right. Before he had settled himself she said, "Well, Captain?"

"In order for me to explain to you how *Denzit* Janeway came to be on Sormana, I will have to violate the Temporal Prime Directive," Chakotay began.

Janeway exhaled her frustration slowly. "For the purposes of this meeting, that directive is suspended. Mister Decan, stop all recordings. No officer present will discuss anything Captain Chakotay is about to reveal. Understood?"

Nods all around the table were swift and sharp.

"The event in question occurred on stardate 54391. In order to avert a catastrophe I was forced to overload *Voyager*'s deflector dish."

"I remember that," Janeway said softly.

"As required, I filed a classified incident report and scheduled it for transmission to the Department of Temporal Investigations as soon as *Voyager* was in range. After we returned, I attended a brief meeting with an agent from the DTI and was ordered to maintain my silence regarding the incident."

Chakotay went on to explain as succinctly as possible the events of that day; the encounter with the temporal rupture, the shattering of the ship into more than three dozen time frames, the chroniton-infused serum the Doctor devised and how he used it to restore the ship to his timeframe with the assistance of the version of Captain Janeway from *Voyager*'s past. He then added the information *Denzit* Janeway had given him, including the Zahl attack and their capture of the *denzit*. Finally, he confirmed that the *denzit* had died, along with every other version of Kathryn Janeway in June 2380, but had been revived by a Rilnar physician.

"You believe her?" Admiral Janeway asked once Chakotay had finished his recitation.

"I do," he replied.

"So do I," Commander Paris added. When Janeway shifted her gaze to him, he continued, "It was downright eerie to meet her. She's *you,* Admiral, and at the same time, she isn't."

"Explain," Seven requested.

"Over the years, I've had the opportunity to observe the admiral under many stressful situations. This *denzit* has the same strength and determination I've come to see as one of Admiral Janeway's defining characteristics. But the woman I met is also incredibly angry. I can't imagine that she's happy with the turn of events that led her to Sormana."

"I agree with that assessment," Chakotay said.

"That's to be expected, isn't it?" Cambridge asked. "True, in the last five years she's gone from living in hell to ruling over it, but it's still hell."

"I assume you advised her that our fleet would arrange to return her to the Alpha Quadrant immediately," Janeway said.

"I did. She refused. She says she won't abandon the Rilnar on Sormana."

"Isn't there a name for that neurosis?" Farkas asked.

"It's similar to Stockholm syndrome," Cambridge began.

"Not precisely," the Doctor interjected before the counselor could continue. "Had she grown to sympathize with the Zahl, the case would be cut-and-dried. But she has transferred her allegiance to the Rilnar."

"She's still a Starfleet officer," Janeway said. "Her first duty is to the Federation."

"She resigned her commission, Admiral," Chakotay reminded her.

"Under extreme duress," Janeway clarified. "Given all she has endured, it is understandable, but there must be some way to reach her and convince her that the path she is choosing to follow is . . ."

"Is what?" O'Donnell asked.

"Inappropriate," Janeway finished. "It is clear that the Rilnar are technologically advanced, perhaps even on par with the Federation, but the expertise she gained as a Starfleet officer is specialized. Regulations don't allow for her to use it in the service of anyone's interests other than Starfleet's."

"You're worried that she is violating the Prime Directive?" O'Donnell asked, incredulous.

"She very well could be," Janeway replied. "The Nihydron indicated that the Rilnar were on the verge of losing this fight until she took command of their forces. If she is the reason for that, the case is cut-and-dried, whether she used her knowledge to improve the Rilnar's tactics or weapons, or simply put existing ones to better use. She's interfering with the development of two civilizations and may be the determining factor should the Rilnar ultimately prevail."

"Don't we have a bigger problem here?" Farkas said.

"The Zahl intelligence that caused them to attack *Voyager* in the first place," Seven said.

"Where did that come from?" Farkas asked.

"The *denzit* was convinced that the evidence was authentic," Chakotay said. "But I can't imagine where it came from either. She also said that it has long been believed, but never confirmed, that the Zahl have some unique facility with temporal weapons."

Janeway sat back in her chair, clasping her hands on the table. She appeared to consider the situation from multiple angles.

"Obviously, we need to investigate that claim," Janeway said. "If *Voyager* did encounter the Zahl and none of us remember it, that suggests that the current timeline has been corrupted."

"Not necessarily," Seven said. "Depending on the Zahl's level of expertise, they may have misunderstood whatever intelligence led them to capture the *denzit*. She said they were attempting to revise history with a chroniton torpedo and failed. They've *mastered* nothing. It is possible that whatever events they took issue with never affected this timeline."

"You think they are looking at information from an alternate timeline and aren't aware of that fact?" Farkas asked.

"Without analyzing the data's source, it is impossible to reach any conclusion."

"Do you suppose the Zahl would turn that intelligence over to us if we asked nicely?" Farkas asked.

"Hang on," O'Donnell interrupted. "If the Zahl were concerned enough about *Voyager*'s presence in this quadrant to attack the ship and capture its captain, why haven't they responded more forcefully to us?" he asked.

"Maybe they've detected the entire fleet and are wary of engaging it," Farkas suggested.

"They've got more than twenty ships patrolling the perimeter of that minefield. I'm guessing that's just scratching the surface of their entire fleet. Our four ships are no real threat to them. They should never have answered Chakotay's hail in the first place. They should have opened fire the moment they detected *Voyager*," O'Donnell insisted.

"He's got a point," Cambridge said.

"Could the *denzit* have been lying to you about the Zahl?" Janeway asked Chakotay. "She might have named them as her captors in order to justify taking the Rilnar's side in this fight."

Chakotay paused before replying. "I didn't sense any deception from her. I sensed pain, regret, and defensiveness, but for all that, she was more open than you might expect under the circumstances."

"Kes," the Doctor muttered.

"Doctor?" Janeway asked.

"Stardate 50786.1, Kes reported experiencing a time paradox. She was moving backward in time and instructed me to construct a bio-temporal chamber to purge her system of chroniton particles. She said she was exposed when a Krenim torpedo became lodged in the ship and she came in contact with it in order to determine its precise temporal variance," the Doctor summarized.

"We're not that far from Krenim space," Chakotay said.

"The year from hell," Janeway said softly. "No, the Year *of* Hell," she corrected herself.

"I beg your pardon, Admiral?" Farkas asked.

"Kes reported a number of troubling facts from the future she saw during that experience. One of them was a sustained battle between *Voyager* and the Krenim that the crew referred to as the *Year of Hell*," Janeway clarified.

"Kes left the ship not long after that," Paris reminded her. "There's no way to know if anything she remembered of that future actually happened."

"It is true that an individual's experience of an alternate time thread does not automatically correlate to the permanent existence of that thread," Seven interjected. "It might have existed briefly, or never, once you were able to eliminate the chroniton particles from Kes's body."

"But it's still intriguing, isn't it?" O'Donnell asked. "We now have reports from two sources—that as best we can tell, never met each other—of a sustained conflict in this sector in which *Voyager* participated. I, for one, think that requires follow-up."

"I agree," Janeway said, "but the greater priority is convincing the *denzit* to come to her senses." After a moment, the admiral added, "I should speak with her."

"No," Cambridge said immediately.

"Why not?" Janeway asked, not irritated but predisposed in that direction depending on the counselor's answer.

"Objectivity is a challenge for anyone in your position, Admiral. In this case, you cannot be expected to summon *any*, let alone enough to effectively advocate for your position in that argument."

"She's *you*, Admiral," Farkas said. "She knows every tactic you could possibly devise to convince her to change her mind. She's had that conversation with herself already and apparently you lost."

"At the time she made the choice to aid the Rilnar, she must have believed that rescue by Starfleet was no longer a possibility," Janeway countered. "Now that it *is* . . ."

"She doesn't want to be rescued," Chakotay said. "She was very clear on that point."

"Then she has a reason beyond what she already communicated to you that she has not yet revealed," Janeway said.

"How do you know that?" O'Donnell asked, then added immediately, "Apologies. I retract the question."

"She did mention a Rilnar officer named Dayne with whom she apparently shared an intimate relationship," Chakotay said. "I have no idea if he is still in the picture. I didn't really press her for details about her personal life. But either way, I don't believe you will be more successful than I was in convincing her to come with us. Apart from you and I, there's no one who knows her well enough or who she would trust, to even make the attempt. I'm willing to try again, but . . ."

"There's no one here *now*," Paris said. "But there is someone."

Janeway looked to Paris and smiled. "You're right." After a moment she continued, "Captain Farkas, prepare the *Vesta* to begin a search of the area between here and Krenim space for any evidence of this Year of Hell. Commander Glenn, I want you to take the *Galen* into Zahl space. Seven will accompany you. Commander O'Donnell, you'll take *Demeter* into Rilnar space. Given his expertise in comparative mythology and alien psychology, I'd like you to continue working with Counselor Cambridge. I want all of you to learn all you can of the history of the conflict on Sormana from each of these species' points of view. While you do that, Captain Chakotay will take *Voyager* to the Beta Quadrant."

"To rendezvous with *Titan*?" Chakotay asked.

"I'll prepare a formal temporary transfer request for you to present to Captain Riker," Janeway said, nodding. Rising sharply, she added, "Dismissed."

7

VOYAGER

"There you are," Lieutenant Harry Kim said as he moved to stand behind Lieutenant Conlon at the main holodeck control panel. She said nothing as he wrapped his arms around her waist and began to lightly kiss the back of her neck. "Shift ended an hour ago, Lieutenant," he reminded her. "We're both off duty at the same time for the first time in days."

A pleasant shiver ran up Conlon's spine but she continued entering the parameters for the simulation she was creating. A large screen hung suspended before her, lines of programming code in a continuous string. In the center of the lab, a holographic representation of *Voyager*'s computer core had been re-created.

Kim was not dissuaded by her silence. As his caresses became more insistent, Conlon paused the simulation she was running and began entering a new set of parameters into the holomatrix.

"I don't have a lot of time tonight," she said, her voice uncharacteristically low.

"I could order a site-to-site transport to my quarters," Kim suggested, "or yours, if you'd prefer."

Conlon shook her head, finally turning to face Kim. "We're on a *holodeck*, Harry," she reminded him.

Kim smiled, puzzled. He then looked past her to see that the setting had changed to a moonlit glen filled with fragrant night blossoms. A pool of water was edged by a long bank of soft earth.

"Computer," Kim called, "secure main holodeck and lock the door. Accept no overrides, authorization Kim pi gamma epsilon."

A few hours later, Kim was still lying on the warm ground counting his lucky stars. Conlon began to extricate herself from his arms and search the landscape for the various pieces of her uniform.

"I'm starved," Kim said, rolling onto his side and resting his head on his hand as he watched her dress. "Want to go to the mess for a midnight snack?"

"Tempting," she agreed, "but I really need to get back to work."

"On what?" Kim asked. "Engineering is finally back in one piece again, isn't it?"

Having located and donned her undergarments, trousers, and shirt, Conlon settled herself beside him, sitting cross-legged. "Yes. It's not that. I'm working on a redesign of our security authorization parameters."

"Why?" Kim asked, intrigued.

"I understand the need for command-level officers to be able to access primary systems and modify them as needed in an emergency situation," Conlon replied. "But twice now in the last year, we've had aliens using those clearances, which left the rest of us at their mercy. We need to stop countering these attacks and instead, prepare for them."

"That sounds like something you should discuss with *Voyager*'s chief of security, don't you think?" Kim teased.

"I would, but he can't keep his hands off of me when we're alone together," she said, smiling.

"You want me to put him on report?" Kim asked.

"I'd rather he just helped me."

Kim sat up. "Glad to. Let me get dressed while you tell me what you're thinking."

As he rose to do so, Conlon said, "Right now, various operations require unique command level clearances. As long as you are an officer with appropriate clearance, the chief of security, for example, and can enter your personal codes, like you did when you locked that door, the computer will accept limited changes to any standard protocol you are allowed to access. The higher up you go, or depending upon your area of specialization, the range of modifications you can make becomes greater, as do the number of systems you can access. But anyone with your command codes can make changes on your behalf."

"That's not always true. There are voiceprint recognitions required as well," Kim noted. "If I try to use Admiral Janeway's command codes, which change every few days and which are encrypted within our databases, the computer won't allow it unless I can also access her voice. A recorded sample won't work. It has to be her."

"But if an alien takes control of Admiral Janeway's body and can access her memories, he's got her voice and her most recent codes, and we're in trouble."

Kim's face softened. He quickly put on his tank top and rejoined her, wrapping his arms around her. She relented, leaning in to rest her head on his chest.

"I understand your concern," he said. "What happened to you was unacceptable. And I'll never forgive myself for not finding a way to prevent it."

"But now that we know that it can happen, we have to make sure it doesn't happen again," Conlon insisted. "And that's not even our greatest vulnerability."

"What is?" Kim asked, brushing his lips over her hair.

"Admiral Batiste was our commanding officer briefly, and managed to not only override all security parameters but also to plant forged logs into the database to deflect suspicion. It was too late when we realized what he had done and suddenly we're opening a rift to fluidic space."

"Yes, but you're not going to restrict the access profile of the admiral of this fleet," Kim said.

"That's not my intention," Conlon said. She gently pulled herself upright and stared into Kim's eyes. "We have bioneural circuitry now. We've moved light-years beyond binary programming options. The computer has the capability to *reason*, within limits, but we've never maximized the potential of that function. The gel packs were designed to allow for all previous data to be included in any analysis the computer performs. It considers the past before it makes a recommendation or performs a requested function. But its results can be countermanded by anyone with appropriate command codes. We could expand that potential. We could allow the computer to question commands that present risks to the entire system or ship. An added level of accountability might have prevented Batiste and Xolani's actions."

"It might also have killed us fifty other times," Kim replied. "I don't know about you, but I don't want to find myself arguing with the main computer when I give it an order in an emergency situation. 'Computer, raise shields.' *'Why, Lieutenant?'* And just that fast, *boom.* We're all dead."

"I'm not talking about standard functions," Conlon argued. "But when Admiral Batiste ordered the computer to open that rift, I wouldn't have minded if that request were at least verified with the next officer in line or the chief engineer."

"What if those officers had just been killed and there wasn't time for discussion?" Kim asked. "What if entering fluidic space was the only, admittedly terrible option on the table? An armada of angry Voth are a few seconds behind us and there's nowhere else to run."

"Now you're just being a jerk," Conlon said.

"I'm playing devil's advocate," Kim countered. "Starfleet has experimented in the past with sentient computers and none have ever been developed that were safe enough to consider using. I'm all for new ideas and new solutions to old problems, but something like this takes years of work and a team of dedicated professionals. This isn't something you and I can come up with in our spare time, let alone consider implementing in the middle of a deep-space mission."

Conlon's face tensed, stricken by his rebuke. "Then you won't even look at the new protocols I'm developing?"

"I didn't say that," Kim replied. "But there's no way B'Elanna is going to sign off on something like this. And even if she did, it would be over my official protests."

Conlon came quickly to her feet. "Open the door, Harry," she demanded.

He rose and tried to take her hands, but she pulled back.

"Computer," she called, "override security lock-out of the main holodeck, authorization Conlon beta beta six delta."

"Override not permitted. Security clearance required."

"Come on, Nancy," Kim pleaded.

"How many times has an alien presence wreaked havoc on this ship?" she demanded. "How many times does it have to happen before you realize that *security* is all too often a comforting illusion around here? If you wanted to hurt me right now, *boom*, I'm dead already."

"Computer, override security lock-out of the main holodeck," Kim ordered.

The computer complied instantly with a series of short trills. *"Override terminated,"* it reported.

"I would never hurt you," Kim said gently. "You have to know that."

Conlon shook her head. "You just don't get it." She left the holodeck too quickly for him to respond.

VESTA

"Icheb, hi," Lieutenant Bryce greeted the ensign when he approached the diagnostic interface panel located at the main engineering station adjacent to the *Vesta*'s combined warp/slipstream drive assembly.

"Lieutenant Bryce," Icheb began, "I was hoping we could review your efficiency evaluation. I know I'm a little early, so if you need more time . . ."

Bryce checked the chronometer on the display as he replied, "You're not early. Okay, you're exactly twenty-six seconds early but around here we call that 'on time' so, sure."

Icheb glanced nervously at the three other crewmen who were busy running other operations at workstations. "Is there somewhere else you would prefer to . . . ?"

Bryce's face fell into confusion. He almost looked as if he was having trouble following Icheb's words. "You mean somewhere other than main engineering?" Bryce asked. "Because I sort of have to be here right now and, *oh*," the lieutenant suddenly corrected himself, "you mean somewhere else like *my office*. No. Well, we could but it's sort of, well . . ." Bryce trailed off as he bit his lower lip in consternation. Shifting gears briskly, he continued, "You know what? That's fine. Come on. It's just . . ."

But his next words were lost as he hurried past several other engineers and swiftly climbed the ladder that led to a catwalk above the drive. Icheb followed dutifully and by the time he reached the chief's small private office Bryce was already grabbing stacks of padds and random spare parts from the only chair in the room and throwing them into a corner that was already piled high with Icheb-could-not-even-tell-what. The area immediately surrounding the office's three display panels and interfaces was similarly cluttered and with a wave of his arm, Bryce ruthlessly cleared it, leaving just enough space to perch on the edge of the surface as he motioned for Icheb to take the chair.

Icheb had seen worse while visiting the homes of some of his fellow Academy cadets during short semester breaks. Had any of their quarters looked this way they would have been reprimanded or summarily dismissed. He found it difficult to understand how anyone, let alone a chief engineer, could work in a room like this and was pleased he had not seen it as part of his initial evaluation.

"I know it's awful," Bryce admitted sheepishly, "but there's just never enough time, you know?"

Icheb did not. But he nodded as if he did. "I guess."

"Anyway, go ahead. Give it to me straight."

"Well," Icheb said, trying to remember how he had intended to begin this conversation, "In many respects, your department is excelling."

Bryce seemed surprised. "Really? Because by my count we're behind in scheduling standard maintenance to forty-three systems, all of which are running fine but without checking the standard diagnostics we're probably missing some minor wear and tear and necessary replacements. I counted ninety-one protocol deficiencies the day you were here because frankly, I don't care if my people call me *Phinn* or *Bryce* or *hey, you* when they need to get my attention, and that sort of thing trickles down. By the way, you should definitely call me Phinn. I was planning to use your report to prioritize our upgrade schedule, unless you've found some glaring issues I've missed, which I'm sure you have. I mean, I'm new at this and right now I call it a good day when everything keeps running and Captain Farkas is happy. I know I have to do better, but, take this afternoon for example. I've got Kurtz and Simensky checking our benamite crystals for microfractures, Yolanda is running down a glitch in our industrial replicator because it gave me a type-six conduit junction when I specifically requested a type-nine, which could be a programming error but might be something more serious, and everyone else is running standard system checks or raiding our inventory for a few things Lieutenant Conlon just requested. Meanwhile, I've got a much bigger problem to solve right now and if you've got a minute I could really use your help."

Icheb actually managed to follow all of this. That Bryce had already come up with many of the same numbers he had was extraordinary. But what was most intriguing to Icheb was the amount of information currently running at warp speed through Bryce's mind without driving the young man to either madness or despair. Setting the padd he had brought with him down on the nearest pile, Icheb said, "How can I be of assistance?"

Bryce smiled infectiously. "Captain Farkas gave me a new assignment this morning. Somewhere out there is evidence of actions *Voyager* may have taken in this sector that were later erased by an alteration to the timeline. So the question before us is, 'How does one begin searching for something that should no longer exist?'"

"Upon what do you base the assumption that the evidence in question ever existed?" Icheb asked.

"Personal testimony from two reliable sources," Bryce replied, "one of whom apparently *heard* pieces of it firsthand."

"Heard? So we're talking about what? Logs?"

"Probably."

"Logs that were transmitted and somehow captured before the timeline was altered?"

"Maybe," Bryce allowed. "But not likely. I keep wondering," Bryce said, scratching his head vigorously, "if I were a starship captain and I found myself at war with someone I knew was capable of altering the timeline, what would I do to make sure that current data wasn't lost by a temporal reset? Better yet," Bryce continued, "you actually served on *Voyager*. What would Admiral Janeway have done in those circumstances?"

Icheb did not have an answer. But he was determined to find one as soon as possible.

VOYAGER

As Doctor Sharak completed his review of the records Doctor Sal had forwarded to him, he marveled at the innovation of his Starfleet counterparts. Vega Nine was, as Sal had suggested, an extremely complex organism, and the damage it did to those it infected was horrific. The treatment regimen Sal devised had included the creation of a nanovirus specifically designed to interrupt Vega Nine's replication sequence. Purging the virus had involved numerous transfusions and, in several instances, organ replacement. The final stage of the treatment had consisted of gene replacement therapy to correct for the damage done by the virus.

That anyone had survived Vega Nine was testament to Sal's perseverance and brilliance. That she would prefer to forget the experience was also perfectly understandable. Many who chose to enter the medical profession brought healthy egos along with them. Only those blessed with exceptional self-regard could meddle with such casual arrogance with the complex inner workings of living beings. Physicians were often accused of "playing God." Sharak doubted that anyone could have done better than Doctor El'nor Sal in ending Vega Nine's ruthless devastation. But he shared Sal's discomfort with the work. It had been necessary. But each step in the process had undoubtedly been terrifying to attempt. Her personal logs attested to the weary days fraught with frustration and countless dead ends, all of which she had eventually overcome. The experience had not left her eager to scale even higher mountains. The logs simply ended with the hope that Vega Nine had been the worst the universe would ever show her of such merciless organisms.

Sharak was inclined to agree with her assessment. After comparing the blood work of those who had succumbed to Vega Nine with that of the members of the *da Vinci*'s crew who had been infected six years earlier by a similar alien virus, *appia veraba*, that had severely compromised their immune systems prior to attacking their DNA, he had concluded that the two strains had less in common than he had initially feared.

A thorough review of Lieutenant Conlon's medical records had suggested to Sharak that her current panels might indicate a resurgence of *appia veraba* organisms that could have lain dormant within her body until *Xolani's* attack. He would have to conduct new tests in order to verify his suspicion that this was unlikely, but should that prove to be true, he was no closer to understanding the current irregularities present in the chief engineer's immune system. He hoped fervently that as the Doctor suspected, her levels would return to normal soon.

Time would tell.

Ensign Icheb found Commander Torres standing outside Counselor Cambridge's quarters. She appeared to be at something of a loss. As gamma shift was well under way, she must have assumed the counselor would be sleeping, but would surely answer her summons.

"Commander," he said as he approached.

Torres turned toward him. "Icheb? Why aren't you sleeping?"

"I wished to speak with you prior to *Voyager's* departure," Icheb replied. "The computer advised me of your current location."

"What is it?"

"Request permission to remain with the *Vesta* until *Voyager* returns from the Beta Quadrant."

"Why?"

"I started my review of *Vesta's* engineering department but we got a little sidetracked working together on a new critical issue Captain Farkas assigned to Phinn."

"Phinn?" Torres asked.

"Lieutenant Bryce," Icheb corrected himself. "We're making excellent progress and I would really like to continue assisting him, unless you feel my presence here is required. I have created an automated program to flag any unusual crew assignments Lieutenant Conlon might make in the interim. You will receive daily reports at your personal station while we are separated."

Torres considered the request along with the fact that this was the most excited she had seen Icheb since his reviews had begun. Progress was being made, even if it wasn't happening precisely how she had envisioned it. And the ensign was certainly honoring her needs as well as those of the fleet. Nodding, she said, "I think we can manage for a few days without you. Be prepared when we get back for a thorough briefing on your work with Lieutenant Bryce."

Icheb nodded. "Thank you, Commander."

"Computer," Torres called, "locate Counselor Cambridge."

"*Counselor Cambridge is not aboard,*" the computer replied.

"He was ordered by Admiral Janeway to accompany *Demeter*," Icheb advised Torres.

"Damn it. She's already left, hasn't she?"

"Two hours ago," Icheb confirmed.

"I guess it will have to wait."

"What will, Commander?"

"You'd better get back to the *Vesta* before *Phinn* leaves without you."

Icheb did not understand the heat that rose to his cheeks at this typical, good-natured ribbing from Commander Torres.

8

STARSHIP TITAN

This is an unexpected pleasure," Captain William Riker said, offering Chakotay his hand as *Voyager*'s commanding officer was ushered into *Titan*'s ready room.

"The pleasure is mine, Captain," Chakotay replied.

"How is the Delta Quadrant these days?" Riker asked as he moved to sit behind his desk and motioned for Chakotay to take the nearest chair opposite it.

"Never a dull moment."

Riker grinned gamely. "I know what you mean."

"We spent the last few months initiating diplomatic relations with a confederacy of planets that rivals the Federation in size and strength."

"I hope you parted on good terms."

"We did," Chakotay assured him, "in spite of some vast cultural differences."

"It's those differences that make our missions worthwhile, don't you think?"

"If you'd like I can leave you with our most recent logs; might make for some interesting late-night reading."

"I'd appreciate that. And I'd be more than happy to return the favor." After a moment Riker asked, "How is Admiral Janeway adjusting?"

"To what?"

"I understand Ken Montgomery has retired. I believe that puts the vice admiral directly under Admiral Akaar's supervision."

Chakotay shrugged. "Honestly, I think she's relieved."

"Your fleet has suffered significant losses since you left the Alpha Quadrant a year ago. You were what, nine ships?"

"Three of those are still with us. One was reassigned and replaced with the *Vesta*."

Riker chuckled. "The last time I saw the *Vesta* she was in pieces at Utopia Planitia."

"Admiral Janeway convinced Admiral Akaar to rectify that situation."

"I've known Kathryn Janeway since we were both cadets and I've yet to meet anyone who could stand against her when she had her mind set on something."

"I hope the request I've come to make won't prove the exception to that rule," Chakotay said, offering Riker the padd containing the transfer request Janeway had written.

As Riker started to read, a chime sounded. "Come in," he said.

Commander Deanna Troi, Riker's first-contact specialist, wife, and one of the few former *Enterprise* officers that Chakotay had met, hurried into the room, her face radiant. She still carried herself with a powerful grace and serenity. He remembered being struck with her poise when she first boarded *Voyager* to assist the crew with their reintegration to life in the Federation after their unexpected return home four years earlier. Chakotay had formed a distinctly positive impression and found himself wishing for a counselor more like Troi in the early days of Cambridge's service aboard *Voyager*.

"Chakotay, I couldn't believe it when Will told me we were about to intercept *Voyager*. How are you?"

"Never better," Chakotay replied honestly.

"I would have met you in the transporter room, but I had to get Natasha settled."

"Natasha?"

"Our daughter," Riker interjected as he continued studying the padd.

"A little over six months old now," Troi added.

"Congratulations to you both," Chakotay said sincerely.

"Thank you," Troi said with unrepressed delight. "But what brings you here? I hope all is well on *Voyager*."

"Admiral Janeway is requesting that we temporarily transfer Tuvok to *Voyager*," Riker informed her.

Troi's face fell into more serious lines, clearly aware that Janeway would never make such a request lightly.

"Why?"

"We have encountered a temporally displaced version of Kathryn Janeway in the Delta Quadrant," Chakotay replied. "Her timeline starts shortly after she took command of *Voyager* but prior to its journey to the Delta Quadrant. She was captured and tortured by an alien species. I've spoken with her, and she is refusing to abandon those who took her in when it seemed all hope of rescue by Starfleet was lost."

"Then she wouldn't have known you," Troi said. "Is it any wonder she might have greeted your offer of rescue with suspicion?"

"Actually, we *have* met before, but I can't explain that situation without violating the Temporal Prime Directive."

"Don't," Riker said, rising from his chair and offering the padd to Troi. "Some of my crew, including Tuvok, have worked closely with agents from the DTI, and I just can't face that much paperwork right now."

"You are convinced that she *is* another Kathryn Janeway," Troi said.

"We are."

Riker and Troi exchanged a meaningful, somber glance. Chakotay wondered if it had something to do with another duplicate Starfleet officer, Thomas Riker, a transporter-created twin of Will's. Chakotay had actually met him a decade earlier while still a member of the Maquis. He was suddenly struck by the realization that as with the *denzit,* two identical people choosing very different paths became pale reflections of each other.

"Tuvok is the one officer we can think of who might stand a chance of reaching her," Chakotay continued. "Their friendship predated their service on *Voyager.* We believe *Denzit* Janeway is more likely to trust him than any of us."

"Even the admiral?" Riker asked.

"Especially the admiral,*"* Troi corrected him.

Riker turned away from his wife's penetrating gaze. "I understand, and I agree that this situation is vital to Starfleet's interests." Tapping his combadge, he said, "Riker to Tuvok."

"Tuvok. Go ahead, Captain," a resonant and familiar voice replied.

"Please report to my ready room immediately."

"Acknowledged, Captain."

"Just promise me one thing," Riker said.

"Yes?"

"Bring him back to us. He is an outstanding officer and one whose skills are essential to *Titan*'s mission."

"I can't promise you that Admiral Janeway will part with him willingly, but I doubt she will argue with your assessment. Nor would she wish to separate him from his wife, who I understand is aboard *Titan* as well."

"She is," Troi confirmed.

Tuvok entered moments later and did not display even faint surprise to see Chakotay standing between his captain and Counselor Troi. As Tuvok was Vulcan, this wasn't unusual.

"Captain Chakotay," Tuvok said, neither pleased nor displeased.

For his part, Chakotay was quite happy to be reunited with a man he considered a friend, one he had missed keenly over the last few years.

"It's good to see you again, Tuvok. You look well."

A faint nod to Chakotay was followed by an abrupt lifting of Tuvok's chin to await *his* captain's next words.

"Admiral Janeway has requested a temporary transfer to *Voyager* for you and I have approved her request," Riker said.

Tuvok did not blink, but he did pause just long enough for Chakotay to intuit that this news was not being greeted with the repressed pleasure he might have suspected.

"I trust, Captain, that the admiral's request is not personal?" Tuvok asked.

"No," Riker replied, somewhat surprised. "There is a mission you are uniquely qualified to perform. Otherwise I'd be sending Captain Chakotay back to the Delta Quadrant disappointed."

What an odd question, Chakotay thought, but held his peace. Both he and Tuvok knew Kathryn better than to imagine she would send him here on a personal matter.

"I'll brief you fully once we get to *Voyager*," Chakotay said. "We've got a bit of a journey ahead of us and time is of the essence."

"In more ways than one," Troi offered kindly.

"Very well, sir," Tuvok said. "I will collect my things and bid farewell to my wife."

"I'll transport back with you when you're ready," Chakotay said.

"Dismissed," Riker ordered.

When Tuvok had departed, a brief silence descended over the

room, marring the convivial atmosphere. Finally Troi said, "You should be prepared for a period of adjustment, Captain. Tuvok has endured a series of personal struggles since the Borg Invasion. His service here has done a great deal to restore him, as has the constant presence of his wife. I don't believe he is unwilling to assist you, but he is well aware that returning to *Voyager* will be a challenge for him."

Chakotay nodded to Troi. In theory, Tuvok's transfer had seemed like an excellent solution to the problem the fleet was facing on Sormana. Now Chakotay found himself wondering if it was really going to be that simple.

VOYAGER

"What's taking them so long?" Commander Torres asked.

"Maybe Chakotay's touring *Titan* before they return," Paris suggested.

"You think that's possible?" Lieutenant Kim asked. "I'd give anything to spend some time on *Titan*."

"Are you bucking for a transfer?" Paris asked.

"Of course not," Kim replied. "I just . . ."

"You want to meet Captain Riker, don't you?" Torres teased.

"*Don't you?* I saw him once, at a distance. He was taller than I'd imagined."

Their conversation was cut short by the sound of the transporter activating. Seconds later, Captain Chakotay and *Voyager*'s former chief of security appeared on the pad before them. As the two men stepped down, Paris, Torres, and Kim immediately surrounded Tuvok.

"Welcome back, stranger," Paris said, extending a hand, which Tuvok accepted stiffly.

"It's been too long, Tuvok," Kim added immediately, matching Paris's gesture and receiving the same response.

"Oh, *come on*," Torres said, brushing past them and opening her arms to embrace Tuvok. He bent slightly to accept Torres's firm hug, but his face betrayed nothing as he did so. As

Torres pulled away, she said, "You look wonderful, Tuvok. I can't believe you're really here."

"Nor can I," Tuvok said.

Paris and Torres exchanged a brief glance of consternation but Torres continued, "So much has happened since the last time we saw you. Join us for dinner tonight in our quarters. We'll catch up."

"Thank you for the offer, Commander," Tuvok said, "but once Captain Chakotay has completed my pre-mission briefing, I will retire to my quarters to begin my preparations."

"You're not going to eat?" Paris asked.

"Unless your replicators are malfunctioning, sufficient nutrients will not be difficult to obtain."

"It will take us a couple of days to get back to the Delta Quadrant," Kim said. "Maybe tomorrow night?"

Tuvok tensed visibly before responding, "My limited understanding of Admiral Janeway's request suggests that it will be necessary for me to spend as much time as possible reflecting on our past relationship prior to meeting with the duplicate you encountered in the Delta Quadrant. I would prefer not to distract myself from my duty until the mission has been completed." Looking toward Chakotay, he said, "Captain?"

"This way," Chakotay said. "Commander Paris, you're with me. When we're done, you can show Tuvok to his quarters."

"Aye, sir," Paris said, falling in line behind them.

Torres and Kim watched Tuvok depart with wide eyes. Paris looked back to them briefly, offering a slight shrug indicating he didn't quite know what to make of Tuvok's behavior either.

When they were alone, Kim turned to Torres. "What was that?"

"I don't know," Torres said.

"It's almost like he wasn't happy to see us."

"In all the years we've known him, have you ever seen him happy?"

"In his own way, yes," Kim insisted.

"Maybe he's worried about the mission."

"He's been doing this longer than any of us. You'd think by now nothing would shake him."

Torres thought for a moment. "It hasn't been that long since he lost his son," she said softly. "I meant to tell him how sorry I was to hear about it."

"He'll be with us for several weeks. You'll get a chance," Kim assured her.

"So, the three of us for dinner then?" Torres asked.

"No. I need to talk with Nancy."

Torres noted Kim's trepidation. "What happened?" she demanded.

"I don't know," Kim replied. "Things were going great. I mean, really, epically great."

Torres was a little shocked by the implication. It wasn't an unexpected development, just maybe a little sudden, especially considering all Conlon had just been through.

"But I said some things a few nights ago that really made her angry. She's been avoiding me since then. I need to fix that."

"Yes, you do," Torres agreed. After a long pause, she asked, "Harry, do you think Nancy has completely recovered from what happened? Do you think she's been able to put it behind her?"

"Until our last conversation I would have said yes," Kim replied. "Now, I'm not so sure."

"Why not?"

"I know she doesn't remember losing control of her mind and body. And I know the counselor and the Doctor cleared her to return to duty. But there's something different about her now. She's more aggressive, more assertive than she used to be. Not that that's a bad thing, you understand."

"I'm worried about her," Torres admitted.

"Me too."

"Will you let me know how it goes?"

"Are you asking as her commanding officer or her friend?"

"Both."

Kim paused. "Okay."

* * * * * *

For the first time in a year, Lieutenant Nancy Conlon's quarters resembled regulation order. It had taken her the better part of the last two days and the volume of matter she had recycled had been alarming, but the work had helped her to clear her mind as much as her personal space.

This was a new beginning for her, a rebirth of sorts. The person she had been before had wasted time and squandered resources. On duty her work was exceptional, but she had never before extended the same level of precision and care to her personal life. Now that she truly understood how precious time was and how quickly the illusion of endless days ahead could be shattered, she was determined to never again lapse into such carelessness. It was strange to think that she had confronted loss before—Galvan VI came vividly to mind as did her first view of the Omega Continuum—and she had come close to breaking under the existential terror they presented, without fully incorporating the most important lesson such losses could teach. The terror of those days had *felt* personal, but they had nothing to do with her. They were beyond her control. Throughout those events she had been little more than a witness, a bystander.

What Xolani had done, *that* was personal.

She could not continue to pretend that her universe would ever again be what it once was or that procrastination was an option. There just wasn't time.

When Harry requested entrance to her quarters, she considered playing possum. Instead, she moved to the door and confronted him.

"What do you need, Harry?" she asked, and immediately regretted her tone. His face betrayed a wide range of conflicted emotions but paramount was his concern for her, his desire to mend what he had unintentionally broken.

She could not explain to him why that wasn't possible.

"Tuvok just came aboard," Kim replied. "We're about to head back to the Delta Quadrant."

She continued to stare at him in silence, insisting he do better.

"I'm sorry, okay?" he finally said. "I hurt you. I didn't mean to. Please let me come in so we can talk about it."

"Have you reconsidered your previous position on the modifications I am considering?"

Kim was a terrible liar. That had initially been one of his more attractive qualities. His lack of guile had been comforting. She would always know exactly where she stood with him. It was all written clearly on his sweet, gentle face. "Right now, I'm willing to consider anything that will get you to lower your shields a bit and talk to me."

When she did not step aside, Kim glanced past her at her quarters. She read his surprise.

"What happened in there?"

"I'm just sorting things out."

"Can I help?"

She knew what her response would do to him. She cared, but not enough to change her mind.

"Not right now," Conlon replied, and stepped back to allow the door to slide shut between them.

Commander Tuvok was not surprised when Captain Chakotay requested entry to his quarters a few hours after the start of gamma shift. As with most humans, complicated or unresolved emotional situations unsettled him deeply. Unlike many, he typically refused to allow them to fester, preferring to confront them and move beyond them as soon as possible.

Tuvok had decreased the ambient illumination in the room to almost nothing. A small meditation lamp rested in the center of the floor, a single flickering flame dancing atop it.

"I'm disturbing you," Chakotay said as soon as he stepped inside. He paused, staring at the long robe Tuvok wore over his uniform. It had been a recent gift from his wife, its wide lapels of black *viteen* embroidered with Vulcan symbols meant to focus a chaotic mind.

"Yes," Tuvok agreed.

"Forgive me."

"Of course, Captain."

Anyone else might have taken this as their cue to leave. Chakotay did not.

"I thought Tom was going to give you one of our VIP suites," the captain said as his eyes adjusted to the dimness and took in the relatively small size of the room.

"He did. I requested the change as soon as the slipstream drive was brought online. I found the constant turmoil of the corridor visible through the port distracting."

"As long as you're comfortable."

"Was there something else, Captain?"

"Have I, or have we, done something to offend you, Tuvok? I know it's been a while, but I would have expected you to take at least a passing interest in the lives of your former crewmates. You seem determined to keep all of us at roughly the same distance that existed when *Voyager* was back in the Delta Quadrant and you were still on *Titan*."

"Upon what do you base that assumption?"

"You haven't said more than five words to me or anyone else that didn't directly relate to the mission since you came on board."

"Forgive me. Aboard *Titan* I have found little cause to interact with her crew with the same familiar intensity that was commonplace during our years together in the Delta Quadrant. I prefer the distance, as it allows me to focus on my duties rather than complicated interpersonal matters.

"I see. Then I guess finding yourself facing what will likely be a series of *very personal* interactions with *Denzit* Janeway is disconcerting?"

Tuvok paused, allowing the emotional turbulence that rose when he contemplated the coming days to move through him—observed but powerless to affect his equilibrium. "Yes and no," he finally replied. "While it is true that I have known this *Denzit* Janeway longer than anyone else in your fleet apart from the admiral, I expect that the experiences she has endured over the last five years have changed her in many ways. Just as she likely bears little resemblance to the Admiral Janeway we both know so well, she will likely also share little in common with the Captain Janeway who first assumed command of *Voyager* and was sent to retrieve me from your ship. I intend to listen closely to what she says and to observe her current circumstances and interactions. Only once this process is complete will it be possible for me to determine how best to advise her."

"If it isn't the existence of the *denzit* that's troubling you, may I ask what is? Kathryn told me that she sent you a personal message advising you of the circumstances of her return from the Q Continuum. She said you never responded."

"Until several months ago, I believed that I would never again see Kathryn Janeway. My friend and my former captain was dead. I mourned her loss. When I received word that she had returned from the Q Continuum, I was understandably surprised. Initially, I found it challenging to reconcile this development with the natural order of the universe. It seemed inappropriate to me that this *one* individual should have been granted a reprieve from the constraints of mortality when so many others had perished under equally devastating circumstances without the benefit of such attention. That response troubled me, given that it conflicted with an equal, if not greater sense of relief that Admiral Janeway had, against all reason and logic, survived the destruction of the evolved Borg cube that assimilated her."

"You aren't the only one who has struggled to come to grips with Kathryn's return. She traveled through more than a few circles of hell on her way back. The rest of us had each made our own peace with her loss. Personally, it was the worst thing I have ever endured. It came very close to breaking me completely. But I can't see her presence among us now as anything less than a miraculous blessing. What I'm suggesting is that if you are still struggling, it might help to talk with the rest of us. We're all walking the same strange path, Tuvok, and we're here for you, if you'll let us in."

"Thank you, Captain."

"Good night, Tuvok."

9

DEMETER

During the first several months Lieutenant Commander Atlee Fife had served as Commander Liam O'Donnell's first officer, he had dreaded moments like this. Fife would arrive to present a report on *Demeter*'s status. On a good day O'Donnell would ignore him, muttering softly to himself. On a bad day, the commander would take Fife to task for repeatedly ignoring his standing order that unless Fife had appeared to report that something was on fire, O'Donnell was content to allow his first officer to run the ship while he pursued his personal scientific projects.

Demeter's was like no command structure with which Fife had become familiar at the Academy or his early Starfleet posts. He had found himself constantly on the defensive. Before long he had decided that O'Donnell had no place aboard a Starfleet vessel, let alone commanding one.

That had changed the day Atlee Fife had suborned mutiny, killed countless innocent life-forms, and instead of being cashiered out of the service, had received his captain's forgiveness and commitment to make their unusual command structure work.

There had been plenty of days since then when Fife had questioned the wisdom of O'Donnell's choice to give him a second chance. Not a single day passed without Fife doing his damnedest to prove himself worthy of it.

He found *Demeter*'s captain in his personal lab completely absorbed, scrutinizing an astrometrics display of Rilnar territory along with the data they had received from the Nihydron on the major Rilnar colonies.

Fife paused, as was his custom now, to allow O'Donnell whatever time he might require to complete the task at hand prior to requesting his captain's attention.

"What have you got, Atlee?" O'Donnell finally asked.

"The helm is requesting confirmation of our destination, Captain. We are three light-years from Rilquitain. At warp six we could make orbit within the hour."

"That's their largest colony," O'Donnell noted.

"Aye, sir, and the location of their capital city. The planet is densely populated with over twelve billion inhabitants and well-defended."

"And you think that's where we should begin?"

"Given the fact that the Rilnar have accepted *Denzit* Janeway as commander of their forces on Sormana, it seems likely that they will be receptive to any request we might make of them for information regarding the history of the planet and the conflict," Fife replied.

"Possibly," O'Donnell said.

"You disagree." It wasn't a question. Fife had become accustomed to O'Donnell's fondness for the Socratic method. "If we announce our presence as representatives of the Federation, we will likely be assigned a diplomatic liaison."

"I'm guessing half their diplomatic corps will want to meet other citizens from the Federation that gave them their *denzit*."

"And we don't have that kind of time."

"Not if we want to get the whole story."

"Sir?"

"We already know that there is an ideological division between the Rilnar on Sormana and those in the colonies. According to the Nihydron, the Rilnar and Zahl both developed interstellar travel capabilities around the same time on Sormana, several hundred years ago. The preceding century had been marked by a lengthy and unusual period of relative peace during which their conflict took the form of an old-fashioned space race. Today, the vast majority of the Rilnar were born in the colonies. They might have a passing interest in Sormana, but their attention is directed elsewhere, toward more local concerns and cultural development. What we will learn from the diplomats will be the party line, the official position."

"Isn't that what we are seeking?"

"It's not what I'm seeking. Look here," he said, gesturing to the chart of Rilnar territory displayed on his monitor. "Rilnadaar VI."

Fife studied the display and accompanying data. "It's an agrarian colony, population two hundred thousand."

"And it was founded less than a century ago by a group of Sormana's natives who apparently came to the conclusion that *living* was more important than *being right*."

"Then you would prefer I lead an away team to Rilnadaar VI?"

O'Donnell smiled. "No."

Fife considered the situation.

"*You* would prefer to investigate Rilnadaar VI," he realized.

O'Donnell nodded. "One of the few prerogatives afforded me by the technical difference in our positions, Atlee. You get to do the unpleasant work."

"Of course, sir."

"You'll drop me and a small away team off on Rilnadaar VI. We'll take some of our most recent harvest with us and offer to trade for seed and other foodstuffs. You and the counselor will make best possible speed to Rilquitain and meet with the diplomatic delegation. When you've had enough of diplomacy, you'll come back to the colony and retrieve us. Between the two of us, we'll get the whole story, not just the official one."

"I will order Ensign Falto to alter course. We should arrive at Rilnadaar VI in twelve hours at maximum warp."

"Very good, Atlee."

Fife departed, hoping it would not take another full year to better anticipate his captain's thoughts and intentions but satisfied that at least he was making progress.

VESTA

The *Vesta* was equipped with two large astrometrics labs, both similar to the one Seven had created for *Voyager*. Captain Regina Farkas did not know the former Borg drone well, but it never ceased to amaze her how much this single individual had done to refine and improve upon standard Starfleet equipment. The main lab was currently being used by her best science officers, led by Lieutenant Skaiden, whose team was searching the heavens for any sign of Federation technology that *Voyager* might have left behind.

The secondary lab had been commandeered by Lieutenant Bryce. Farkas hadn't questioned her chief engineer's request. She had learned to give the young man as much rein as possible. Thus far, he hadn't disappointed her.

Skaiden's team worked with silent intensity. The main lab's display was filled with a single chart of several sectors between Sormana and Krenim space, and operations experts worked diligently to acquire any faint signal that might indicate a Federation presence.

Entering Bryce's lab, Farkas wondered if the chief engineer could possibly be working on the same project. The massive screen had been broken into nine discrete areas, each displaying different spatial grids, none of which were the same areas Skaiden's team was analyzing. Bright red, orange, green, and gold lines ran throughout each grid, possibly denoting potential flight paths. Nine pairs of engineers worked at separate control stations, each pair engaging in animated conversations and in some cases, arguments.

Bryce moved among them, followed by a young ensign Farkas recognized immediately as the fleet's most recent transfer, Icheb.

"No, no, no," Bryce's voice sounded, rising above the din. "Run the simulation to completion. As soon as we can access long-range sensors, we'll test it, but I don't want to waste time on incomplete courses."

Farkas stood back for a moment, enjoying the chaos. Bryce caught sight of the captain and moved toward her.

"Captain," he said.

"Whatever this is, I'm already intrigued," Farkas said.

"It was Icheb's idea," Bryce said, smiling. "Ensign, come here."

Icheb hurried to Bryce's side. "Good afternoon, Captain."

"Skaiden tells me you're threatening to revoke her access to long-range sensors in the next two hours. You know how I feel about my senior officers working and playing well with others, Bryce."

"She's not going to find anything," Bryce insisted.

"That's probably news to her."

"It's not her fault. She's doing the logical thing. She has limited her search to current Zahl space, assuming that's where they must have found their evidence of *Voyager*'s previous journey through their territory," Bryce explained.

"I'm having a hard time seeing the flaw in that reasoning," Farkas admitted.

"If, as we suspect," Icheb spoke up, "the evidence in question originated in another timeline, we must consider the possibility that *in that timeline*, Zahl territory could be configured quite differently."

"Never mind the fact that the Zahl have probably already found anything in their space and have it locked down in a lab somewhere. So we're ignoring the Zahl's current holdings," Bryce added.

"Rather than focus on the Zahl or the Rilnar, we are focusing on *Voyager*'s previous course through these sectors," Icheb continued. "The only local species *Voyager* contacted was the Krenim. According to the logs, it was a brief conversation and after being advised that this area of space was in dispute, Captain Janeway ordered a new course set which avoided it entirely. What we are extrapolating are the most likely courses *Voyager* would have followed based upon interstellar phenomena rather than political designations, had she chosen to ignore the Krenim's warning. There are several notable features Captain Janeway might have ordered investigated, including a young binary system and four large nebulae."

"Interesting premise," Farkas agreed. "But aren't there a lot more possibilities for such a hypothesis than we could realistically consider?"

"No," Icheb replied. "In theory, there are infinite variations, but based upon the captain's standard methodology, these are the most likely courses she *would* have chosen."

"But doesn't all that go to hell if, as we also suspect, *Voyager* was repeatedly attacked during that time?"

"Our simulations include calculations that allow for several battle scenarios, as well as naturally defensible areas," Bryce replied. "We could still be wrong, but we're looking at a lot more territory than Skaiden's team and we're utilizing different search parameters."

"How different?"

"For any artifact to have survived within multiple timelines it cannot simply exist in a single reality. It is likely lodged in subspace," Icheb said, "and must contain some rudimentary temporal shielding."

"Starfleet doesn't have temporal shielding," Farkas noted.

"The Borg did," Icheb advised her.

"And if you and Seven were on board during that so-called Year of Hell, *Voyager* would have had access to that technology," Farkas realized.

"I was not," Icheb said. "But assuming these events occurred near the time of *Voyager*'s only contact with the Krenim, Seven was."

"Okay," Farkas said. She had seen enough. "How long until you are ready to test your theory?"

"Another hour at most," Bryce replied.

Farkas shrugged. "I'll go give Skaiden the bad news."

LILLESTAN STATION

Galen's chief of security, Lieutenant Ranson Velth, was uncomfortable with the amount of attention his team was attracting. It was understandable. His and Seven's were the only human faces to be seen on the small spaceport, and Seven's striking physical beauty was noteworthy. The pair received several long, questioning glances as they moved through the wide halls leading from the docking ports to a central business arena that included various shops and dining establishments.

The station was heavily trafficked by numerous alien species Velth could not name. A few, he could, including several Rilnar and Zahl. While those he saw seemed to give one another a wide berth, Velth noted that there were no direct confrontations between them.

Commander Glenn had been advised when she requested clearance to dock that Lillestan was considered neutral territory and serviced a diverse range of local species. No weapons were permitted on the station and the proprietors requested only that their patrons leave any disputes between species at the airlock. That the Rilnar and Zahl were honoring that custom confirmed that the conflict on Sormana did not extend beyond the surface of the planet, and that most likely, consequences for disturbing the peace on Lillestan were severe.

This small backwater station was an ideal destination for those who wished to engage in personal business and recreation beyond the bounds of their particular governments, which meant it could be an excellent source of intelligence on a wide range of topics. It was also likely the epicenter for a thriving illegal trade in illicit, banned, or rare commodities.

Velth and his officers would spend the next several days here attempting to blend in and glean what they could from talkative patrons. Seven's intentions were different. Despite the courtesy their perimeter defense ships had extended to Captain Chakotay, Commander Glenn believed that a direct contact with Zahl leadership would be too risky for her small ship and crew. From Lillestan, it should be easy enough to secure passage aboard a private transport to one of several large Zahl colonies. Seven and the Doctor would travel as anonymously as possible, research the conflict on Sormana from the Zahl's perspective, and hopefully return to Lillestan leaving the Zahl none the wiser.

The center of the port contained a large display listing the variety of services that were publically available. Seven discreetly scanned the map with her tricorder, which translated the alien script. After a few moments, she turned her head toward a darkened doorway barely noticeable between two brightly lit establishments; one offered a wide variety of clothing, the other was some sort of restaurant where patrons sat on tall stools imbibing colorful beverages and small living animals served to them in delicate, edible cages.

"This way," Seven directed him, obviously having chosen their course without the need for input from him.

"Where are we going?" Velth asked.

"To secure passage aboard a ship."

"There is a public transportation platform on the third level of the arena. Why not seek passage there?"

"Because anyone availing themselves of public resources here will be questioned and their destination will be noted for the station's logs," Seven said.

"We're not doing anything illegal. Why shouldn't we submit ourselves to a little scrutiny?"

"Because Captain Glenn would prefer that the Zahl government remains ignorant of our intentions at this time."

"Hundreds of people pass through this station daily," Velth argued. "Our presence isn't likely to be noted."

"You're willing to risk that, given the Zahl's attack on *Voyager* that resulted in the *denzit*'s capture and torture?" Seven asked.

Velth paused. He had been ordered to accompany Seven aboard the station for her protection but not to interfere with her choices. She held no rank, so it wasn't a question of following orders. It was just Velth doing what he always did: analyzing everyone's decisions in light of how likely they were to get someone killed.

"What are we going to find behind that door?" he finally asked.

"Jewl, I presume. The establishment is her private club. If you prefer, you may wait here until I return."

"Not a chance. Lead the way."

Seven was not nervous, but she was eager to conclude their business on Lillestan as quickly as possible. The moment she entered the dimly lit, smoky room filled with semiprivate and likely unseen private alcoves, live music provided by a quartet of identically attired Hedeomiks—Species 9552—whose instruments were partially submerged in large tanks of murky, green liquid, and scantily clad service personnel, she knew she had chosen correctly.

"Welcome to Jewl's," said an obsequious host with vivid neon-blue tattoos covering his bald scalp, face, and neck. The rest of his body was encased in a skintight black ensemble and emitted a strong, musky stench that almost brought tears to Seven's eyes. "May I inquire as to your patronage?"

"You may not," Seven replied.

The man took only a few moments to size her up. Should he insist that they identify a member of this club to gain admittance, they might be forced to retreat. Seven hoped that pretending as if they belonged would be enough to discourage questions, along with the small chits of local currency she slipped to him casually while allowing her eyes to nonchalantly search the room.

When he did not reply, but pocketed the small bribe, Seven continued, "I was told that Jewl's was an establishment that prioritized discretion."

"You were not misinformed," the man said with a deep bow.

"I require specialized services," Seven whispered.

For a moment the man's eyes met hers and his desire to personally provide whatever those services might be was clearly visible. "Name them and they shall be yours," he replied huskily.

"A ship with a discreet pilot," Seven said.

The host's disappointment was clear, but he nodded again. "This way," he said.

10

VESTA

Admiral Kathryn Janeway awaited Tuvok's arrival with mingled anticipation and trepidation. She had transmitted a private message to her old friend shortly after the Omega Continuum crisis had been resolved. To her surprise, Tuvok had not responded. His wife, T'Pel, had sent a letter instead indicating that Tuvok was struggling at the time to regain his emotional equilibrium and believed that contacting the admiral would threaten the progress he had made.

For someone long accustomed to placing the needs of others ahead of her own, it had been relatively easy for Janeway to convince herself that Tuvok had every right to ignore her message until he felt ready to respond. As the moments leading up to this final, significant reunion dwindled, she found a little anger surfacing unexpectedly. Apparently her needs had not factored into Tuvok's thought process. That stung more than she had admitted to herself.

Chakotay had briefed her while en route and shared Tuvok's desire to keep his former friends at a distance. This troubled her. Tuvok had never been emotionally demonstrative. As a Vulcan, it was simply not his way. But the admiral had never doubted that Tuvok deeply respected all of his crewmates, and he had spoken often of the intensity of the bond that existed between him and Kathryn. Many of those Janeway had been close to had changed after her death, but those had been positive changes.

Tuvok was the only one of her close friends who seemed to be moving in a direction she did not understand.

Tuvok entered her private office alone, as requested. Janeway would have held similar meetings with any other officer in the main briefing room and asked the *Vesta*'s senior officers to attend. This reunion was different and she wasn't going to pretend otherwise.

Despite her fears, the only thing she felt when their eyes met was tremendous relief. There was no outward indication of his internal struggle, which was promising.

"Hello, Tuvok," she said simply.

"Admiral," he began, but paused. He looked away briefly, clearly not to compose himself, but almost to confirm an internal revelation. When his eyes returned to hers they were noticeably softer. "I have anticipated this moment since I received your letter. Forgive me for not responding sooner. While I was relieved when I learned of your return, it was also rather difficult to accept. I am pleased to report that the only sensation of which I am conscious now is gratitude that your death was apparently presumed in error."

Janeway could not repress a wide smile. "I'm glad to see you too," she said. After a long pause, she continued, "I am so sorry for the loss of your son and daughter-in-law. For a long time, I blamed myself for their deaths as well as the other sixty-three billion the Borg annihilated."

"Your order to destroy the Borg's transwarp hub was not a tactical error. I concurred with it. To attempt to assign blame for the Borg's subsequent choices to anyone *but* the Borg is irrational."

"It felt like the only rational response for a long time."

"Many responses born of deep and complex emotions initially *feel* that way. Only patient reflection and the application of logic can reveal the flaws in such thought processes."

"T'Pel indicated in her letter that you were struggling with your son's death. Is that still the case?"

Tuvok did not respond immediately. Finally he said, "While the all-consuming anger has become controllable. I do not believe I will ever reconcile myself with Elieth's death."

This stunned Janeway. Her long relationship with Tuvok had given her a great deal of insight into the nature and limits of Vulcan mental discipline. Many assumed that a Vulcan's stoic demeanor was evidence that they did not possess the same depth of emotional responses as many other species. She knew that the opposite was true. A Vulcan's range of instinctive emotional responses was powerful. They had driven primitive Vulcans to levels of violence that rivaled humanity's. By following Surak's teachings of the strict application of reason and the elevation of logic, Vulcans had brought order to their deep emotional storms and paved the way for their evolution into a highly civilized culture.

Acceptance of a loved one's death was a challenge, but Janeway had difficulty believing that Tuvok would not rise to meet it.

"Have you considered working with a professional counselor to assist you with this?" Janeway asked.

"I have not. My son's death was meaningless. Counseling will not change this fact. My goal has been to control the emotional responses that surface whenever I recall his death. I can report that over time I have succeeded in doing so. Constant mindfulness of this priority coupled with my duties aboard *Titan* has resulted in renewed emotional control."

"But, Tuvok," Janeway began. "Acceptance is the most critical stage of grief. Without it, you will never fully integrate this loss or begin to heal from it."

"There have been numerous times in the past when I have experienced acceptance of loss. In this case, absent any evidence that Elieth's death served any purpose and cognizant of the reality that this will not change, I must content myself with acknowledging the randomness of this existence. I do not allow this to affect my ability to perform my duties as an officer, a husband, or a father. I have no desire, however, to forget the lessons Elieth's death have taught me. Indeed, they are all that his loss has left me."

"What lessons?"

"That we must never allow ourselves to underestimate the

brutality of which those with whom we share this universe are capable; that we must carefully consider what we are willing to sacrifice in the name of preserving peace; that peace is but a temporary illusion; and that in the absence of certainty of our own security, constant vigilance is required."

This troubled Janeway deeply. She knew that Tuvok had access to an excellent counselor aboard *Titan* and wondered why he had not availed himself of this resource. She was curious to know if Will Riker suspected the depths of devastation Tuvok was masking. On some level, she knew he could not endure in this state, but Janeway was absolutely certain that only *Tuvok* could choose to move beyond it.

The admiral wasn't sure she wanted to know the answer to her next question, but in light of recent events, it seemed imperative that she ask. "Tuvok, was my death also meaningless?"

"No, Admiral. If I understood your communication correctly, it is clear that your death, while *assumed* by those who witnessed the evolved cube's destruction, was never actually final. Your *katra* was separated and safeguarded by your godson until you were able, with his assistance, to restore your physical body. While these are admittedly extraordinary circumstances, well beyond what most would consider the natural order of things, upon close inspection it seems that those who reported your death were simply not in possession of all relevant data. In addition, your apparent death was in the line of a duty, striving to safeguard the lives of those you serve. While your death was difficult to accept, it served a purpose."

"How is that different from your son's death? Wasn't he a public safety officer on Deneva?"

"He was a civilian and undoubtedly chose to sacrifice his life by giving up his space on one of the few transports that escaped the planet prior to the Borg's attack."

"How can you call that meaningless? How is that not the very definition of honor and duty?"

"His choice is not the issue. That he was forced to make that choice is unacceptable. The Borg chose to attempt to annihilate the Federation. This was as tactically unsound a proposal as it was an obvious exercise in futility. While no one could have foreseen the Caeliar's existence, let alone the unusual solution they provided—eliminating the threat the Borg posed by integrating them into their gestalt—even the Borg had to know that we would never cease to resist them and that some would escape their genocidal rampage. Still, they chose to slaughter billions of innocents. Sixty-three billion perished. There is no logical defense for the Borg's actions. It was evil. Surak teaches us to accept that such things are inevitable and unavoidable, yet each time I turn my thoughts to my son's last moments, I find only rage."

Until this moment, Janeway had not doubted for an instant that Tuvok would be capable of convincing *Denzit* Janeway to abandon the Rilnar and return to Starfleet. Now she wondered. In his current state of mind, Tuvok might actually find himself sympathizing with the *denzit*; the only development that might make this situation worse.

"I know Chakotay has told you everything we know about the *denzit*. Do you believe you can convince her to see reason and return to Starfleet?"

"The basis for any argument I could make in support of her return is grounded in my personal knowledge of your life as I observed it in the years that have passed since the day your life and hers diverged. Her survival is not surprising, given that she must share your obstinacy and strength. But in truth, I cannot image *any* series of events that would ever cause you to turn your back on Starfleet. That she has suggests psychological damage I might be ill-equipped to address. *Logic and reason* should already have led her to conclude that returning to the Federation is the only appropriate course before her. Neither of those tools will prove effective if she has already abandoned them."

"I don't know about that," Janeway said. "While I have always appreciated your counsel, your ability to help me think through the challenges we have faced together was never the thing I valued most in our friendship."

"Indeed?" Tuvok asked, doubtful.

"No. It was the clarity with which you always saw *me*. You have been a mirror for me. Many times you have reflected things I might not have wanted to see, but I always concluded that your expectations were based upon your understanding of who I can be at my best. I never wanted to fail to live up to that. Whatever she has endured, whoever she has become, she knows that your disapproval is a clear indication that she had strayed from the path. I believe she will trust you to guide her back to us."

"Your confidence is, as ever, appreciated."

"Bear this in mind," Janeway continued, "she's hiding something. I can't imagine what it is, but it's keeping her on Sormana."

"I concur. The explanation she offered to Captain Chakotay was compelling, but hardly convincing. Clearly, she has personalized this conflict with the Zahl as a result of their treatment of her, but revenge has never really been a prime motivating force in your psyche."

Or yours, Janeway thought, realizing that now this was no longer the case. Still, she had to hope that Tuvok would resist the urge to identify with the *denzit* and their better angels would prevail. "Are you ready for me to contact the nearest Rilnar vessel and advise them that you wish to speak with the *denzit*?" Janeway asked.

"With your permission, Admiral, I would prefer to make contact."

"Why?"

"She knows you are here. She knows you are determined to bring her home. You must not initiate any direct action unless all other strategies fail."

"Why is every single officer in this fleet terrified of allowing me to speak with her?"

Tuvok stood passively, allowing her to reach her own conclusion.

"History?" she finally asked.

"Not entirely. You cannot help but take her choices personally, to see them as a reflection on your character."

"Believe me when I tell you that I've learned in the most excruciating way possible how pointless that exercise would be."

"Perhaps, with *one* alternate version of yourself."

Janeway considered Tuvok's inscrutable face. "You are right," she finally admitted.

SORMANA

"Forgive the interruption, *Denzit,* but we have received a secured priority transmission from the Federation *Starship Voyager.*"

The *denzit* was acutely conscious of the wary glances of the twelve regional *tilzitar* assembled in the operations center. They had been engrossed in an analysis of the Zahl's most recent troop movements near Jirscha and Sepseta. The reinforcements that had arrived over the last two days might have been inexplicable given their close proximity to the current Rilnar stronghold of Ketleh. They suggested that another attack on Ketleh was imminent, but the powerful defense grid had proven in dozens of engagements how fruitless such attacks would be.

It was likely that the arrival of the Federation fleet had inspired these actions. The Zahl would undoubtedly believe that the *denzit* intended to bring her Starfleet into this battle and that an alliance between the Rilnar and Federation could prove decisive. Their fortification of Jirscha and Sepseta was a sign the *denzit* couldn't miss.

The suspicion she saw in the eyes awaiting her response to this latest contact was disconcerting. Cabriot had been by her side since she arrived on Sormana and pledged herself to Kal Uthar. She had elevated Limlesh to his present position. Most of the others had served with her for more than two years and had personally witnessed how ruthlessly she had driven the Zahl from the occupied territories. That *they* could doubt her loyalty was painful. They knew what she had sacrificed to their service. They knew the scars she bore in their name. Perhaps one more display was required.

"Advise *Voyager* that our discussions have concluded. Should they attempt to approach Sormana again, they will only have themselves to blame for the resulting casualties."

"Yes, *Denzit*," the messenger acknowledged.

When he returned only a few minutes later, she seriously doubted the young man's sanity.

"Pardon, *Denzit*," he interrupted, "I was asked to advise you that the individual attempting to make contact is a Lieutenant Commander Tuvok."

Janeway's heart stilled briefly in her chest.

Tuvok?

Chakotay had not mentioned his presence with their fleet. She had assumed he had either perished along the way or been assigned elsewhere. Worse, she understood what this meant. Chakotay had conveyed her message to the Admiral Janeway commanding the Federation fleet and clearly she was not going to give up without a fight.

Rising from her seat she said, "I want the latest situation reports from the bases at Jaxom and Fressa when I return."

The assembled *tilzitar* stood as she left the room. She could imagine what they would whisper to one another in her absence and cursed herself and her other self for sowing seeds of discord.

That frustration gave way to a burning wave of anger that rose through her chest the moment she saw Tuvok's face.

"You didn't make contact just to say 'hello' did you?" she asked without preamble.

"As you are well aware, Denzit *Janeway, Starfleet regulations require that its officers refrain from offering tactical support to species that are not members of the Federation except in very specific instances. Moreover, you know who commands this fleet and that in the absence of compelling evidence supporting the choice you have made to join the Rilnar, she will not consider the matter settled."*

"I told Captain Chakotay everything I had to say on the subject."

"Unfortunately, everything you had to say was insufficient. Permit me to join you on the surface and allow me to assist you in rectifying that situation."

"Then *you* understand my choice?" the *denzit* asked. They had been friends for such a long time. Was it possible he sympathized with her? His face was unreadable as ever, but she knew that he would never betray her.

Chakotay she trusted, but only to a point. Any version of her that had risen to the rank of admiral was also unlikely to be moved by her arguments. *She just wouldn't understand.* But Tuvok?

I could make him see, she realized. "I will provide you with transport protocols shortly," the *denzit* replied. "End transmission."

VOYAGER

"*Do you want the good news or the bad news?*" Captain Farkas asked. Admiral Janeway and Captain Chakotay were seated in his ready room, awaiting the results of Tuvok's contact with Sormana.

"Let's start with the good news," Janeway replied.

"*We've found something. Bryce and Icheb found something, to be more specific. It's faint, but it's definitely a Federation signal.*"

"How did the Zahl miss it?" Chakotay asked.

"*That's part of the bad news. The signal is being transmitted over a secured Federation frequency. The transmission was apparently triggered by our scans. No one else searching for it would have been capable of finding it.*"

"That doesn't sound like a bad thing," Janeway observed.

"*It's not in Zahl space. It's in the outskirts of Krenim territory.*"

Janeway and Chakotay exchanged a meaningful glance.

"We already suspected that contact with the Krenim might be unavoidable," Chakotay said. "Now is as good a time as any."

"*I agree. I just wish we knew more about what we are getting ourselves into,*" Farkas noted.

"Perhaps we're about to find out," Janeway said. "I'll return to *Vesta* shortly. Plot our course and prepare to depart as soon as possible. Advise Ensign Icheb that I want him to continue to work with Lieutenant Bryce until we have retrieved whatever is generating that signal."

"*Aye, Admiral. Vesta out.*"

"Maybe the *denzit* will refuse Tuvok's request and *Voyager* can accompany you to investigate this signal," Chakotay said.

"I want you to remain here in case *Demeter* or *Galen* run into trouble," Janeway replied.

"Understood."

A chime sounded and Chakotay called, "Enter."

Tuvok did so, immediately addressing the admiral.

"I have spoken with the *denzit* and she has approved my request to transport to the surface."

"Good," Janeway said, somewhat relieved.

"Then I guess we all have our work cut out for us," Chakotay observed.

"We do," Janeway agreed. "Captain Chakotay, you will facilitate Tuvok's transport to the surface and await further contact from him or the other fleet vessels. *Vesta* will return as soon as we retrieve the source of the signal they detected."

Once Janeway departed, Chakotay called Commander Paris to the ready room. As soon as he entered, Chakotay said, "Tuvok's request to meet with the *denzit* on Sormana has been approved."

"That's good, isn't it?" Paris asked.

"Yes. But it also means that unless we can devise a safe means of navigating that minefield, he's effectively at her mercy once he departs."

"I do not believe the *denzit* accepted my request in an attempt to further complicate relations between the Rilnar and the Federation," Tuvok noted.

"Nor do I," Chakotay agreed. "But she's not the only military leader down there who might try to take advantage of your presence. The Zahl might respond more forcefully, or the *denzit*'s subordinates might fear that she is about to betray them."

"Obviously, you must take any precautions you feel are warranted, but take care not to act precipitously. I will be in constant contact and will advise you at any sign that the situation is deteriorating."

"Do you have any suggestions before you go as to how we

might safely navigate several million kilometers of space filled with undetectable subspace mines?" Paris asked of *Voyager*'s former chief of security and tactics.

"If you are unable to acquire an accurate map of their locations either from the Rilnar or by sensor enhancements, you might consider utilizing a dampening field," Tuvok advised.

"The mines appear to have hair triggers," Paris said, shaking his head.

"I am certain you will rise to the occasion, Commander," Tuvok said. "On the off chance my survival depends upon it, I would appreciate your best efforts."

"You'll have them, Tuvok," Paris confirmed.

"Let's not keep the *denzit* waiting any longer," Chakotay said. "Bring her home."

"Should my analysis determine that to be the best course of action, I will not hesitate to do so, Captain."

As he turned to go, Chakotay caught the look of consternation on Paris's face that Tuvok's remark had provoked.

"Tuvok," Chakotay added, "whether or not you believe her choice to be valid, your *duty* is to bring her back to Starfleet."

"I understand my duty, Captain. I also understand that this Kathryn Janeway has suffered over the last several years and that we are obligated not to add to that suffering. I have no intention of betraying Starfleet or the *denzit*. You brought me here to use our friendship to strengthen your argument. But that friendship also makes it impossible for me to ignore her needs, whatever they may be. I will listen to her and I will act according to the dictates of my conscience, bearing in mind that those actions may affect my standing with Starfleet as well as hers."

Tuvok departed the ready room without another word. When he had gone, Paris asked, "What the hell is the matter with him?"

"I don't know," Chakotay replied.

Icheb's automated reports on Lieutenant Conlon had been innocuous during *Voyager*'s trip to the Beta Quadrant to retrieve

Tuvok. Commander Torres had hoped this might signal that Conlon had reconsidered her proposed modifications or that she had encountered enough stumbling blocks to deter her from the project altogether.

Torres had hesitated to confront Conlon without further evidence that she was disregarding orders until she could speak with Counselor Cambridge. *Demeter* was not expected to return for several more days, and Torres had begun to wonder if that conversation would even be necessary until her morning report highlighted a request Conlon had made at the start of alpha shift. Apparently she had requested the transfer of six gel packs stored aboard the *Vesta* and Lieutenant Neol had signed off on receipt of them.

Torres couldn't wait for Cambridge's return. Instead she activated Kula to watch over Miral and Michael and hurried to main engineering.

The moment Nancy Conlon caught sight of Commander Torres's face as the fleet chief entered main engineering she knew there was a problem. When Torres ordered her briskly to her small private office, the list of possibilities shortened.

"Lieutenant," Torres began as soon as they were alone, "I ordered you not to begin working on the security modifications you proposed until I had reviewed them thoroughly."

"I know," Conlon said.

"You have not followed that order."

"Yes, I have."

Torres's eyes narrowed. "You assigned Ensign Mirk to begin testing augmented samples of bioneural fluid several days ago. Today you pulled six new gel packs from storage aboard the *Vesta*."

"Yes. Our last diagnostic showed that the gel packs in section nineteen-alpha-c are showing wear. I was going to replace them this morning."

Torres was puzzled.

"I asked Mirk to conduct a random series of tests of our

existing functional gel packs to make sure there were no unforeseen complications as a result of Xolani's presence in them."

"Oh," Torres said.

"*On my own time*, I have continued to review the main computer's security protocols and have written some sample code to enhance the computer's reasoning capabilities, but I haven't begun testing it. I understand you don't want me working on this while I'm on duty. You do not have the right to order me not to *think* about it during my off hours."

"Why didn't you record your orders to Mirk in your main duty log?" Torres asked.

"I did."

"No you didn't."

"Then I meant to, but forgot. We've been a little busy around here undoing the damage your new assistant did while I was recuperating."

Torres's face flushed.

"Should I assume that your knowledge of Mirk's orders came from Icheb as well? What's he doing, going through all of my staff's logs every day to make sure I'm not stepping out of line?"

"It's not like that, Nancy."

"*Now* it's Nancy? Two minutes ago it was *Lieutenant* and you came in here looking for blood, *Chief Torres*."

"I'm sorry, all right? Harry said you were having problems. I've been worried about you."

"*Harry* said?" Conlon demanded, her voice rising. "I'm sorry, Commander. I know we're all good friends and this is a small ship, but if you have questions or concerns about my work I'd appreciate it if you would take it up with me and not my former boyfriend."

"Former?"

Conlon felt her cheeks beginning to burn. "We're . . . *I'm* taking a little break. Things got intense pretty fast and I needed to step back."

"Do you want to talk about it?"

"Absolutely not."

"Nancy, I really am sorry. I'm still trying to get my bearings too. What happened to you and to this ship when Xolani attacked us was my responsibility. I failed us."

"No, you didn't. We all failed. And we all need to figure out how to make sure it can't happen again. Both you and Harry think this is some personal vendetta. It's not. I'm just trying to do my damn job and what I need is your support, not your suspicion."

"You have it," Torres tried to assure her.

"It doesn't feel that way right now."

"I know. I misjudged this. I should have just asked you directly the moment I had any questions. I've had some issues in the past, trying to handle stuff that was too big for me to work through alone. I guess I was just projecting that onto you."

"I'm still seeing Counselor Cambridge whenever I can. He's been pretty busy lately, but I'm doing all right."

"Good. Great. I'll let you get back to work."

"Thank you."

Torres nodded and departed, clearly still troubled. Conlon felt for her. But as with Harry, she could not prioritize B'Elanna's feelings over her own. There was too much to be done and far too little time in which to do it.

As soon as the doors to main engineering had closed behind Torres, Conlon called Ensign Mirk to her office and ordered him to cease his tests of the bioneural fluid. She doubted B'Elanna would continue to scrutinize her staff's logs, but on the off chance she did, Conlon couldn't afford any more questions.

11

SORMANA

Upon his arrival, Tuvok was greeted by a young woman in uniform who advised him that the *denzit* was waiting for him in the "Center." After following the young officer through a warren of dimly lit, windowless hallways and down several flights of stairs—suggesting that this part of the Rilnar base was located underground—the room into which he was ushered reminded him unexpectedly of the bridge of an advanced space vessel.

The Center was arranged in a dodecagon formation. Each of its twelve sides was structured in similar fashion with a wide viewscreen running from the ceiling to the wall's midline. Below that, several operational panels and smaller data screens were grouped. All were wide enough to allow four officers to work comfortably at each of the stations. A waist-high railing circled the room dividing the stations from an open space that contained two rectangular tables, each covered with large maps that appeared to represent the land masses in each of the planet's hemispheres. Small markers on each map likely denoted Rilnar and Zahl troop placements. Several officers stood at each of these tables altering the markers as intelligence was fed to them from the twelve larger stations.

A single chair sat on a slightly raised platform in the room's center. In that chair sat Kathryn Janeway.

Denzit *Janeway*, Tuvok reminded himself. The mere sight of her should not have evoked surprise. The physical resemblance was to be expected. As she swiveled in her chair to face him, he was immediately struck by the scarring on her neck and wondered how she had sustained that particular injury.

He read determination in eyes that too rarely had held anything else. The force of will emanating from them turned the deep blue pools to steel. She was already on the defensive, but given the level of activity in the room, that might not have anything to do with Tuvok's arrival. The images on the viewscreens were constantly shifting. Two of them featured what appeared to be real-time ground engagements.

The *denzit* rose from her seat and moved toward Tuvok. "Welcome to my command center, Commander Tuvok. As you can see, it's a busy day, or I'd offer you a tour."

"Please do not allow my presence to distract you from your duties, *Denzit*," Tuvok said.

She inclined her head and motioned for him to join her at one of the map tables. A set of markers was moved off the board as she approached. Turning, she checked one of the two battles and noted that the display had stabilized to exterior scenes of a city's perimeter, distorted by the haze of an energy field.

"Jaxom's energy field repelled the latest attack, *Denzit*," an older male advised her.

"Excellent," the *denzit* said. "The power grid has stabilized?"

"The attack on the lines running from the Analepsis Dam resulted in Zahl losses of one hundred fifty-nine," the officer reported. "The tunnels had to be collapsed."

"Have Renada dispatch a team to start digging them out immediately."

"Yes, *Denzit*."

Turning to Tuvok, she said, "Jaxom, like all twelve of our city-states, is protected by an advanced defense shield. The technology was still in development when I first came here and I made the installation of those shields my first priority. Since they came online, our casualty rate among the civilian population has dropped by more than seventy percent."

Tuvok listened attentively, but said nothing.

"The problem at Jaxom and three of our other smaller cities is that the infrastructure does not exist to provide all of the energy the shields require. Auxiliary sources such as Analepsis have been secured and power lines run underground to provide additional resources, but those lines remain vulnerable to constant attacks."

"How frequent are these attacks?" Tuvok asked.

"Weekly," the *denzit* replied. "You could set your chronometer by them."

"How many Rilnar currently inhabit this planet?" Tuvok asked.

"The largest city has almost two hundred thousand. Most are between seventy and eighty thousand."

"And how many Zahl?"

"They have been reduced to nine settlements from fifteen in the last few years," she replied, clearly proud of this achievement. "Four were completely destroyed; the other two were rendered uninhabitable by unfortunate infestations."

As biological warfare had never been approved by Starfleet, Tuvok was surprised to hear Janeway suggesting their casual use on Sormana. "Infestations you caused?" Tuvok asked.

"No," she clarified. "Ones we chose not to prevent. The Zahl's remaining nine settlements are larger than ours. The total Zahl population at this time is still a little over a million."

"How can the Zahl, even with a population that size, absorb weekly casualty rates like they just suffered at Jaxom?"

"They seem to have an unending supply of new recruits and to be honest I still don't know how they're bringing them here. At first I thought they must breed like voles, but my medical staff assures me that's not the case. There was a noticeable drop a few decades ago when the proximity mines went online, but that didn't slow them down for long. We've managed to secure our off-world supply lines to provide for necessary reinforcements from sympathizers within the colonies, but the Zahl have found another solution, one that eludes me at present."

"Fascinating," Tuvok noted.

The *denzit's* face broke into a wide grin, characteristic of Kathryn, but not the battle-hardened leader she had clearly become. She stared up at him for a moment as a sudden light in her eyes warred with regret. Stepping closer to him, she said softly, "Are you well, my old friend?"

"During the years that have separated us I have endured a number of difficult losses accompanied by developments of great personal fulfillment. I am as I have ever been."

Her smile faded. Placing a hand on his arm and giving it a gentle squeeze she said, "You have no idea how much I have missed you."

"I believe I can imagine," Tuvok replied.

HAVERBERN, RILNADAAR VI

Under any other circumstances, Counselor Cambridge would have thrown himself into the harvest revelries of Haverbern's small farming community body and soul. The colony's inhabitants were a technologically advanced community. They specialized in tiered hydroponic farms that left a great deal of arable land untouched. The rustic annual ritual they were in the process of enacting was a rarity among most species as technologically advanced as the Rilnar. It was beautiful, noble, and completely without artifice. Each piece was performed as it must have been on Sormana by these people's ancestors.

Several large fires had been lit around which men and women of all ages danced with abandon. They were clad in ceremonial cloaks, colorful vests, tunics, and broad skirts accented with images of ripe grains and vegetables. Children ran wild chasing packs of domesticated animals from group to group, their hands dripping with the juice of fresh fruits that were piled on tables surrounding the fires.

At the far end of the grounds, a platform had been erected from which occasional announcements were made in between the exotic sounds—Cambridge hesitated to call it *music*—being coaxed from a variety of percussive and small wind instruments.

Had he not known better, the counselor could have imagined that he had been transported back in time to the earliest years of Rilnar civilization. It was a vivid reminder of the magnificent, simple power of life's most primal cycles and the way they continued to inform and ignite the imagination.

Several of the local participants had invited him to join their dance—as soon as they had advised the local alderman that they were friends of Commander O'Donnell and Lieutenant Elkins, who had been left at this settlement four days prior. The alderman was an ancient Rilnar man whose entire body was covered with faded green tattoos. He embraced Cambridge and Lieutenant Url, *Demeter*'s tactical officer, like long-lost kin. Clearly

Commander O'Donnell had managed to completely ingratiate himself among these people.

Cambridge and Fife had also enjoyed a series of successful and enlightening discussions among the Rilnar diplomats at Rilquitain. Their story had been unsurprising.

The Rilnar and Zahl were one species. They had evolved on Sormana tens of thousands of years earlier and from the moment two disparate tribes had made contact, there had been conflict. The Rilnar already had written communications and rudimentary mathematical skills when their territorial expansion brought them into contact with the somewhat less-advanced Zahl. They had enslaved the Zahl. The Zahl had rebelled. For a student of comparative anthropology, such as Cambridge, it was an old story he felt he had heard one too many times.

Centuries passed. Both cultures evolved. Lines were drawn on maps. Weapons became more deadly, tactics more complex. Vast resources on both sides were expended. Occasionally the lines on the maps were redrawn. Brief periods of peace were followed by outbreaks of new hostilities with relatively little provocation.

Rilnar scientists had first unlocked the potentials of the atom. Spaceflight followed and on its heels, the development of rudimentary warp capabilities. Those that had emigrated from Sormana were content to leave the conflict behind. They were the first among their people to grasp how insignificant their petty differences and tortured history was when measured against the vastness of the rest of the universe.

Those who now led the Rilnar colonial worlds were a proud people. Their artists, philosophers, and scientists could stand easily beside their counterparts among other warp-capable species. Their military showed surprising restraint. It seemed there was one lesson Sormana's past had taught them well: development was the child of peace.

Defensive capabilities were prioritized as the Rilnar set their sights farther and farther from their homeworld, and from similar colonies constructed by the Zahl. There was, after all, plenty of space for both.

The leader of the Rilnar diplomatic delegation, a slight woman named Halaah, spoke frankly of her and her predecessor's attempts over the years to establish a true and lasting peace on Sormana. For her people and their Zahl counterparts, Sormana had become a cultural blight. Those who remained on the planet, relatively few by the colony's standards, could not under any circumstances be convinced to part with their ancient hatred. When decades of negotiations failed, the Rilnar and Zahl had come to an uneasy and dispiriting truce of their own. Those who lived on Sormana were free to continue to do as they wished. The rest of their people would move on without them. The minefield had been established along with the blockade, staffed equally on both sides. Each tended to their own humanitarian needs. Each had a fair number of sympathizers among the diaspora, but never enough to tip the balance toward one side or the other.

Sormana was like a cancer: a growth that could be contained, never eliminated. That it had not metastasized was encouraging. Whether or not it might one day prove fatal had yet to be determined.

Despite the fact that after such a dispiriting history lesson they could have used a little release, Cambridge and Lieutenant Url were duty-bound for the moment to restrain themselves. Several hours prior to Cambridge's arrival, O'Donnell and Chief Elkins had joined the local elders in a massive tent that occupied the center of the field. They were attending a ceremony that was part historical re-enactment, part spiritual observation. While waiting for this ceremony to conclude, Cambridge had initially attempted to engage those who approached him in simple conversation, inquiring about their costumes and dances. The sad fact was that most of them were already too intoxicated by constant helpings of a concoction that smelled like refined deuterium to speak intelligently.

The horizon was a riot of orange, purple, and deep blue when

O'Donnell and Elkins finally emerged from the tent, arm in arm with three farmers who appeared to be helping them to stand upright. Both had removed their uniform jackets and tunics. At least they'd had the good sense to affix their combadges to their belts. Their pasty chests and bellies had been decorated with wide green markings. They laughed loudly at some inside joke, O'Donnell staggering toward Elkins as he doubled over with mirth.

If they both weren't blind drunk, Cambridge would eat his socks.

The alderman led their small procession, winding his way through the crowd to the raised platform. Elkins disengaged himself unsteadily from two of the farmers who hurried to follow the alderman. Lieutenant Url moved swiftly to keep the engineer from falling flat on his face.

"Chief Elkins," Url asked softly, "do you require medical attention?"

Elkins laughed, slapping Url much too hard on the back. "That'll be the day, son," he replied cheerily.

Cambridge moved toward O'Donnell, who held him at arm's length as he waited for a dizzy spell to pass before peering at the counselor through narrowed eyes. "Counselor," he began, before breaking into a chuckle at what had to be a joke only he understood. When it had subsided, he said, "How nice to see you again. Would you be so kind as to return to venerable Griveth's tent and retrieve my jacket for me? It's a bit chilly out here, isn't it?"

"Of course, Commander," Cambridge replied. "As I sincerely doubt you could find it in your current condition," he added under his breath.

"I'm not so very drunk," O'Donnell said with a wink. "When you return, we'll be ready to leave."

"Url, keep an eye on these two. I'll be back momentarily," Cambridge said.

Cambridge hurried into the tent and paused briefly to allow his eyes to adjust to the brightly candle-lit interior, a stark contrast to the dusk he had inhabited moments earlier. He paused, his breath catching in his throat, as he began to study the walls of the tent. Dozens of panels were painted with various scenes, most of them battles. Alien script ran beneath each panel and Cambridge automatically pulled out his tricorder and began to scan and translate them. He had assumed that the history now before him must be Haverbern's, or Rilnadaar VI's. He had been wrong. The oldest panel, located at the rear of the tent, opposite the entrance, featured a view of the planet Sormana resting in the dark vastness of space. Crudely rendered above the planet were two male figures facing each other with their arms outstretched. Whether they intended to embrace or strike each other was unclear.

After scanning each panel thoroughly, a task he could have completed only in the solitude he currently enjoyed, Cambridge turned his attention to the center of the tent, where a large, low stone table sat. Dun-colored cushions surrounded it: fourteen in all. Cambridge searched among them for O'Donnell's uniform. He noted that on the table before each cushion sat a small dish with partially eaten chunks of bread, cheese, fruit, and a few pickled vegetables with sour stenches. Beside each cushion sat a cup that had been turned over onto the dirt floor once it had been emptied. Next to each cup, a small, leather-bound book rested. Hundreds of pages of the small script filled these books, and Cambridge wondered at their significance. They might be letters, myths, legends, or recipes, for all he could tell.

He toyed with the idea of borrowing one indefinitely, but hesitated to steal from such gracious hosts. Hopefully, O'Donnell and Elkins had learned more than the limits of their tolerance for alien moonshine during whatever ceremony they had experienced in this tent.

He finally located two cushions behind which his fellow officers had abandoned their uniforms and their dignity and he bent low to retrieve the rumpled clothing. As he lifted them from the dirt, a single leather-bound book fell from inside O'Donnell's jacket.

Either O'Donnell had less compunction about acquiring the data they needed, or possibly, this book had been a gift from their hosts. Cambridge decided to assume the latter, folded the book back into the jacket, retrieved Elkins' jacket, and exited the tent.

He emerged into a crowd so somber it was almost unrecognizable. The entire assembly had abandoned the fires and moved to sit and stand near the platform. They all held small flickering candles. The alderman had clearly been speaking for some time, and rapt faces gazed at him reverently from the crowd.

". . . we cannot know if the brothers will return. We believe in the promise they made to our ancestors. We believe the time of peace is at hand. We eagerly await the day when we will be reunited with our families, when Sormana is free."

"When Sormana is free!" the crowd chanted in aggressive unison.

"Until then, who will rise to defend what is ours and to secure the blessings of future generations?" the alderman asked.

"I will," a voice responded from the crowd, followed by dozens of others. Cambridge watched in morbid fascination as a small group of young men and women, their faces flushed with the exertions of the last several hours, moved to the platform to form a line behind the alderman.

"Children of Rilnadaar VI, inheritors of Sormana," the alderman shouted.

"Inheritors of Sormana," the crowd responded, lifting their candles as one and cheering with a rabid intensity that Cambridge feared could erupt at any moment into something much darker and more frightening.

A song began somewhere in the crowd. Soon every voice was raised. It was largely unintelligible, but Cambridge got the drift. It was a dirge of sorts, mourning those who had sacrificed themselves on Sormana's red hills.

"Are we ready to go?" a clear voice demanded.

Cambridge turned to see O'Donnell, Elkins, and Url

standing behind him. To his astonishment, both the captain and chief engineer stood steadily, their eyes clear and their faces quite somber.

"I believe I have acquired the data you wanted," Cambridge replied to O'Donnell.

With a brisk nod, O'Donnell tapped his combadge, requesting immediate transport. He did not slur, nor did he stumble. The last image Cambridge saw before the transporter took hold was the face of Liam O'Donnell, etched with unutterable sadness as he gazed at the crowd before him and those who had just volunteered to join the ongoing slaughter on Sormana.

CELWINDA

The pilot Seven had met at Jewl's might have been anywhere from forty to ninety years of age. Her name was probably not Rukh, but that was the only designation the woman had offered when they had begun their negotiations, along with the name and location of her vessel, a small cargo ship called *Celwinda*.

Seven did not recognize Rukh's species. Deep-brown flesh was covered with fine white hair. Incredibly narrow eyes rimmed with black lids and a small, pale nose gave her a feline appearance. Her hands were hairless and their flesh was deeply lined. Her eyes darted around nervously whenever she deigned to speak. Rukh seemed constantly on alert.

Once they had boarded for the journey to Zahlna II, the Doctor had attempted to engage Rukh in light banter, to no avail. Seven had encouraged him to join her near the rear of the passenger cabin and to speak only when absolutely necessary.

It was somewhat shocking as they began to approach their destination's orbit when Rukh invited Seven to join her in the cockpit. There was only a single chair for the pilot, and Seven had to bend at the waist to avoid hitting the overhead panels, but she did so, unwilling to insult their current host. Rukh had demanded a small fortune in local currency for their passage, which had been easy to obtain through trade on Lillestan, and a few medical supplies, which Commander Glenn had been less willing to part with. She relented only when it became clear that the light analgesics and antibiotics would seal the deal in obtaining anonymous passage to a Zahl colony.

"Is there a problem?" Seven asked.

"Once we make orbit and obtain clearance, we're going to land at the Port of Ngbel. I have cargo to offload and will be on the ground for six hours at most. Is that enough time for you?" Rukh asked.

"Depending upon how far the port is from the city's other municipal facilities, that should be more than sufficient."

"You're looking to make contact with a local official?" Rukh asked. "I don't want any trouble."

"We are not. We require specialized information that should be readily available in any public records or library facility."

"Public library . . . you mean that anyone can use?" Rukh asked.

"Yes."

"There's no such thing here. The *germschled* is about five klicks from the port. That's the center of education for all Zahl. But you won't be able to access their research buildings without identification. You'll need visitor's credentials."

Seven sighed, understanding where this was going. "Would you be able to acquire those credentials for us?"

"For another ten thousand *Zelcheks*."

"That's outrageous," the Doctor said. Seven turned abruptly to see that he had joined her at the cockpit's doorway.

"Do you have a better suggestion?" Seven asked archly.

When the Doctor did not respond immediately Seven said, "You'll have twice that when we return to Lillestan, assuming the credentials you provide us with prove effective."

"Oh, they'll work," Rukh said. "Funny thing, though, I never figured you two for students."

"Really? And what did you *figure us for*?" the Doctor asked.

"Spies."

LILLESTAN

"I'm telling you, we're being followed," Lieutenant Reginald Barclay insisted.

Lieutenant Velth sighed. This was his fifth tour of the station in two days and he was already comfortable navigating its crowds and commercial establishments. While escorting Commander Glenn, they had discovered that the *sigkn* bar's unusual live appetizers were dense with nutrients and well-seasoned. Lieutenant Benoit had spent more than an hour in earnest conversation with a local cargo pilot who claimed that his vessel was powered by protomatter. Ensign Drur had managed to lose his uniform jacket in a friendly game of *haskik*. Velth had stepped in before the ensign had succumbed completely to the wiles of a Rubenesque alien female with whom Drur had appeared willing to bet the *Galen* in order to impress.

Velth had no such issues with Lieutenant Reginald Barclay. The ship's resident holographic specialist had refused to contemplate shore leave until Commander Glenn had ordered him from his lab. Organic officers were in short supply aboard her ship and she wanted the widest possible array of personal impressions gathered as she prepared her report on her ship's stay at Lillestan.

To say that Barclay had been uncomfortable from the moment they had stepped foot onto the docking platform would have been an understatement. Velth's constant reminders that thus far, everyone they had encountered had been friendly and respectful, and that Velth was more than capable of subduing any attacker even without his phaser, had done nothing to calm the lieutenant's nerves. He had complained of debilitating stomach pains three times in an obvious attempt to cut their visit short before becoming spooked by an individual he was certain was now trailing the pair of officers.

Velth had taken note of the single Zahl male, tall and fleshy, dressed in nondescript civilian clothing. While he had maintained a safe distance, and paused on several occasions near enough Velth's position to stand out, he did not appear to be paying the Starfleet pair any heed. His eyes had a glazed, unfocused look. He might be intoxicated. He was not, however, a threat.

"Why don't we move to the third platform?" Velth suggested softly. "We can check out the transport facilities and try to get a sense of the frequency of local traffic and typical crew complements."

"That would require us to utilize the public lifts," Barclay moaned.

"You think your stomach can handle the stairs?" Velth asked.

"I don't like small, confined spaces," Barclay said.

"This way," Velth replied with a shrug. The narrow, dimly lit staircases situated in the far corners of the arena were probably a greater tactical threat than the lifts, but Velth saw no reason to point this out to Barclay. The echoing of their footsteps as they ascended added to the eerie atmosphere and Velth was about to activate his SIMs beacon when the unmistakable sound of an additional set of footsteps entering the stairwell below them caused him to reconsider. Instead, he glanced toward Barclay's bulging, alarmed eyes and said, "Double-time."

The lieutenant nodded vehemently and quickened his pace. They exited the stairway at the third level without incident only to find themselves in another equally dim but slightly wider corridor. Velth didn't pause to consult his tricorder. He knew the general direction of the transport offices and given that the station was constructed in a circular orientation figured that either direction they chose would take them to their destination eventually.

The hallway was carpeted, so Velth did not hear the individual behind them exit the stairwell. But as he and Barclay reached a T-junction, a pain-filled grunt sounded behind him, followed by the muffled thump of a large form impacting the deck.

Velth paused, looked to Barclay, who was lifting his hand to his combadge, probably to request emergency transport, and pulled Barclay's arm down, whispering, "Stay here."

Barclay nodded and Velth hurried to retrace his steps. Moments later he came upon the Zahl male Barclay had spotted earlier. The alien was in no position to threaten anyone, lying on the deck, curled into a ball and moaning softly.

"Sir, do you require medical attention?" Velth asked, stepping closer but on guard in the event of a ruse.

The man continued to moan, but said nothing.

Velth risked a few more steps and his nose was assaulted by a rank odor. The man was tearing at his tunic and beneath his fingers rotting flesh was clearly visible.

Velth retreated, tapping his combadge. "Velth to *Galen*. Can you lock onto my signal along with that of an alien within one meter . . ." he began. Before he could complete his request, however, a shrill whine sounded and the unfortunate soul before him vanished in a whirl of red particles—a sight Velth already knew indicated the activation of Lillestan's transporter system.

Velth turned to see Barclay approaching. "Don't get too close," he ordered. He then ordered both of them transported immediately to *Galen*'s sickbay behind forcefields, hoping against hope that whatever their pursuer suffered from was not contagious.

12

VESTA

Captain Regina Farkas had grown accustomed to Admiral Janeway's presence at her right hand on the bridge. It rarely felt intrusive, though Farkas had initially worried that it would become so. Commanding a Starfleet vessel was challenging enough without a member of the brass literally looking over your shoulder.

But Janeway was proving to be an exception to common mythos about Starfleet admirals. Her rank came with privileges she chose neither to flaunt nor abuse. She rarely questioned Farkas's orders and never in front of her crew. The admiral seemed content to observe when she chose to appear on the bridge. Conversation was frequent, discussion enlightening, and she never made Farkas feel that her opinions were not both welcome and duly considered. The captain couldn't help but feel that many of Janeway's peers could learn from her example, were it possible to *teach* an admiral anything.

However, it was painfully clear that the closer *Vesta* drew to the source of the Starfleet signal, the more anxious Janeway became.

The starscape visible on the main viewscreen had not altered for several minutes when Jepel advised her from ops that they were essentially right on top of the signal.

"Have you identified the source?" Janeway asked before Farkas had the chance—a rare impolite interjection.

"No, Admiral," Jepel replied. "Altering sensors now to broaden the search of local subspace bands."

"What do you think it is, Admiral?" Farkas asked.

"I have no idea. A message buoy, perhaps?" Janeway replied.

"That would make sense," Farkas agreed.

"Captain," Lieutenant Kar advised from tactical, "long-range sensors have detected a vessel approaching. It is Krenim and at current speeds will intercept us within the next ten minutes."

"Yellow alert," Farkas said. "Raise shields but be ready to drop them if we can lock onto the signal's source."

"Aye, Captain," Kar replied.

Janeway rose from her seat and moved to stand behind Ensign Jepel at ops. Farkas didn't think that was going to make the young man work any faster, but one never knew. After observing in silence for a full minute the admiral said, "Try scanning for antichroniton residue along the fourth and fifth bands."

Jepel dutifully altered his search parameters, and Farkas was pleased to hear a faint series of trills erupt from his control panel.

"That did the trick, Admiral," Jepel said.

"Bryce and Icheb were right," Janeway said as she moved back toward Farkas. "Its temporal shielding has begun to decay. Otherwise, it might have taken us days to find."

"What is it?" Farkas asked.

"Its size and configuration suggest a standard Starfleet message buoy," Jepel replied. "We will be ready to transport it aboard within the next three minutes."

"The moment transport is complete, set course to rendezvous with *Voyager* and engage at maximum warp," Farkas ordered.

Janeway resumed her seat and gestured for Farkas to lean closer. "I wouldn't mind saying hello to the Krenim."

"Really?" Farkas asked, surprised. "I would have thought it better to avoid them until we know more about what we're dealing with."

"They know we're here. We've violated their territory. Better not to add insult to injury by trying to outrun them."

"New friends." Farkas sighed.

Janeway nodded. "Let's hope so."

"Admiral, we have retrieved the buoy," Jepel reported. "It has been transported to our main science lab on deck six."

"Order all officers to refrain from initiating analysis until I arrive," Janeway said. "And ask Lieutenant Bryce and Ensign Icheb to join me there."

"Will do," Farkas said as Janeway rose and hurried toward the bridge's turbolift. "Are you sure you don't want to speak personally to our new acquaintances?" Farkas asked.

"Keep it short," Janeway suggested. "And if diplomacy fails . . ."

"It won't," Farkas assured her.

And it didn't. The Krenim scout ship that intercepted *Vesta* inquired perfunctorily about their presence in Krenim space. When Farkas identified herself as the captain of a Federation vessel her counterpart didn't even blink. He simply ordered one of his officers to make note of it in their logs and advised Farkas as to the quickest route out of Krenim territory, accepting at face value her protestations that she had no idea her ship had wandered into their space.

Later, in her personal logs, Farkas would note that her brief first contact with the Krenim had left her with the impression that they were one of the more civilized Delta Quadrant species she had yet encountered.

Admiral Janeway wondered if she had entered the wrong science lab when she arrived to find only an empty analysis table.

The admiral stepped out and asked the security officer standing guard, "Where is the buoy?"

"It's right there, Admiral."

Janeway stepped back in and double-checked the table's display panel. The sensor readings clearly indicated the presence of the buoy, as well as more antichroniton residue.

The first order of business was to disable the buoy's temporal shielding without triggering its self-destruct mechanism. If the buoy's internal workings had degraded at a similar rate as its shielding, that might prove challenging.

The lab's door slid open and a breathless Lieutenant Bryce entered, Icheb trailing a few steps behind. "Got here as quick as we could, Admiral," Bryce said.

"Clearly," Janeway observed.

Icheb took over the main data station and began a series of new scans. He worked with silent intensity as Bryce peered over his shoulder.

"Do you have any idea how to disable the temporal shielding?" she asked.

"I'm not sure that will be necessary, Admiral. I just have to find . . ." Icheb began, but before he could finish, Bryce added, "There it is."

"What?" Janeway asked.

"The buoy's specs," Bryce replied.

"The temporal field surrounding it has been masking its exact dimensions," Icheb added.

"This thing has to be five generations behind our current standard," Bryce noted. "I'm pretty sure I trained on one of these at the Academy."

"Lucky for us," Janeway said, realizing for the first time that Bryce hadn't even entered the Academy when *Voyager* was first lost in the Delta Quadrant. "But what exactly . . . ?"

"The basics of the temporal shields aren't that different from a Scheinen phase displacement field, but you have to augment for the temporal variable. This particular field has already been modified to interface with our systems," Icheb explained.

He fell silent for a few moments as Bryce whistled softly. "Holy cow, that's brilliant."

It was rare that Janeway could stand in the presence of a scientific problem and feel lost. "Icheb?" she demanded.

"Sorry, Admiral. It's just that when you dropped this, you really didn't want anyone else to find it," the ensign replied.

"How could you possibly know that?" Janeway asked, somewhat taken aback at Icheb's certainty that she was personally responsible for the buoy's presence here. Of course, there weren't that many other possibilities.

"The decay of the temporal shielding was triggered by our scans. This device was designed to probe the space-time continuum for our specific scanning frequencies, by which I mean frequencies that correspond not just to Starfleet technology, but technology that shares our quantum resonance. When that is detected, the temporal shields fall away slowly to make sure that the device is fully integrated into our time period prior to dispersing. Do you see the rate of decay increasing?"

Janeway checked the readings and immediately understood. "But why would anyone limit the buoy's potential discovery to a single timeline?"

Bryce scratched his head vigorously. "The temporal shields would have been activated prior to launch, right?" Following Icheb's nod he continued, "At that moment it essentially became the property of all timelines. If the data contains information that could corrupt multiple timelines by its discovery, you might have been trying to prevent more damage."

We did this, Janeway thought in wonder as the invisible device on the table before her began to appear in a distorted haze. While it was true that Starfleet believed that only *Voyager* and *Equinox* had been lost in the Delta Quadrant, it was always possible that another vessel had found its way here in another timeline and they might be responsible for the temporal mess this mission was becoming. *But a Starfleet message buoy standard to roughly eight years earlier that had been enhanced by Borg temporal shields?* The odds against it having originated anywhere but on her *Voyager* were staggering.

The buoy emerged into the present moment in fits and starts, eventually materializing in the center of the diagnostic station.

"Scan for quantum resonance," Janeway ordered as soon as the buoy had stabilized.

Icheb did. When his scan was complete, he shook his head. "As expected, according to this scan, the buoy originated in *this* exact timeline."

This time Janeway was ahead of him. "If it originated in this timeline and its shields prevented it from being affected by any alterations to the timeline, that means that this device couldn't have come from anywhere but *my Voyager*. Whatever happened was somehow erased from our memories without creating an alternate timeline."

"Maybe," Icheb said. "It is also possible that we are now occupying a timeline that was reintegrated with a temporary alternate line where this buoy was launched and its quantum signature is now identical to ours."

"The buoy is requesting an access code. Do you remember your codes from that period of time?" Bryce asked Janeway.

The admiral shook her head. "We don't even know exactly *when* this happened."

"Does knowing that Seven had to have been aboard to help you create the temporal shields narrow it down? Or the stardate of *Voyager*'s single contact with the Krenim?" Icheb asked.

Janeway thought back as best she could. Assuming she *had* launched this buoy, she wouldn't have used a command authorization that would have been hard to remember. Codes changed regularly for different security functions, but she would have made sure this one was familiar.

Her hands were shaking slightly as she placed them on the data interface and entered her initial clearance code, the first she had created when she became *Voyager*'s captain: *Janeway pi alpha four seven.*

The buoy's data interface screen darkened. Then a series of log entries appeared.

Janeway selected the first log for playback and her voice, distant and unspeakably cold, echoed through the lab.

"Asking you to stay would be asking you to die."

She abruptly halted the playback and turned to Bryce. "Thank you both. I'll take it from here."

"If you run into any problems, Admiral, just contact us," Bryce said.

Janeway nodded, then pulled up a stool and perched on it before continuing. She quickly realized that the logs were out of order. They had all been downloaded within seconds of one another, a data dump prior to the buoy's launch, and had never been refiled by the stardate on which they had been originally recorded. She took a few moments to correct this and began the log's playback at the beginning.

The story recounted for her in her voice and her words was the most chilling, disheartening, and terrifying thing she had ever heard.

VOYAGER

Lieutenants Harry Kim and Gaines Aubrey had been studying various sections of the minefield on the astrometrics lab's screen forever. At least it felt that way to Kim. No algorithm they had yet devised had revealed the subspace frequency or band that indicated the location of the mines. The best they could do at this point was attempt to extrapolate the mine's locations based on their logs of other ships' journeys from the checkpoint to Sormana's orbit, but even that task was proving frustrating. The fact that Seven hadn't made any progress beyond this point either soothed Kim's ego more than he liked to admit.

It didn't help that Kim found it unusually difficult to focus. Normally a problem like this would have consumed him until he found the answers he sought. Now his attention was divided between studying the minefield and figuring out how to undo the damage he'd unintentionally done to his relationship with Nancy. Of the two issues, only one felt truly pressing, and it wasn't the one that duty forced him to address.

"Tell me you have something, gentlemen," Commander Tom Paris said as he entered the lab.

Kim sighed deeply. "We do. You're not going to like it."

"Come on, it can't be that bad," Paris said.

"We have analyzed the routes of fifty-eight vessels that have traversed the minefield since we first detected the checkpoint," Aubrey began. "None of them took the same course from the checkpoint to the planet's orbit."

"In some cases this makes sense because they were clearly headed for different areas." Kim picked up the report. "Others seemed to indicate that the configuration of the minefield is constantly shifting."

"A design flaw?" Paris asked.

Kim pulled up four separate scans so that Paris could study them simultaneously. "I don't think so. Watch this."

Each ship began at the checkpoint and made at least a dozen course corrections before arriving at the same orbital entry point. "This is the same ship seen moving in and out of the field on four consecutive days," Aubrey reported. "Each time it took a completely different course."

"Okay, but maybe the courses are randomized to prevent anyone from reverse-engineering the coordinates of the mines," Paris suggested. "I mean, we can't be the first to try and figure this out."

Kim maximized the display of a single vessel. "This ship entered the field the day before you took the *Tuccia* in." Kim then added the doomed journey of Paris's shuttle to the screen for comparison.

"I'll be damned," Paris said. The ship in question had moved well within proximity of the mine his shuttle had triggered without suffering the *Tuccia's* fate. "But if they are moving the mines, couldn't we detect *that*?"

"I don't think it's that complicated," Aubrey noted.

"No?" Paris asked.

"I think the field is probably a lot denser than we suspect and that on any given day, the only people who know which mines are actually live are the ones controlling the field," Aubrey continued.

"Which means one of the ships out here is constantly activating and deactivating the mines," Paris said. "Have you searched for that signal?"

"Nothing yet," Aubrey reported.

"Damn," Paris said, impressed in spite of himself.

"Yep," Kim agreed.

SORMANA

"What was it like?" *Denzit* Janeway asked, leaning toward Tuvok while taking a generous drink from the fluted metallic cup she'd been nursing over the last few hours. It contained a local wine. Tuvok found its fragrance repellant and he had no intention of dulling his senses as he gently probed the *denzit's* emotional defenses.

"Assimilation?" Tuvok asked.

The *denzit* nodded somberly in response.

"It is difficult to describe, as I was only briefly aware of the sensation of absolute submission to the Collective. The anticipation of the loss of self is definitely more frightening to contemplate than the reality. As the neural suppressant that the Doctor had given all of us began to fail, I recall the absence of fear. To submit seemed not only inevitable, but preferable to any other state of being. I am not certain how Borg nanoprobes accomplished this feat, but I do believe that the overwhelming certainty that accompanies assimilation was a significant factor in the Borg's ability to function so cohesively."

"That and the power of the Queen," the *denzit* noted.

Tuvok nodded. "Yes."

"Still, your captain's choice to risk your life and hers to save these mutated drones seems incredibly reckless."

"Perhaps. But you must understand that by the time we learned of the existence of Unimatrix Zero, we had already faced and defeated the Borg on several occasions."

"Defeated?"

"Survived the encounters without suffering the destruction of our ship or the assimilation of our crew."

"An important distinction, don't you think?" the *denzit* said.

"I do," Tuvok allowed.

"Were you still aboard *Voyager* when this Borg Invasion began?"

"No. By then, I had accepted a position with Captain Riker aboard the *Titan*."

The *denzit* smiled. "Will Riker. I can't believe it's taken him this long to get a command of his own. Tell me honestly, do you prefer serving under him, or *your* Captain Janeway?"

"Both present their fair share of challenges," Tuvok replied diplomatically. "Both share the same devotion to Starfleet's principles and ideals. Both are incredibly demanding. But I do not share a similar or even comparable personal relationship with Captain Riker. He seems to prefer the company of those with whom he has a greater shared history and while his trust is not difficult to gain, I have always found you to be more accepting."

The *denzit* smiled again, accepting the compliment. She sat back in her chair across the small table they shared in her private dining room. Draining the last of her wine, she said, "Part of me misses Starfleet. I'd be lying if I said otherwise."

Tuvok remained silent. To push her would be pointless.

Kathryn Janeway could be mercurial in her passions, but her defenses were formidable in the presence of any genuine threat.

"Why are you still out there, Tuvok? Seven years of a deep-space mission wasn't enough for you?"

"It seemed logical to transition to the Academy when *Voyager* first returned home," Tuvok admitted. "It was a refreshing change. But when I was asked to join Starfleet Intelligence, I could not deny that I still harbored a strong desire to seek out new challenges. *Voyager*'s journey home was difficult, but it never failed to provide fascinating insights into our universe and those with whom we share it. I remain content with Starship duty because I have not yet had my fill of exploration and discovery. I don't know that I ever will."

"You don't miss your family?"

"My wife is with me on *Titan*. Our surviving children have their own lives and we remain in constant contact."

"Your *surviving* children?"

"My son Elieth and his wife, Ione Kitain, were killed when the Borg attacked Deneva. Nothing I have ever . . ." he began, but trailed off.

The *denzit*'s eyes were suddenly filled with tears. She reached forward and took one of Tuvok's hands, squeezing it firmly. "I am so very sorry," she said.

They remained like that for several moments as tears began to flow freely down her face. Tuvok could not conscience a similar display, nor could he deny that her raw compassion touched him deeply. Her response could not help but remind him of the earliest years of their relationship and the competent but vulnerable woman she had always been.

The admiral was very different. They had only spoken briefly, but Tuvok had clearly felt the walls that now fortified her emotions, allowing her a new dispassionate perspective from which to examine the tragedies of the past. Tuvok could not say exactly why the *denzit*'s simpler, overwhelming suffering was more satisfying to witness. It did, however, mirror his emotional state more closely than the admiral's had.

This Kathryn understood. She had already shared some of what she had suffered at the hands of the Zahl. She had clearly compartmentalized the trauma. She spoke of it almost as if it had happened to someone else. But she had not lost her empathy. The violence she had endured had not severed her heart from her mind. She seemed driven by her pain to destroy those who had inflicted it upon her. She refused to release the anger that fueled her, unwilling to sacrifice the power it kindled within her.

What Tuvok had learned since his descent into near madness following Elieth's death was that rage provided a double-edged sword. It cut decisively into oneself as easily as those one sought to destroy. He understood well how necessary pain could become.

"I appreciate your sympathy," Tuvok finally said. "Thank you."

The *denzit* released his hand and wiped her ruddy cheeks dry. She looked past him for a long time, then returned her eyes to his. In the distance she had seemed to glimpse briefly some unspoken horror. It was quickly buried.

"How long can you stay?" she finally asked.

Tuvok considered the question before replying, "As long as it takes."

The *denzit* nodded, understanding. "I can't go back."

"So you have said."

"I'm too close now."

"To what?" Tuvok asked. "This war has continued for thousands of years. You are no more than a temporary player on this stage. It will continue long after you have sacrificed your life on the altar of revenge."

"Is that what you think I'm doing here?"

"It is logical to wish to destroy those who injured you. It was logical for you to embrace those who could best aid you in this cause. However, it is illogical to assume that anything you might do to aid the Rilnar will prove decisive in this conflict. Given that, your commitment is misplaced."

"This isn't about the Rilnar, Tuvok."

"No? I do not—" Tuvok began as she rose abruptly from her chair.

"Tomorrow will be another long day. You'll find me in the Center when you awaken."

Without another word she departed the room. An aide entered shortly thereafter to guide Tuvok to the quarters that had been prepared for him.

VESTA

Admiral Janeway had found it impossible to remain seated as she reviewed the contents of the message buoy. Stillness had given way to fretful pacing. She had paused only when the body blows of certain specific events had halted her, with the force of their visceral revulsion.

It was an unnerving sensation to hear herself speak of things she could not remember. She'd felt sympathy for the *denzit* when Chakotay had described the role similar logs had played in her torture at the hands of the Zahl. Now she felt she had shared some of the *denzit*'s suffering. Even in the absence of brutal interrogation techniques, to listen even once to the voice of the woman she had been was to bear gut-wrenching witness to her own descent.

The initial entries had been filled with resolve, determination not to allow what had appeared to be minor setbacks to sway her course. As the situation had continued to devolve, the cracks in her personal defenses had widened under the vast weight of the mounting obstacles to *Voyager*'s survival. The toll was unmistakable. The final logs had been composed of short, terse phrases, filled with equal parts of anguish and rage. The admiral doubted that the few officers who remained aboard had been privy to the depths of her torment. But these personal logs testified to her despair.

On her worst days in the Delta Quadrant, Janeway had never imagined miscalculating so thoroughly. To believe for a moment that the fate *Voyager* had suffered at the hands of the Krenim was possible would have given rein to paralyzing fear. She had no idea how much of Kes's Year of Hell resembled the events of these logs, but she was certain that the crew's designation of that period of time was accurate.

It had begun innocuously enough. On Stardate 51268.4, *Voyager* made contact with a large battle cruiser that identified itself as part of the Krenim Imperium. They were ordered to leave Krenim space. Going around their territory would have added years to their journey, and Janeway opted to attempt to cross through undetected. Within weeks they were engaging the Krenim on a regular basis. The ship suffered heavy damage. Several crew members were killed or seriously injured, including Lieutenant Commander Tuvok, who was blinded by the detonation of a chroniton torpedo that had become lodged in the ship. Seven and B'Elanna had developed temporal shields for *Voyager* as a defense against the chroniton torpedoes. Eventually they realized that the shields also had a more significant effect. They made *Voyager* immune to further alterations in the timeline that they realized were happening all around them. Two and a half months into their struggle, they were contacted by a Krenim leader named Annorax who said that he bore *Voyager* no malice, but could not allow them to continue to thwart his designs. He had taken Commander Chakotay and Lieutenant Paris prisoners in order to "study" them. The battles had raged on for months as vast sections of the ship had suffered irreparable damage and *Voyager* had been stripped of her defensive capabilities. Eventually, Janeway had been forced to order most of the crew to abandon ship.

The logs had ended there.

The admiral did not wish to review the logs again but had no choice. A cursory analysis revealed the power the Krenim had once wielded in this area of space and the lengths to which they had gone to secure their supremacy. While still formidable, their current holdings were dwarfed by those reported in the logs. The present-day reality suggested that Janeway had managed to somehow alter that timeline, wiping away the Krenim's vast gains and possibly leaving them none the wiser. *But how?* The only contact she remembered with the Krenim had taken place on the exact same stardate as the one referenced in the buoy's first log entry.

As she struggled to organize her thoughts, separating her true memories from what she had just learned, the door to the lab slid open and Captain Farkas entered. One look at Janeway's face halted her in her tracks.

Squaring her shoulders, Farkas said, "We have departed Krenim space, following the course given to us by the scout ship we encountered. We kept sensors engaged along the way, but did not detect any additional Federation signals. We're preparing to engage the slipstream drive to regroup with the rest of the fleet, unless you have new orders."

Janeway nodded. "For now, we must go back. We need to know what intelligence the others have acquired. But as of this moment, our mission here has expanded beyond the situation on Sormana."

"It has?"

"We need to know everything there is to learn about the Krenim Imperium, and we need to know it yesterday. In addition, Lieutenant Bryce and Ensign Icheb should begin work immediately integrating that Borg temporal shielding into all of our defensive systems."

"You think we're going to need them?"

"I hope not, but until we know more, I can't rule out the possibility."

13

ZAHLNA II

The forged identification cards Rukh had provided to Seven and the Doctor had granted them access to the *germschled*'s largest research library. The residents of Zahlnerest, the planet's capital city, sent their children to this campus to be educated from kindergarten through post-graduate studies. The centralized arrangement appealed to Seven's sense of order but the Doctor wondered how robust an education anyone could acquire from any system that was so strictly regimented. It was an ideal establishment for indoctrination, less so for rigorously expanding developing young minds.

However, for their purposes the facility was certain to provide all the data they required regarding the history of the Sormana conflict.

They presented their credentials and asked to be directed to the library's records on Sormana. The attending aide looked up at them quizzically. "A moment please," he said.

"Perhaps we should simply instigate our own search," the Doctor suggested softly.

Seven was about to concur when the aide returned, accompanied by an aged Zahl female wearing a diaphanous robe in shades of purple and green that fell almost to the floor.

"Hello," she greeted them pleasantly. "I am Wichella, this facility's chief archivist. Mev has advised me that two students from off-world have come to study Sormana. If you could provide me with more specific information about the nature of your search, I will be better able to direct you to the appropriate resources."

The Doctor warmed to Wichella immediately. Seven had witnessed a similar response from him many times when they had first joined the Federation Institute, before they had both realized how tedious many of their fellow scholars could be.

"We wish to understand the history of the conflict as well as the Zahl's interests in perpetuating it," Seven said.

Wichella seemed taken aback by the inference. "It appears you have already been misinformed, Miss . . . ?"

Seven paused a moment too long to remember the name on her forged credentials. "Pranlit, Shenra Pranlit," she finally said.

"I am Ginalis Trawk," the Doctor added. "Perhaps you have read my thesis on—"

Seven cut him off by shooting the Doctor a glare that could melt duranium, as Wichella's eyes darted between them, perhaps wondering if she had found herself on the receiving end of an alien joke. She continued without losing her composure, "Miss Pranlit. Mister Trawk. I regret to say that I am not familiar with your academic achievements. From whom have you already heard tales of Sormana?"

"An alien species several light-years distant," Seven replied. When Wichella continued to stare at her expectantly Seven added, "The Nihydron."

"Hm. Never heard of them either," Wichella mused. "But if they suggested to you that the Zahl Regnancy has done anything other than attempt to end the conflict on Sormana, they were mistaken."

A few other students had begun to form a line behind the Doctor and Seven. Wichella gestured for them to follow her into a nearby study carrel. Once the door had closed behind them, she continued. "Sormana remains, to this day, our greatest cultural tragedy. It is not difficult to understand what drove the conflict in its earliest days. The Rilnar are an aggressive species. They subjugated the Zahl on Sormana and it took more than a thousand years for our Zahl ancestors to throw off the yoke. As our civilizations advanced, side by side, there were periods of relative peace. But neither group ever seemed willing to let go of the disputes of the past in favor of an enduring peace. It's more complicated than that, of course. We're talking about thousands of years of history. Once our people ventured out among the stars, however, everything changed for us."

"But not for those who remained behind?" the Doctor prodded gently.

Wichella's face became wistful. "No. The educational system on Sormana is quite different from ours. Children are raised on ancient disputes. They are taught, and rightfully so, that the fault lies with the Rilnar. They have always wanted more. They have never been satisfied with any territorial exchanges, nor have they honored previous settlements. And with so much of the planet now laid waste, habitable areas are even more valuable than they once were."

"The Zahl are an advanced species," Seven said. "Why have they simply not forced the residents to abandon the planet? Surely there is ample room in the colonies to absorb Sormana's Zahl population."

"Sormana's political leaders have always claimed authority over the colonies, given that their rule is hereditary and predates the founding of the colonies," Wichella replied. "The regnancy doesn't see it that way, but has never been willing to officially disabuse them of this quaint notion. There is no practical point in doing so. A fair number of children born on the planet are sent here or to some of the other *germschleds* to be educated. Few return to Sormana when they come of age. Once they begin to understand the futility of the ongoing conflict, as we do, it is difficult for them to rejoin the war effort. It is impossible to say when the settlements on Sormana will be no more, but it seems inevitable to everyone who lives beyond them. The situation, as it stands, simply cannot endure."

"And yet it has," the Doctor noted.

"Yes, but the present age is different. Even a hundred years ago there were still many colonists with friends and family members on the homeworld. Today, there are almost none. The current regnancy and its predecessors have gradually distanced themselves from Sormana. While I cannot say that we enjoy particularly warm relations with our Rilnar neighbors, there is, at least, so much space between us as to make ongoing conflict unnecessary. The goal now is to contain the fighting on the planet's surface and hopefully, within the next few generations, to see it fade, like any fire denied sufficient oxygen."

"What can you tell us about the work of Zahl researchers or scientists in the field of temporal mechanics? Whom do you consider to be your most promising or preeminent voices on the subject?" Seven asked.

Wichella chortled to herself. "*Temporal* mechanics?" Shaking her head, she continued, "I must find these Nihydron and provide them with better data on our people. Undoubtedly they told you of Rahalla. As a historian, I understand well how mundane the truth can appear when set beside such vivid and sensational tales."

"Rahalla?" Seven asked.

"He was a Zahl scientist who was born, oh, almost three hundred years ago on Sormana. He claimed to have discovered particles of matter that mutated time. He was an old man when he first boarded a colony transport vessel and began to spread his ridiculous theories."

"You are saying that no one else verified his findings or has continued to pursue his work?" Seven asked.

"There is a single office at this *germschled* dedicated to Rahalla's theories. Its small staff is led by Frem Albrec. His work is permitted, though not officially sanctioned. The provost is content to allow a few frivolous pursuits when they have some basis in historical fact. One never knows, I suppose, what ancient tidbits might be worth remembering. But there are no reputable Zahl scientists here pursuing research in that field. In fact, the only species of which I am aware that is rumored to take the study seriously are the Krenim."

"The Krenim?" Seven repeated, consciously avoiding a pointed glance the Doctor directed toward her at this revelation.

"Theirs is a vast Imperium whose territory once bordered ours. Long ago, when the Zahl first ventured into space, they encountered the Krenim and there was a period of sustained territorial disputes. But they have kept to themselves for most of the last century, if not more. Still, some of our exploratory vessels that have ventured into the Krenim's space will return with terribly interesting, if completely unverifiable, rumors; nothing that would stand up to serious academic scrutiny."

"Could you direct us to Frem Albrec?" the Doctor asked.

"With pleasure," Wichella replied. "But only if you promise to remember that his tales are more myth than fact."

"We promise," Seven assured her.

GALEN

"You can relax," Commander Glenn said as she deactivated the force field behind which Lieutenants Velth and Barclay had waited while they had been scanned for any contagions. "You are both in perfect health and free of any unknown viral or bacterial agents."

Velth smiled in relief. Barclay, who was sweating profusely, seemed dubious. "Are you certain, Commander?" he asked. "I really don't feel well."

"I wouldn't let you rejoin the rest of us if I had any doubts, Reg," Glenn replied. "Get cleaned up and eat a decent meal. Drink lots of water over the next several hours. You'll be fine."

"If whatever incapacitated that man is loose on this station, we might want to consider suspending further tours," Velth suggested.

"Agreed," Glenn said. "I've already checked the other officers who have boarded the station and nothing contagious has shown up, but it's not worth risking. We did get a brief glimpse of the victim's bio-readings. When you called for transport, Gevais was trying to establish a lock on both of you. It was interrupted by the station's internal transporter, but the fact that he was pulled out of there so quickly suggests that someone on Lillestan knows there's a problem. They found him and removed him too soon for it to have been random. He was under surveillance, or they have some fairly unique protocols in place to handle their medical emergencies."

Velth shook his head and came perilously close to rolling his eyes. He'd gotten to know the *Galen*'s captain pretty well in the last several months. They'd shared a particularly grueling experience in their tour of the First World's medical facilities during the fleet's recent mission to establish diplomatic relations with the Confederacy of the Worlds of the First Quadrant. He clearly knew where this was heading and was already dreading the prospect.

"You're going to personally investigate Lillestan's medical offices, aren't you?" Velth asked.

"Damn right I am. The victim was Zahl. Seven and the Doctor are on one of their colonies right now. If this isn't an isolated incident, we need to be ready."

Velth nodded. "When do you want to do this?"

"No time like the present, Lieutenant. I just need to collect a few supplies."

"Aye, Commander."

DEMETER

Lieutenant Commander Atlee Fife was the last to join Commander O'Donnell and Counselor Cambridge to begin their analysis of the data they had collected on Rilnadaar VI and Rilquitain. *Demeter* was en route to rendezvous with *Voyager*, and Lieutenant Url had taken the watch. Fife had not seen Counselor Cambridge put down the small, leather-bound book O'Donnell had liberated from Haverbern since their return to the ship. Even now, Cambridge sat at the briefing table with it open before him. His tricorder was near at hand and consulted frequently.

"Well, Atlee, what did you learn?" O'Donnell asked.

"That I do not share your distaste for diplomatic exchanges," Fife replied amiably, eliciting a wide grin from O'Donnell.

"Really?"

"The food was excellent," Fife noted.

"The wine was better," Cambridge added without looking up.

"The party line, as you described it, Commander, is summarized in my report," Fife continued, nodding toward the padd that sat on the table before O'Donnell.

"Sormana is a great tragedy, a blight upon the otherwise stunning cultural achievements of the Rilnar," O'Donnell said, quoting from the padd.

"Yes, sir."

"And the *denzit*?"

"She is something of a curiosity among them. I did receive verification that the Rilnar rescued her several years ago. The facts tracked with those she reported to Captain Chakotay. They further confirmed that they attempted to assist her in locating *Voyager* again, but to no avail."

"By the time she would have started looking we were back in the Alpha Quadrant, exploring the Yaris Nebula, if memory serves," Cambridge offered.

"There is an unspoken but clearly implied confidence in her abilities among the diplomats," Fife said.

"They don't want to get their own hands dirty, but are cheering her on from the sidelines?" O'Donnell asked.

"Something like that."

"Does it go further? Are they secretly sending her supplies and reinforcements?"

"Not that they would admit to me," Fife replied. "What about Rilnadaar VI?"

"It's different for them. Some of them still have family members living on Sormana. They have a tradition at the annual festival of asking for volunteers to return and join the fight. But they are also absolutely convinced that peace is coming to Sormana and they await that eventuality with a confidence that is both heartening and inconceivable."

"What has led them to believe that?" Fife asked.

"Counselor?" O'Donnell said.

Fife turned toward Cambridge, who seemed disappointed at having to terminate his studies and join the discussion. "I have no idea if any of this can be substantiated, but it is absolutely one of the most fascinating cultural relics I have ever examined," the counselor began.

"What is it?" Fife asked.

"It's part mythology, part devotional."

"There's more in there than the story of the two brothers?" O'Donnell asked.

"Much more," Cambridge replied.

"The two brothers?" Fife asked.

"There is a legend among this group of the diaspora that has been handed down for several hundred years," O'Donnell said. "I'm not sure how seriously the rest of the Rilnar take it, but for the residents of Rilnadaar VI, it is almost a sacred belief. We reenacted it with them as part of the festival."

"Approximately two hundred years ago, if this document is to be believed," Cambridge said, picking up the story, "just after the slaughter at Batibeh—think Wolf 359 or the Azure Nebula, acts of violence so extreme that they stand out among others for their depravity and devastation—there was a moment when it appeared, that the fighting on Sormana might come to an end once and for all."

"Batibeh was an ancient Rilnar city, one that had never been attacked, despite its value and significance to the Rilnar," O'Donnell explained. "Its destruction sent shockwaves through both the Rilnar and Zahl colonies. It was a line no one believed anyone would ever cross. It horrified the colonists who had left Sormana and at the time it did a great deal to turn them against the conflict entirely."

"Two brothers from different settlements came to Batibeh. One was supposedly Rilnar, one Zahl. Don't ask me about their parents or how they *could possibly have been brothers* because there's nothing here on it, so we'll just have to take them at their word," Cambridge reported bitterly.

"What were their names?" Fife asked.

"Also lost to history," Cambridge replied, "which makes me wonder if they actually existed."

"I think they did," O'Donnell said.

"Yes, well, you haven't read this while sober have you?" Cambridge asked.

"I was exaggerating my condition for the benefit of Griveth," O'Donnell insisted.

"The brothers came to Batibeh," Cambridge continued with a wry nod toward O'Donnell. "There was a stone table that survived the destruction in the center of a park. They began to speak publically about the possibility of peace, the necessity of ending the war. Soon enough the public outcry they fomented began to spread and led the civilian and military leaders on Sormana to enter into serious peace negotiations."

"Roving diplomats?" Fife asked.

"They were inspirational speakers—prophets, if you will," Cambridge offered him. "But their timing couldn't have been better. After Batibeh, the bloodlust that had driven so much of the conflict was momentarily spent. Both sides were exhausted and demoralized. And both the military and civilian leaders of the time seem to have had more sense than most."

"Tell him about the pools," O'Donnell suggested.

"Yes, well, this is where the story starts to really get interesting," Cambridge said. "The brothers told the Rilnar and Zahl leadership that they could prove to them the futility of eternal war. They claimed to be able to see Sormana's future in these sacred pools hidden somewhere on the planet—again, their location lost to history."

"You'd think something that important, somebody would have left a map or at least dropped a few bread crumbs," O'Donnell noted.

"The brothers took several leaders from both sides to visit these pools. When they returned it was as if the scales had fallen from their eyes. A new peace accord was to be established. Sormana was to be evacuated. It was to be left to heal from the damage its residents had inflicted upon it and to serve future generations as a reminder of how close they had come to complete annihilation. Apparently whatever they saw in those pools scared the living daylights out of them."

"When did this happen?" Fife asked.

"Two hundred years ago, give or take," Cambridge replied. "What we have here is a series of journal entries, secondhand accounts of what the brothers said and did. The oldest sources had only heard rumors about the sacred pools. But it doesn't matter. Before the peace accord could be finalized, the two principal Rilnar and Zahl commanders were murdered. The brothers vanished from Batibeh and history. Both sides accused the other of treachery. The stone table was broken, and the war continued."

"What do the residents of Rilnadaar VI believe?" Fife asked.

"They think these brothers might have been more than men.

Not gods. No one goes that far. But *exceptional* beings. They say that the brothers departed Sormana on the eve of the accords, believing their work was done. The hope is that one day the brothers will come back and finish what they started. So once a year, the people of Rilnadaar VI set the stone table and eat and drink to peace, calling out into the void and begging the brothers to return."

"Why not eliminate the middlemen and just end it?" O'Donnell asked. "And why the hell would they send their children to fight in a war they believe to be futile?"

"As long as the war persists, they will not abandon the cause," Cambridge replied. "But as far as I can tell, these are the only people on either side of this equation who honestly believe that one day peace could prevail."

ZAHLNA II

"No, no, no, you misunderstand," Frem Albrec insisted. "Rahalla has never been given the credit that he is due, but one day that will change."

The Doctor and Seven had already spent the better part of an hour listening to Albrec wax rhapsodic about the Zahl scientist. Albrec's faith was something, especially when one considered that he had never in his life so much as laid eyes upon a single chroniton particle.

"Rahalla had seen the chroniton particles. He was never able to transport them off Sormana, nor was he able to bring others to the surface. The conflict deterred even the most devoted of his followers. But the theories he developed for their potential uses were profound. We have yet to be able to apply them, as no one has ever located other chroniton particles, but it is only a matter of time, no pun intended, of course." Albrec chuckled to himself.

"And you are certain that the Zahl military is not conducting experiments based upon Rahalla's findings?" Seven asked.

"With the military, nothing is certain," Albrec admitted. "But were they so inclined, they would certainly be utilizing the skills of myself or some of my colleagues, and that has never happened. We've shared our theories in hopes that the science officers aboard our vessels will seek out other sources of chroniton particles. But nothing has come of it."

Seven and the Doctor exchanged perturbed glances. Albrec seemed sincere and equally misinformed if the *denzit*'s story was to be believed.

"Do you believe that the particles Rahalla discovered might still be on Sormana?" Seven asked.

"They're incredibly unstable in a natural state, so it's hard to know so many centuries later. Personally, I doubt it," Albrec replied.

"Where did Rahalla go after he left Sormana?" the Doctor asked.

"To spread word of his discoveries. I'm afraid our people were not terribly accommodating. He was written off as something of an eccentric. But he found fellow believers among other species. Even some Rilnar scientists attended a few of his symposiums."

"Are there extant records of any of those gatherings?" Seven asked.

"A few. We have pieced together fragments of data acquired from other reference materials, but nothing Rahalla touched or left behind has survived."

"Why not?"

"Rahalla traveled on a small ship he had been given by the Zahl science institute. It was lost, along with all of his research, two hundred years ago."

"Could we look at those fragments?" Seven asked.

"How long will you be here?" Albrec asked. "Our records would take weeks, if not months, to properly review. They have to be understood in context."

"Did Rahalla ever make contact with the Krenim?" Seven asked. "We've heard from others that it is believed the Krenim have some facility with temporal mechanics."

"So they *claim*," Albrec said, clearly dismissing the notion. "They share nothing, convene no appropriate interdisciplinary conclaves. I wouldn't be surprised if the Krenim simply allow these rumors to flourish in order to discourage Zahl territorial expansion."

That one of the Zahl's most prominent academic proponents of the study of temporal theories could make such a claim was dispiriting. It did suggest to Seven that there was a distinct line between Zahl civilians and military officers. Why the two would be completely segregated made little sense. It was common in the Federation for civilian scientific institutes and Starfleet to share research and findings. But it was also possible that the Zahl military recruited only the best and brightest to further their knowledge of temporal theory. Albrec, while clearly enthusiastic, was neither of these.

Seven checked the chronometer on Albrec's wall. Rukh would be departing the planet in a little less than an hour. Nodding toward the Doctor, she said, "Thank you so much for your time, Mister Albrec."

"A moment, please," he requested, and began to tap quickly at his data console. After an excruciating wait he continued, "I've written my own treatise on every known individual or institute that mentioned direct contact with Rahalla either during his life or within a hundred years of his passing. Most of the citations have only single sources, which I know is insufficient by academic standards, but nothing else has survived or yet come to light."

Seven accepted a small data card from him with thanks and assurances that should they have any other questions, they would be in touch.

"Please do," Albrec said, beaming. "I do allow a select number of exchange students to audit my upper level courses. Both of you would be welcome."

"You are too kind," the Doctor said. Seven understood that he was speaking ironically. Fortunately, Albrec did not.

LILLESTAN

The infirmary's waiting room was filled with unhappy people. None were suffering from severed limbs or anything resembling an emergency, but a fair number obviously nursed nasty respiratory ailments and a few moaned softly, bent over in their chairs.

Commander Clarissa Glenn didn't feel right about asking these poor souls to wait while she interrogated the local doctor. But she had no intention of lingering among them long enough to catch whatever alien bugs had attacked them.

She ordered Velth to wait outside the room, then moved briskly from the entrance to the front desk, where a weary young man barely glanced at her before handing her a small, flat device.

"What's this?" Glenn asked.

"Your evaluator," he replied. "Place your palm flat on the panel and this will check your vitals and scan your system for infections. Your priority on the waiting list will be determined by the results of this scan."

Glenn gently pushed the device aside and said, "I did not come here for treatment. I came to speak with the infirmary's chief physician."

The young man's eyes finally lifted to meet hers. "The doctor doesn't take meetings. If you have any general questions, you should visit Lillestan's public safety division. I'm sure they'll be more help to you than us."

Glenn had come prepared for this eventuality. Nonetheless, she chaffed at the transactional nature of places like Lillestan.

"Does the doctor accept donations to his infirmary?"

The young man's eyes widened.

Glenn handed him a padd that listed several items from *Galen*'s stock she would trade for the intelligence she required. It had taken her less than a day at Lillestan to understand that nothing was freely offered here.

After perusing the list, the man made a notation on his data terminal. "The doctor will see you momentarily," he advised her almost cheerfully.

Less than ten minutes later, Glenn was ushered into an examination room with musty gray walls. There were automated diagnostic systems and a data terminal, but to her well-trained eyes, the facility was barely adequate. A fine layer of grime rested on most surfaces and a foul stench mingled with the burn of a cleaning solution filled the air.

The doctor who eventually entered, knocking softly before the door slid open for him, was an unfamiliar alien species. He was a dozen centimeters shorter than Glenn and a shock of spiked white hair sat atop a long face that bore two distinct demilune-shaped structures framing it on either side. His flesh was mottled gray and black and a flat pointed tongue flicked rapidly over thin lips.

He moved immediately to his data panel to call up her identification, then turned toward her puzzled. "I am Doctor Pakho," he said in a high, nasal voice. "You have questions for me?"

"I do."

"The generosity of your donation is sufficient to purchase five minutes of my time, Miss . . . ?"

"Commander Clarissa Glenn," she replied, choosing not to offer the designation of her ship. She hadn't spent much time on places as unsavory as Lillestan, nor was she accustomed to subterfuge on this level. But her gut told her that the less she said the better. "I'm curious about a patient you might have examined a few hours ago. He collapsed in a corridor near two of my crewmen and was almost immediately transported out. He seemed quite ill . . ."

"And you want to know if there's any chance your men caught what he had?"

Glenn nodded, despite the fact that this was not her concern at all.

"Obviously I cannot reveal the patient's history or condition to you," Pakho began. "Privacy is a valued commodity on Lillestan."

Glenn made a notation on the padd she held and offered it to Pakho, who reviewed it and emitted a long, slow hissing sigh.

"The illness is not communicable," Pakho said. "It is species specific. Your men are in no immediate danger."

"He was Zahl," Glenn said, showing a few of her cards. "If I decided to visit one of their colonies, should I be worried about contracting this infection there?"

Pakho stared at her briefly, then grabbed the arm of a device extending from the examination table and pointed it toward her. "Don't move," he ordered.

Glenn stepped back immediately.

"It's a level-six bio-scanner. It will not hurt you."

Glenn moved back into the scanner's range. A pop and a click completed the evaluation and Pakho paused for a moment to study the results. Finally he said, "Neither you nor anyone else sharing your quantum signature is at risk, Commander."

"I beg your pardon?" Quantum scans were familiar to her, but she was amazed to see them integrated into this room's standard functions.

"I can't tell you more about the illness, Commander." She lifted her padd again but Pakho raised a hand to stop her. "It's not a question of willingness. I simply don't have the resources here to analyze it properly. Doesn't matter. It's fatal. The man your people encountered died a few minutes after he arrived here and was immediately incinerated. It's our standard protocol in these cases."

"How many do you see?"

"Maybe a hundred each year. It only affects the Zahl deserters with variable quantum signatures."

"You're telling me that there are Zahl present here who originated in different quantum realities?" Glenn demanded.

"I'm not telling you anything," Pakho reminded her.

"Can you give me copies of your evaluations? I don't need to know the identity of the patients, just their physical condition upon admission. I might be able to analyze them more thoroughly and should a treatment regimen present itself, I'd be willing to share it with you."

Pakho stared at her, his tongue playing over his lips. He then took her padd and made a few notations of his own. Glenn blanched when he handed it back to her. He had just requested ten times the supplies she had already offered.

It was worth it. Glenn nodded her consent.

"Don't bother with the cure, if you find it," Pakho added as he started to retrieve the files she had requested.

"You wouldn't help them, even if you could?" Glenn asked, surprised.

"The Rilnar wouldn't like it."

"I thought Lillestan was neutral territory."

"It is. And we'd like to keep it that way." A small chip emerged from the data panel and Pakho handed it to Glenn.

"Thank you," she said.

"No, thank you, Commander. It's been a pleasure doing business with you."

By the time Glenn and Velth had returned to the *Galen*, Seven and the Doctor had arrived. Glenn turned the records Pakho had given her over to the Doctor and asked him to begin evaluating them immediately. She ordered the helm to advise the station that they were departing and to set course for the fleet's rendezvous point.

Glenn then retreated to her quarters and took a very long sonic shower. She'd seen worse in her travels than Doctor Pakho's moral and ethical depravity. The intelligence she had gained might prove critical to the fleet's efforts on Sormana. But the means she had used to acquire it left her feeling filthy, long after her flesh had been scoured clean.

14

SORMANA

Tuvok awoke several hours before the first shift's duty chimes sounded. He spent that time in meditation, clearing his mind of the unwanted and dangerous emotional responses that had stirred during the previous evening's conversation with the *denzit*.

Once he was assured of his own equilibrium, he attempted to leave the room that had been allocated for his personal use while a guest of the *denzit*. Its furnishings suggested that normally four people would share these quarters, but he was its sole occupant. The moment Tuvok opened the door, he found a young Rilnar officer facing him.

"Good morning, Commander Tuvok," she greeted him. "I am *Linzatar* Kresch. I have been ordered to direct you to the mess and to advise you that the *denzit* will be unable to speak with you for several hours. As soon as she returns, you will be notified."

"Returns? From where?" Tuvok asked.

"Titha's power lines were attacked a few hours after you retired for the evening. Given their proximity to our base, the *denzit* chose to personally lead a team to secure them."

"Does the *denzit* usually undertake missions of this nature?" Tuvok asked.

"Yes, sir," Kresch assured him with pride. "She won't order anyone to do something she's not willing to do herself. It isn't always practical, but when it is, she prefers to lead the charge."

Tuvok nodded, wondering if this was actually true. He sensed no intentional deception on Kresch's part. The young woman seemed truly proud of the commander of the Rilnar forces. It was possible, however, that others saw the arrival of Starfleet as a test of the *denzit*'s loyalty. As long as she had no choice but to remain on Sormana, she would likely do so. Given the option, many might question her choice to remain. Some might even hope for her departure to secure their own advancement.

While Kathryn Janeway did not balk at direct engagement when necessary, she was also not reckless in her command decisions. She must have chosen to lead this mission for a reason, and that reason might have more to do with Tuvok's presence on the planet than any other tactical consideration.

"I would like to monitor the *denzit*'s progress from the Center. Would that be acceptable?"

"I suppose so," Kresch replied.

A few minutes later, Tuvok found himself again in the heart of the Rilnar's operations on Sormana. Kresch was kind enough to direct him to the screens that displayed the movements of the *denzit's* team through the tunnels beneath Titha. The first thing to strike Tuvok was that the Rilnar detachment was outnumbered three to one. He also noted that one of the officers operating a data panel seemed to be having trouble raising the *denzit's* team.

"Center to alpha squad, do you read?" she said urgently.

Even Tuvok could hear the sharp burst of static that was the only reply.

A Rilnar man of middle age approached the console. "Z-three has regrouped. Advise alpha squad to dispatch six to engage in southwest twelve. Three should meet those pursuing in southwest nine."

"I cannot raise alpha squad, sir," the woman advised.

"Comm failure?"

"The signal is being jammed."

"Is the *denzit* aware of the current tactical situation?" Tuvok asked.

"Two additional Zahl squads have entered the caverns since her team arrived," the woman replied.

"Will you dispatch another squad to aid the *denzit's*?" Tuvok asked.

"I'm sorry, who are you?" the officer asked dismissively.

"I am Command Tuvok, of the Federation *Starship Titan*, and an old friend of the *denzit's*."

"Since you're her *old* friend, I'm surprised you would ask such a ridiculous question. She is more than capable of routing these Zahl *finlits*. She would not approve of any decision to risk further resources."

"And who are you?" Tuvok asked.

"*Tilzitar* Limlesh," he replied.

Nodding, Tuvok turned to Kresch. "Would it be possible for you to take me to her current position?"

Kresch paused, clearly taken aback by the suggestion. "I'm not sure—that is, the *denzit* did not specify . . ."

"Is it possible?" Tuvok demanded.

"Yes, but you'd be placing yourself in great danger."

"That is a state with which I am familiar. I am a highly trained and experienced tactical officer. I can assure you that my presence will not compromise the *denzit*'s mission, nor will it place any of your team at risk. Unless you are afraid . . ." he trailed off, allowing Kresch's pride to finish that sentence for him.

Kresch looked to Limlesh, who shrugged. "If he wants to risk the *denzit*'s displeasure, it's his choice. I will not be permitted to provide you with a sidearm or personal armor."

"Neither will be necessary."

"This way, Commander," Kresch said.

Less than ten minutes later, Tuvok materialized beside the *linzatar* in a narrow, dimly lit cavern. The sounds of shelling were deafening as they echoed throughout what appeared to be a system of underground tunnels. With each blast, fragments of rock and curtains of dust fell from the ceiling. It was almost as difficult to breathe as it was to see.

Undaunted, Tuvok turned to his companion. "Where is the *denzit*?" he asked.

In response, she removed a small handheld device similar to a tricorder but with a larger screen, and activated it. A single cluster of glowing golden lights burst into view, surrounded by three distinct small teams identified by red motes. Tuvok immediately absorbed the tactical situation, which was not exactly promising for the *denzit*'s team.

An ear-splitting roar sounded. Tuvok and Kresch were immediately covered by a fresh coating of dust. As she brushed her screen clean, Tuvok noted that one of the three hostile teams had just been eliminated.

"Did Rilnar forces destabilize that tunnel, or was it a result of Zahl fire?" Tuvok asked.

Kresch shrugged. "Sounded like ours. Most of these tunnels have been pre-wired to collapse."

"Can the *denzit*'s team be transported to safety directly from their current position?"

Kresch shook her head, pointing to a junction of tunnels a hundred meters distant from the *denzit*'s team. "This was their point of ingress. They'll have to return here in order to evacuate."

One of the two remaining Zahl teams was moving steadily toward the *denzit*'s position, blocking the only path to the evacuation point. Not that the *denzit*'s team seemed mindful of this obstacle. They pressed forward toward the second remaining group, and the sounds of weapons fire could clearly be heard through the din of another round of surface shelling.

Should the *denzit*'s team succeed in neutralizing the threat posed by those they were pursuing, they would still have to fight their way back to their only exit.

"This way," Tuvok said, leading Kresch forward. As soon as she realized where he was headed, she placed a hand on his shoulder to stop him.

"As long as we stay here, we can return to the Center without engaging the Zahl. Beyond this point, our signal will be jammed."

"Assuming we can safely access the evacuation point, we can be transported out along with the *denzit*'s team."

"Yes, but the Zahl might anticipate the arrival of reinforcements. See how they are moving into these three adjacent tunnels? They're leaving part of their squad behind to surround the evacuation point."

"They intend to ambush the *denzit*."

Kresch nodded.

"And you are content to allow them to do so?"

Their eyes met and eventually, the *linzatar* shook her head.

"Follow me," Tuvok said.

When Commander Tuvok had advised *Linzatar* Kresch that he was among the Federation's best tacticians, she had assumed he spoke the truth. Until she had seen him disable the first team of Zahl infiltrators, she had no idea what that really meant.

The man moved with the grace of a *jhanqrekar*, an extremely stealthy predatory beast native to her homeworld of Rilnadaar VI. Kresch did her best to match the rough scuffles of her boots to his silent treads. The constant shelling in the caverns meant that everyone's ears were ringing by now, but a stray footfall at an inopportune moment could mean death.

She wondered at his temerity, given that he possessed no means of defending himself. Wonder gave way to admiration when she watched him creep silently toward the single Zahl stationed in the nearest tunnel and place a hand on his shoulder. When the man crumpled to the ground unconscious, Kresch wanted to cheer. She was also determined to take the first possible opportunity to beg the commander to tell her how he did that. Tuvok then retrieved the man's weapon, studied it briefly, dismantled its power core, and tossed the other remaining pieces into the darkness beyond the Zahl's position before backtracking.

When he returned to her side and pointed on her display to the tunnel they would target next, Kresch whispered, "You could have taken his weapon for yourself."

"I do not wish to see the *denzit* harmed, *Linzatar* Kresch, but I will not kill for her or her cause," Tuvok retorted.

The second Zahl they encountered met the same unfortunate fate as the first. The third and final member of the ambush party had clearly been alerted, likely by the comm silence of his fellow Zahl, and turned on Tuvok, opening fire when the commander was only a few meters from his target. What followed was a brisk lesson in hand-to-hand combat. Tuvok hit the ground well before the Zahl's phase-pulse rifle had discharged. He then sprang upon his would-be killer and with a few quick jabs, completely disabled him. Another Zahl was left unconscious, though in slightly worse shape than his comrades.

Tuvok then led Kresch toward the evacuation point. According to her display, the *denzit*'s team had taken out the squad they had pursued. They had separated into three small groups and were returning along separate paths, sweeping the tunnels for any explosive devices the Zahl might have planted when they infiltrated the area. Two of those groups arrived at the evacuation point before the *denzit's* team could be seen approaching.

The *denzit* brought up the rear of her group as they made their way forward. Her three *palzitars* were moving double-time. She kept pace, discreetly checking her own surveillance scanner as she ran. She pulled up twenty meters from the evacuation point. Gesturing for the others to continue, she ducked down an adjacent tunnel alone.

Kresch turned to Tuvok, who did not appear in the least dismayed by this development. With a barely perceptible nod, Tuvok brushed past the arriving *palzitars* and followed the path the *denzit* had taken.

Throughout the engagement, Tuvok had told himself he was not violating his oath as a Starfleet officer. Strict adherence to regulations demanded that while observing any alien encounter, he was not permitted to join the fight except in self-defense. It had also occurred to him that should the *denzit* perish during this battle, Admiral Janeway's present dilemma would be immediately resolved. No further action on Sormana would be warranted or permitted.

But Admiral Janeway had taken the position that no matter what *Denzit* Janeway called herself, and in spite of any contrary oaths she had taken, she was a Starfleet officer. As such, Tuvok was duty-bound to defend her. Taking the initiative and disabling enemy combatants who intended to ambush her certainly approached but did not technically cross the line. He had spent twenty-five years analyzing tactical situations and devising combat strategies to neutralize threats. Disabling hostiles was always preferable to killing them. Had he waited to see how the situation unfolded, and had it done so as he expected, such measured tactics might have been impossible.

Without Kresch's scanner to guide him, Tuvok moved on instinct. Immediately entering the tunnel the *denzit* had taken, an irritating hum swept over his body. Tuvok stopped in his tracks and studied the walls around him. An energy field had been activated, likely by the *denzit*'s passage through the tunnel. Tuvok did not know what its purpose was but her apparent ignorance of it suggested a Zahl origin and devastating intent. Allowing the humming sensation to guide him, Tuvok gently ran his hands over the walls and ground. Soon enough, he detected the source. An explosive device had been hastily buried a few meters from where he stood. The *denzit* had not tripped it, but it had activated based on her proximity and it was clearly ready to detonate should she retrace her steps.

"Tuvok?"

He rose from his crouched position. Janeway stood at the far end of the tunnel, fifteen meters from his position and ten from the explosive. The surprised smile on her face and flush of her cheeks suggested she was insensate of the danger facing both of them.

For a split second, Tuvok considered his next action. This woman was a temporal anomaly. Her absence would restore integrity to this timeline. She was responsible for the choices that had led to this moment. Had he not been present, she would likely have died in the line of what she would have considered to be her duty.

The moment their eyes met, Tuvok understood that such considerations were irrelevant. Kathryn Janeway had been his friend for more than two decades. There was no *version* of this woman who could perish without removing something essential from his existence. He had lost too much already.

"Stop," Tuvok commanded, and watched her smile falter.

A sharp tone pierced his ears as the hum that had first alerted him to the presence of the explosive intensified. Clearly, it was sensitive to multiple types of pressure, including, perhaps, sound waves. It suddenly struck Tuvok that for the last several minutes the surface shelling had been silenced. He wondered if this was a random coincidence or if someone was tracking and targeting the *denzit*.

There was only one course of action open to him. With one hand he grabbed the largest rock he could find; with the other, he gestured for her to retreat.

She did not question his order. As Tuvok stepped back and tossed the rock onto the proximity explosive, he saw her sprinting in the opposite direction.

As the rock flew from his hand, Tuvok mirrored her actions, sprinting full-out toward the evacuation point. As the ensuing concussive blast erupted and the tunnel collapsed upon him, he wondered if either of them was meant to survive.

The first time Tuvok regained consciousness his immediate thought was to wonder why the room around him was completely dark. A high-pitched alarm rang in his ears. Its piercing quality grated and he wondered why no one had though to silence it. A sluggish wave washed over him before he could consider the matter further. Darkness descended again.

The second time he awoke, two incongruous sounds met his ears. The first was a light, regular snoring. The second was the sweet trilling of a songbird. The room was no longer absolutely dark. Brightness assaulted his eyes through bandages that had been secured around them. A quick physical inventory told him that he had apparently suffered no serious physical damage. He could gingerly move his arms and legs, fingers and toes, though the effort left him weary and several muscles in his low back protested painfully.

"Kathryn?" Tuvok said through parched lips. His throat was dry and the word sounded more like multiple croaks than an attempt at communication.

Almost instantly, a soft, warm hand gripped his. "There you are," a familiar voice said in clear relief. For an instant he thought he must have been returned to *Voyager*'s sickbay. Surely this was Admiral Janeway seated at his bedside.

Then he remembered the song of the bird.

"Where?" he attempted.

"Shh," she hushed him. Seconds later he felt something

touch his lips. He opened them to allow cool water to begin to slake his desperate thirst.

Her voice sounded again, calm and clinical. "You were evacuated to Felstar. This is the only Rilnar settlement on Sormana that the war has never touched. It's located in an isolated mountain range more than five thousand kilometers from my current command center. It was built seven hundred years ago and to this day, the Zahl don't even know it exists. It's also the home of our finest doctors, including my personal physician. After you saved my life four days ago, I couldn't possibly offer you less than our best."

Tuvok reached for the bandages covering his eyes.

"Don't," she reprimanded him. "Doctor Mastin will be along in a few hours to remove them. You suffered a concussion and the pressure on your optic nerve was worrisome. There was considerable trauma to your spine, which took the brunt of the impact of the ceiling of that tunnel. You'll be sore for a few more days, but we repaired the fractures."

"Thank you."

The *denzit* laughed dismissively. "I think I owe you much more than you owe me at this point."

"Were you injured?"

"A minor concussion and some soft tissue damage. Your warning saved my life. I'd actually forgotten what that felt like, even though it was hardly the first time, was it?"

Tuvok sighed, content.

"I thought about sending word to *Voyager* but once Doctor Mastin advised me that we could easily treat your most critical injuries here, I agreed to the procedures on your behalf. It's probably silly, but I simply couldn't bear to send you back to Admiral Janeway while you were at death's door."

This amused Tuvok. No sign of that response touched his face.

A long silence followed. Tuvok wondered if she might have left the room. When she spoke again, her voice was thick with emotion.

"She was right to send you here. I half expected her to come herself. I'm still not sure why she hasn't. It's not really like us."

"You know as little of her life as she does of yours," Tuvok reminded her.

"Someone with some sense tied her to a chair, didn't they?"

"In the course of her travels, she has interacted with more than one alternate version of herself. It is a difficult situation and one that must be approached delicately."

"I'm not sorry to have been spared that."

Tuvok said nothing, waiting for her to continue.

"I understand why she thinks it is her duty to bring me back. I might do the same in her place. But I cannot leave now."

"Unless I am able to present her with a rational argument to the contrary, I am certain that the next visitor you receive will be the admiral."

"I don't have to authorize her transport."

"Do you honestly believe that would stop her?"

"No." After a long pause, she continued, "She doesn't deserve the truth. She has no right to it. It's mine, not hers. But you do."

Her hand gripped his again, this time much colder.

"I know I can't make you swear not to reveal anything to her. But I have to believe that once you understand, you won't."

"Please do not ask me for assurances you know I am unable to give."

Her thumb brushed the back of his hand before she released it. As she continued to speak, it became increasingly difficult for her to form the necessary words through the emotional response they evoked.

"When Captain Chakotay came here and asked me about stardate 57445 I thought he must know. I thought the Zahl must have gotten to him too. Nothing else made sense. But he was satisfied when I told him that I had died. Why was that?"

"I cannot explain in the detail you require. Admiral Janeway is the best person to answer that question," Tuvok replied. "You know that she, too, apparently died on that day. According to the admiral, who was taken at the moment of her death to the

Q Continuum, every single version of Kathryn Janeway who has ever existed in any quantum reality died at the same fixed point in time. She witnessed those deaths in a moment of expanded consciousness granted to her by a Q. Knowing that you had suffered the same fate was the conclusive evidence Chakotay needed to confirm your identity."

"Every single version of us . . . but why?"

"It is a long story."

"Don't weary yourself telling it. Honestly, nothing the universe does surprises me anymore."

"What is the significance of that stardate apart from your death and resuscitation?"

"Did Chakotay tell you about Dayne?"

"The Rilnar officer who assisted you when you were first rescued from the Zahl and with whom you shared an intimate relationship?"

"We did more than that. We were married in a private ceremony three years ago."

The obvious pain in her voice made Tuvok refrain from congratulating her.

"Shortly thereafter I learned I was pregnant. I went into labor at the Center in the middle of an unusually fierce attack, even by Zahl standards. Ours was the first advanced shield grid to come online and they were determined to bring it down, understanding what would happen if we were able to secure all of our settlements with similar defensive systems. They failed, but it was a very long day.

"My death was not the result of injuries sustained in battle. I'd been isolated in the most secure sector of the Center since my contractions began at daybreak. I died in childbirth. I bled out. Mastin still can't tell me who the doctor was that brought me back or how he did it. But whatever he did, it obviously worked.

"At the moment of my death, Dayne kept a promise he'd made to me months earlier. Our only concern, beyond liberating Sormana, was securing the safety of our daughter. He took her from the Center, believing I was dead. They were both captured by the Zahl attempting to leave the surface. The Zahl have never acknowledged this. They insist that they don't have them. On bad days I wonder if they're telling the truth and we've just never managed to find their bodies. But several eyewitnesses have sworn to seeing Dayne and our child surrounded and transported away.

"I honestly believe that if she was dead, I'd feel it. And I never have. She's out there, somewhere. Dayne is with her. Even if the Zahl don't know what he was to me or who the child is, they do not negotiate the release of prisoners. The only way for me to get them back is to win this war."

Tuvok had believed until this moment that whatever the *denzit*'s true reasons for staying were, he would be obligated to convince her to abandon them.

That was no longer the case. It wasn't the raw anguish of her voice that moved him. It was their shared tragedy. They had both lost a child. But in her case there was still a chance, slim though it might be, to correct this unacceptable reality.

"I see," he finally replied.

"But . . ."

"You need not fear. For me to reveal what you have told me might further endanger the life of your daughter."

"*That* I will never do."

15

VESTA

"Let's start at the beginning," Admiral Janeway told those assembled in. the *Vesta*'s main briefing room. Captains Chakotay and Farkas, Commanders O'Donnell and Glenn, were joined by Counselor Cambridge, Seven, the Doctor, and Tuvok. The commander had returned from Sormana a few hours earlier and reported having been seriously injured while on the planet. Doctor Sharak had performed a thorough physical evaluation and advised Janeway that while evidence of trauma to Tuvok's spine and central nervous system was present, the Rilnar's medical treatment had been more than adequate. Sharak had authorized Tuvok to continue on duty without reservation.

"Unless anyone here can go back before the Rilnar and Zahl tribes on Sormana first started throwing rocks at one another, I'd say that's the beginning," Counselor Cambridge offered.

"Tribes?" Admiral Janeway asked. "They're the same species?"

"Yes," Cambridge replied.

"So this has always been a civil war?"

"There's nothing civil about it," O'Donnell said.

"Go on, Counselor," Janeway ordered.

Cambridge, O'Donnell, and Fife recounted in detail the history lessons they had learned. Seven and the Doctor were quick to point out that the Zahl's version of this story was essentially the same. Both away teams also agreed that the ideological division between the vast majority of the Rilnar and Zahl populations living on the colonies and the planet's natives had never been starker.

"That just doesn't make any sense," Captain Farkas said. "These are two advanced, spacefaring civilizations. They have the resources necessary to transport every single person on that planet to a cargo ship, relocate them to existing safe territories, and end this thing in a matter of weeks. Instead, they're content to wait until it burns itself out?"

"I'm not sure removing the natives from the planet would actually solve anything," Cambridge said. "Give them access to the advanced technology of the colonies and interstellar fleets, and the hatred might simply spread and grow into a sector-wide conflict. This way, the colonists and their leaders can look sadly down on their misguided cousins on Sormana, claim to respect their right to self-determination, and remain smug and complacent while risking very little."

"That minefield has become a barrier between Sormana and the rest of the sector. As long as the fighting doesn't spread, it's really not a problem for the colonial leadership, just an embarrassment," Chakotay observed.

"I understand that oftentimes political will can go absent without leave," Farkas agreed bitterly. "But thousands of years later, the residents of Sormana have learned nothing? Each side honestly believes they can still win?"

"I can't speak for the Zahl," Cambridge said, "but there are a fair number of Rilnar who cling to a desperate hope that peace might still prevail."

"Based on what?" Janeway asked.

"A myth, or an unverifiable historical incident that occurred a few hundred years back," Cambridge replied. He proceeded to present a brief summary of the legend of the two brothers and how close they had come to ending the conflict once and for all.

"If the Prime Directive didn't prohibit it, and there was any chance they were still alive two hundred years later, I'd suggest we try and track those silver-tongued devils down," Chakotay said.

"I don't think it was just the brothers," Cambridge noted. "A critical component, at least as I read this legend, was *the moment* they arrived. Only after something like Batibeh were both sides willing to seriously consider trying to find another way."

"Give them enough time on Sormana and there will be another Batibeh," Farkas said sadly. "There always is."

"So there is little to no chance that the colonial leadership is going to expend any effort to end the conflict, unless the natives come to their senses," Janeway summarized.

"In a nutshell," Cambridge agreed.

Turning to Seven, Janeway asked, "Were you able to locate any data supporting the *denzit*'s claim that the Zahl used a chroniton torpedo to attack *Voyager* and capture her, or that the Zahl would have had any reason to do so?"

"No," Seven replied. "The sources I spoke to, while not terribly well-informed, indicate that there is little civilian research under way in the area. If the Zahl have temporal technology at their disposal, it is a military asset and well-hidden from the general public."

"Then it might not exist?" Janeway asked.

"It does," Glenn interjected. When all eyes turned toward her, she related Velth and Barclay's discovery of the dying Zahl at Lillestan.

When she had finished, the Doctor picked up the story. "I have analyzed the patient records Commander Glenn was able to obtain, and what they reveal is very disturbing. A number of Zahl soldiers, identified at Lillestan as 'deserters,' have died over the last few years from a degenerative condition caused by quantum misalignment."

"Quantum misalignment?" Janeway repeated. "The Zahl are bringing reinforcements to this timeline from other quantum realities to fight their war?"

"It appears so," the Doctor replied.

"How?" Janeway demanded.

"I don't know. What is clear from the records that I was able to review is that the longer they remain in this timeline, the worse their condition becomes. I can't tell if returning them to their timelines would reverse the degenerative damage. Apparently finding out isn't high on the Zahl's list of priorities either."

"Wait a minute," Janeway said. "We've encountered individuals from alternate timelines. We've never seen any who suffered from a similar condition."

"It is possible that the illness is caused not merely by crossing over into this timeline, but by some subtle difference in our quantum reality to which their bodies cannot acclimate," Glenn suggested.

"It is also possible that the method used to bring them here is the real culprit," Seven suggested. "They could have been injured in transit without showing immediate symptoms."

"The *denzit* did say that the Zahl seem to have an endless supply of reinforcements and even she doesn't know where they're coming from or how they're getting to Sormana," Chakotay added.

"There is a Zahl academic," Seven began but paused when the Doctor coughed loudly at her use of the term.

"Very well, Doctor," Seven conceded, "a Zahl *historical enthusiast*, who told us that a Zahl male from Sormana named Rahalla claimed to have discovered chroniton particles on the surface several hundred years ago. He studied them for much of his life and eventually left the planet to share that knowledge with other scientists."

"I wonder if Rahalla's chroniton particles could be related to the pools the brothers supposedly used to show Sormana's leaders the horrors their future held," Cambridge said.

"When two sources from opposing camps reference similar legends they become harder to dismiss, don't they?" O'Donnell asked.

"Those sources are a myth and a barely credible historian," Janeway reminded him.

"But the deaths of those Zahl deserters is fact," Chakotay said.

"If there is temporal technology on that planet and it is being used to corrupt the timeline . . ." Janeway began.

"We call the DTI?" Farkas asked.

Janeway smiled wanly. "I'm afraid this is a little outside their jurisdiction."

"*Ours* too," Chakotay noted.

"One of the Zahl sources we spoke to also mentioned that it is widely rumored that the Krenim possess some sort of temporal technology."

"*That* I do believe," Janeway said.

"Did you encounter the Krenim when you went to retrieve the source of the Federation signal?" Chakotay asked.

"We did," Farkas replied. "They didn't seem troubled by our presence in their territory, although they were quick to point us to the nearest exit."

"The Krenim once possessed incredibly advanced temporal

technology," Janeway said. "The message buoy we retrieved indicates that the Year of Hell did happen and our present condition suggests that its horrific effects were ultimately reversed by *Voyager*."

Tense silence gripped the room as everyone absorbed this.

"Does the intelligence you gathered suggest that the Krenim still utilize that technology?" Chakotay asked. "If *Voyager* prevailed over them, was the timeline sufficiently altered to prevent them from following the same path again?"

"There is no way to know based solely on what I heard," Janeway replied. "What is interesting to me is that none of the logs we discovered, which were admittedly incomplete, referenced the Zahl or the Rilnar *at all*. Even if we hypothesize that the Zahl did find one of our buoys—a long shot, as they were designed to be activated only in the presence of a Federation signal with our quantum signature and encrypted using my personal access codes—I haven't discovered anything yet that would have caused the Zahl to target *Voyager*."

"And if, as you suspect, the end result of *Voyager*'s encounter with the Krenim was a complete reset of the timeline, even the Krenim might not be aware of it," Seven said.

"I don't know," Janeway mused. "It's possible the Krenim aren't connected to this. Their Imperium is large and well defended and hasn't so much as troubled their neighbors for a cup of sugar in a century."

"There are reports that Rahalla invited the Krenim of his day, as well as the Rilnar to study his discoveries," Seven noted.

"He hoped to use the mysteries and majesty of science to bring those occupying this area closer together?" Cambridge asked sarcastically.

"Which Krenim?" Janeway asked. "Do you have any names?"

"A few," Seven replied. "The fragments we have reference a symposium on one of Zahlna's starbases that was attended by a Krenim delegation led by a scientist named Annorax."

Janeway dropped her head into her hands and began massaging her temples. "Annorax built the weapon ship that *Voyager* encountered."

"How can space be so big and the universe so small?" O'Donnell asked rhetorically.

Janeway turned to Tuvok for the first time since the briefing had begun. "Did the *denzit* mention the Krenim?"

"She did not," Tuvok replied.

"Were you able to discover a good reason for her refusal to abandon the Rilnar and return with us?" Chakotay asked.

"Yes, Captain. Her personal concerns far outweigh any ideological commitment to the Rilnar."

"What personal concerns?" Janeway demanded.

"The *denzit* believes that the Zahl captured the Rilnar officer who first assisted her when she was rescued. They did more than share an intimate relationship prior to his loss. They were married. She is determined to save Dayne and believes the only way to do that is to defeat the Zahl."

The admiral sat back, exhaling slowly as she absorbed this information.

"Does she know where he is being held?" Chakotay asked.

Tuvok shook his head. "The Zahl have never acknowledged his capture or his existence as their prisoner. She does not find this response convincing enough to abandon the search."

"We can't take on the Zahl on her behalf, nor can we assist her in defeating them," Farkas noted.

"We also can't force her to return, can we?" O'Donnell asked.

"If we could get close enough to Sormana to capture her, I don't think Starfleet would mind," Chakotay suggested.

"*She* would mind," Tuvok said. "Although currently operating in defiance of her Starfleet oath, it is neither illegal nor immoral for a Federation citizen to renounce that citizenship and become a naturalized citizen elsewhere. She chose this course when she had good cause to believe that rescue by Starfleet would never come. She will not change her mind now. Any effort to force her to do so will not succeed."

"You believe we should abandon her to her fate?" Janeway asked.

"I believe she has the right to determine her own destiny.

Extreme circumstances have dictated her choices but she is not behaving unreasonably or illogically. Her priorities are no longer ours but that does not make them less worthy of respect."

Admiral Janeway knew that Tuvok could read the disappointment on her face. She also knew that he no longer had the ability to assist her in this matter. The *denzit* had somehow gained his sympathy. Shared loss might have brought them closer. She silently cursed herself for not weighing Tuvok's current emotional state more heavily before allowing him to meet with the *denzit*.

"How were you injured on Sormana?" Janeway asked.

"I was observing the *denzit* during an engagement with the Zahl. I interceded when I believed her life to be endangered and I took the brunt of an explosion meant for her."

"You saved her life?" Chakotay asked.

"I could not have done otherwise, Captain. Could you?" he asked pointedly.

Janeway spared Chakotay the need to answer that loaded question. "The Prime Directive limits our options here even as our duty to a fellow Starfleet officer demands action. We cannot interfere directly in this conflict. However, what we have learned—about our history with the Krenim and the evidence of ongoing temporal corruption—definitely impacts our interests, as well as those of every inhabitant of this quadrant."

"Are we going after the Krenim?" Farkas asked.

"I have a few questions only they can answer," Janeway replied. "Have Bryce and Icheb completed their work installing temporal shields aboard the *Vesta*?"

"They need another day at least," Farkas replied.

"I want their final specifications forwarded to every fleet vessel and integrated into our defensive systems before we proceed," Janeway ordered. "In the meantime, I'm going to speak to the *denzit*."

"Admiral," Tuvok began.

She immediately raised a hand to silence him. "I understand the delicacy required by this situation. But I'm also not going to hide from it. Neither you nor Captain Chakotay was able to convince her to return to us. I would be negligent in *my* duty if I didn't at least make the attempt."

"Request permission to accompany you to Sormana?" Tuvok asked.

"Request denied," Janeway replied. "We will reconvene when I return from Sormana."

VOYAGER

"You asked to see me, Doctor Sharak?" Lieutenant Conlon asked, after tapping on the doorframe of his office in sickbay.

Sharak rose immediately, his face uncharacteristically stern. "I asked to see you three days ago, Lieutenant."

"We've had our hands full in engineering, Doctor. I'm sorry for the delay," Colon replied.

Sharak nodded and gestured for her to precede him into the main sickbay and to take a seat on one of the biobeds. "Our last round of tests suggested some ongoing irregularities with your immune system. I have taken it upon myself to conduct a complete analysis of all of your medical records to search for any cause beyond your experience with Xolani. I am pleased to report that no prior exposure to alien contagions appears to be related. I need to conduct a new round of scans and blood work in order to determine your current levels and to see if your immune system is returning to normal on its own."

"I feel fine," Conlon said.

"No unusual weariness?"

"No."

"Headaches?"

"No."

"How are you sleeping?"

"Well enough, when I can."

"That's a good sign," Sharak noted as he continued to run his medical tricorder over her. "I'm going to take some blood now, and then I'd like to do a complete genetic scan."

"Why?" Conlon asked, tensing.

"It's possible that you have been exposed to something we've never found, something that could have remained dormant that was activated as a result of your immune system's attempts to rid you of Xolani's essence. If there is genetic damage present, we need to know about it and begin taking steps to correct it."

"What kind of genetic damage?" Conlon asked.

"There are a handful of genetic abnormalities that affect DNA's ability to replicate properly. These damage repair syndromes are degenerative and usually lead to death through secondary causes before they prove fatal on their own. Most are evident at birth. Starfleet has encountered a few alien contagions that act on human DNA in a similar fashion. The treatment protocols are unique to each infectious agent. There are some odd hormone levels that have been present since Xolani's attack that might suggest exposure to such an agent, but I cannot confirm that without further tests."

"Engineering to Lieutenant Conlon," Lieutenant Neol's voice sounded over the comm system.

Tapping her combadge quickly, Conlon replied, "Go ahead, Neol."

"We've just received the specs on the new temporal shielding the admiral ordered installed. We need you down here right away."

"Understood," Conlon said, pushing off the biobed. "I'll be right there."

"No, you won't," Sharak said as soon as she had closed the channel.

"Doctor, I appreciate your concerns, but I'm needed in engineering right now. I'll come back as soon as I can for you to complete your tests. I really do feel fine. I want you to finish your work, especially if my levels are still off. But this is a direct order from the fleet commander. I can't tell her we don't have the new shield system integrated because I was prioritizing your medical curiosity over my duty to this ship."

Sharak was clearly frustrated. "You will return to sickbay at the end of your current duty shift, or I will speak to Commander Torres about your negligence in tending to your medical issues."

"It won't come to that, Doctor Sharak. I promise," Conlon assured him.

DEMETER

Although it felt like a lifetime ago—a thrilling and complicated lifetime—Ensign Icheb had not forgotten his failure with Commander O'Donnell during the weeks that had passed since their last conversation. His work with Lieutenant Bryce had gone a long way toward repairing his flagging self-esteem. Phinn respected his experience and never seemed to care that he was allowing a green ensign to take the lead in the fleet's search for the message buoy or in developing the temporal shields they now required. It might have been that despite the difference in their ranks, Bryce was only a few years older than Icheb. Their rapport was instantaneous and effortless. It had been a long time since Icheb had met anyone who he honestly felt might one day become as close to him as *Voyager*'s original crew.

Commander Torres had ordered him to drop the matter, but this only made it worse. He had failed her *and* failed Commander O'Donnell. He had to know why.

As soon as the specs for the new shields had been completed and disseminated throughout the fleet, Icheb had again turned his attention to *Demeter*'s evaluation and after careful consideration, eliminated all but three critical system deficiencies he wished to bring to the attention of Commander Elkins. He felt this effort went beyond personal compromise. Had this been a test at the Academy, he would have expected to fail in presenting such a woefully incomplete analysis. But Commander O'Donnell was now the immovable object that stood between Icheb and his peace of mind. If O'Donnell could see Icheb's genuine desire to be of use rather than taking an adversarial position, perhaps they could both move past this and Icheb could return his attention to more interesting and exciting duties.

Commander O'Donnell didn't look up when Icheb entered his private lab. Icheb stood just inside the door for a full five minutes before O'Donnell even seemed to take notice of him.

"Ensign?" O'Donnell asked in surprise.

"Good afternoon, Commander," Icheb said. "Pursuant to our last conversation, I have again revised my evaluation of Lieutenant Elkins and with your permission, would like to present this report to him."

Silently O'Donnell extended a hand to accept the padd Icheb held. He had barely glanced at it when he passed it back to the ensign.

"Nope."

"Nope?"

"Nope."

"Commander, I don't understand," Icheb said, flabbergasted at this outright rejection of the olive branch he had so generously offered.

"I know," O'Donnell agreed.

"I . . . but . . ."

"Don't come back until you do," O'Donnell said, dismissing him.

Icheb did not allow the deep sigh of disappointment to escape his lips until he had left O'Donnell's presence and was on his way back to *Demeter*'s transporter room. He only hoped that word of this latest failure would not reach Commander Torres's ears.

SORMANA

When the enhanced transporter released Admiral Janeway from its confinement beam, she wondered at the efficiency of this extraordinary technology. It used a series of subspace pattern enhancers to relay officers from ships that would normally be outside transporter range to Sormana's surface. *It might have a few bugs in it.* The admiral expected to arrive in the Center's transporter room, just as Chakotay and Tuvok had. Instead, she found herself surveying a wasteland.

That this had once been a magnificent city was obvious. Where tall buildings had once stood, twisted metal beams rose from the rubble like sickly, misshapen trees. The surface had been cleansed by years of erosion. Nothing grew here.

Visible in the distance were smaller buildings, all that remained of ancient homes. People had lived here. *Families* had lived here. How long ago, the admiral could not say. Their ghosts surrounded her and seemed to press close to her as she made her way toward a pile of large stone fragments in a relatively clear area where the lone figure of *Denzit* Janeway awaited her arrival.

The sky was filled with low-hanging clouds, casting a gray pallor over the devastation. The air was slightly chilled even without the tension rolling off of the admiral in waves.

The *denzit* stood beside the rubble. On one of the larger stone fragments rested a tall thermos and two metal cups. She seemed more relaxed than the admiral, or perhaps simply resigned. Janeway struggled to match her demeanor to that of the woman whose face she shared but whose life she could barely imagine.

"Welcome to Sormana," the *denzit* greeted her when only a few meters separated them.

"What was this place?" Janeway asked without preamble. She understood that the *denzit* had chosen this location intentionally. She was setting a stage, attempting to provoke an emotional response from the admiral. Janeway couldn't allow that—not with so much at stake—but she knew a stacked deck when she saw one.

"Batibeh," the *denzit* replied. "This was once the most ancient Rilnar settlement on the planet. Like its Zahl counterpart, Hillresh, it was designated as a sanctuary thousands of years ago. The war might rage elsewhere, but here Rilnar were free to learn about their past and build the kind of city that would endure in a better future. For over five thousand years, the Zahl refrained from attacking this small, completely defenseless city just as the Rilnar left Hillresh in peace.

"Eventually, an armed perimeter was established as much to keep the Rilnar in as any new settlers out. But its historical significance was respected until two hundred years ago when, apparently, the Zahl changed their minds. Almost a hundred thousand men, women, and children perished in a sustained bombardment that lasted eight days. Despite this atrocity, Hillresh still stands."

"The Zahl are the problem here?" Janeway asked. "Is that the point of this exercise?"

"The Zahl are monsters, Admiral," the *denzit* said simply. Civilian casualties have always been an unfortunate reality on Sormana. But without civilians willing to continue to occupy the planet, Sormana's ultimate loss would be inevitable. Essential pieces of Rilnar history would be lost forever. The Rilnar wouldn't still be here were it not for the Zahl's utter barbarity."

"A characteristic with which I understand you are well acquainted," the admiral said.

The *denzit* smiled bitterly. "This isn't about me," she said. "What the Zahl did to me when I was captured was no more than we were trained to expect from the Cardassians. It was degrading, merciless, and unbelievably painful. But I had already learned how to defend myself, how to keep enough of myself separate from what they were doing to my body to survive. They made me wish for death, but they never made me forget the extraordinary beauty life can hold."

"What's in the thermos?" Janeway asked.

This time the *denzit*'s smile was briefly genuine. She poured a steaming liquid black as pitch into both cups and offered one to Janeway as she sipped from hers. The admiral accepted it and drank. The burn going down had nothing to do with the liquid's temperature and Janeway had to admit it was invigorating. What it was missing were the mellow tones of really great coffee, the smooth finish that followed the bite. Instead, she felt instantly enervated, not entirely unpleasant, but just this side of uncontrolled.

"What do you think?" the *denzit* asked.

"I think this stuff could probably fuel a warp core. And I think it's time you told me exactly what you're doing here."

The *denzit* seemed disappointed, but not surprised. "I'm ending a war, Admiral."

"You could have fooled me," Janeway said.

"Do you really think I am any less nauseated by the state of affairs here than you are? This conflict has taken lives and treasure well beyond what anyone would consider rational. It has become a way of life for the Rilnar and the Zahl and in the process significantly limited their potential."

"So end it. There are dozens of habitable worlds, many of them not that far from here that could easily absorb the population of Sormana. Lay down your arms. Agree to declare this planet neutral territory, accessible by any who wish to study it, but uninhabitable for a set period of years until both parties can figure out how to share it in peace."

"Did you really come down here to give me a refresher course in basic diplomacy?"

"I wasn't sure you remembered."

"The Rilnar leadership will never agree to those terms."

"Why not?"

"Because the Zahl would never honor them, even if they accepted them in principle."

"If I were speaking to the Zahl right now, would they say the same thing about the Rilnar?"

"Probably."

"Then this is pointless. It seems to me that both parties have amply demonstrated that they are incapable of having nice things. I could bring my fleet through that minefield into Sormana's orbit and fry every millimeter of this planet. I could render it uninhabitable for centuries. Everyone here now is going to die sooner rather than later. Why not cut to the chase, put you all out of your misery, and remove the source of the conflict?"

The *denzit* considered Janeway evenly. Finally she said, "I wouldn't put it past you. Starfleet Command would strip you of your rank but you might consider it worth the sacrifice to make your point."

Had the *denzit* thrust a dagger into Janeway's heart, the injury done by those words could not have been more severe. *I would never.* The admiral was simply testing the limits to which the *denzit* might be willing to go. That she could *believe* this of Janeway suggested that the *denzit* had already given in to the darkest impulses nurtured by sustained conflict.

Without warning, the sound of her own voice recounting a Krenim attack that had rendered all but six decks of *Voyager* uninhabitable during a war neither of them remembered echoed in Janeway's mind. What chilled the admiral was the determination in that voice to make the Krenim pay for what they had done, with no thought to the choices *she* had made that had prolonged the conflict or led to those losses.

Perspective was everything in life, and one of the easiest things to lose, particularly in this region of the Delta Quadrant it seemed.

"You're wrong," Janeway finally said. "That would not only be an illegal and immoral act, it would also solve nothing. Until the people on this planet recognize the futility of the present struggle and the benefits of peace, this is merely a question of geography. But I'm not sure how you think you're going to end this war by doing anything less than annihilating the Zahl. You've already dehumanized them. Isn't genocide the next obvious step?"

"Not from where I'm sitting," the *denzit* replied. "It's taken me a few years, but in that time I've shored up every aspect of Rilnar defensive capabilities. The Zahl are reaching the end of their resources. The public outcry from both the Rilnar and Zahl colonies to end this conflict grows louder each day. All that remains is to discover the last of the Zahl supply lines and sever them. It's somewhere on this planet and when I find it and eliminate it—game over."

"This isn't a game."

The *denzit*'s face hardened.

"For one man?" Janeway asked.

The stone face cracked as the *denzit*'s cheeks flushed.

"You know about Dayne?"

"Of course I do."

"What happened to Mark?"

Janeway sighed and looked briefly away. She was in no hurry to add to the list of the *denzit*'s valid grievances, but she deserved the truth.

"When *Voyager* was officially declared lost, he moved on with his life. He married a lovely woman named Carla. They have a child. Disappointing as it was, I don't blame him." Finally meeting the *denzit*'s eyes again, she added, "And he's so happy now."

"I'm glad to hear that. He deserves it."

"He does."

"Have you allowed yourself to love anyone since then?"

Janeway inhaled and released the breath slowly. "I have."

"Anyone I know?"

"Yes."

"Chakotay?"

"Yes."

"That must be nice for you, commanding the fleet that includes his ship."

"It has its moments."

The *denzit* reached inside her uniform jacket, removed a tattered, worn image of a Rilnar man, and handed it to the Admiral. His skin was fair, and his face held fewer traces of the characteristic epidermal pitting common to the species. A mop of sandy blond hair sat over piercing hazel eyes. It was a kind face, and the eyes seemed to be those of an old soul.

"No one was more surprised than I was when I realized what Dayne had given me. When I learned that I could feel that again. It was . . ."

"I know," the admiral said, handing the picture back to her.

"He wouldn't want me to continue this fight just for him."

"Good."

"But he wouldn't want me to abandon it either, not when I'm so close to winning it."

"Are you aware of the illness plaguing the Zahl deserters right now?"

"I've heard rumors."

"Do you understand its source?"

"No. I've lost six teams trying to infiltrate local medical facilities. They are more heavily guarded than the Zahl armories."

"Then you don't even know what you're looking for."

"Do you?"

Janeway said nothing.

"You do," the *denzit* said, struck by the realization.

Janeway struggled to keep her face neutral. "Come with us. You don't belong here. You'll do more good from outside this conflict than leading a doomed charge. Help us discover the truth, to learn what's *really* at stake here and then you can use the trust you have gained from the Rilnar to bring their leaders to the negotiation table."

"You'll never get the Zahl to join us there."

Janeway couldn't help the disparaging glance that flew unbidden from her eyes.

"Look, I understand that challenges like this get us out of bed in the morning, but I'm telling you, the Zahl are a special case. They may look civilized to the outside observer, but their obstinacy and tactics are more reminiscent of the Borg."

"Don't waste our time on meaningless hyperbole. The Borg is the only species that was *anything like* the Borg. And even they met their match."

"Sixty-three billion lives later."

"I'm past that too."

"How?"

"Come with me and I'll tell you."

The *denzit* shook her head. "It's too easy. Here you are promising me everything my heart could possibly desire. All I have to do is give up my control, hand it over to you, and you'll solve everything."

"That's not what I'm suggesting. I am trying to help you, but you know that in many respects my hands are tied."

"By choice. That's what you haven't learned yet. Every day we make choices and only as long as we can are we truly free."

"This isn't freedom. This is a prison of your own making. The Zahl didn't have to kill you to beat you. They still own you. You're doing their bidding whether you acknowledge it or not."

The *denzit* stepped back. "We're done here."

"Did I hit too close to home?" Janeway asked, closing the distance between them again.

"*Home*. That word. Tuvok said it was your sole obsession for seven years. I saw some of what you suffered along the way. I understand what you felt you'd lost and what you thought you owed *Voyager*'s crew. But home isn't a place. It's something you create. It's something that lives inside you. And once it's yours, you'll never misunderstand the difference again."

Janeway felt her brow furrow. "I don't follow."

"I know. And I doubt you ever will. I know what's within my grasp. I won't walk away from it for you or anyone else. I don't need your help, Admiral."

Janeway paused. "Would you consider giving me yours?"

The *denzit* was intrigued.

"How?"

"You know I can't take a side in this conflict. But there are larger concerns at play. I need to send a team to the surface to confirm some intelligence we've gathered about the Zahl. Thanks to that damned minefield I can't even get a ship close enough to perform the necessary sensor scans. Give us a clear course. Allow *Voyager* to assume orbit to guide the team. Don't do anything to endanger them as long as they're here."

"That's all?"

"That's all."

"You will share with me whatever you learn."

Janeway shook her head. "I can't promise that right now and you know it."

"Then no sensor scans. Your ships don't come anywhere near Sormana. Send down your team. Assign Tuvok to lead it."

"I don't think—" Janeway began.

"I'm not negotiating with you. I'm giving you my terms. You will accept them or this conversation is over. Tuvok will lead a team of three of your finest. I will allow them access to whatever intel I have that might assist them. If they are captured or killed, that's your problem."

Janeway nodded, grudgingly.

"And Admiral, if, in their travels, they learn that my characterization of the Zahl is accurate, please reconsider how much you can share with me about whatever you discover. I have every intention of ending this on my own, but it's likely that countless lives could be saved if we work together."

Janeway smiled wistfully. "The last time I decided to work with another version of me—who had dubious personal motivations—the Borg ended up invading the Alpha Quadrant and killed billions. Tempting as it is, I don't plan on making *that* mistake again."

The *denzit* activated a handheld comm device and signaled for Janeway's transport. While they awaited confirmation she said, "When Chakotay told me you were still alive, I decided that of the two of us, you were undoubtedly living the best possible version of our life. Now, I'm not so sure."

"I am," Janeway said as the Rilnar transport beam took hold of her.

16

VOYAGER

Chakotay hadn't bothered trying to sleep while Kathryn was on Sormana. He'd spent his time on the bridge, an unusual state of affairs during gamma shift. Lieutenant Kim, who technically had the watch, had updated him on their frustrating search to find a way through the minefield surrounding Sormana. Thus far, no usable patterns had been detected, nor had the source of the field's ever-shifting activation transmissions.

The typically garrulous Kim had reported this in as few words as necessary. The captain watched as Harry left his ready room. Chakotay wondered if something was troubling him, but was pulled away by an incoming transmission from *Vesta*. Farkas advised Chakotay that Lieutenant Bryce had discovered another Federation signal and she was anxious to set course and retrieve what she hoped would be another message buoy. They knew the admiral hadn't shared most of what she had learned from the first one with them, and there was only so much they were willing to discuss, even over an encrypted channel, but both captains had a healthy respect for the Krenim. Fear was too strong a word, but it was definitely waiting in the wings.

Voyager received word a little more than an hour after Janeway had departed that she was ready to transport back. Chakotay ended his contact with Farkas and leaving the bridge to Kim, hurried to the transporter room to greet her.

The admiral's face betrayed nothing. He started to lead her toward the briefing room but when she directed the turbolift to deck three, he realized she intended to conduct this conversation in a different setting.

Only when the doors to his quarters had slid shut behind him and she had moved close to allow his arms to encircle her did he ask, "How did it go?"

She savored the embrace for a few moments, then stepped back. "Better than I expected. Not as well as I'd hoped."

"She's not coming back, is she?"

"No."

"Because of Dayne?"

"Because she seems to honestly believe she can end this conflict."

"Do you have any interest in letting her do that?"

"I don't really have a choice. She said the strangest thing, something about home being what you create, what lives inside you."

"I can relate to that. Can't you?"

"Yes and no. I don't think she considers Sormana her home. But something is keeping her here. She says this isn't personal, but I don't buy it."

"The *denzit* didn't give you any clues?"

"No. But she did agree to allow a small team to the surface to investigate the Zahl. She requested Tuvok. Although I'm hesitant to permit them further contact, I understand. Send Harry and Seven with him. I trust them to be more objective than Tuvok is."

"More objective than a Vulcan?"

"More objective than Tuvok can be right now."

"You want them to find the temporal technology the Zahl are using to bring their soldiers to Sormana?"

Janeway nodded.

"Does the *denzit* have any idea what our team will be looking for?"

"No, and we can't tell her."

"Will she allow *Voyager* to make orbit so I can monitor them and pull them out if things go badly?"

"No."

Chakotay sighed. That wasn't what he wanted to hear. "We still can't get through that minefield without permission and a safe course."

"Keep working on it."

"Captain Farkas has located another Federation signal. She thinks there's another buoy out there."

"We'll pick it up on our way to the Krenim homeworld."

Chakotay was surprised. "You don't want to wait and see what Tuvok's team finds before you approach them?"

"I'm ready to confront them now. I'm taking the *Vesta* and I'd like Counselor Cambridge to join us."

"I think the next time one of us goes home I'm going to put in a request for a new counselor. He hasn't had time to do much of that for the last several months, and it's not like we don't need him."

Janeway smiled bitterly. "I need him more right now. His perspective is critical, particularly in first-contact situations like this. I don't know how objective *I'm* going to be able to be with the Krenim."

Chakotay's smile in response was genuine. "Kathryn Janeway acknowledges the fact that she needs help. I'm going to make a note of that in my personal logs."

"Do it and I'll have you sent home in an escape pod."

They embraced again, this time for a long, comforting moment.

"Don't get yourself in any trouble while we're apart. I'm going to have my hands full making sure Tuvok and his team get off that planet in one piece," Chakotay said softly.

"Keep the fleet safe until I get back," she said softly.

"Always."

Relieved that the admiral had returned safely from Sormana, Lieutenant Harry Kim allowed his thoughts to drift back to the endless circular course they had taken since the last time he had spoken to Nancy Conlon off duty. He knew she was hurt and angry with him. He thought she just needed some time before she would be willing to open up to him. This had been a pattern between them over the last year. The cheerful openness of her demeanor had always masked murky unsettled waters beneath the surface. She was an outstanding engineer and a fine officer, but the volume of tragedy she had witnessed and endured in her career had been understandably overwhelming. You never knew it with Nancy until you were in the middle of a full-blown crisis. One minute she was doing her job, the next, paralyzed by unspeakable fears. She kept it all buried so deep that even Harry had a hard time seeing when he was close to tripping an internal mine.

He understood. He had his own painful past with which to contend. He shared her desire to keep it at bay, focusing on the positive, the here and now. Some people might have mistaken it for shallowness or lack of character. What they missed about him and Nancy was the amount of strength required to keep pushing past it, or maybe just running as fast as they could to keep ahead of it. Their friends expected them to hold it together. So they did, until they no longer could.

Kim didn't think Nancy had ever shared what lay beneath those effervescent waters with anyone else. When she had decided to initiate intimate contact, he had finally felt he could relax. She knew his darkness almost as well as he knew hers. They would walk through it together.

And then she'd shut him out completely.

Another mission might have allowed them a little time and space to find their way back to each other. The Full Circle Fleet's habit of careening from one massive crisis to another did not. Duty had to come first for both of them. But right now, Kim would have given anything for a few weeks of impulse travel through uninhabited space with nothing more interesting to discuss than astrometric data.

He was considering his next move when to his utter amazement Conlon stepped onto the bridge from the turbolift. She did not move immediately to the engineering station. Instead, she walked toward the center seat and said, "Do you have a minute?"

Kim didn't, but under the circumstances he would make one.

"Waters, the bridge is yours," he advised the acting operations officer. As she moved to take his seat, he led Conlon toward Chakotay's ready room.

The moment they were alone, Conlon moved to Kim, wrapped her arms around him, and initiated a long, deep, incredibly passionate kiss. It was tempting to forget the awkwardness of the last several days. Perhaps that storm had passed as quickly as it had broken. But when Nancy began to tug urgently at his uniform jacket, pressing her body close enough to his to feel the effect her presence and actions were having, Kim took both her hands in his and held them steady as he stepped back.

"What are you doing?" he demanded.

"Using you," she teased.

Except that part of Kim understood that she wasn't actually kidding. Taking back her hands, Conlon unzipped her uniform jacket. She had started to lift her tank top when the ready room door slid open and to Kim's absolute mortification, Chakotay entered.

He paused the moment he understood what he had inadvertently stumbled upon. "Lieutenants," he snapped.

Kim's cheeks were now burning for two reasons. He moved to stand at attention as Conlon picked up the jacket she had just discarded and joined him.

"I don't even know what to say," Chakotay growled. "It's not possible that two of my most trusted senior officers don't know better than this. You're both going on report. Lieutenant Conlon, you are dismissed. Lieutenant Kim, you'll stay."

By the time Conlon had made her brisk exit, Kim's ears were pounding as blood rushed to his head, fleeing his extremities.

"Captain," he began.

"Don't," Chakotay warned. "We're in the middle of a ridiculously complicated mission here. Your priorities are completely out of order. You've been moping around this ship for days. You've been unable to solve a tactical problem I'm reasonably convinced is well within your capabilities and now I'm starting to think that the reason why is that your head is simply not in the game. I get that balancing your duties with your personal life can be challenging, and I'm not claiming to have always stayed on the right side of that line. But damn it, Harry, *this* is unacceptable."

Kim wanted to protest that it hadn't been his idea. He knew better. The only thing worse than transgressing so grievously was refusing to accept responsibility for it. His instinct was to protect Nancy as best he could. He didn't really understand what had just happened between them but it set off every internal alarm he had.

They were interrupted by the sound of the door chime.

"Enter," Chakotay ordered.

Tuvok and Seven did so.

"I'm sorry to wake you, but I have a mission for the three of you, a complex one, and I want you ready to move out in the next few hours."

To his credit, Kim gave his captain his complete attention as Chakotay laid out the work ahead of them on Sormana. He knew whatever was happening with Nancy needed his attention. He also knew that it didn't matter until he had found a way to undo some of the damage he'd just done.

Commander B'Elanna Torres hadn't been surprised when she received Chakotay's contact. They hadn't spoken about Conlon since Torres had expressed her concerns in his ready room just before he went to Sormana. Since then, between her misreading of Conlon's intentions, the new issues that had arisen for the fleet, and caring for both of her children, she really hadn't given the matter as much thought as it might have deserved. She hadn't even found time to grill Harry about how his last conversation with Conlon had gone or how he felt about the "break" Conlon had decided to take from their relationship.

After shaking Tom gently awake and advising him that he was on call, Torres dressed quickly and hurried to Conlon's quarters. She was granted immediate access and found the chief engineer seated on the edge of the bed tucked into a corner of her quarters beneath a long port. She had drawn both of her knees to her chest and though she looked up to acknowledge Torres's entrance, she was clearly withdrawing further into herself. Apart from the starlight, the room was dark.

Torres took a moment to wonder if she should simply contact Counselor Cambridge. The few details Chakotay had provided of Conlon's most recent indiscretion were enough to tell her that Nancy was out of control. Torres had little faith in her personal counseling abilities, but she had a great deal more in her heart. Seeing Nancy like this, she didn't want to berate her or demand an explanation. She wanted to help. She wanted to make whatever was wrong better. She wanted to reach inside

Conlon, find the pain that was eating her alive, and rip it out with her bare hands.

Warily, Torres moved to the bed and perched herself on its edge. "Several years ago, right around the middle of *Voyager*'s first tour out here when we'd finally managed to get word back to the Alpha Quadrant that we were alive, we received a huge transmission of messages from home. Chakotay got a letter from one of our old Maquis friends, Sveta. That's how we learned that almost all of the Maquis were massacred by the Cardassians and the Dominion while we were lost in the Delta Quadrant. The ones who didn't die were in prison.

"I was furious at first. I had never been so angry and believe me, that's saying something. But I didn't know what to do with all of that anger. So I kept it inside. I continued doing my duty. I kept thinking it would go away if I just left it alone.

"It didn't. Instead, by refusing to feel that pain, I lost the ability to feel anything. I thought that might be a problem. I didn't realize it was just a symptom. I tried to solve it by putting myself in the most dangerous situations I could find. When our missions weren't exciting enough, I created holo-deck programs. I let aliens three times my size beat the living hell out of me on a daily basis. I broke I don't know how many bones. It hurt, but at least it was *something*. The pain I inflicted on myself became the only assurance I had that I was still alive.

"I learned later that it's called survivor's guilt. Chakotay finally figured out what I was doing and forced me to accept the fact that I needed help. I haven't thought about it in a long time, but it's always there. Knowing that I could do that doesn't ever go away. But I know now that no matter how bad things get, they could always be worse, because they have been."

Torres sensed Conlon's face turn toward her. She shifted her gaze and saw cold, dead eyes staring back at her. "Why are you telling me this now?" Conlon asked.

"I don't know what's happened to you," Torres replied. "I just know that something is wrong and I want to help."

Conlon turned away and again settled her gaze directly ahead. "Has Chakotay ordered me off duty?" Conlon asked.

"Not yet," Torres replied. "He said he would leave that at my discretion as your immediate superior officer. He did recommend it in the event you were unwilling or unable to explain yourself."

Conlon nodded thoughtfully. Finally she said, "It wasn't Harry's fault. I am the only one who should be held responsible. Make sure Chakotay knows that."

"I will. But even if that's true, I don't understand. *The captain's ready room*?"

"I honestly wasn't paying that much attention to where we were, just that we were alone."

"You told me you needed a break. What changed your mind?"

Conlon shrugged. "I had a bad day."

Torres struggled to remember the day's reports she had hastily reviewed prior to turning in for the evening. Nothing that could account for Conlon's behavior jumped out at her.

"In engineering?" Torres asked.

"No."

Torres rose from the bed and stood above Nancy, absent mindedly shifting her weight from one foot to the other. It was her default when standing these days. The motion calmed her newborn son.

"Nancy," she began, "we can play twenty questions all night, or you can tell me what is going on. Is this about those modifications you wanted to make? Are you still afraid we're all too vulnerable?"

Conlon exhaled quickly through her nose in a huff that never made it to her throat. "I think you'd call that a symptom," she finally admitted.

Torres knelt so that they were eye-to-eye. "A symptom of what?"

Conlon lifted her eyes to look past Torres's. "I'm not sorry I survived Xolani's attack. I'm not sorry I survived the Omega Continuum. I'm not sorry I survived the Borg Invasion. I'm not sorry I survived Galvan VI. I don't feel guilty that I'm still alive when so many I have cared about are dead.

"My problem is the opposite."

"I don't understand."

"My problem is that I'm about to join them."

Torres felt as if she had been slapped. "What the hell does that mean?" she demanded.

Conlon dropped her feet to the floor and rose, moving past Torres into the darkest corner of her cabin. Torres could see her shadow pacing the small area between her replicator and the door to her quarters.

"I told you and everyone else that I didn't remember what happened when Xolani attacked me."

Torres quickly reclaimed the edge of the bed and sat absolutely still, fearful of doing anything to break Nancy's train of thought.

"That was a lie."

Torres's heart began to burn. It wasn't disappointment so much as shared devastation. She had blamed herself for Xolani's attack and had taken a small measure of comfort in the thought that Conlon had no memory of what had to be a harrowing experience. She would resume beating herself up about it later. This was not the time.

"Not the only one I've told lately, by the way. You were right. I have been ordering my staff to begin testing our gel packs and some synthetic amebocytes."

"I don't care," Torres said honestly. "Tell me about Xolani."

"At first, it was like a pressure at the base of my neck. My head started to pound. I got a little dizzy. My skin started to feel like it was too tight, like I was a balloon filled with too much air. I started to tingle all over.

"The next thing I knew I was floating in darkness. The first thing the asshole said to me was, *'That's right. You're free now. Don't be afraid.'* But I was afraid. I was terrified. I started pulling at the nothingness with my arms and kicking my legs, like I could swim to some surface and breathe again. He kept trying to convince me to calm down and I kept fighting him with every ounce of strength I had.

"Suddenly, I was sitting up in my bed. *Oh, God, it was just a dream*, I remember thinking. I was so relieved. But then he was there, sitting beside me. He reached out and touched my face. *'You're so beautiful, and so strong,'* he said. *'You will make a fine host.'*

"I told him to drop the schoolboy flattery. Somewhere along the line, I had put it all together. I knew who he was. I knew he was inside me. And I also knew that unless I gave him permission, he could never take all of me. The longer we sat in that imaginary room, the stronger I grew. No matter what he said, no matter what he offered, I refused. He said the pain would go away. He said I would always be part of him, but that no suffering would ever touch me again. He would protect me. I just kept screaming at him over and over to get out.

"There's a story I heard as a child about a girl who grows larger when she eats a certain cookie or piece of cake. I was like that. I was growing and he was shrinking. I was winning.

"So he came clean. He admitted that to submit to him was to die. By then, my head was brushing the ceiling of this room. All I could think was that I'd won. I was kicking his ass and there was nothing he could do about it. He had chosen poorly when he attacked me.

"But then he asked why I was so afraid of death when I was already dying."

"What?" escaped Torres's lips before she could help herself.

Conlon stepped out of the shadows. She had relayed this much of the story in a cold, detached voice. Only now could Torres see the tears streaming down her face.

"There was a moment of blinding pain, like every muscle in my body had just exploded. Suddenly I was small again. And then I was smaller. I was moving through my own body, through my bloodstream, until I reached a white mass. I got even smaller as I entered it. So small I was finally able to see the cells of that mass and the molecules that make up those cells. It was obvious to me that something was wrong. These large, sick black patches were growing, absences where there shouldn't be any. I think I was looking at my own DNA.

"He told me that the cells of my body had already turned against me. A foreign substance had been introduced years earlier and mutated my DNA. It was a slow process, but it was accelerating."

"Nancy, he had to have been lying," Torres said.

"He wasn't. I knew exactly what he was talking about. Several years ago, while I was on the *da Vinci*, we'd encountered this alien pathogen. It only affected a few of us, but two died before a treatment could be developed. I survived, but this was one of those cases where the cure was almost as bad as the disease. The mutated strain they created to attack the virus is still inside me. It's had years to move slowly through my body, making small enough changes to my DNA to remain undetected. It's killing me."

"Then we'll find a treatment," Torres insisted.

Conlon shook her head. "Once I knew, I realized something. If I kept fighting him, he was just going to find another host, someone who wasn't already dying. I couldn't let that happen. It wasn't fair. I decided then and there that if I was going to die, it would be *my* choice. And I could accept it as long as it meant no one else would have to face him."

Conlon paused to wipe her face clean with her bare forearms. When she was again composed, she continued, "After that, I really don't remember anything. I was gone. No one was more surprised than I was when I woke up on board the *Galen*. It didn't all come back to me at first. But over the next few days, I started to remember. I assumed the Doctor would find evidence of the illness and I kept waiting for the bad news. But it never came.

"*I know* it's still in there. Nothing has changed. But it's still undetectable. So I thought about it. *Why tell anyone now?* If I do, I'll spend what little time is left to me in some hospital back home. I don't want that. I love my life. I love my life *here*. I love Harry Kim, at least, I think I do. Tomorrow doesn't matter. Today is what I have. And I'm going to make the most of every single moment I have left.

"I pushed Harry into a closer relationship than I think he was ready for. I tried to push you into making those system modifications and I'm going to keep pushing you on them because if it's the last thing I have a chance to do, I'm going to make damn sure that no one on board this ship gets hurt by something we could have prevented. I'm going to *live* for as long as I can.

"Does that make sense?"

It did. It was a variation on a theme Torres knew well.

It was also a temporary fix at best, not a solution.

Torres rose from the side of the bed and approached Conlon as carefully as she would a wounded animal. "It makes perfect sense, Nancy," she said. "I'm so sorry you thought you had to carry this alone for so long. But that ends now. We're serving with an incredible team of doctors. They will find a cure. I'm relieving you of duty, and I'm ordering you to sickbay. I'll go with you. We'll tell Doctor Sharak everything you just told me and we'll let him start doing what he has to do. We're going to get through this together, do you understand me?"

Conlon nodded.

Torres felt more relief than fear. She knew what the Doctor was capable of and that Sharak would likely consult with him on this. For weeks now she'd struggled with this amorphous problem. Now it had a name and a precise shape. Now it could be attacked. Now it could be solved. She smiled reassuringly at Nancy.

Conlon did not smile back. She seemed resigned, defeated.

The look on Conlon's face did not change when they entered sickbay and called for an emergency consult with Doctor Sharak. It didn't change when Conlon told Sharak the same story she'd told Torres. It didn't change when Sharak thanked her for her honesty and assured her that all would be well.

Torres departed as Sharak began a new physical work-up on Conlon. She couldn't stop thinking about Nancy's haunted face or the hopelessness that now permeated her eyes.

17

VESTA

*C**hief Medical Officer's log. Stardate 51558.6. As of nineteen hundred hours, thirty-nine minutes, I have, in my capacity of Chief Medical Officer and in accordance with Starfleet Medical Regulation 121, Section A, officially relieved Captain Kathryn Janeway of her active command of the Federation Starship Voyager.*"

Admiral Janeway immediately paused the log playback on the second message buoy and looked to Counselor Hugh Cambridge. Given the fact that she wanted his perspective to be as well informed as her own when they eventually made contact with the Krenim, Janeway had decided to brief him fully on the contents of the first message buoy and to allow him to listen to the recordings on the second with her. He sat beside her in the science lab, his long legs stretched out before him and crossed at the ankle. His hands were clasped behind his head but he had sat up the moment he heard the Doctor's voice. This was the only log either of them had heard from any officer aboard *Voyager* other than her captain.

"Problem, Admiral?" Cambridge asked.

Janeway took a deep breath and gave him a knowing look.

"I see," Cambridge said. "You've nurtured your own misgivings about the choices you made during this trip down forgotten lane, but hearing those of a fellow officer takes this to a whole different level, does it?"

The admiral shook her head, not in denial of this statement, but to forcibly remove the thought from her head. "On the one hand, everything I did was in the interest of preserving my ship and her crew."

"And on the other?"

"It's hard to believe I allowed the situation to degenerate to this point."

"Just as it's hard to believe that *Denzit* Janeway could continue to apply her considerable skills to fighting the Zahl on Sormana?"

Janeway paused. "Looking back, it seems like there were so many better choices I might have made. But in the heat of the moment, apparently none of them occurred to me."

"She said from the comfort of a perfectly climate-controlled science lab aboard one of the Federation's most advanced starships. It can be constructive to second-guess command decisions. But it's difficult for me to take you to task when I have never spent more than a hundred days aboard a barely functioning vessel, struggling merely to survive while facing an enemy with the ability and the determination to eradicate me from history. Don't judge yourself too harshly."

"But I'm so very good at it," she said semiseriously before resuming the playback of the Doctor's log.

"For all the good it did me. I explained to the captain my suspicion that she has been suffering from traumatic stress syndrome for several weeks now. The symptoms include irritability, sleeplessness, obsessive thoughts, and reckless behavior. She attempted to rationalize her behavior. I asked her to remain in my temporary sickbay for a few days of observations. She refused. When I reminded her that I had the authority to relieve her of duty she said that if I did so, she would deactivate my program. I should note that she apologized immediately, but the fact that she would even temporarily entertain the notion in the interest of maintaining her position is further evidence of her obvious mental strain. Ultimately, she acknowledged my order, then refused to obey it. While it pains me to besmirch the record of one of the strongest, bravest, and most dedicated officers I

have known, duty obliges me to enter this incident in my formal log. Should charges result from this event, it will be for others to determine which of us acted appropriately or whether the captain's actions in this case rise to the level of severance from Starfleet."

Janeway paused the playback again. "It's interesting, isn't it? In theory, I would have been the one to review all of the logs contained in this buoy before it was dropped."

"You're wondering why you would have included the Doctor's log?"

"Yes. It doesn't reflect terribly well on me, does it?"

"Your choice to include it certainly does. You and the Doctor were *both* right," Cambridge noted. "I can't tell you how pleased I am that the Temporal Prime Directive prohibits either of us from ever telling him that I said that," he added.

The logs ended on stardate 51682.2. By that time, Captain Janeway had managed to collect a small allied fleet, including the Nihydron and the Mawasi. She had received an encrypted communication from Lieutenant Paris, who was still captive aboard Annorax's weapon ship. It was her intention to lead this small force into a direct attack on the Krenim vessel. *Voyager's* continued existence and the absence of any of these events from the memories of those that had endured them were the only indications available that Janeway's attack had somehow succeeded in restoring a timeline where the Krenim had posed no threat to *Voyager* or the Delta Quadrant.

SORMANA

"Unacceptable," *Denzit* Janeway insisted.

Tuvok understood her reaction but was unwilling to allow it to affect his decision. The fact that Lieutenant Kim and Seven were seated beside him in the *denzit's* office had nothing to do with his determination. Captain Chakotay and, by extension, Admiral Janeway were correct that the mission Tuvok and his team were about to undertake could directly affect the conflict between the Rilnar and the Zahl. That the *denzit* had agreed to bring them safely to the planet to perform it did not earn her the right to track the movements of Tuvok's team on the surface. Even knowing where they intended to go could affect her tactical calculations. It was a difficult line to navigate but Tuvok had no question about which side of it the Prime Directive demanded he walk.

"Then may I suggest again that you allow *Voyager* to assume orbit so that we may utilize her transporter system in traveling to and from our intended destination," Tuvok said.

"I can't allow that," the *denzit* replied. "The Zahl might take it as evidence that the Federation is about to take a side in this struggle and my own people would question my motives."

"Then what is your suggestion?" Seven asked placidly.

The *denzit* stared at her with bemused curiosity. Glancing at Tuvok she asked, "Are you absolutely certain this woman can be trusted? She's not even in uniform." Turning back to Seven, she demanded, "You were liberated from the Collective how many years ago, have served Starfleet constantly since then, but never accepted a commission?"

"Yes," Seven replied.

"The fact that she was selected for this mission should be all the confirmation you need of my assurance of her loyalty and abilities," Tuvok added.

"My *suggestion*," the *denzit* said, "is that you tell me where you intend to go, allow me to provide you with intelligence on the safest point of ingress, and to track your progress once you have transported there using my secured planetary network."

"Unacceptable," Lieutenant Kim chimed in.

"Thank you, Lieutenant Kim," Tuvok said tonelessly while still communicating his clear desire that Kim remain silent while he continued this difficult discussion.

"I know you're not going to tell me what you find there," the *denzit* said. "I understand the limitations of the Prime Directive."

"Then you also understand how knowing our target might compromise that directive," Tuvok continued.

"You could provide us with one of your shuttles," Seven

suggested, "assuming they possess limited transport capabilities."

"I could," the *denzit* agreed.

"That shuttle will have logs," Kim noted. "She may not be able to track us, but she will still be able to figure out where we went after the fact."

"Unless I wipe the logs in question," Seven said.

"Someone thinks awfully highly of their technical capabilities, considering you've never seen one of my tactical shuttles," the *denzit* observed.

"Yes, *someone* does," Seven agreed.

The *denzit* cracked a smile. "I like you," she said simply.

"Then we have an agreement?" Tuvok asked.

"We do," the *denzit* replied. "Is there anything else?"

"Do you have any spare Zahl uniforms in storage?" Tuvok asked.

"Yes, but you three aren't going to fool anyone in them. You'll need to be surgically altered."

"They will suffice from a distance," Tuvok corrected her. "Should we get close enough to any Zahl officer for them to see our faces, the likelihood of the success of our mission will have dropped to below ten percent."

"Still, I could have my medical staff provide you with cosmetics that might buy you a little time."

"That would be appreciated," Tuvok said.

"And you understand that under no circumstances will I be able to assist you once you've left the Center?" the *denzit* asked.

"We do."

"Very well."

The shuttle the *denzit* provided Tuvok's team was cramped by Starfleet standards, but sufficient to the task at hand. Its scanners were similar enough to those Starfleet utilized that Lieutenant Kim had mastered them within a few moments of activation.

Seven piloted the small vessel, keeping it low to the ground for its flight over the desert that stretched for a thousand kilometers south of the Rilnar Center toward the edge of the continental land mass. No Rilnar or Zahl settlements were located near the coast, which would make hiding the shuttle in a dense wood that covered several kilometers along the cliff-line fairly easy.

The edge of nowhere was not the team's final destination. From here, they would transport to an island only three hundred square kilometers in size. It was located south-southwest of the cliff-line.

When Kim had finally been granted access to sensors to analyze Sormana's surface it had taken him no time to locate a target for their investigation. The parameters were simple. If the Zahl were using temporal technology somewhere on the planet that allowed them to bring soldiers directly to Sormana from other timelines, it would have to be heavily shielded. Chroniton readings were not hard to detect. Shields massive enough to hide chronitons would, by design, be incredibly difficult to find, but the power source for the shields would not be. In the case of the island, some unusual geographic features, currents, and tidal shifts presented anomalous readings. A cursory analysis of anything within a thousand square kilometers wouldn't raise any red flags, unless you were specifically looking for a small dead zone. An area in the middle of an ocean would most likely indicate a series of currents bordering a gyre, a vortex of becalmed waters where all of the incoming currents deposited whatever they carried. Erratic winds would make such an area hazardous to navigate for sailing vessels and would likely be avoided.

It would also be an excellent place to hide temporal technology as the natural magnetic fields generated by the gyre would add conflicting readings to any detailed sensor scan.

Seven and Tuvok had concurred when Kim presented his findings. The next question was how to gain access to the island. Several hours of study suggested that the Zahl were not using sea vessels to move troops on and off of it. This meant they were probably using their own secured transporter system. In order to do that, the island's shields would have to be lowered for several seconds, at least partially, for any signal to be transmitted.

Seven had aided Kim and soon enough they had found an energy pattern that suggested shield permeability on two-hour cycles that were concurrent with the natural shifts in magnetic energy around the island. Both were impressed by the Zahl's integration of natural and technological features to create their virtually impermeable fortress.

It now fell to the away team to determine exactly what was inside that fortress.

They began by studying the island's perimeter to determine their point of ingress. Once they had selected a forest bordering the northern coast on one side of what appeared to be a massive citadel in the center of the island, the last step was to prepare their gear and time their transport to coincide with the next shield drop.

It took Tuvok's team the better part of eighteen hours to collect this intelligence. After ordering Kim and Seven to rest for six hours, four of which he spent in restorative meditation, Tuvok packed sufficient supplies to sustain the team for two days. This was longer than they intended to stay, but it was always better to be over-prepared. They each carried a single pattern enhancer. These would be used to aid the shuttle in locking on the team during their return, as the window of possible transport was so brief.

They transported to the island at o two hundred hours local time and under cover of darkness hiked toward the high-walled structure. It looked ancient. Newer roads led to six different entrances. Tuvok led his team beside the nearest and least-trafficked one, camouflaged by the forest until they made camp a thousand meters from the northern gates. Several small transport vehicles utilized the road, even at this hour. Scans indicated that most were filled with fresh food taken from the surrounding ocean and the volume suggested that the small citadel likely housed thousands of Zahl soldiers.

Fortunately for the away team, the transports were automated.

Stopping one, boarding it, and hiding themselves among the cases of foul-smelling fish—while using their tricorders to generate scrambling fields to hide their presence—was relatively easy.

Once the vehicle was cleared to enter the citadel by an electronic sentry and began making its way toward a large storage building, the team slipped off the transport and melted into the shadows, using their tricorders to map the area and determine their next target.

The first thing to catch Seven's eye was a geothermal hot spot located in the center of the citadel. A newer edifice, fifty meters higher than the ancient exterior walls, had been erected there. The amount of power surging underneath it suggested that this would be the source of the island's shields as well as the safest hiding place for any temporal technology. No chroniton readings were present, but they shouldn't be if the structure's internal shields were properly maintained.

Tuvok's attention was drawn to a very different feature of the citadel. Turning to Kim he indicated both the life-form and force-field readings his tricorder had detected. Kim responded by displaying a larger map of the entire area within the walls. Once this was done, he nodded knowingly to Tuvok.

Finally, in a low voice Tuvok said, "You two will attempt to access the central structure. I will investigate these holding cells."

"Beg pardon?" Kim whispered.

"We should stay together," Seven added.

"We will cover more ground in less time if we separate," Tuvok replied. "Thirty minutes should be sufficient to take the necessary readings. We will regroup here at that time. If any of us fail to do so, we will rendezvous in one hour at our observation post outside the walls."

"We came here to find temporal technology," Seven said. "It is there." She pointed to the central structure. "Where are you going?"

"This island is hiding more than temporal technology," Tuvok replied. "Those buildings there are prisons and they are holding several hundred Rilnar."

Seven nodded her understanding. "If they are keeping the *denzit*'s husband anywhere, it will be here." Despite intense frustration, Seven agreed grudgingly. "Thirty minutes," she said in a tone that dared Tuvok to fail to make the scheduled rendezvous.

The commander concurred with a slight nod.

Denzit Janeway sat in her command chair in the Center and studied the display of the coastal area where Tuvok's team had abandoned the shuttle she had given them more than nine hours ago.

This was not an area of Sormana she had ever analyzed, given how far it was from any Rilnar or Zahl settlement. She puzzled over the topography and the movement of the southern ocean, struggling to ascertain why Tuvok would have chosen this place or anything nearby to investigate. There was simply nothing there.

The shuttle's transporters could operate safely at a range of ten thousand kilometers, so its current location didn't do much to limit her area of inquiry. From that shuttle they could have gone almost anywhere and she wouldn't know precisely where until the shuttle was retrieved and its transporter logs studied. Each of the shuttle's systems had multiple layers of backup, so she doubted Seven's ability to scrub all of them effectively. She might simply destroy the shuttle, but its tritanium-encased computer core could survive anything short of a singularity.

Barring that, the *denzit* could simply activate the tracers she had ordered sewn onto the uniforms she had provided Tuvok's team. That would tell her exactly where they were. But it would also tell anyone else who might be scanning her frequencies where the away team was. Whether or not the Zahl would initiate those scans at the precise moment necessary to capture the signal or understand its significance was another matter. But the *denzit* would refrain from putting Tuvok's team in greater danger unless it became absolutely necessary.

Sadly, patience had never really been one of her virtues.

18

VESTA

*G**reetings*, Vesta," the deep, warm voice of the Krenim Defense Force vessel's captain said. "*I am Commandant Irlin and my ship is the* Brevmon.*"*

"And I am Captain Regina Farkas," *Vesta*'s captain replied evenly. "But then, I'm guessing you already know that."

"*This is the second time in as many weeks that we have found you trespassing within Krenim space. While we are always anxious to make new friends, I am unsure what to make of your actions, Captain. I hesitate to suspect dubious intentions, but I cannot rule them out, either.*"

This was the first time in a long time Admiral Kathryn Janeway had been able to put a face to the Krenim. She barely remembered the brief contact *Voyager* had made years earlier. They were fair-skinned humanoids with large patches of dark mottling running from their hairline to their ears. They also possessed two raised, circular nodes at each temple. They might be protuberances of bone that permanently cracked the epidermal cells above them, or perhaps, vestigial horns. Their uniforms were utilitarian in shades of brown and maroon. Irlin's chest was decorated with several metal pins, likely denoting rank or accomplishments.

"I assure you, there is no cause for concern, Commandant," Farkas said hastily. "We are actually en route to your homeworld. We intend to make official first contact and enter into diplomatic discussions with the appropriate representatives."

Irlin's face broke into a wide smile. "*How marvelous,*" he said. "*We would be happy to escort you to your destination and to send advance notice of your arrival and intentions.*"

"We would be most grateful for that," Admiral Janeway said.

"*And you are?*" Irlin asked.

"I am Admiral Kathryn Janeway, leader of the Full Circle

Fleet dispatched by the United Federation of Planets to explore the Delta Quadrant."

It might have been nothing more than a trick of the light aboard the *Brevmon*, but it appeared to Janeway that for a moment, the bridge's illumination dimmed. A faint hum emitted by the Krenim vessel's engines silenced and was replaced by a low, insistent beeping.

"Is everything all right over there?" Farkas asked, likely picking up what Janeway had noted along with the consternation that was now etched on Irlin's face as he studied a small display screen embedded in his chair.

"Forgive me, Captain Farkas and Admiral Janeway. I am receiving, that is to say, my ship is in the process of alerting me to an unusual protocol. I must sign off for a few moments and make contact with another Krenim vessel that is nearby. I assure you, we bear you no hostile intent. Unfortunately, my ship will not be permitted to escort you farther into our territory. The determination of your progress will be made by a more specialized Krenim division. Again, deepest apologies," Irlin said before closing the channel.

Farkas turned to Janeway, who was smiling in spite of herself. "What the hell?" Farkas asked.

"As a Starfleet captain you are aware of similar specialized protocols that would be activated on your ship in the event certain unusual substances were detected," Janeway said.

Farkas chuckled at the thought. "You think that's what just happened? You think the Krenim feel the same way about you that we feel about omega particles?"

"If they know half of what we do about the Year of Hell, it wouldn't surprise me in the least," Janeway replied.

SORMANA

For an internment camp, the two long single-story structures that housed the Rilnar prisoners were woefully unprotected, at least by Tuvok's standards. Each building contained only one entrance and no windows. Short ventilation slits were cut into the exterior stone walls offering fresh air and no chance of escape. Undoubtedly, these buildings were only the first level of security. Should a prisoner manage to liberate himself from his holding cell, he would have to breach the main door, manned by a single guard who didn't seem particularly attentive to his duties. But even should the prisoner succeed, there was still nowhere to go. There was constant light foot traffic between the other nine buildings encased by the high citadel walls. Then there were the walls themselves. The six entrances to the citadel were more heavily guarded than the prison blocks. Beyond the walls, the energy field shielded the entire island. Beyond the island lay the ocean.

It was a perfect prison. It was built to keep those it housed *in*. It was not, however, terribly efficient at keeping unwanted infiltrators out.

Tuvok chose to assault the door of the northern cellblock nearest the high wall. It was the farthest from the center of the citadel and as it faced the wall, was hidden from the view of anyone not intent on directly accessing it. Tuvok assumed there were security sensors monitoring the perimeter, so he kept well inside the wall's shadow until he had the door's guard in sight. Tuvok then observed the man for ten minutes. His boredom was immediately apparent. From time to time he stood briefly at attention or walked a few paces back and forth before the door. When, to Tuvok's dismay, the guard looked toward his still figure, glanced around himself furtively, and then began to stride away from his post and toward Tuvok, the Starfleet officer readied himself for an attack.

It never came. The guard moved into the shadow of the wall several meters from Tuvok's position and removed something from a pocket of his long jacket from which he proceeded to take two generous swigs. Tuvok did not hesitate. He strode briskly toward the guard and from behind, grasped the man's shoulder firmly, pleased that the Zahl possessed similar enough physiology to most humanoids. The nerve bundle vulnerable to the Vulcan nerve pinch proved the young guard's undoing. Tuvok then rifled through his pockets to find a small security-access key card, relieved him of his jacket, and arranged his body so that it should go undetected for the next several minutes at least.

Tuvok donned the jacket and moved back to the door, keeping his face down, assuming the man's position briefly in the event he was being monitored. He then cupped a hand over his ear, feigning receipt of a comm signal, took the key card from his pocket, and used it to enter the cell block.

Just inside the door was a small office. Large windows provided visual access to the long hall of sealed doors that lay beyond another closed metal door. Inside the office, a single Zahl soldier slept with his feet up on his console.

For a moment, Tuvok wondered if this might be a trap. These were by far the least-effective security forces he had ever encountered. The only possible rationalization for their criminal dereliction of duty must be the fact that they believed outside infiltration to be impossible. He had no idea how long this prison had been in operation. Given the Rilnar's ignorance of its existence, it might never have been targeted for attack. But it still seemed ridiculous that those entrusted with its protection took such a lackadaisical attitude.

Still, Tuvok was willing to accept his good fortune. Using the same key card that had opened the exterior door, he entered the small office. Its attendant immediately jerked awake and peered at Tuvok through sleepy eyes.

"Who are you?" the guard demanded.

"Your replacement," Tuvok replied, wondering how long the uniform and makeup he wore would fool his adversary.

"You new here?" the guard asked as he stood up and yawned.

"This will be my first shift."

"Who'd you piss off to pull this lousy duty?"

Tuvok forced his mouth into an uncharacteristic, knowing smirk, which seemed to satisfy the other guard. Nodding, he turned his back to Tuvok, placing his hands on a data interface panel and entering a few commands.

Again, Tuvok did not hesitate. He disabled the guard in the

same way he had his counterpart outside and after depositing him carefully on the floor, addressed himself to the data panel. Using his tricorder, he was able to tap into the computer system and immediately began to search the prison's records for a Rilnar named Dayne. When this provided no results, he searched for prisoners who had entered the camp around the time of Dayne's disappearance. Only one current resident of the cellblock came up: N19471.

Noting the cell number, Tuvok left the office and made his way down the long hallway. When he reached the door, he again inserted his key card into the appropriate slot. A loud buzz alerted him to his error. It also brought the cell's resident to the door. A small square opening just above eye level was covered by two thick metal bars. Sound was the only thing likely to come through them.

"You forget your key again, Limpis? Where's my breakfast?" a gruff voice sounded.

Apparently prisoner N19471 wasn't the only hungry resident on the block. Several other voices began to call out up and down the hall, echoing in the dimness. None of them thought highly of Mister Limpis, or seemed overly concerned with mocking him openly.

"I am not Limpis," Tuvok replied. "I require information about a man I have been told is a fellow prisoner."

"Why don't you come in and get it then?" N19471 asked.

"I was sent here by *Denzit* Janeway," Tuvok added.

The hall fell suddenly silent.

"She's still alive?" N19471 asked.

"I told you she was," another voice sounded.

"Yeah, but you're an idiot," yet another added.

"Shut up, all of you," N19471 insisted. When the chatter subsided he said, "She finally found this place?"

Because Tuvok could not answer truthfully that she had, he asked instead, "You were captured almost two years ago. Did you know a Rilnar officer named *Dayne* who would have been captured around the same time?"

N19471 fell strangely silent.

"Did you know—" Tuvok began again.

"Who is asking?" N19471 demanded.

"A friend," Tuvok replied almost honestly.

"Dayne wasn't captured," N19471 said. "He didn't even take the field that night. Rumor is he defected."

"He was the *denzit*'s man," another voice shouted. "He would never have betrayed her."

"You didn't know him," another insisted. "None of us did. He claimed he was from Pyral but no one I know there ever heard of him."

"He's dead," someone shouted from down the hall. "He has to be."

"Silence," Tuvok said, cutting through the din. "Can anyone here offer me definitive intelligence regarding Dayne's current whereabouts?"

"What's in it for us if we do?" N19471 demanded.

"I'd like to know the same thing," a new voice called from down the hall. Tuvok looked immediately back toward the cell block's entrance where the guard he had first subdued now stood jacket-less, leveling a fierce-looking rifle directly at him.

"Your freedom," Tuvok replied without hesitation.

As expected, this brought a fresh round of raucous cheers from the inmates, who began banging on their doors with fists and metallic objects—likely cups, bowls, or possibly waste receptacles.

The guard turned to be sure the doors all around him weren't about to swing open. Tuvok used the momentary distraction to raise his phaser and stun the man. He dropped to the ground and Tuvok charged forward as the second guard he had disabled stepped into the doorway, lifting his weapon hurriedly.

The second guard fired, but his shot went wild. Tuvok had thrown him to the ground, taking the rifle in both his hands and thrusting the side of it into the guard's face before the next shot hit the wall beside them opening a large, fuming hole in the stone.

They wrestled briefly to the cheers and jeers of the residents. Tuvok eventually landed a strike with the butt of the rifle into the man's nose, leaving him bleeding and unconscious. Tuvok rose from the ground, assessing the situation. The cell block was in chaos. Even guards as lazy as these Zahl would have to respond momentarily. He required a diversion. The only one available was likely to severely compromise his team's ability to escape, but less likely to result in his immediate capture.

Tuvok returned to the main office and again linked his tricorder to the main computer system. After bypassing a series of overrides, he gained access to the security grid and simultaneously unlocked every single door in the cell block.

Turning, he saw six guards come through the main door. One looked immediately to the office where Tuvok stood. The glance was brief, as his attention was suddenly captured by the flood of prisoners now evacuating their cells and pouring into the hallway. They formed a living battering ram. Those in the front, seemingly heedless of the danger, ran forward like wild raging beasts. They were fired upon. A few fell and were immediately trampled by the momentum of those who followed.

Tuvok watched the chaos he had just unleashed work its will. Alarm buzzers cut through the air all around him and the sound of boots running in unison toward the cell block was soon clear.

Tuvok joined the rear of the fray. Once outside, he saw prisoners fighting guards hand to hand. Some who managed to avoid being shot claimed a few weapons of their own and the result was tumultuous confusion. Tuvok used it to slip again into the shadows of the wall, hoping that he could somehow find Seven and Lieutenant Kim.

VESTA

The next Krenim vessel to intercept the *Vesta* was a third of the size of the *Brevmon* and configured quite differently. Commandant Irlin's ship was considerably smaller than Farkas's while still quite formidable. The main body was a long tube large enough to hold ten decks. The nacelles affixed almost at the midpoint of each side were a similar shape, but shorter and angled slightly toward the control module.

The new vessel was a small disc surrounded by a superstructure connected to the disc at eight points. On one side the structure extended like a lattice around a long strut terminating in a luminescent sphere of energy. The purpose of this appendage was not immediately clear but it brought to mind a much smaller version of Annorax's weapon ship described in the logs Admiral Janeway had reviewed. A shorter, thicker strut extended from the other side of the superstructure. The computer's analysis indicated this was the smaller ship's single propulsion array.

As soon as the disc ship arrived, the *Brevmon* departed without so much as a farewell. *Vesta* was hailed by the newcomer and when the channel was opened, the bridge of the ship was revealed as a small circular room filled with a wide variety of computer displays but apparently manned by a single individual who stood at a low railing. An empty chair was secured to the deck behind him.

His face had a certain boyish charm. Fine, golden hair sat atop pleasantly arranged features and all but hid the characteristic temple protrusions. Bright hazel eyes beamed at Admiral Janeway, but every muscle below them was taut with tension.

The admiral's stomach lurched. She had only seen this man once in a tattered photo, but there was no mistaking his true identity. His intentions were another matter.

"Greetings to the Federation Starship Vesta *from the Krenim Temporal Defense Agency vessel* Truon."

"You have got to be kidding me," Admiral Janeway said, stepping toward the main viewscreen.

"Hello, Kathryn," the man said.

"Dayne," the admiral said with obvious disgust.

The faint smile that answered her was replaced immediately by mingled regret and embarrassment.

"I am certain you have as many questions for me as I have for you. Permission to come aboard?" Dayne asked.

"Granted," Janeway replied without hesitation.

SORMANA

Lieutenant Harry Kim wasn't certain why Seven had so easily acquiesced to the sudden wrench Tuvok had thrown into their carefully planned infiltration of the citadel. Although he hadn't participated in all of the high-level briefings regarding *Denzit* Janeway, Chakotay had included the broad strokes of her past during their current mission prep and Tuvok had filled in the blanks during their journey to the coastline. While finding a way to convince the *denzit* to abandon Sormana was a goal Kim shared with the rest of *Voyager*'s senior staff just on principle, it did not take priority over the only part of this mission regulations actually permitted them to undertake—locating any temporal technology the Zahl might be using to alter the timeline. Tuvok's choice to add finding a potential Rilnar prisoner to their agenda, coupled with the distance he had maintained from his former friends since he had returned to *Voyager*, only served to raise more questions about Tuvok's priorities than Kim was comfortable with.

Seven had concurred with Tuvok, but then she was not bound by Starfleet's rules the same way Kim was. True, she always did her best to follow them, but it wasn't as if she could lose her commission should she stray a little outside the lines.

Kim would definitely bring this to Chakotay's attention later. For now, his duty lay elsewhere.

Their tricorders displayed a schematic of the building and noted several pockets of anomalous energy readings. The smallest would be easiest to investigate. They originated on the roof of the building, which could only be accessed from one of four internal stairways. The others were located on the five lowest levels of the structure, three of which were below ground level and shielded by small internal force fields.

As it was still the wee hours of the night, there was little activity around the building. A direct assault on the main entrance seemed foolhardy, even in their Zahl disguises. The north-facing side of the structure could be accessed in two ways. A set of formidable, metal double doors sat at one end. At the other was a wide rolling door that was currently raised. One of the automated transport vehicles was backed into the opening and four Zahl soldiers could be seen offloading its cargo.

Timing their ingress perfectly, Kim and Seven waited until the officers' backs were turned, moved swiftly to the vehicle, and retrieved the two smallest crates they could find. Each took one and followed the others into the building. They met no resistance. Depositing their crates on the first available stack, they continued deeper into the storeroom, a vast rectangle that took up a quarter of the square footage of this level. Along the far wall another set of double doors sat open. Kim and Seven hurried through them after consulting their tricorders and confirming that the adjacent hall was empty. They made their way briskly to the nearest stairwell and used it to ascend to the roof. The access door required a security key. Kim used his tricorder to override the panel and spring the locking mechanism.

In the center of the roof sat a massive shield generator. It was protected by a series of overlapping force fields, almost strong enough to protect a starship. A single square room sat at one corner of the roof and likely contained the shield system's primary control mechanism.

From the safety of the stairwell, Kim and Seven studied the assembly to their satisfaction, then retraced their steps, descending to the lowest level they could access. They reached the first sub-basement and exited the stairs into a hallway lit by a sickly orange glow. Again studying their tricorders they found the central staircase that accessed the three lowest levels of the structure. Twice, they passed other Zahl officers hurrying about their own business. None of them paused to question the unfamiliar faces. Clearly they were not terribly concerned that anyone who was there might not belong. Kim was beginning to believe that they might complete their work with time to spare when, upon unlocking a door to a storage room on the second sub-basement, a voice behind them shouted, "You there. You know this level is restricted."

Seven did not hesitate. She turned calmly and began to walk toward the Zahl officer as if prepared to take him to task for his insolence. When they were no more than a meter apart, Seven fired a single shot from the phaser concealed by her uniform jacket, stunning their new acquaintance. Kim dutifully dragged him into the storage room as Seven began to study its contents.

The room housed enough arms to sustain the Zahl's efforts on Sormana for another ten years. Crates of hundreds of rifles were present along with additional stocks of power cells. Smaller disruptors, grenades, and other explosives were also in abundance. It was a singularly depressing sight.

"Why so many?" Seven asked softly.

Kim did a few mental calculations and immediately understood the problem. "This island is too far away from the Zahl settlements for it to be easy to ship these to where they are needed most," he agreed. Kim looked past the crates and found a data control board near the doorway. After studying it for a few moments and applying his tricorder's translation matrix he said, "Stores one-one-nine-six and one-two-seven-eight are scheduled to be distributed tomorrow. That's four hundred rifles and sixteen hundred power cells."

"Where are they going?" Seven asked.

"Here," Kim replied. "Four hundred new recruits will be arriving here tomorrow and will be armed from this stock."

"This is the access point for the Zahl's temporal transporter," Seven said. "It's here, somewhere."

"Something like that would give off massive chroniton radiation," Kim noted. "But I'm not reading any."

"You shouldn't be," Seven said. "Even a small leak would render the island uninhabitable."

"So how do we find it?"

Seven studied her schematics further and said, "This way."

Kim followed her back into the hall. She led him past another large storeroom to a dead end.

"Seven?" Kim asked.

She responded by tuning her phaser and cutting a hole in the wall just large enough for them to crawl into. She did her best to pull the large piece of metal back into place, although it would not fool anyone who inspected it closely. She had led him into a ventilation shaft and they crawled on hands and knees through the claustrophobic space for several minutes until Seven cut another access hole.

Wiping the sweat dripping from his face onto his jacket, Kim followed Seven out of the hole and onto a small catwalk. Below them was a massive space that took up most of the two lowest levels of the building. In the center of it, four doorways had been erected on discrete octagonal platforms. Glowing orange crystals burned in the pediments of each, and the sides were covered with blinking panels and tubing that ran into the ground beside the clear raised platforms. Directly beneath each was a pool of liquid, a complex energy source of swirling orange whorls reminiscent of a warp core. Along the far wall, a set of data control interfaces stood abandoned. Kim was searching for a path that would lead them down to those panels when Seven began to move in the opposite direction.

"Where are you going?" Kim whispered. "Those have to be Rahalla's pools."

Seven responded by gesturing impatiently for Kim to follow. In the corner they found a large trunk of interconnected cables. She ran her tricorder over them and then pointed to a ladder imbedded in the wall which led to another catwalk one level above. Once they had reached the next level, Seven began to follow the path of one series of cables breaking off from the main trunk. Kim knew her well enough not to argue. Instead he took a quick reading of the cables and noted the odd patterns of energy flowing through them.

The cables ended at a transparent window. Through it, a harsh yellow light could be seen. Leaning closer, Kim saw space almost as vast as that which housed the temporal transport system he thought they should be studying. In the center of that space, suspended by a massive energy field were dozens of pallets. Each of them held hundreds of torpedoes.

Kim swallowed the panic that surged through him at this sight.

"Are those?"

"Chroniton torpedoes," Seven said flatly. "Enough to destroy this entire planet and an area of subspace several billion kilometers beyond it. This entire system will be rendered uninhabitable should a significant portion of these be detonated."

"Who the hell would be dumb enough—" Kim's words were drowned out by a piercing wail that suddenly began to sound all around them.

It paused long enough for a harried voice to report, *"Attention all personnel. Security breach in cellblock Beta-One. Repeat, security breach in cellblock Beta-One. Dispatch armed containment teams to ground level and subdue with deadly force."*

As Kim wondered whether or not Tuvok might have triggered the alarm, Seven's gaze shifted from her tricorder to Kim's jacket, her eyes wide.

"What?" Kim asked.

Seven's head cocked to the right. This gesture was traditionally followed by a request that he explain himself. Instead, Seven pointed to the opalescent buttons of his jacket.

They were now lit by a faint red pulsing light.

Kim looked immediately at Seven's jacket and saw the same luminescent display.

Both of them immediately removed the jackets and dropped them into the open space below. Then they started to run.

Denzit Janeway could not believe what her eyes were telling her. After allowing more than thirty-six hours to elapse with no sign of movement from the shuttle the Starfleet team had taken, she had activated the personal tracers embedded in their Zahl uniforms.

The signal that came back to her was intermittent, indicating that something was jamming it at the source. It gave her coordinates that made no sense. According to her readings, Tuvok, Seven, and Lieutenant Kim were floating just above sea level several miles off the southern coast of the continent.

The *denzit* immediately ordered a recon team dispatched. Within half an hour she had her answer.

"An island?" she demanded of *Tilzitar* Limlesh.

"Yes, *Denzit*. It is located in a remote area, several thousand kilometers from the nearest Zahl settlement. Scanners are unable to detect it. It is heavily shielded. However, visual recognizance has confirmed its presence and noted a single large structure at its center."

"Dispatch infiltration teams. Low air approach. I will take the first shuttle. You will coordinate our efforts from here."

"Very good, *Denzit*."

19

VESTA

When Dayne entered the *Vesta*'s briefing room, his eyes lit first on Admiral Janeway before glancing toward Captain Farkas and Counselor Cambridge, who stood on either side of her. He appeared puzzled by their presence to the point of disconcertment.

"Welcome aboard the Federation *Starship Vesta*," the admiral greeted him. "This is her captain, Regina Farkas, and this gentleman is one of our fleet counselors and first-contact specialists, Lieutenant Hugh Cambridge."

"I see you finally found your people," Dayne said, stepping forward to shake hands with Farkas and Cambridge. "A pleasure to meet you both."

Janeway had wondered, until this moment, if he truly

believed her to be the *denzit*. She had her answer. While cognizant of the vast intelligence she might gain from Dayne by allowing him to continue their conversation in error, the thought sickened her, perhaps even more than her discovery that the Rilnar man *Denzit* Janeway had loved and married was actually Krenim. At some point the truth was going to come out. There was no telling how he might respond to intentional duplicity on her part, but she doubted it would help. The answers she sought were likely ones he would never share with the *denzit*.

"I am surprised to find you among them again," Dayne continued when he finally took Janeway's icy hand in both of his. "I thought, as did the Rilnar leadership, that when you renounced your Federation citizenship, you meant it."

"Forgive me, Commandant, is it?" Janeway asked, retrieving her hand.

"*Agent* Dayne," he corrected her gently.

"Agent Dayne," Janeway repeated cordially. "I believe you have me confused with *Denzit* Kathryn Janeway, the current commander of the Rilnar forces on Sormana."

Dayne's face lost its polite deference. He failed miserably to hide his shock. "Are you telling me there is more than one Kathryn Janeway still alive in this timeline?"

"Yes," Janeway replied.

"That's not possible."

"And yet, here I am," Janeway said.

"Agent Dayne," Counselor Cambridge interjected, "what branch of the Krenim military forces do you serve?"

"Might we sit?" Dayne asked. There were more than two dozen chairs in the room resting idly before four conference tables. Janeway gestured to the nearest small one and the group assembled themselves around it. Normally the admiral would have called for refreshments, water at the very least. She found herself strangely immune to the niceties of hospitality in Dayne's presence. He hadn't done anything to her. But his multiple betrayals of the *denzit* had already soured her stomach.

"I am a primary incursion analyst with the Krenim Temporal Defense Agency," Dayne told them once they were settled.

"And how often do the Krenim offer commissions to former Rilnar citizens?" Cambridge asked, feigning ignorance.

"As you have no doubt surmised by now, Counselor, I am not Rilnar. I am Krenim. At the time of *Denzit* Janeway's recovery, I was working undercover with the Rilnar to assess any activities in which they were engaged that might be detrimental to the integrity of this timeline. I was, in fact, ordered to undertake that mission when it came to our agency's attention that the Zahl had captured Captain Kathryn Janeway using what we believed was a stolen chroniton device. The Rilnar had no idea who Kathryn was, or of her significance to the Zahl or the Krenim. I was given a great deal of latitude by my Krenim superiors in the rescue operation and in assisting with her integration into Rilnar society."

This revelation brought dozens of new questions to Janeway's mind. Captain Farkas interjected before she could ask any of them.

"What is the Krenim Temporal Defense Agency?" Farkas asked.

"We are an organization comprised of individuals from a broad range of scientific, academic, and philosophical backgrounds dedicated to the study of space and time, in particular temporal anomalies and the analysis of the integrity of any and all timelines that may, on occasion, intersect with our own."

"Are you part of the Krenim military?" Cambridge asked.

"The Imperium's defense force is controlled by the government. Our agency is civilian, although we are permitted to call for military assistance when necessary."

Janeway and Farkas exchanged a meaningful glance. On the surface, it appeared that the KTDA held a similar position among the Krenim as the Department of Temporal Investigations had within the Federation. The Krenim's use of temporal technology under Annorax's leadership, however, suggested a very different mandate. The interesting thing was that *both* might be true.

"Is your agency currently led by a man named Annorax?" Janeway asked.

Dayne smiled. It was disarming in its genuine warmth. "Someone has found a temporally shielded buoy, haven't they?" he asked. "I suspected you might have detected one of their signals. It was the only way to make any sense of the Federation's sudden interest in our territory. I always believed we hadn't found all of them," he added with a shrug.

Janeway's review of those buoys had chilled her to the very core of her being. That Dayne could speak of them so casually was worse.

"Then you know who I am?" Janeway asked.

"I know who you *must* be, since you aren't my Kathryn."

"*Your* Kathryn," Cambridge huffed. "You speak of her warmly when you must know that right now she is leading one side of a senseless, brutal war in hopes of rescuing you from the Zahl."

Dayne's face again lost all traces of lightness. Shaking his head, he said, "I know what I have done to injure Kathryn. Had there been any way to avoid it, I would have found it. There wasn't. But the *denzit* isn't still leading the Rilnar because of me. She must think me dead by now, and she might hold that against the Zahl. Believe me when I tell you that her devotion to the Rilnar cause is genuine. I helped guide her to it."

"For a rational man, you don't seem to appreciate the gravity of that particular transgression," Cambridge noted.

"If you shared my perspective on the situation, you might judge me less harshly," Dayne retorted. "As it is, I know what a heartless bastard I must seem to you."

"I would be most interested in your perspective, Agent Dayne," Captain Farkas interjected. "What little we know of it so far doesn't reflect terribly well on you or your people."

"You think you know who the Krenim are, because you know who we were in one terribly misguided version of our history," Dayne said. "We, too, were horrified when we discovered the first of *Voyager*'s temporally shielded buoys in our territory. My agency was actually having trouble maintaining sufficient funding for our operations at the time. *That* discovery changed everything for us. For the first time, we had concrete evidence to support many of our temporal theories, as well as a new mandate: to further our studies and ensure that the tools envisioned by Annorax would never be used as he once apparently did."

"Then Annorax . . ." Janeway began.

"Annorax is revered among the Krenim as the father of temporal theory. He was the first among us to grasp the possibilities, the fluidity, the malleability of time. He designed elegant technologies that allow us to study multiple timelines, to witness the effects of the smallest actions, to understand time in all of its vast complexity. But the man the Krenim now remember also wrote and spoke extensively on the restraint required of all who dared to immerse themselves in the study of time. There were many temporal technologies based upon the discovery of chroniton particles that were natural extensions of his work, but he refused to create them. He believed time must be our teacher, never a weapon."

"That doesn't sound at all like the man I encountered so long ago," Janeway said.

"I know. *We* know. Yours is a cautionary tale, Admiral. I can't tell you exactly what made the difference between the Annorax you knew and the one we remember. Our analysis of your logs suggests that eventually, *Voyager* was able to force the weapon ship Annorax had designed into normal space-time and to destroy it. That is the only scenario we can imagine that would have resulted in a complete restoration of the timeline we now enjoy. None of our current scans reveal the existence of the timeline your logs reference. It has completely collapsed. Those shielded buoys you launched are the only records of it that exist.

"For you, Annorax was a monster, a warped, deeply misguided man who believed time had a personal vendetta against him. For us, he was one of our greatest thinkers. He lived a long, incredibly productive life, and died peacefully at his home on

Kyana Prime surrounded by his family and friends almost two hundred years ago. I understand that what you endured to bring about that reality was horrific. But on behalf of the Krenim, I thank you. Only those of us who know how dark the other roads could be can truly appreciate the light in which we now live. You did all Krenim a great service."

"Is that why you were so keen to come to Kathryn Janeway's aid when you learned of the Zahl attack?" Farkas asked.

"How did you learn that the Zahl had captured her?" Cambridge said over her.

"As I said, our agency monitors various timelines and scans the continuum regularly for temporal incursions. Limited knowledge of our alternate pasts has made us mindful and incredibly protective of what we consider our 'prime' timeline. We also do our best to make sure that temporal technology does not come under the control of other species. While I will not disparage our neighbors, the Rilnar and the Zahl, I cannot pretend that at their current level of development it would be wise to allow them unrestrained access to technologies that could prove so dangerous to all of us. Without the centuries of study that have accompanied our development of temporal scanners, it is impossible to fully grasp the magnitude of temporal manipulation."

"The Zahl have had access to temporal technology for at least a few hundred years. Didn't Rahalla share his discoveries with Annorax?" Janeway asked.

Danye nodded grudgingly. "Rahalla was a uniquely gifted Zahl, a visionary in some respects. But we have never been able to confirm his findings on Sormana. What temporal technology the Zahl utilize now they have stolen from us."

"That technology would have to have been stolen by Zahl *military* vessels," Janeway noted. "They have made it clear that they have no interest in continuing the war on Sormana. Even if they had stolen your technology, why would they turn it over to Sormana's natives?"

Dayne shook his head. "I don't believe the official position on the war is shared by all of the colonists on either side. There are more sympathizers out there then you might suspect.

"My ancestors clashed with the Zahl and Rilnar regularly during the early years of their colonial expansion. Eventually we negotiated mutually acceptable borders. This agreement has allowed all of us to continue our development in relative peace. We do not interfere with the Zahl or Rilnar, except when it becomes clear that our technology has been compromised. Often our hands are tied until those technologies—chroniton torpedoes, for instance—are used. They are simply too hard to locate. But once an incursion is detected, our agents planted on both sides of the conflict do what they can to mitigate the results."

"Are you aware that the Zahl are currently using some sort of temporal transporter to bring reinforcements to Sormana that are not native to this timeline?" Janeway asked.

Dayne sighed. "We are. We suspect the transporters were created from schematics stolen from our agency more than fifty years ago. They are located on Sormana, which makes it all but impossible for us to retrieve them without engaging both the Rilnar and the Zahl. No doubt the Zahl initially intended just to hide them there, but it is clear that they are now under control of the Zahl forces on the surface. My superiors have decided to allow them to continue this devastating practice, as the consequences are greatest for them and the individuals they have coerced into using them."

"You claim to be dedicated to the preservation of the integrity of the timeline, but *this* isn't your problem?" Cambridge asked, incredulous.

"We are not gods, Counselor," Dayne replied. "We do what we can, though obviously, not all we would wish."

SORMANA

Seven and Lieutenant Kim managed to escape the building they had infiltrated more by luck than skill. They departed the lower levels by finding the quickest route to a stairwell that led them into a squadron of Zahl soldiers utilizing the same route to exit the building and join the battle. By keeping their heads down and following the others, they secured their freedom from the frying pan only to find themselves in the blazing-hot center of the fire.

Dawn was still hours away. Nevertheless, the wide paths and yards between the structures of the citadel were drenched in brassy white illumination, courtesy of long banks of lights that had been placed at the top of the wall and angled inward. Seven and Kim emerged into absolute chaos. There was no sense, no pattern to the battle before them. A few loud voices shouted commands and in the confusion they were taken as suggestions rather than orders. Zahl soldiers shot wildly into the groups of prisoners that could be seen. Most of the inmates had struck out on their own and were wrestling with guards hand to hand. Some of the Rilnar had acquired weapons and were using them against their Zahl counterparts, hitting fellow prisoners and guards alike.

Seven linked her arm through Kim's and pulled him around the side of the building, turning away from the most concentrated area of fighting spreading out from the north side of the citadel. A mad dash across an opening between a transport and a smaller building brought them a brief measure of safety, allowing them to consult their tricorders.

"We will never make it back to our rendezvous point," Kim said.

"Each of the six gates has been sealed with two squads ready to defend them. We will not escape the way we came either," Seven added.

"We have to find Tuvok."

Seven nodded, retuning her tricorder.

"Seven, there's no time," Kim insisted.

"I am attempting to access the Rilnar frequency the *denzit* is using to trace us."

"Call me crazy, but I didn't honestly think she'd compromise our security like that," Kim admitted.

Seven shook her head. "The *denzit* is not the Kathryn Janeway you and I know." A series of short beeps indicated success. A green flashing light was moving furtively along the wall toward their position. "This way," Seven said.

Moments later, they caught sight of Tuvok and signaled to him. Checking his surroundings, he dashed across a clearing and joined them huddled behind a series of large crates located outside a smaller building near the southwest corner of the citadel.

"What happened?" Kim demanded.

"I was forced to improvise," Tuvok replied.

"There is no longer any way for us to evacuate the citadel. We must find a safe place to hide," Seven suggested.

"No," Kim countered. "We're getting out of here now."

"How?" Seven asked.

Kim replied by removing a small beacon from his pocket. "In the event we were stranded, Chakotay ordered me to activate this signal beacon. *Voyager* will come for us."

"Have they devised a means to safely transit the minefield around Sormana?" Tuvok asked.

"I hope so," Kim replied.

"Even if they have," Seven said, "they will not be able to lock onto us as long as the island's shields are operational."

"I know," Kim said. "It will take them time to reach orbit. Our job now is to bring down that shield."

"We must not contact *Voyager* and put the lives of the crew at risk without exploring every other option," Tuvok noted.

"Tuvok, the minute you freed those prisoners, you eliminated any other option," Kim pointed out. "We found the temporal transporters and more. The Zahl are storing hundreds of chroniton torpedoes here, enough to destroy the entire planet should they detonate."

"All the more reason to refrain from bringing down the shields that protect this island," Tuvok insisted.

Seven shook her head. "We don't have to destroy the shield generator. We could create a small power overload, just enough to momentarily drop the shields and allow for our transport.

The Zahl will surely restore them as soon as they realize the shields are down."

"Then timing this maneuver will be critical. How will we know when to bring the shields down?" Tuvok asked.

"*Voyager* will signal us through this beacon when they are in position," Kim said.

"Do we know where the shield controls are located?" Tuvok asked.

"We do," Seven replied.

"Very well. Signal *Voyager*," Tuvok ordered Kim.

VOYAGER

"Captain, Lieutenant Kim has activated the emergency beacon," Lieutenant Kenth Lasren reported from ops.

"I see it," Captain Chakotay acknowledged. A report had been sent to the data panel embedded in the arm of his chair. Turning to his first officer Chakotay asked, "Where are we with the minefield?"

Commander Paris immediately tapped his combadge. "Paris to Lieutenant Aubrey. Report."

"*Aubrey here, sir. At this point I can recommend six different courses, all of which should be safe.*"

"Should?" Chakotay asked gravely.

"*We still don't know how often the Rilnar and Zahl alter the activation patterns of the mines. The courses I would recommend have all been shown to be free of active mines within the last twelve hours.*"

"That's not good enough," Paris warned.

"If it's the best we can do, we don't have a choice," Chakotay replied. "Kim wouldn't have activated that beacon if there was another option."

"Lasren, open a channel to *Demeter* and *Galen*," the captain ordered. Seconds later, the main viewscreen was split, showing the faces of Commanders O'Donnell and Glenn.

"*Voyager* is about to attempt an emergency evacuation of our away team. Both of you should fall back at least a light-year and wait for our signal or *Vesta*'s to regroup."

"*Whichever comes first?*" O'Donnell asked grimly.

Chakotay nodded. "*Voyager*—"

Before he could conclude, Commander Fife interjected, "*Captain, may I ask how you intend to safely navigate the minefield?*"

"We're going to follow a course recorded over the last few hours," Chakotay replied.

"*As soon as you run the blockade, won't the Rilnar and Zahl respond by activating all of the mines?*" O'Donnell asked.

"Let's hope not," Chakotay replied. "We will advise them of our intentions. We've been totally accommodating up to this point. If they understand we are on a rescue mission . . ."

"*Didn't the* denzit *prohibit us from assuming orbit?*" Commander Glenn asked.

"Circumstances have changed," Chakotay said. "We'll just have to hope she understands where our loyalties lie and remembers where hers once did."

"*There might be another option,*" Fife said.

"Go ahead," Chakotay ordered.

"*My tactical officers and I have been studying the minefield for the last few days. We have mapped several sections of the field near the Rilnar checkpoint based upon the courses utilized by vessels that have safely transited it . . .*"

"We did the same thing," Paris interjected. "But given the fact that only certain mines are active at any given time, it's impossible to create an accurate map of any section of the field."

"*I know, Commander Paris,*" Fife said. "*Our scans suggest that the density of the field is its only weakness. If we assume that all of the mines will be activated once* Voyager *breaches the blockade, the only potentially viable alternative is to detonate a wide range of the field prior to entering it, setting off a chain reaction and clearing a safe course between you and the planet.*"

Chakotay sat back in his chair and turned to Paris. Both were clearly sharing the same thought. Neither liked the idea of stripping the natives of Sormana of their defense against orbital attacks. But, then there were no other options at this point.

"Excellent idea, Commander Fife," Chakotay acknowledged. Commander O'Donnell was beaming at his XO with considerable pride.

"Would you care to borrow Fife for the next hour or so?" O'Donnell asked.

"I would," Chakotay agreed. "Transport over at once, Commander Fife, and report to Lieutenant Aubrey in astrometrics."

"Aye, sir," Fife said, and could be seen moving immediately to exit *Demeter*'s bridge.

"We will be ready to depart once Fife is aboard," Chakotay continued. "I want both of you clear of the area by then."

"Acknowledged," Glenn said. *"Safe travels, Captain. Galen out."*

"Chakotay," O'Donnell said. *"I want Atlee back in one piece when all this is done."*

"What about the rest of us?" Chakotay asked.

"Meh," O'Donnell offered with a shrug and a knowing smile.

The gallows humor brought the same smile to Chakotay's lips. "*Voyager* out."

"Attention all hands. Red alert. Helm, set course to intercept the blockade. Ready all weapons and prepare full spread of phasers and torpedoes," Paris ordered.

"Coordinate firing solutions with astrometrics," Chakotay added. "Lasren, as soon as we can establish transporter lock, signal the away team."

"Aye, sir," Lasren said.

"Transmit a message to the nearest Rilnar and Zahl vessels," Chakotay ordered. "Advise them that we are entering their secured no-fly zone on a rescue mission."

"And when they order us not to proceed?" Paris asked.

"Advise them to stay back and close the channel," Chakotay replied.

20

VESTA

It was incredibly difficult for Admiral Janeway to accept Agent Dayne's story. Part of her problem was the dull, sickening ache that rose in her gut every time she thought of the logs she had heard, the sound of her voice itemizing damages, casualties, and the wanton destruction of multiple species by the Krenim. It would have been nice to believe that all *Voyager* had once suffered had not been in vain. If in this restored timeline the flutter of a butterfly's wings had led Annorax down one path rather than another, one that opened his eyes to the dangers as well as the destructive power of temporal manipulation, it was almost worth it.

But the admiral's understanding of multiple timelines gained through her experiences of them within normal space-time and beyond during her brief sojourn with the Q, made it hard for her to accept Annorax's change of heart and the resulting whole-sale changes in Krenim society.

Anything was possible. *Probable* was another story.

While it was true that multiple timelines existed, not all of them were created equal, nor did they all endure. What made the "prime" timeline so significant was the fact that even minor disruptions, intentional or natural, usually birthed alternate realities that eventually merged again with the original line. The anomalous ones rarely existed because of a simple choice or cause. The choice of coffee over tea for breakfast did not nec-essarily create a new reality—one for coffee, one for tea—that then led to a vastly changed version of history. Yes, some would argue that it *could*, but the preponderance of evidence suggested it did not. While with the Q, Janeway had witnessed the deaths of countless incarnations of herself. The vast majority had died under similar circumstances as those she suffered on the evolved

Borg cube. Most of the others had still been Starfleet captains, many of whom had served on *Voyager*. The few whose deaths had been most shocking were those who died under clearly different circumstances. Those numbered no more than twenty. She would never know what temporal corruption or anomaly had given rise to these radically different paths—with the notable exception of *Denzit* Janeway. But there was something comforting in their scarcity. It suggested that there was a course to be followed and that major events, including the developmental trajectory of most individuals and species, were not meant to be subject to the whims of temporal fate.

If what Dayne had said was true, the Krenim might have to be considered an exception to that rule. Flattering as it might be to imagine that her struggle had resulted in a better life for billions over centuries, Janeway was hesitant to accept the credit, or the proposition at face value. Many of the choices the Krenim, and Dayne, had made didn't make sense to her.

"Agent Dayne," Janeway finally said, "even if I were willing to accept that *Voyager*'s previous encounter with the Krenim had resulted in a massive change for your people, I still don't understand many of your present actions. Setting the conflict on Sormana aside just for the moment, why did you lie to *Denzit* Janeway? If the chroniton torpedo that the Zahl used to capture her was stolen from the Krenim, and you were dispatched to handle whatever circumstances arose from that torpedo's use, why not simply tell her the truth when you recovered her?"

"The only way to rescue the woman who became *Denzit* Janeway without bringing the Krenim into a state of open war with the Zahl was to do it covertly, working through the Rilnar," Dayne replied. "I had been posing as a Rilnar agent for months prior to her retrieval. When she was rescued, her unique situation made her an object of intense curiosity among them. Her species was unknown and she had clearly suffered cruelly at the hands of the Zahl. Everyone wanted to know who she was and why she had been targeted. Kathryn and I were able to convince them that her capture had been accidental. Her ship had ventured unknowingly into Zahl space and been badly damaged. Its technological advancement had made her a target for intense interrogation. The Zahl were willing to go to any lengths to acquire her technological expertise. The Rilnar were never told that she was taken from another quantum reality."

"The Krenim Defense Force was backing you up, weren't they?" Farkas interjected, "Why not transport both of you to safety once she was secured? Why not fake your deaths to cover for your absence? Why not let the Krenim military undertake a covert mission to rescue her?"

"We considered every option," Dayne replied. "The path we chose was the one least likely to result in failure and most likely to return Kathryn Janeway to some semblance of a normal life. My hope was that we would find *Voyager*. I convinced my Rilnar superiors to allow us to search for her ship and we did, for months. I was aware that the chroniton device the Zahl used had the capacity to lock onto *Voyager* no matter where the ship was in space. The ship might be too far away for us to locate using conventional warp drives. Kathryn had no way of knowing what *Voyager*'s position was when the Zahl fired on her. I could not utilize any Krenim technology to aid our search, as it would have tipped our hand to the Rilnar."

"But to this day you have allowed her to believe a lie," Cambridge insisted. "Her continuing allegiance to the Rilnar is based primarily on the fact that they were her saviors, but *they weren't*. The Krenim were."

Dayne paused, dropping his head and briefly analyzing his folded hands. When he lifted his face to theirs again, his cheeks were flushed and his eyes glistened. "I didn't plan on loving her, Counselor. It was the furthest thing from my mind when I began my mission. I have never felt for anyone what I shared with Kathryn. Her happiness became my only concern. It was wrong. It was unprofessional. It should have resulted in my termination from the Temporal Defense Agency. But it was also *true*. When I realized that I could not return Kathryn to her people, I tried to give her a life that was as close as possible to the one she knew best, a leader devoted to a cause where her skills and abilities would be appreciated and utilized. Too much time had passed, too much had happened between us for me to be able to tell her who I really was. I'm afraid I'm not that brave. She had already impressed the Rilnar. I helped her transition to their service, first to repay the debt she felt she owed them for her rescue and later to assist them in achieving victory over the Zahl on Sormana. It was the only choice that would not undo the progress she had made in recovering from the Zahl's torture.

"I advised my Krenim superiors of my intention to continue indefinitely as a covert operative among the Rilnar. I cited the ability to continue to oversee Kathryn's case and they agreed. But they also told me something I never expected to hear. A new analysis of the continuum had yielded a surprising finding. They understood Kathryn's significance to the Krenim by then. They could not explain the calculations that also indicated that her death was imminent and fixed across multiple timelines. She was going to die. There was nothing I or anyone else could do to prevent it. I decided to make the final years of her life as happy and fulfilling as I possibly could.

"I don't expect you to understand my choice. I don't need you to agree with it. Had she not been the single most extraordinary woman I have ever known, things might have gone differently. But she was. She still is."

Silence descended around the small table as everyone absorbed this revelation. Finally Janeway said, "So you abandoned her moments after her death, the death your own people told you was inevitable?"

Dayne nodded. "My evacuation was planned to coincide with the event. I watched her die. I left, certain I had made the right choice."

"And what did you do when you found out she had somehow, miraculously survived?" Cambridge asked.

"My duty," Dayne replied bitterly. "I couldn't go back. I had to allow the charade of my capture to endure. I was given no choice in the matter."

"Why not?" Janeway asked.

"Do you understand and agree with every order you receive from your superiors?" Dayne asked. When the admiral did not respond, he continued, "I didn't think so. But you follow them anyway, don't you?"

"Usually," Janeway finally admitted.

VOYAGER

"Captain Chakotay, this is Ornzitar Rileez. Your vessel's current course will take it into Sormana's defensive field. Your ship will be destroyed. You must alter your course immediately. Please respond."

"It almost sounds like he really cares," Commander Paris noted.

"Maintain course and speed," Chakotay ordered. "Commander Fife, are our firing solutions ready?"

"Aye, Captain," Fife replied over the comm. *Demeter*'s XO had taken Aubrey's place in astrometrics and quickly augmented the tactical officer's research on the minefield. Aubrey had returned to the bridge to execute Fife's plan.

"Captain," Aubrey reported from the tactical station, "the Zahl vessel *Tascara* is on an intercept course."

"Hail them," Chakotay ordered.

"I have Shipmaster Pilusch," Lasren reported seconds later.

"Onscreen."

"Captain Chakotay, your vessel has been designated as a hostile agent acting to aid the Rilnar on Sormana and will not be permitted to continue to approach the planet. Voyager and the other Federation vessels are hereby ordered to leave and refrain from returning here or to Zahl space. Should you refuse to honor this request, you will be destroyed."

"Shipmaster Pilusch, you are operating under faulty intelligence," Chakotay said evenly. "We dispatched an away team to the surface with the Rilnar's permission yesterday to investigate reports of possible misuse of temporal technology on Sormana. We have not nor will we take sides in this conflict. Our research is intended to safeguard the entire quadrant and falls under the mandate of the Federation's goals of peaceful exploration."

"I assure you, Captain, we are completely aware of your intentions and the dissembling you have done to hide your true allegiance. Had your goals been peaceful contact, you would not have sent spies to Zahlna II to infiltrate our germschled or to interrogate our scientists. The civilian pilot of the Celwinda *you bribed has confirmed the actions of your officers while in our territory, as has Frem Albrec and the archivist Wichella. Your away team has not yet been identified, but early reports suggest that they have illegally accessed a Zahl settlement and breached the security of one of our prison camps. Several of your officers have been in constant contact with the Rilnar leadership on Sormana. These are not the actions of a neutral party. These are the actions of an aggressor and we will not permit them to continue. Fall back or I will open fire."*

"If you open fire on us, we will defend ourselves," Chakotay said.

"So be it," Pilusch said, and closed the channel.

"Captain, four other Zahl vessels are now moving to intercept as well."

"Distance?"

"Two hundred to five hundred thousand kilometers. It will take them between ten and fifteen minutes to reach our position."

"We'll be in orbit by then," Chakotay said. "Shields?"

"Already at maximum, sir. Ready to absorb the impact of the mines," Aubrey replied.

At that moment, streaks of violet light shot forth from the *Tascara*, jolting the bridge officers without unseating them.

"Ensign Gwyn, evade what you can, but keep us on course to destroy the minefield," Chakotay ordered the helm.

"Aye, sir," Gwyn acknowledged.

Tascara's second weapons volley was more intense, but did not reduce *Voyager*'s shield strength perceptibly.

"Are they just trying to annoy us?" Paris asked. "Because those weapons don't have the power to put a dent in our shields. They have to know that already."

"Return fire, sir?" Aubrey asked.

"Not unless it becomes absolutely necessary," Chakotay replied.

Tascara's response was to alter course with a burst of impulse speed and maneuver directly between *Voyager* and the minefield. Chakotay could not deviate too far from his current course without recalculating the firing solutions Fife had so painstakingly constructed. Given the report they had received of the prison breach, Chakotay now had a much better understanding of the danger the away team was facing. He had absolutely no intention of keeping them waiting.

"Lieutenant Aubrey, target the *Tascara*'s shield generators and fire," Chakotay ordered.

Aubrey did so and while not seriously damaged, the *Tascara* veered off and a small explosion on their hull suggested the phasers had found their targets.

A thunderous boom rattled the deck despite the fact that the Zahl ship had yet to answer *Voyager*'s first shots.

"What was that?" Paris demanded.

"The *Golant* fired a torpedo at us," Aubrey replied. "Aft shields are down to eighty-two percent."

"Maintain maximum power to forward shields," Chakotay ordered. "Distance to minefield?"

"Two thousand kilometers and closing, sir," Gwyn reported.

"We need to pick up a thousand more without taking another shot," Chakotay said.

"Understood," Gwyn said. "Hang on."

The bridge crew had grown accustomed to taking their pilot at her word when she made such statements. Chakotay gripped his armrests, stabilizing his torso against the back of his chair. Gwyn punched the impulse engines briefly to maximum, evading the *Tascara*'s next shot in the process and bringing *Voyager* in range of their true target.

"We are in position to destroy the minefield, Captain," Aubrey reported.

"Fire at will," Chakotay ordered.

On that command, every phaser *Voyager* possessed along with a full spread of photon torpedoes flew forward, each targeting an individual mine on the outskirts of the field. Anticipating what was to come, Gwyn immediately dropped the nose of the ship and executed a dive meant to avoid the impact of the nearest mines.

Chakotay watched a series of small explosions erupt almost simultaneously. Fife's chain reaction, however, appeared to have failed. It was possible that the Rilnar and Zahl had not responded as anticipated to *Voyager*'s course and activated all of the mines.

Gwyn maintained her course keeping *Voyager* clear of the initial explosions but bringing the ship gently up in a slow curve meant to follow the trajectory of subsequent detonations.

The *Golant* and *Tascara* had broken off their attack momentarily in an effort to avoid impact from the mines *Voyager* had detonated.

"It didn't work," Paris said softly.

"Fife to the bridge. Our course corrections to avoid enemy fire rendered the first set of firing solutions obsolete. I have recalculated and am transmitting the revised data now. Maintain current course, fire when ready, and brace for impact," Fife ordered over the comm.

"Aubrey?" Chakotay asked.

"Firing, sir."

A second volley of torpedoes was launched, impacting a cluster of mines deeper into the field and much more closely arrayed.

This time it was like watching a starfield burst into being. Dozens of small explosions became hundreds, then thousands. Just as Fife had intended, Sormana's planetary defense system destroyed itself.

"Gwyn, get us in standard orbit," Chakotay ordered.

"With pleasure, sir," Gwyn said.

Voyager moved at low impulse into the detonated area, carefully timing its progress to avoid the wake of explosions that continued to erupt before them.

"*Tascara* is following us in," Aubrey reported.

"The other Zahl vessels are altering course to intercept, moving through the areas we just detonated," Lasren added.

"Maintain course and speed," Chakotay ordered.

A few more phaser exchanges forced the *Tascara* to break off. Chakotay was relieved Pilusch had accepted the futility of her efforts without forcing him to destroy her ship.

The other Zahl vessels were about to become a problem when Chakotay noted an unexpected movement of ships on the main viewscreen. More than a dozen Rilnar vessels had responded to the attack on their minefield by entering it at full impulse. They were forming a line between *Voyager* and Sormana and within the next few minutes Chakotay would be forced to fight his way through it or abandon his away team.

"Lasren, hail Rileez again," Chakotay ordered.

"No response," the ops officer reported.

"As soon as we're in range, target two or three of the closest ships simultaneously," Chakotay said.

"We can't take all twelve of them," Paris noted.

"We just need to get close enough to the planet to lock onto our team and transport them out. Once that's done we can do a quick jump to warp to extricate ourselves from this situation."

"Inside the planetary system?" Paris asked.

"I'm pretty sure that even at full impulse we'll be easy to pick off. The rest of the Zahl will have arrived by then. We're only going to get one shot at this."

Paris nodded. "Okay."

SORMANA

A number of things had changed in the minutes that had passed since Seven and Kim exited the building that housed the shield generator, regrouped with Tuvok, and made their way as carefully as possible back to the central edifice. The first was that the intensity of fighting around the north face where the cargo door was located had decreased. The remaining free prisoners had fled, using the other structures as cover and continued to engage the Zahl one-on-one. A number of dead and injured were strewn on the ground between the center of the citadel and the prison barracks.

The second was that the cargo door Kim and Seven had previously utilized had been sealed and several armed Zahl now stood at every entrance to the building. This might have frustrated someone less accustomed to unwinnable scenarios than Lieutenant Harry Kim. As it was, he simply scanned the area for another option and quickly located one. With a brisk gesture for Tuvok and Seven to follow, Kim led the trio toward the automated cargo vessels parked fifty meters from the one that still sat at the closed door. The nearest was already aflame, and everyone in the area was giving the others a wide berth. Kim targeted the vessel farthest from the flames and ushered the team into its empty hold. He then forced his way through the access doors to the main compartment and activated the vehicle. He had no time to program his course. He selected the manual operation mode.

"Secure yourselves as best you can and hold on," Kim ordered as he nudged the vehicle forward and brought it around, aiming it directly at the transport blocking their way to the building's cargo door. Most of the soldiers who saw the attack coming jumped out of the way. A few stalwart Zahl stood their ground and opened fire on the vehicle as it approached. Kim ignored them, accelerating to top speed, which wasn't as much as he'd have liked, and rammed the vehicle into the stationary transport, sending it careening backward into the cargo door, ripping it from its moorings.

The moment the shock of impact had dissipated Kim followed Tuvok and Seven out the rear doors. Both had raised their phasers and stunned the few Zahl now running toward them. Those who had guarded the door were in no position to put up a fight. Kim took the lead and Seven brought up the rear as he hurried into the storage room, shot the interior doors off their hinges, and entered the hallway leading to the nearest staircase accessing the roof.

The bodies that lay on the final stairs and roof landing alerted Kim to the reality that their plan might have just become more complicated. The shouting and intermittent weapons fire coming from the roof, beyond the now-open door, was more bad news. Tuvok settled himself in position to cover Kim, who placed his back to the door, peering as best he could through the opening to access the situation.

Roughly twenty prisoners and half that many Zahl were engaged in a fierce battle for control of the island's shield generator. From this vantage point, Kim had a clear view of the corner control room located directly across from the stairwell. Its metal door had been ripped from its hinges and was being used as cover by a trio of Rilnar prisoners. A single prisoner stood in the doorway, firing at anyone who approached. Beyond him, two more could be seen working furiously at the shield control panels.

Taking a deep breath, Kim poked his head around the door and noted the intermittent flashing of the force fields that protected the generator. Two other armed Rilnar prisoners were exchanging fire with the Zahl, but every other inmate with a gun was firing it at the shield generator.

It was good to know that within moments the island's shields would be coming down and should *Voyager* safely transit the minefield, they could rescue the away team. Kim's knowledge of the existence of the chroniton torpedoes stored in the bowels of this building made the thought of *no* shields less comforting. With the island completely unprotected, the planet and much of the system depended upon the ability of the Zahl to defend the island from a Rilnar attack.

The chaos that had descended upon the citadel in the last fifteen minutes told Kim all he needed to know about the likelihood of the Zahl's security skills and the odds that they were going to be able to protect the island for any significant length of time. A hiss, followed by an abrupt clap of thunder and slight tremor in the building beneath him turned Kim's eyes upward. The edge of the island's shields extended approximately a hundred meters above the citadel. Something had just impacted them from the air.

The *denzit* was attacking the citadel.

Retreating over the bodies and down the stairs, Kim crouched at the next landing beside Seven and Tuvok. "The good news is that the shields are about to come down. With any luck we'll be transported to safety in the next few minutes."

"The bad news is that those shields are going to stay down and it is highly unlikely that any of us will live long enough to make our rescue worthwhile, correct?" Tuvok asked.

"Yes," Kim replied.

Tuvok bowed his head briefly, then removed his combadge from beneath his Zahl jacket and tossed it to Kim. "When the shields fall, use the beacon to alert *Voyager* to your coordinates and transfer back to the ship."

"Where are you going?" Kim demanded.

"To save all of us from the *denzit*," Tuvok replied.

Before Kim or Seven could protest further, Tuvok hurried back down the stairs, disappearing into the darkness below.

"Denzit *Janeway*, Voyager *has destroyed the planetary defense field and is approaching Sormana's orbit. The Rilnar Colonial Command ships are preparing to destroy the Federation vessel. What are you orders?"* Limlesh asked.

The supreme commander of the Rilnar forces on Sormana could see the island Tuvok's team had infiltrated through her shuttle's forward ports. A dozen low-flying vessels were already coordinating an aerial attack on the island's shields. They were the strongest of any Zahl defensive shields she had seen on Sormana. It would likely take several runs to bring them down.

That they would be brought down was inevitable. The *denzit* still had no idea why Tuvok's team had targeted this island, but the fact that it had gone undetected by her forces for so long and was so well defended meant that its destruction was necessary. This might be the decisive blow in ending thousands of years of conflict.

She did not want to see Tuvok or his team suffer for having given her the opportunity to achieve her goals, despite the fact that they had never intended to do so.

Voyager's actions were another story. Captain Chakotay was clearly trying to rescue his people. That he had rendered

Sormana vulnerable to orbital attacks by the Zahl had probably not weighed heavily on his mind when he gave the order to destroy the minefield, but his choice would be devastating should the war continue after this day. She didn't blame him. In his position she knew she would have done the same.

As the Rilnar's leader, she could not allow his attack to go unanswered. As a former Starfleet officer and *Voyager*'s captain, however briefly, the thought of ordering her ship's destruction was unimaginable.

In the end, the choice was simpler than she had expected. After Tuvok had saved her life in the tunnels beneath Titha, she had sat a weary vigil by his bedside at Felstar wondering why he had risked so much on her behalf. She was not the woman he had served with in the Delta Quadrant. She was a traitor, a deserter. She had violated her oath and ran roughshod over the principles that had once bound them to each other. Still, he had come for her. He had suffered a life-threating injury meant for her. He had refused to abandon her, even before she had told him why she must secure a Rilnar victory on Sormana.

She could not fail to repay his devotion; not when the only casualty would be her pride.

She issued her orders to Limlesh, knowing he would not understand, certain he would disapprove, and not giving a damn. Then she opened a channel and hailed the commander of the Rilnar Colonial Fleet.

21

VESTA

Counselor Hugh Cambridge was the last person any would ever accuse of harboring romantic tendencies. His courtship of Seven had stalled and nearly faltered on numerous occasions as a result of his deficiencies. That did not make him completely insensitive to the reality that it was easy to abandon all reason when Eros called.

He had listened intently to Agent Dayne's story. He wanted to believe the Krenim man, if only for the *denzit*'s sake. If anyone in the multiverse deserved a little compassion, it was any version of Kathryn Janeway who had ever existed. It was nice to think that the *denzit* had found something worth living for, misguided as it might have been, in the midst of the wreckage that had become her life after she was captured.

But sincere as Dayne seemed, Cambridge couldn't square the man's words with his eyes. The words were unambiguous. The eyes were calculating, clearly measuring the impact of his story as he told it. Dayne was lying, but like all great liars, he was seasoning those lies generously with bits of truth. Separating the two was no easy matter.

Cambridge rose from the table to give himself a little distance from Dayne's emotional display. He began pacing a circuit around the other tables, conscious of the fact that the admiral and captain seemed somewhat disconcerted by his rudeness. Dayne hardly seemed to notice.

Crossing his arms at his chest the counselor said, "Temporal mechanics is not my area of expertise. *People* are. I'm intrigued by your story, Agent Dayne, but there are a few points where I'd like a little clarification."

"Please," Dayne offered, opening his hands in a gesture of patient acceptance.

"According to you, we are all now living in the timeline the admiral *created* when she confronted Annorax," Cambridge began.

"*Restored*," Dayne corrected him gently.

"My apologies, an important distinction, as it clearly indicates which was the aberration and which the appropriate one," Cambridge allowed. "But in this *restored* timeline, the Krenim, the Rilnar, and the Zahl all hold vast territories, enjoy great technological advancement—and apart from the people on Sormana—have learned to live with one another in peace."

"Yes," Dayne said.

"So even if the Zahl learned of the Year of Hell as we did, why would they want to change anything?"

"I beg your pardon?" Dayne asked.

"If the Zahl stumbled upon one of the same temporally shielded buoys we did, they would have had no reason to target Kathryn Janeway. We've heard the logs the captain recorded during her battles with Annorax and none of them so much as mention the Zahl or the Rilnar."

Dayne remained absolutely still, keeping his eyes fixed on Cambridge. "There's more to it than—" Dayne began.

The admiral cut him off. "There really isn't. One of two things must be true. The Zahl, whose only demonstrated proficiency with temporal technology seems to be stealing it, found and decrypted a temporally shielded message buoy from yet *another* timeline that actually referenced the Zahl and *Voyager* or . . ."

"Or the Krenim, who by your own admission learned about the Year of Hell a long time ago, created a buoy for the Zahl to find—one that changed the story just enough to make capturing Kathryn Janeway a priority for them," Farkas finished.

"Actually, there's a third and much more intriguing possibility," Cambridge said. "What if the Zahl had nothing to do with this? The first thing that happened to the *denzit* when she was captured was a period of interrogation and torture. I doubt seriously she was given names, ranks, and serial numbers when that process began. The Krenim are the only species in this quadrant that had a vested interest in Kathryn Janeway prior to the *denzit*'s arrival on Sormana. They could have captured her, and eventually realized that they had the *wrong* Kathryn Janeway. The Krenim then fabricated a Zahl conspiracy to convince the Rilnar to free her from her 'Zahl' captors and utilize her skills on Sormana. The Krenim's hands remain clean. Further seeds of suspicion and discord are sewn between the Rilnar and Zahl. After securing her absolute devotion by gaining her trust and her heart, Kathryn Janeway is sent to a place where she can never again do anything to harm the Krenim."

"It takes a lot of Rilnar and Zahl ships to patrol that blockade on Sormana," Farkas noted. "One wonders what those ships might do were they not otherwise occupied."

"Spend some time exploring Krenim space perhaps?" Cambridge suggested.

"At the very least," Farkas agreed. "You know, that's the only version of this story that actually makes sense to me."

Dayne had kept his eyes fixed on Cambridge throughout this discussion. When Farkas had finished, he lowered his head and began to study his hands. Finally, he rose from his chair and shook his head. "I can't tell you how many times Annorax warned us not to underestimate chaotic variables."

"*Chaotic variables?*" the admiral asked.

"You have to understand time as we do. You have to know its moods, its colors, its petty torments," Dayne said with a bitter smile that had lost all of its boyish charm.

"The first time *Voyager* was detected on any Krenim temporal survey, it was classified as an inert component, one that had no potential impact on our history. Ironically enough, Annorax made that determination personally using his earliest temporal scanners.

"Every time *my* agency scans the continuum, you, Admiral, and all Federation ships are classified quite differently. We call you *chaotic variables*. There is simply no way to predict what the outcome will be when you become involved. You are the only components currently designated as such."

After a long, thoughtful pause, Dayne finally admitted, "The Krenim Temporal Defense Agency *had* to know the reason why. Kathryn Janeway had to be captured and studied so that she could be properly classified."

"The Krenim captured her," Janeway said softly. "You wanted *me*," she continued through gritted teeth, "but you got *her*. She couldn't have begun to answer your questions, to account for her actions during the Year of Hell, but you tortured her anyway."

"Why didn't you just kill her?" Farkas asked.

"If you try to tell us again it was because you were in love with her, Agent Dayne, I'm going to escort you to the nearest airlock myself and push you out of it," Cambridge warned.

"To kill her would have produced more counter-indications than any other scenario," Dayne said. "We transported her to a stolen Zahl vessel. I helped the Rilnar 'retrieve' her, with the intention of ultimately placing her on Sormana, where her range of possible actions became limited to a finite set.

"Almost as soon as she was settled there, our calculations began to change. Her death began to appear with a shocking consistency across multiple timelines. We didn't understand why. We assumed it might have something to do with our actions. But it didn't matter. It seemed that time had decided to solve the Janeway problem permanently and for that my superiors were grateful."

"Until she came back to life?" Cambridge asked.

Dayne laughed half-heartedly. "Once that happened, my agency was forced to revise its position. It was determined that no further interference in the fate of Kathryn Janeway could be permitted. That changed a few weeks ago when this ship first ventured into Krenim space. Obviously, I didn't expect to find *you* here, Admiral," Dayne said pointedly, "but according to our most recent calculations—the ones that now include the interference of your fleet on Sormana—the entire planet and much of the space around it will be destroyed in the next few hours."

Dayne moved to stand directly across from the admiral, who rose to meet his eyes. "Congratulations, Admiral Janeway. You have once again managed to insert yourself into a situation that has nothing to do with you and by your actions have damned millions, if not more, to untimely death."

VOYAGER

Whenever *Voyager* was in a position where it was necessary to open fire on an alien vessel, Captain Chakotay stopped thinking about all of the different decisions he might have made that could have rendered this moment unnecessary. He focused on the only part that mattered, making sure his ship survived the engagement.

As *Voyager* approached the Rilnar picket line he was thinking about attack patterns. He didn't need to destroy every ship out there. He needed to punch a hole in their blockade. Even if he could seriously damage one or better yet, two of the ships in *Voyager's* path, the other ten would quickly close the gap. Once the away team was recovered, Gwyn was going to have to spend at least a minute plotting a point of orbital release that would allow the ship to go to warp and avoid colliding with both the Rilnar and the Zahl moving into the area of engagement.

That wasn't going to be easy, but Gwyn had extricated them from equally fraught scenarios. The captain knew that Tom's faith in Gwyn's piloting shills exceeded even his. When Commander Paris left his seat at Chakotay's left hand, moved to the conn, and began to speak softly to Gwyn, the captain wondered if he had finally asked too much of her. If Paris felt it necessary to personally direct her efforts over the next few minutes, their odds of safely executing this rescue were probably lower than he'd calculated.

"Lieutenant Aubrey, attack pattern beta six," Chakotay ordered.

"Aye, sir," Aubrey acknowledged.

Gwyn made a slight course correction in response to the chosen attack pattern. *Voyager* was about to fire on two Rilnar ships at once. Depending on the alien vessels' shield strength and weapon's systems, this might be enough to create the gap Chakotay required.

A few heartbeats passed in tense silence. The timing would be critical. *Voyager's* forward motion had already alerted the Rilnar vessels to Chakotay's intentions. If they broke formation or opened fire, an alternate attack pattern would be required.

"Steady as she goes, Ensign Gwyn," Chakotay ordered.

"Aye, Captain."

Chakotay was poised to give the order to open fire when the two ships in his sights altered their courses. They were breaking the line but moving toward *Voyager,* closing the distance between the ships while simultaneously eliminating *Voyager*'s ability to take them both out at once.

Chakotay always gave those he met in battle the benefit of the doubt. He assumed they were as smart as he was, if not smarter, and never dared hope that they would fail to anticipate his tactics. This was one time he wished he had overestimated the Rilnar. Then he remembered that they had Kathryn Janeway on their side. He should have known better than to hope for a tactical error.

"Helm, alter course heading—" Chakotay began.

Lieutenant Lasren quickly interjected, "Captain, Rileez is hailing us."

"On-screen."

"Hold your fire, Captain," Rileez said the moment his haggard face appeared before Chakotay. *"I have conferred with the* denzit *and she has made a personal request of our fleet that we permit your vessel to assume orbit and transport your away team to safety."*

Chakotay watched in great relief as half of the main viewscreen showed the rest of the Rilnar vessels following the lead of the first two, forming a corridor through which *Voyager* could pass on her way to orbit.

A new and terrifying thought struck the captain. *This could be a trap.* Even at high impulse, there would be several minutes ahead when should the Rilnar choose, they could destroy *Voyager.*

"Did the *denzit* happen to mention what changed her mind?" Chakotay asked as congenially as possible.

"The denzit *does not make a habit of explaining her orders, Captain. Although she is not technically part of our chain of command, we tend to defer to her wishes when they directly affect her engagements on Sormana. In this case, she indicated that she is about to destroy the location where your team is trapped. I can only assume that for her own reasons, she does not want their blood on her hands."*

"Thank you, Rileez," Chakotay said sincerely. "Please pass along my thanks to the *denzit*. I'm not sure the Zahl are going to be quite as accommodating," he added.

"You let us worry about them, Captain," Rileez replied.

"Understood. This will be over in a few minutes. We'll signal you when our transports are complete."

"Very good. End transmission," Rileez said.

"Helm, best possible speed to assume orbit," Chakotay ordered. "Aubrey, stand by to execute attack pattern delta four. Transporter room, signal the away team. Lasren, drop our shields as soon as the transporter room has a lock on the away team's signal."

Brisk acknowledgments followed these orders. His part done, Chakotay sat back, wondering if he had just caught an incredibly lucky break or fallen for one of the oldest tricks in the book.

Time would tell.

SORMANA

As Tuvok made his way toward the building's lower levels, he checked his tricorder as often as possible. He was watching for two things: confirmation that the shields surrounding the island had fallen and the safe evacuation of Lieutenant Kim and Seven.

He already knew where he was heading. Not far from the area where the chroniton torpedoes were stored was another large room where many of the building's power lines terminated. This was likely the command center of the entire citadel, and Tuvok hoped that it was also the secondary control station for the island's shields. Tuvok understood the Zahl's choice to place the shield generators and primary controls on the building's roof. Once they were operational, the island became invisible to most sensors. The only real threat was posed by a loss of control within the citadel, and if the attitude of the guards Tuvok had already encountered was any indication, no one had ever believed that to be a likely scenario.

Any critical system must have back-up generators and operational controls. If the Zahl had failed to institute this most basic of all tactical requirements, there was little Tuvok would be able to do to prevent catastrophe. Assuming they had, there was still time.

The chaos gripping the citadel was Tuvok's ally. He moved purposefully through the halls and stairways, keeping his head down. None of the few Zahl who ran past him, bothered to look up, let alone stop him.

He would blame himself should *Voyager* or the away team come to harm as a result of his choice to release the Rilnar prisoners to ease his escape. The *denzit* could not be blamed for targeting the island. It had been a calculated risk on the admiral's part to advise the *denzit* of her intention to send an away team to the surface at all. That she could not grasp the complementary nature of her goals and the away team's was also not her fault. The Prime Directive had tied everyone's hands.

The tension created by his fears for those he served with was difficult to subdue. When Tuvok considered how likely his own imminent death had become by his choice to infiltrate the Zahl command center, there was no fear.

Tuvok had faced death in the course of his career many times. Until this day, he had never welcomed it.

Had there been time, Tuvok might have paused to study this odd sensation more deeply. As it was, he increased his pace when he turned the corner and saw a row of six armed Zahl soldiers standing between him and the entrance to his target.

"Identify yourself," a rough voice demanded from the end of the hall.

Tuvok halted immediately and raised his hands in the universal signal of defenselessness. "I am Commander Tuvok of the Federation Starship *Titan*," he said, raising his voice and speaking slowly and clearly, as he might have to one of his children when they were very young. "I have come to speak with your commanding officer. It is imperative that you bring me to him or her. There is only one way to prevent this island's destruction. Assist me," Tuvok finished, giving his last words the unmistakable tone of an order.

A massive concussive blast shuddered through the floor and walls. The harsh orange lighting flickered briefly before resolving at a dimmer setting. A programmed ping from his tricorder indicated that the shields were failing. The next several minutes would determine the fate of every living being on and anywhere near Sormana.

VOYAGER

The Rilnar vessels kept their word. *Voyager* cleared their gauntlet and assumed orbit without incident.

"Lasren, report," Chakotay ordered once the image on the main viewscreen showed Sormana's browns and blues veiled by thick gray wisps of clouds.

"I've located the beacon," Lasren replied. "I'm reading three combadges, but only two life-forms: Kim's and Seven's."

Chakotay forced his concerns for Tuvok into the back of his mind. "Coordinate with the transporter room and get them out," he ordered.

"There's an energy field surrounding their location with intermittent intensity readings. Twelve surface vessels are bombing the field."

"That would be the Rilnar," Paris noted.

"Can you estimate how long the field will hold?" Chakotay asked.

"Not long," Lasren reported, "but if the field strength falls low enough, we might be able to retrieve them."

Chakotay waited. Seconds felt like hours.

"Lieutenant Kim and Seven are safely aboard," Lasren said. A collective sigh of relief washed through the bridge.

"Bring them to the bridge right away, site-to-site transport authorized. Scan for Tuvok's bio-signs. Conn, let me know when you have our escape route," Chakotay ordered as the air before his chair began to shimmer, resolving within seconds into the forms of Kim and Seven.

Chakotay rose immediately. "Where's Tuvok?"

Kim opened his hand and offered Tuvok's combadge to his captain. "He stayed behind."

This report didn't surprise the captain. Tuvok's demeanor since they had first met on *Titan* had been off. Chakotay had wondered, along with Kathryn, how much sympathy the *denzit*'s predicament might have aroused in Tuvok. But part of him refused to accept the possibility that Tuvok could betray *Voyager*.

"We located the Zahl's temporal transporters," Kim continued. "They're also storing enough chroniton torpedoes down there to destroy the entire planet and then some. I think Tuvok is going to try and reach the *denzit* from the surface and get her to call off her attack."

"Are the shields already down?" Chakotay asked.

"They're fluctuating. She's getting some assistance from a large group of recently freed Rilnar prisoners who were in the process of destroying the shield generator when we were transported out," Seven advised him.

"Helm, belay my last order," Chakotay said. "Lasren, get me Rileez."

"Aye, sir."

Lasren shifted the image on the main viewscreen from the planet to the field of battle behind the ship. The Rilnar vessels were no longer in formation. A dozen Zahl ships had entered the fray and both sides were now engaged in a fierce firefight.

"Unable to raise the *Golant*," Lasren reported. "She's been destroyed."

"Open a channel to all Rilnar vessels. I just need to talk to one of them," Chakotay said, conscious of the stress in his voice.

"No response, sir," Lasren said.

"Damn it," Chakotay murmured. "Begin searching all frequencies for the Rilnar's surface communications signals. If Tuvok doesn't make it, someone needs to explain to the *denzit* that she's about to kill us all."

"Do those surface vessels have shields?" Paris asked.

"Nothing like ours," Lasren replied.

"Could you get a stable transporter signal through them?" Chakotay demanded, realizing what his first officer was thinking.

"Yes, sir."

"Is the *denzit* on board one of them?"

Lasren paused briefly, running the necessary scans. Finally he confirmed, "She is, Captain."

"I'll go," Paris said. "I can make her listen."

Chakotay shook his head. "No. The bridge is yours, Commander Paris. As soon as I've gone, take *Voyager* out of orbit on the far side of the planet. Do not under any circumstances get in the middle of the Rilnar and Zahl. Lasren, forward the coordinates of the *denzit*'s ship to the transporter room."

Chakotay left the bridge.

22

VESTA

Admiral Janeway considered Agent Dayne's latest revelation as dispassionately as possible. For the thousandth time, she thanked her lucky stars for Counselor Rori Austen. Had Janeway been forced to meet this moment without the benefit of the wisdom she had gained from their counseling sessions, the crushing weight of the imminent devastation Dayne had described might have paralyzed her. Instead, her first thought was not, *What have I done?* It was, *How do I fix this?*

Dayne had already squandered her trust, sympathy, and respect. Every move he made was part of a calculation. Even if the Krenim were not engaged in the alteration of time on a scale as vast as Annorax, Janeway firmly believed that this rotten apple had not fallen very far at all from that tree.

"Should I assume that the destruction of Sormana does not trouble you or the rest of the Krenim?" Janeway asked.

Dayne shrugged. "It's always unfortunate to witness a loss of this magnitude, but all of our agents among the Rilnar and Zahl were recalled several days ago. The Krenim won't be the ones to suffer from your latest misstep."

"You intended for this to happen," Farkas said, coming to her feet and moving to stand beside Cambridge. "You alone of all the species in this sector have the ability to look forward in time. You might not be able to read the future exactly, but your calculations permit you to determine outcomes within some degree of probability."

"That's true."

"So whatever is about to happen will likely cripple the Rilnar and Zahl colonial fleets as well as destroying Sormana," Cambridge said.

"And *Voyager*," Dayne added.

"It sounds to me like the Krenim Temporal Defense Agency is dedicated to preserving the events of the prime timeline so long as those events are advantageous to the Krenim," Janeway said.

"Is your Federation really so different?"

Janeway sighed. It was probably too much to ask that the Krenim should have developed any real understanding of Federation values, despite how much time they must have spent studying her representative in the Delta Quadrant. Turning to her officers, she asked, "Why tell us about it?"

Both considered the question.

"It's not as if he has the upper hand here," Farkas said. "He's on our ship. *Vesta* could destroy his with one shot. Maybe he's concerned about getting back to his people in one piece and thinks this will distract us. But given his track record, I'm not sure I believe what he's telling us about this threat."

"Either way, he's leaving us no choice but to return to Sormana immediately to confirm his story, which we could do in minutes using our slipstream drive," Cambridge noted.

"If we go back to Sormana now, we're taking him with us," Farkas said. "I'd hate for him to miss the resolution of all this, wouldn't you, especially if that includes our destruction upon arrival?"

Janeway turned back to Dayne and squared her shoulders. "Your move, Agent Dayne."

In response, Dayne lifted his left hand with the palm facing up and with the forefinger of his right, tapped a small device embedded in his wrist.

"Bridge to Captain Farkas."

"Go ahead, Commander Roach."

"Six Krenim vessels have just arrived. They dropped out of warp a few thousand kilometers from our present position. Their shields are raised and their weapons are charged. We're surrounded, Captain."

"Thank you, Malcolm. Stand by," Farkas ordered, closing the channel.

"I'm not going with you, Admiral," Dayne said. "As soon as your shields are brought down, I'll be transported to safety before your ship is destroyed."

"I guess we're done talking," Janeway said with a shrug. "Whatever I did to your people it clearly wasn't the restoration of a timeline in which the Krenim are masters of a vast Imperium enjoying peace and prosperity. Once you learned I was the one who beat you, the Krenim captured a woman you thought was me. You tortured her. You warped her loyalties. You turned her into your pawn. And now, she is about to die. *Again.* I guess all that's left is to make *me* suffer as you believe I made the Krenim suffer."

"I wasn't lying about the debt of gratitude we owe you, Admiral," Dayne said. "We've run millions of calculations based upon your recovered logs. By the time you destroyed Annorax's ship, the alterations he had made to the timeline were so massive, the number of counter-indications to our future survival were staggering. But it has taken a long time and a few extremely precise incursions to create the reality we now enjoy.

"You and the *denzit* are the only individuals we can isolate as potentially capable of reversing our work. We cannot allow that."

"He almost sounds sorry, doesn't he?" Cambridge mused.

Farkas lifted her hand to her combadge. "Farkas to the bridge. Red alert. Bring the slipstream drive online and plot a return course to Sormana. All shields to maximum, arm all phasers and torpedoes. Advise sickbay to stand by to receive heavy casualties. We're going to have to fight our way out of here. Commander Roach, await my order to open fire."

"Aye, Captain."

"Is this really what you want, Dayne?" Janeway asked. "You know us well enough by now to understand that we don't go quietly. We won't be the only ones to take casualties in this engagement. We've been here before, the Krenim and I. We fought this war once to the last man and against all odds, this chaotic variable took you down. You really want to try your luck again?"

Dayne blinked.

"Tell me," Janeway said, "what do you want? What can I offer you in exchange for taking a step back? Despite our tortured history, I don't have any vested interest in harming your people. We're here to learn from and to better understand those with whom we share this galaxy. If all you really need is to see me die, maybe you're about to get your wish. But *maybe not*. Tell me that there is another solution. Tell me the Krenim haven't mastered space and time and concluded that the best way to secure their future is by learning nothing from their past."

Dayne blinked again. "Why are you still alive?"

Janeway smiled faintly. *There it is.*

"The odds against the *denzit's* survival were too low to bother calculating. But even still, medical miracles happen from time to time. *Your* survival is impossible."

"*That's* the true nature of a chaotic variable, isn't it? You can't predict us because you lack sufficient data about our capabilities. Some of them you misunderstand because you ascribe malice to our motives that does not exist. The rest is simply a lack of information. For all your advances, you haven't traveled as far as the Federation has. You haven't seen the things we've seen. You haven't learned what we've learned. No wonder we scare the hell out of you.

"I'm willing to end your ignorance, but at a price. Order your ships to retreat and agree to help me prevent Sormana's destruction."

"Tell me," Dayne said. "If the intelligence you provide is helpful, I will consider your request."

"No. Stand down. Help me. Then you get your answers."

"This is the problem with all those lies, Agent Dayne," Cambridge said. "Now we have trust issues."

Dayne inhaled deeply and released his breath slowly.

"You would have to accompany me to the *Truon*, Admiral. You would have to come alone."

"Not a chance," Farkas insisted as Cambridge laughed aloud at the suggestion.

"Very well. *One* other officer may accompany you."

"Where your ship goes, mine will follow," Farkas said.

"Where we are going, you cannot follow," Dayne said.

SORMANA

Rough hands pushed Tuvok through the doorway to the citadel's central command room. The end of a rifle pressed firmly into the small of his back.

"Servitor Silbrit," the rifle's owner shouted.

The room was filled beyond capacity. Those not busy at the dozen terminals and control panels the room held were standing along the walls, studying a large screen at the far end that tracked the aerial assault now in progress. The air was stale and thick with sweat.

"Silence," one of the officers at the center of the stations closest to the screen shouted. Another loud blast shook the room, dropping a mist of fine silt from the roof.

"Servitor Silbrit, you must contact *Denzit* Janeway at once and allow me to speak with her," Tuvok said over the din. Abruptly, the silence that had just been requested descended over the room.

The officer who had given the order turned toward Tuvok. His haggard mien and grim, determined eyes spoke of countless battles. *None as desperate as this one.* He studied Tuvok intently for a few seconds, then said, "You're not Zahl."

"No. I am a friend of the *denzit*'s. She is not aware of the munitions currently housed in this facility. She does not understand that by destroying this installation, she will also destroy the planet. If you tell her the truth, she will never believe you. If *I* tell her, she will break off her attack."

"Nempir, how soon can you get that shield stabilized?" Silbrit demanded.

A series of three consecutive detonations responded for the unfortunate Nempir.

"You are wasting time you do not possess," Tuvok assured Silbrit. "Contact the *denzit*."

The Zahl commander appeared to weigh his pride versus his survival. His shoulders fell visibly as he said, "Bref, see if you can hail the lead Rilnar attack ship."

The only sound that broke the silence was that of continued explosions on the surface above. Each successive blast was louder than the last.

Finally Bref reported, "The *denzit* is not responding, sir."

Silbrit turned back to Tuvok. "Any other suggestions, friend of the *denzit*?"

Tuvok looked down at the Zahl uniform jacket the *denzit* had given him. The buttons flashed. She knew he was still in the citadel. Clearly, that did not trouble her. Or maybe it did, a little. *Just not enough.*

Tuvok shook his head.

"Kill him," Silbrit ordered.

"Squads six through ten, attack pattern R-twenty," the *denzit* ordered grimly. The shields around the island were falling faster than she had predicted. She was moments away from the end of her war.

Glancing at her tactical display, she noted that two of her

tracer signals had been deactivated. The small tracking devices were designed to shut down in the absence of bio-signs. Either Lieutenant Kim and Seven had abandoned their disguises or they had just been added to a long list of casualties on Sormana. Tuvok's signal was still active. He was alive down there.

Come on, Captain Chakotay, she thought. She'd given him clearance to enter orbit and rescue his team. *What the hell was taking him so long?* Her ground-based transporters couldn't penetrate even the weakened energy shield around the island, but *Voyager*'s should have been able to. She wouldn't hold her squad back once the shields came down for Tuvok's sake. She had always hated "needs of the many" scenarios, but in this case she had no choice but to accept it. Tuvok deserved better than to die like this. But his life was Chakotay's to save, not hers.

"*Denzit*, the Zahl installation is hailing us."

"Which servitor?"

"Silbrit."

Silbrit had been a fierce and bloodthirsty warrior in his day, but that day had passed. He had disappeared from the Zahl's ranks two years prior. She assumed he had died. Apparently, he had been transferred to a much more critical post. She knew him only by reputation. In his career he had personally been responsible for the deaths of at least ten thousand Rilnar officers and citizens. She understood why he might want to speak with her now.

He didn't deserve the courtesy.

"I have nothing to say to the servitor."

"Understood, *Denzit*."

A sudden sound of exclamations followed by alarmed shouts forced the *denzit* to turn from her panels toward the rear of her attack shuttle. "Don't move," one of her auxiliary tactical officers ordered.

Captain Chakotay lifted his hands in response.

"I am unarmed," he said evenly.

His composure in the face of four weapons now aimed directly at him by her shuttle's crew was impressive. His timing was inexplicable.

"Lower your weapons immediately," the *denzit* ordered. "Attend to your stations." Rising, she stepped toward Chakotay and pulled him toward the rearmost compartment of the shuttle. It wasn't private, but it was the best she could do under the circumstances. "Why are you here?"

"Kim and Seven are aboard *Voyager*. They told me that the Zahl are storing enough chroniton torpedoes on that island to destroy the entire sector. You have to call off this attack."

"I can't . . ." she began automatically, but paused as this realization sank in. "Did your sensors confirm this?"

Chakotay shook his head. "I don't need confirmation. I have the word of two of my officers."

"This war could end in the next few minutes," the *denzit* argued.

"Oh, it's going to," Chakotay assured her. "Did you plan on living long enough to celebrate your victory? Call off this attack."

"Where is Tuvok?"

"He stayed behind. He was trying to reach you from the Zahl's command center."

The *denzit* turned back toward her crew. "Hail Silbrit," she ordered.

A few seconds later, the Zahl servitor's voice crackled throughout her ship.

"*Denzit Janeway, you must stand down. If you destroy this island, you will kill us all.*"

"So I've been told. Where is Commander Tuvok?"

"*Your friend?*"

"If you try to turn this into a hostage negotiation, Silbrit, I'm going to see you in hell."

"*I just ordered his execution.*"

"Do that, and you're next. I'm coming down there to confirm the intelligence I have just received regarding a store of incredibly dangerous weapons you're holding. Drop what little is left of your shields and await my arrival."

"We're under attack from within our installation. I cannot assure your safety."

"I'm willing to take my chances. Are you?"

"I'll admit it. I've always wanted to meet you."

"Now seems like as good a time as any."

"Our shields will be down momentarily. Keep your officers on a short leash and I will do the same."

"End transmission," the *denzit* ordered. "Open a channel to all squads. Cease fire immediately and hold until further orders are given. Confirmation code *Denzit* Janeway Delta three four seven six two Omega."

"Your orders transmitted and received," her comm officer replied.

Turning to Chakotay, she said, "Go back to *Voyager*."

"No."

The *denzit* sighed. "This isn't your fight."

"It's not yours either," Chakotay reminded her.

VESTA

Farkas hurried onto her bridge just in time to see Dayne's ship vanish from the main viewscreen. The six Krenim warships that had surrounded the *Vesta* during their negotiations had departed shortly before Admiral Janeway and Counselor Cambridge had transported with the Krenim agent to the *Truon*.

"Report," Farkas ordered.

"Prior to its disappearance, the *Truon* raised her temporal shields. As soon as it did, we lost our sensor lock. I can't tell you where or when they went, Captain," Lieutenant Kar said.

"Farkas to engineering. Phinn."

"Yes, Captain?"

"What did you learn about the *Truon* in the half hour that we had a stable sensor lock?"

"She's amazing, Captain."

"I wasn't actually looking for a review."

"Her engines don't just alter the configuration of space and sub-space. She initially emerged from an extradimensional, variable-plane stabilization fold."

"Long story short, that ship can move through space and time at will, right?"

"Yes, Captain."

Farkas nodded. Despite Dayne's cryptic warning, she was pretty sure she knew *where* his ship was headed. The problem was *when*.

"We're returning to Sormana, Bryce. Are you and Icheb ready to bring our new temporal shields online?"

"Yes, Captain, but they aren't compatible with our slipstream assembly."

"So we can't operate both at once?"

"No, Captain."

"Here's how we're going to do this," Farkas said.

SORMANA

The transport coordinates Silbrit had provided deposited the *denzit* and Chakotay in an office adjacent to the citadel's control room. The servitor was waiting for them. Tuvok stood beside him, unperturbed by the tension gripping everyone else.

"Welcome to Rahalla, *Denzit* Janeway," Silbrit said once they had materialized. Nodding toward Chakotay he continued, "My, but you seem to have made a lot of new friends lately."

"I am Captain Chakotay of the Federation *Starship Voyager*," Chakotay replied, extending his hand to the Zahl leader.

Silbrit glanced toward Tuvok as he accepted Chakotay's hand. "This man is one of yours, isn't he? Has your Federation entered into an alliance with the *denzit*'s forces on Sormana?"

"No," Chakotay replied.

"Before I became *denzit*, I was a Starfleet officer. Chakotay's ship came here to retrieve me."

The servitor appeared to warm to the idea. "If you're planning to return to your own people, *Denzit*, you'll get no argument from me."

"I refused their offer, Servitor. I have no intention of leaving Sormana until this war is won."

"If you're not here to help her, why did your people attack Rahalla?" Silbrit demanded of Chakotay.

"When the *denzit* refused to leave Sormana, my fleet began to investigate the conflict. We wanted to understand why two species as advanced as the Rilnar and the Zahl were incapable of ending thousands of years of warfare over a tactically insignificant planet. We learned a great many things, among them, that a Zahl scientist named Rahalla claimed to have discovered chroniton particles on this planet and that the Zahl are reinforcing their swiftly dwindling forces on Sormana using individuals taken from alternate timelines."

The *denzit* shot Chakotay a look of utter astonishment as he continued. "Despite Starfleet's strict noninterference policy, we understand the devastating impact of temporal manipulation. We came here to confirm the intelligence we had gathered and hopefully to convince you that whatever other challenges your people face on the road to peace, further temporal corruption could destabilize anything you might accomplish."

"Rahalla was a madman," the *denzit* said. "No reputable Rilnar scientist gives credence to his supposed discoveries."

"Rahalla was a genius, *Denzit*," Silbrit replied. "We named this place for him when we discovered it a hundred years ago. Among other remarkable features, this *tactically insignificant planet* is home to the only naturally occurring stable chroniton fields the Zahl have ever discovered. In truth, we might have abandoned Sormana long ago, were it not for our determination never to allow this technology to fall into Rilnar hands."

"There's more than naturally occurring chroniton fields on Sormana now, isn't there, Servitor?" Chakotay asked.

Silbrit nodded. "I don't suppose that if I simply tell you, you'll believe me?"

"Not a chance," the *denzit* replied.

"This way."

A small lift carried Silbrit, Tuvok, Chakotay, and the *denzit* to the lower levels of the building. A few minutes later, all of them stared in wondrous horror at the store of chroniton torpedoes the Zahl had amassed.

"You see?" Chakotay asked, once the *denzit* had absorbed the scope of the crisis.

"Where did these come from?" she demanded of Silbrit.

"I won't tell you where we got the specs," Silbrit replied. "But they were constructed here."

"Why?"

"We're going to need them."

"Why?"

"When we succeed in driving the Rilnar from Sormana, we will still have to defend her."

"From whom?" the *denzit* demanded.

"The Krenim?" Chakotay ventured.

Silbrit nodded. "If you'd seen what I have, you'd understand," he suggested to the *denzit*.

"I'd like to see what you've seen," Chakotay said. "I think if you showed the *denzit* as well, it would help a great deal."

Silbrit started to reply but was cut off by the sound of a detonation on the surface above them. The catwalk on which the group stood swayed and creaked as the impact settled. Silbrit shouted into a small, handheld communicator. "Bref, report!"

"The Rilnar assault has resumed, sir. Shields are at eight percent and falling."

Silbrit turned to the *denzit*. He didn't seem surprised by this development, but was clearly infuriated. "This is what I get for trusting you."

The *denzit* activated her communicator. "Cease fire at once," she shouted. "I gave no order to resume the attack."

"I gave the order," a cold male voice replied.

"Limlesh?" the *denzit* asked, stunned.

"From the moment you began to welcome your former comrades to Sormana, I worried that your loyalties might change. I didn't

want to believe it, but when you chose to sue for peace rather than destroy the Zahl's greatest tactical asset on Sormana, I knew you could no longer be trusted to lead us. You are relieved, Kathryn Janeway. I am assuming command of our forces effective immediately. Denzit Limlesh out."

Three more blasts struck the building. Everyone held tight to the railing as they sought out solid ground. Silbrit directed them to a nearby ladder that led to the level below. Chakotay brought up the rear as the group descended. His feet had just touched terra firma when a terrified voice crackled over the building's loudspeakers.

"Shields are down. Repeat, shields are down. All remaining forces, evacuate Rahalla."

What happened next seemed to occur in slow motion. The ceiling high above the level where Chakotay stood cracked and began to fall. The massive blast of the bomb that had caused this destruction echoed through the chamber a fraction of a second later.

There was nowhere to run.

23

VOYAGER

Commander Tom Paris knew that *Voyager* should already have been well on her way out of the system by now. The captain's orders had been perfectly clear.

But *Voyager* was his now, and it was his intention to make sure that *all* of his family, the captain and Tuvok included, survived what now seemed like the inevitable destruction of Sormana.

"We're running out of time, Tom," Lieutenant Kim whispered from the first officer's chair to his left.

Seven stood behind Lieutenant Devi Patel at the science

officer's position on the bridge and reported, "The island's shields have fallen."

"Did the Rilnar finally destroy them?" Kim asked.

"No. The Zahl appear to have deactivated them."

"Why the hell—?" Kim began.

"Chakotay and the *denzit* have transported to the island," Patel reported before Seven had the chance.

Paris sighed, relieved. "He did it. They're talking. It's going to be all right."

"You say that like you know what the *denzit* will do," Kim argued. "You don't. She looks like our admiral, but that's where any similarity ends."

"I know," Paris agreed. "But I also know what Chakotay and Tuvok can do when they set their mind to it. Hold our position, Gwyn."

"Holding, sir."

"The Rilnar shuttles have ceased their aerial assault," Lasren said.

"Aubrey, how are the Rilnar and Zahl colonial vessels doing?"

"The Rilnar have lost six vessels. The Zahl have lost eight. Long-range sensors show reinforcements on both sides approaching."

"Are any of them paying any attention to us?"

"No, sir."

"As long as that holds true, we're staying. Get transporter locks on Chakotay, Tuvok, and the *denzit*. Be ready to pull them out on my order."

"Acknowledged," Lasren said.

Kim brushed the sweat from his forehead with the sleeve of his Zahl uniform. Several minutes later Seven said, "Commander Paris, the Rilnar have resumed their attack on the island."

Paris rose from his seat. "Why?"

"Doesn't matter. We have to go, *now*," Kim insisted.

Paris clenched his jaw in frustration. "Helm, execute orbital release and take us to warp six."

"Aye, sir."

KRENIM TEMPORAL DEFENSE AGENCY VESSEL *TRUON*

There was only one seat on the *Truon*'s bridge. Her captain, Agent Dayne, occupied it for the few minutes it took to enter navigational instructions into his ship's computer and engage the engines. Admiral Janeway and Counselor Cambridge wandered about the small space examining the displays. Even had they been able to read the Krenim language, there was no way they could have understood the significance or purpose of the technology they beheld.

Dayne had a feeling both of them got the general idea.

"How do we do this, Agent Dayne?" the admiral asked once they were under way.

"I will send both of you to Sormana. You will arrive in time to attempt to mitigate the disaster that is about to occur. If you fail, the counselor will die, along with everyone else on the planet and within a few trillion kilometers.

"Once you have succeeded, or failed, *you*, Admiral Janeway, will return to this ship to fulfill your end of our agreement."

Dayne rose from his seat and crossed to a small storage cabinet embedded in the rear bulkhead of the bridge between the causality calculators and the temporal conversion matrix. After entering his security clearance codes, Dayne removed several small devices attached to thin, black bands. He then offered them to Janeway and Cambridge.

"Once you depart this ship you will be vulnerable to the same laws of space and time as everyone else not protected by the *Truon*'s temporal stabilization field. These are personal temporal synchronization disruptors. They are quite safe. Our field agents use them regularly to study unstable timelines."

"So these were designed purely for research purposes?" Cambridge asked wryly.

Dayne was not amused.

"I only have six. Choose those you share them with wisely. Everyone who wears one of these will remember everything that happens, despite any alterations your actions may cause to the timeline once I restore the normal flow at the point of incursion."

"You're not coming with us?" Janeway asked.

"I have to stay here and maintain the integrity of the temporal field."

"You understand that I have to tell the *denzit* about you and the impact the Krenim have had on this region."

"Nothing you tell anyone now will likely change the course of history. Should your actions produce significant counter-indications, we know how to deal with those as well."

"Agent Dayne, we're not going to allow you to . . ." Janeway began, but trailed off as the image on the viewscreen before Dayne's chair stabilized. A battle raged around Sormana. Dozens of Rilnar and Zahl vessels were engaged in a massive conflict. Huge chunks of wreckage suggested at least a few ships had already been destroyed.

"Is *this* what we have to prevent?" Cambridge asked dubiously.

"No," Dayne replied. "*This* is nothing. Activate your synch disruptors and prepare for transport."

Janeway and Cambridge did as they had been instructed.

"Initiating temporal incursion."

Just before the *Truon*'s transporter took hold of her, Janeway was certain she had seen the image on the viewscreen freeze.

SORMANA

The first time Admiral Kathryn Janeway visited Sormana, she wondered if the Rilnar's transporters had malfunctioned. *This time*, it was reality she no longer trusted.

The admiral and Cambridge materialized in what appeared to be a large cavern bathed in orange light. The stillness, the silence, the sense of motion suspended was incredibly disorienting.

The admiral's eyes were immediately drawn to the motes of dust before her. The air was thick with them. She kept waiting for them to move, for gravity to do its job. Instead they hung motionless around her.

Looking up, she saw their source. Forty meters above her head, the ceiling of the cavern had begun to collapse. That probably had something to do with the explosion that was frozen in time. Still flames licked rock, transforming it to a liquid state in some places. It was extraordinary to witness without technological assistance a moment the naked eye could never see.

Metal catwalks that ran along the walls ten meters above were in the process of collapsing. Several people hung in midair, one only a few centimeters from the ground, his face a mass of burning flesh. Two others higher up wore suits of fire.

In the far corner, a group of three men and one woman crouched, their hands raised automatically to shield them from the tons of rock that were about to descend upon them. "Chakotay," Janeway said softly. Tuvok was beside him, along with the *denzit* and a Zahl male the admiral did not know.

Counselor Cambridge's attention was already focused on what would have been the area's most fascinating feature, were it not for everything else there was to see. Four doorways stood on raised platforms above swirling pools of orange liquid. A wave of dizziness flowed over the admiral at the sight of the churning fluid until she realized what she *had* to be seeing. *Rahalla's chroniton pools.* Cambridge was bending low to examine one of them more closely.

"Careful," she ordered.

"What is this?" Cambridge asked reverently.

"Chroniton particles. It looks like we've found the source of the Zahl's reinforcements."

"These are some sort of doorways through time?"

"I'd hate to confirm that without a little more data, but my gut says yes."

Cambridge stood up and stared in wonder. "This is . . . we'll . . . it's just . . ."

"Unnerving?" Janeway suggested.

"Fantastic," Cambridge said. "While I still deplore the

Krenim's tactics, it's impossible to experience this without being awed by the power of it."

"Focus, Counselor."

"Right, sorry."

"With me."

On unsteady legs, Janeway led Cambridge toward the corner where Chakotay crouched, suspended in time.

"How did they get here?" Cambridge asked.

"Time to find out."

They moved to affix the temporal synch disruptors Dayne had given them to each member of the group. As soon as the technology was secured around the arms of an individual, they immediately came to life, continuing the motion they had begun before Dayne's temporal incursion.

After assuring each of them that they were fine, Janeway gave them a few moments to take in their surroundings.

The *denzit* was the first to speak. "I'm guessing this isn't heaven."

This brought an incongruous chuckle from Chakotay, who seemed to be struck by the same sense of marvel as the counselor.

"No," Admiral Janeway said.

"Then what is it?" the Zahl officer demanded.

"I don't think I've had the pleasure of making your acquaintance, sir," the admiral said, stepping toward him. "I'm Admiral Kathryn Janeway, commander of the Federation fleet, engaged in a long-term exploratory mission in the Delta Quadrant."

The Zahl officer looked at the admiral, then at the *denzit*, then back at the admiral. "Oh hell, there are two of you?"

This brought a smile to the admiral's lips. "Is that really so shocking, sir? Am I right in assuming that you have been bringing reinforcements to this planet via those temporal portals over there?"

"Yes, but never duplicates," he replied.

"I'm sorry, I didn't catch your name."

"Servitor Hav Silbrit. I command the Zahl forces at Rahalla."

"Rahalla?" Cambridge asked, delighted.

"I wish we could have met under different circumstances, Servitor Silbrit."

"Admiral," Tuvok said, stepping forward. "Can you explain what it is that we are all experiencing?"

"This is a temporal incursion. Yesterday, I took the *Vesta* to make contact with the Krenim. I learned a number of things relevant to this moment in time, among them the fact that this planet and a great deal of surrounding space was about to be destroyed. I negotiated an agreement with the Krenim that included the possibility of preventing this disaster and was sent here by them to attempt to do so."

"And how, exactly, do you plan to do that?" Silbrit demanded. "If the Krenim have stopped the normal flow of time, the moment this incursion ends and time's passage resumes, we're all dead. Are you certain the Krenim intended for you to survive this mercy mission?"

"I think so," the admiral replied. "I possess information they believe to be critical. I have withheld it from them, pending the outcome of our discussions."

"What happens when the conversation is over?" Chakotay asked.

"One step at a time," the admiral said. Turning to Silbrit she asked, "Does your position within the Zahl forces on Sormana give you the ability to enter into peace negotiations with the Rilnar's supreme commander?"

"It does."

"Wonderful."

"This isn't a negotiation," the *denzit* interjected. "He'll say anything right now to save himself and his men, but he'll never abide by it if we all somehow miraculously survive this."

"Not to split hairs, *Denzit*, but unless I misunderstood your man up there, you're no longer in charge of the Rilnar."

"Surely a minor point at such a moment," Cambridge said. "Obviously a thousand hours of mind-numbing diplomatic meetings will have to follow this day's events. The only thing we must acquire is both of *your* commitments to counsel everyone on your side to end this futile war. Unless of course either of you look at *this*"—he opened his arms as if to embrace the room—"and call it victory. Whatever led you to this moment, surely you can agree that the loss of every life on the planet and the thousands more on the ships above you who have been manning the blockade cannot be considered an acceptable outcome."

"How exactly did we get to this point?" Janeway asked.

In bits and pieces, each of them told their tale. Tuvok explained the away team's discoveries. The *denzit* admitted to placing tracking devices on the team, following them to the island, and instigating the aerial attack. Chakotay described his efforts and the *denzit*'s assistance in saving his away team. Silbrit confirmed his willingness to attempt to negotiate some sort of cease-fire, given his knowledge of the stored chroniton torpedoes and the scale of destruction that would occur should the *denzit*'s attack succeed.

"You're saying you ordered the Rilnar attack to end *before* you came down here?" Cambridge asked of the *denzit*, glancing up at the still firestorm above.

"One of my subordinate officers staged a little coup," the *denzit* replied. "He questions my loyalties."

"Okay," Janeway said, satisfied. "Obviously this is the chain of events we were sent to disrupt. The question is how can we possibly intercede now?"

"This looks pretty final to me, Admiral," Cambridge noted.

"But we wouldn't have arrived at this precise moment unless it was critical," Janeway argued.

"Batibeh," Cambridge said softly.

"What?" Silbrit asked.

"Just like Captain Farkas said. It would happen again because it inevitably does. Someone goes too far."

"Counselor, I don't see—" Chakotay began.

"If we had come at any earlier moment, would either of you have believed that you would end up here?" Cambridge asked of the *denzit* and Silbrit. "Of course not. You've all been fighting this war for so long, you've lost sight of the fact that *this* was the most probable outcome of your conflict. You wouldn't even admit to yourselves that you had driven one another into corners so small that mutual annihilation was the only endgame. You lied to yourselves, believing you could end this war on terms acceptable to your side. But you can't. Nothing short of a moment like this would have ever forced you to confront your lunacy."

"While I might have phrased that a little more delicately, your point is well taken," Janeway said. "If I told you I knew your future, if I told you this would happen, you wouldn't have believed me. Now you don't have to. You see it for yourselves."

"Fine, but that doesn't change anything between us," Silbrit said.

"Doesn't it?" Tuvok asked. "Do you remain unconvinced of the futility of this course of action?"

"No, but this is just me. How do we convince anyone else that this *will happen*, unless it does?"

Cambridge looked to the temporal transporters. "Do these things work both ways?"

"How do you mean?"

"Can you venture into alternate timelines as well as bringing others here?"

"Yes."

"Do you really want us to move further along into this timeline?" the *denzit* asked. "Do you have any idea how this temporal incursion really works? I don't want to step through one of those things and find myself floating in the debris of a planet that was just destroyed."

"That might not be necessary," Silbrit said, moving to the control panels that rested opposite the platforms along the far wall. Cambridge accompanied him while Tuvok, the *denzit*, and Chakotay closed ranks around the admiral.

"What did you promise the Krenim in return for this?" Chakotay asked.

"A little information. Nothing I'm unwilling to share."

"Why would the Krenim even help you?" the *denzit*

demanded. "I've heard of them, but as far as I know they keep to themselves."

Janeway turned to face her. "When you were being tortured, the voice you heard on those logs, *my voice*, was describing a year-long conflict between *Voyager* and the Krenim."

"No, it wasn't. It was the Zahl."

"The logs you heard were altered by the Krenim to make you think that. They wanted you to believe it was the Zahl who captured you and tortured you. They programmed you to hate the Zahl so that they could bring you into this conflict on the side of the Rilnar and leave you on Sormana to die. The Krenim are responsible for everything you have suffered. They possess powerful temporal technology, as you can see, and it is my belief that they have used it more than once to create the status quo in which you find yourselves. They use these temporal incursions to revise history in their best interest. *Voyager*'s original encounter with them left them much weaker than they had been. They've set about restoring their losses and seem reasonably content with their current lot, but you and I are what they call chaotic variables."

"That sounds about right," Chakotay noted.

"They meant to capture me when they took you. They wanted to study me, to understand why I'd beaten them and to make sure that I could never do it again."

"The Zahl have chroniton torpedoes, Admiral," the *denzit* argued. "We just saw them."

"The Zahl didn't know you existed until you entered this war on the Rilnar's side," Janeway assured her.

"But Dayne," she began, struggling to make sense of this revelation, "he couldn't have known. They were using him too?"

Janeway felt an immense heat, part anger, part pain on the *denzit*'s behalf, begin to burn in her chest. "Dayne . . ." she began.

"Admiral," Cambridge shouted, "over here."

Janeway moved swiftly toward the control panels. Tuvok took her arm to hold her back as the *denzit* and Chakotay went ahead.

"What about Dayne?" he asked.

"He's Krenim," Janeway whispered.

Tuvok's startled response was small, but clear to the admiral. He immediately composed himself, then hurried with the admiral to join the rest of the group. Several screens embedded in the wall were lit and scrolling through scenes of battles.

"Why is this technology working when everything else here is frozen?" the *denzit* asked. "Is this some sort of illusion?"

"These monitors are tied to the chroniton pools beneath the temporal transporters. In their natural state, chronitons exist in temporal flux. They aren't subject to whatever is causing this incursion," Silbrit explained.

"What are we looking at?" Chakotay asked.

"These displays," Silbrit said, pointing to a set of screens, "are our standard recruitment lines. If you think that our lives are bad here, you should see how these people live. They line up to join us whenever my officers cross over. They know the war is still going on in our timeline and that if they don't die in battle they will likely suffer debilitating symptoms of quantum misalignment, but they don't care. We have food and water and roofs over our heads. They're barely eking out an existence. These are several slightly different versions of Sormana's future, from fifty to a hundred years from now."

"You never recruit from your past?" Tuvok asked.

"Too dangerous," Silbrit replied.

"How refreshingly wise of you," the *denzit* noted.

"This is what you need to see," Silbrit said, pointing to a single screen where nothing but large chunks of debris could be seen floating in space. "These portals are fixed on the other side. This one comes out near Batibeh. As you can see, even the ruins are no longer there. I've studied more timelines than I care to remember using this technology. I've never seen this one before. I never looked at *our* timeline because it is normally in constant flux, but not anymore. This is *our* quantum signature. That's how this moment is going to end."

"Will this record still exist if we are able to change the course of this moment somehow?" the admiral asked.

"It should," Silbrit said with a shrug. "*This* is happening right now. Any new timeline created by our actions subsequent to your arrival will branch off from this one."

"Assuming we find a way to survive, could you show this to your superior officers and to the planet's political leaders?" Chakotay asked.

"If you people get us out of here in one piece, and the technology survives, that would be my first priority."

"The Rilnar would have to see it too," the *denzit* said.

"Can you convince them to look?"

"I can try," the *denzit* said.

"Will that be enough?" Chakotay asked. "Self-preservation doesn't seem to be the priority around here one would think it should be."

"They'd have to believe that peace is also possible. They'd have to know that there is a better alternative and that the Zahl would honor any agreement they made," the *denzit* said.

"There's no record of anything like that here," Silbrit said.

"There might be," Cambridge interjected.

Silbrit shook his head. "The only timelines I've ever seen through these portals that don't show constant warfare are the handful where Sormana is unoccupied, where sentient life never arose here for one reason or another."

"Set new parameters for the Batibeh portal," Cambridge said. "Show us all of the unoccupied timelines."

Silbrit adjusted the controls before him and began the search. A number of scenes appeared on the display screens, most showing landscapes untouched by people. A few small creatures skittered among tall green and brown stalks. Larger animals could be seen roaming freely. It was almost painful to see these pristine vistas and to wonder what the rest of space surrounding Sormana might look like in these alternate realities.

"Go back," Cambridge said suddenly.

"What?"

"There. Timeline 024.51899.012. Show me that again."

Silbrit did as Cambridge had requested. It was a scene similar to the others; a field of green grass spilled over a low hill, but at its edge stood a configuration of rocks that on close inspection could not have been naturally occurring.

"What is that?" Silbrit asked.

"The stone table," Cambridge said. "Do you think we have time for a little recon mission, Admiral?"

"I do."

"What do you expect to find there?" Silbrit asked.

"Peace."

VESTA

Captain Farkas had assumed she would see something like the image now before her on the main viewscreen if her plan worked. That didn't make it any easier for her eyes to accept.

Bryce, Icheb, and her flight controller, Lieutenant Hoch, had perfectly executed her instructions. The moment *Vesta* arrived a billion kilometers from Sormana and the slipstream corridor began to disperse, the temporal shields had been activated. Against long odds they had done it without turning *Vesta* into dust in the process.

Sensors had already detected the *Truon* orbiting Sormana. It was the only visible object within a billion kilometers of the planet that moved. Everything else was frozen, a grisly still-life painting; the subject: war.

Within the next few minutes Farkas would have an exact count of the number of starships now positioned in what had once been the minefield surrounding Sormana. She guessed twenty or more were engaged in what looked like a dog fight. Both sides had suffered losses, as evidenced by the large pieces of broken starships conspicuous among those still intact.

One very important ship was missing.

"I've got *Voyager*," Jepel reported from ops.

"Where is she?"

"She's holding position, or rather, stuck like everyone else out here on the far side of the planet. It looks like she was just breaking orbit when . . ."

"When time stopped," Farkas finished for him. "Mister Hoch, give me a one-second burst of our impulse engine."

The flight controller did so and *Vesta* moved ever so slightly closer to the battle.

"Bryce?"

"Go ahead, Captain."

"Am I right that as long as our temporal shields are stable, we will not be affected by whatever the Krenim have done here?"

"Yes, Captain."

"Hoch, wait until the *Truon* syncs with the dark side of the planet and bring us into a slightly higher orbit. Continue to match the Krenim ship's speed. I want the planet to stay between us at all times. Understood?"

"Aye, Captain."

"It would be preferable if the *Truon* did not see us approaching," Roach added.

"We're the only other thing moving out here. That might not be possible. At any rate, I don't think Agent Dayne considers us to be much of a threat. He'll leave us alone, but I want a little warning if I'm wrong about that."

"Understood."

"Whenever you're ready, Hoch."

It took a few minutes for the flight controller to execute her command. Farkas spent that time marveling at the fact that right now, a number of people on the frozen starships out there were alive. Within seconds of the restoration of normal time, some of them were going die. Their families would receive word of their sacrifice. The lives of those who loved them were going to change forever. She wished fervently for the power to board those ships, to show their commanders what she was seeing. She wanted to force them to look at the faces of the men and women under their charge who were about to die and ask if, given that knowledge, they might have done anything differently. Sometimes conflict was unavoidable. Farkas knew that. *This* was a choice, not a last resort.

When the *Vesta* had finally reached orbit, Farkas ordered, "Jepel, begin a full sensor sweep."

Kar exclaimed, "Captain, there's a massive source of chroniton particles on the surface."

"Really?"

"I'm only detecting six life-forms on the planet," Jepel said.

"That can't be right."

"The sensors don't read anything that is suspended by the temporal field," Jepel clarified.

"I don't suppose you can tell me who any of those six life-forms are?"

"Four humans, one Vulcan, I assume: Admiral Janeway, Captain Chakotay, Lieutenant Tuvok, Counselor Cambridge, and the *denzit*. I can't identify the other one."

"Let's hope he's friendly."

"Captain, ninety percent of the chroniton readings we're getting are coming from a single source. There appears to be a huge cache of chroniton torpedoes located on an island in the southern hemisphere," Kar said.

"Let me guess: our officers are on that island too?"

"Yes, Captain."

"There are also a dozen Rilnar shuttles in proximity to the island. Their positions suggest they are in the process of attacking it," Jepel added.

Farkas turned to Roach. "Agent Dayne told us that Sormana was about to be destroyed. Is there anything else going on here that could account for that?"

"Not that I can see," Roach replied.

"How many torpedoes are we talking about?"

"Five thousand," Kar reported.

"Bryce, clear out cargo bays two and three. Jettison anything you can't find room for."

"Of course, Captain, but may I ask—"

"I'm about to transport five thousand chroniton torpedoes into our holds."

"Captain, that's not the best idea you've ever had."

"The moment normal time is restored those weapons are going to detonate. They are going to destroy the planet and everything in the vicinity, including us. Can you think of another way to prevent that from happening?"

A long pause followed.

"Bryce?"

"It's all right, Captain," Icheb's voice replied. *"I'm walking the chief and his staff through the creation of a suitable containment field for our cargo bays. It's based on Borg designs."*

"I'd suggest *running* them through it, Ensign."

"Understood. We'll need fifteen minutes."

"I'm giving you five. And I'm not exaggerating. I don't do that."

"Five minutes, it is," Bryce said.

Closing the channel, Farkas turned to Roach, "I never thought the day would come when I'd be grateful for Borg ingenuity."

"What are we going to do once we've got the torpedoes aboard?" he asked.

"Put as much distance between us and the planet as possible. We will likely become the *Truon's* target at that point and I have no idea how quickly he can call for reinforcements."

"Lieutenant Kar, begin an immediate search for a good hiding place and transmit the coordinates to the conn," Roach ordered. "Should we go to red alert?" he asked.

"Not yet. One more thing, Jepel. Can I talk to Admiral Janeway?"

"Yes, Captain, I can open a channel . . . wait."

"What?" Farkas asked, tensing.

"Admiral Janeway is gone."

"What happened to her?"

"I don't know, Captain. She, the counselor, the *denzit*, and that unidentified individual just vanished from our sensors."

"What about Chakotay?"

"I've still got him and Commander Tuvok."

SORMANA

Chakotay watched with great trepidation as the admiral, the counselor, the *denzit*, and the servitor vanished through one of the Zahl's temporal portals. Silbrit had assured everyone that the process was completely safe. He had visited other timelines before and never experienced any adverse effects. The deadly quantum misalignment syndrome was only a concern for individuals who entered this timeline from one of six other future lines. The Zahl believed it was a genetic issue related to mutations caused by biogenic weapons that were going to be put into use on Sormana in the next twenty years. While somewhat comforting, it hardly put the captain's mind at ease.

The admiral had ordered Chakotay to stay behind. She didn't know how much latitude Dayne intended to give her in resolving the crisis and she wanted to make sure that someone could keep him talking, should he take exception to her choice to leave the present timeline. Tuvok had asked to stay as well, to provide security for Chakotay.

Both officers stood before the display screens and were able to watch the admiral's party arrive at Batibeh. The group soon moved beyond the range of the portal's visual sensors but at least Chakotay knew they had reached their destination safely. He had no idea how long they would be gone.

"I wish to apologize to you, Captain," Tuvok said softly.

"Why?"

"I must take full responsibility for the chain of events that precipitated this crisis."

"That's awfully big of you, Tuvok, but I think the counselor was right. *This* was going to happen eventually. You might have just hurried it along."

"I did more than that. When we arrived, I chose to separate from Kim and Seven. When I realized that this island was also a Rilnar prison, I decided to investigate the cell blocks."

"You were hoping to find Dayne, weren't you?"

"Yes."

"Even though that wasn't your mission?"

"Yes."

"Tuvok, the moment you decided that the *denzit*'s choices could be justified, you betrayed your oath."

"You do not possess sufficient data, Captain."

"I don't? Then enlighten me. I understand how complicated this is. I imagine that even for you, it's difficult to separate your love for our friend the admiral from the *denzit*. But you had one job. You, among all of us, had a real chance to bring her to her senses. But you chose not to. Why?"

"Vesta to Captain Chakotay. Do you read us?"

The sound of Captain Farkas's voice echoing through the chamber startled both Chakotay and Tuvok and immediately dissipated the tension flaring between them.

"Hello, *Vesta*," Chakotay said. "How—?"

"Just before we returned we activated our new temporal shields. They work. We're not subject to the temporal field Agent Dayne's ship is generating."

"Everything down here, but us, is frozen in time," Chakotay reported.

"So is everything out here. We were reading six life-forms in your vicinity until a few moments ago. Are the admiral and counselor all right?"

"They are. They had to . . ." *How to explain?* "They should return to this location shortly."

"We've also detected a massive quantity of chroniton torpedoes down there. I thought we might take them off your hands, if you don't mind."

"Can you do that?"

"We're going to try. We need a few more minutes."

"We could use a little more help than that if you're up for it," Chakotay said.

"What did you have in mind?"

"Removing the torpedoes will save the island and the planet, but not those of us in this building. It's collapsing around us."

"I can transport you and Tuvok back here right now," Farkas offered.

"We need to stay until the admiral's team returns. When they do, can you be ready to get all of us out of here simultaneously?"

"*Vesta*'s transporters could also be used to move the other people on the island to a safe location while we await the admiral's return," Tuvok suggested.

"*We can't get a lock on their life signs while this temporal field is in effect. Yours are the only clear signals.*"

"Tell your transporter operators to search for trace minerals consistent with Rilnar and Zahl bio-signatures. They might be able to extrapolate individual readings from those."

"*We've got our hands full at the moment, Tuvok, but we will try. Our priorities are the torpedoes and our officers, in that order.*"

"All of this might be for nothing if the *denzit* and the Zahl commander don't survive as well. They should be returning with the admiral and counselor."

"*We've got clear readings on them. We'll get all six of you as soon as they return.*"

"That was not our arrangement," a new voice said.

Chakotay and Tuvok turned to see that an alien male had just materialized in the center of the cavern. Chakotay could only assume that he was the Krenim officer Kathryn had met and the man currently holding countless lives in his hands.

"*Is that Agent Dayne?*" Farkas asked.

Dayne, Chakotay realized. *He was Krenim?*

Of course he was. Kathryn had just told them that the Krenim were behind the *denzit*'s capture. It made sense that her "savior" was also Krenim. *But he had been so much more than that, at least according to the* denzit. *Where did the lies end?*

"Whatever you can do, *Vesta*. Chakotay out."

It was strange to realize that despite the fact that time did not exist in the reality he was occupying, Chakotay's duty now was to buy exactly that for both the admiral and Captain Farkas. Assuming the most casual demeanor he could muster despite the disgust he automatically felt for Dayne, Chakotay started toward him saying, "So you're the *denzit*'s husband?"

"Spare me your judgments. I agreed to allow the admiral to attempt to salvage this situation, but I did not authorize her to remove those weapons. Contact your ship and advise them that the torpedoes must stay where they are."

"I'm not sure how any of us will survive this as long as they're here. It sounds to me like we're doing precisely what you authorized the admiral to do." Chakotay said, "Unless *you* were planning to handle that detail?"

Had Chakotay been less focused on Dayne, he might have sensed the shift in Tuvok's demeanor before the security officer unexpectedly emitted a feral growl and ran straight toward the Krenim man, easily tackling him to the ground. To Chakotay's shock and horror, Tuvok began to assault Dayne brutally with his fists.

"Tuvok!" Chakotay shouted in alarm.

"Where is she?" Tuvok demanded, punching Dayne one last time before wrapping his hands around Dayne's neck.

Chakotay was already moving to try and pry the commander off of Dayne when the next words Tuvok spoke stopped him.

"Where is Kathryn's daughter?"

24

BATIBEH

The *denzit* was hardly convinced that trusting Silbrit and his temporal portals was a good idea. However, she was certain that no matter what the admiral did or discovered on the other side, when they returned to the cavern they were all going to die. She didn't know if she still had the strength to hope for a better outcome. When she had first learned of the island and seen its defenses she had known in her bones that this was the last target for the Rilnar. This engagement was going to end the war. She was finally going to learn the fate of her husband and daughter. The nightmare was almost over.

The admiral's revelation that the Krenim had been her enemy all along, coupled with the fact that she had never even suspected this to be true, had shaken her down to her core. *How many other things have I been wrong about? What happened to Dayne?*

What has he done with our child?

Half expecting her life to end the moment she stepped through the portal, it was a shock to the senses to emerge in a fragrant field of tall grass beneath clear, sunny skies. The energy of this place was electric. Life hummed and buzzed and chirped and croaked all around her. Trees stood tall and proud, their leaves rustling in a gentle breeze. The sound of running water in the distance made her suddenly conscious of a desperate thirst.

The portal was the only feature to mar the landscape, but on this side it was not a metal doorframe. Here, a small stone pillar stood beside the entrance and only a vague distortion of the air, like a ripple of thermal energy, denoted the access point to another time. A circle of small rocks surrounding the area would have prevented anyone from simply wandering into it unaware.

Batibeh's resemblance to Earth in this timeline was overwhelming. If she closed her eyes and simply allowed her senses rein, she could have easily convinced herself that she was walking around her mother's farm in Indiana. The visceral memory was as agonizing as it was comforting. It made her heart beat faster, her hands tremble, and her arms ache to hold the life she had created and once dreamed might grow up in a place like this.

Unbidden, a thought rose to her mind, momentarily blinding her eyes with tears.

Home.

"*Denzit?*" the admiral's soft voice sounded.

She locked eyes with the woman she had once planned to

become. They were strangers to each other. Still, the admiral had brought her home.

The counselor had rushed ahead with Silbrit to examine the stone table. The two women settled into a more leisurely pace as both soaked in the simple natural beauty around them. As they crested the rise of the hill where the table sat, they could see in the distance below a small, rustic village. They sensed no movement and saw no signs of habitation. But the *denzit* did not doubt that these buildings had been erected hundreds of years earlier. She'd seen images of Batibeh before it was destroyed. While there had been pockets of historical districts left untouched, a small but advanced city had been built around them. There was no trace of the tall buildings that had been the central trade district, or streets teeming with smaller service industries. The high metal fences that had bordered the city in its final years were also non-existent.

The *denzit* liked *this* version of Batibeh much better.

When she reached the stone table, an artifact she had never seen in one piece, the counselor was already deep in discussion with Silbret.

"I'm telling you, the Rilnar know this to be true. They have records of it," Cambridge was insisting. "I've spend the better part of the last week poring over written accounts that describe this place almost exactly."

"The Rilnar have never been granted access to the chroniton pools or our portals," Silbrit retorted. "I don't know what evidence you think you saw—"

"But it makes perfect sense if you believe the story of the two brothers."

"The two brothers?" the *denzit* asked.

Cambridge settled himself on the side of the stone table, his long legs dangling from its surface, and began to explain. "Two brothers, one Rilnar, one Zahl, came here after Batibeh was destroyed. They convinced the public and the authorities to sue for peace. This table was the site of the negotiations. In time, they succeeded. The war on Sormana was set to end. But they left before the final accords could be signed and an act of treachery derailed their efforts."

"This place hasn't been touched by war for a long time. Those trees," Silbrit said, pointing to a grove that lay nestled at the base of the hill near the ancient buildings "are *urulian jastins*. They don't grow anywhere on Sormana now, but those are at least two hundred years old."

"According to that journal you found, the Rilnar believe that the brothers were real and that they *almost* ended the war. Why does this place make me think they actually succeeded?" Janeway asked.

"Maybe *here* they did," the counselor said, pushing himself off the table's edge. "How long has that temporal portal existed?" Cambridge asked of Silbrit.

"About fifty years. At first, we simply used them to map as much as we could of some of the alternate timelines. Our resources are extremely limited. They've only seen significant use as transporters in the last decade."

"Do we know exactly *when* we are?" Admiral Janeway asked.

"Assuming the portal was functioning properly, it's the same as the timeline we left, a little over two hundred years after the destruction of Batibeh," Silbrit replied.

"So that portal has only been *here* for fifty years as well," the *denzit* confirmed. Turning toward Cambridge, she asked, "But you believe the Rilnar accessed them one hundred fifty years earlier than that?"

"Yes. Even before the portals were constructed, those chroniton pools were there. Rahalla discovered them more than two hundred years ago. The legend of the brothers said they used the pools to show the leaders of their day what would happen on Sormana if they failed to make peace," Cambridge said, pacing restlessly as he struggled to put the pieces together.

"That still doesn't explain why this place exists if these brothers ultimately failed to bring peace about," Silbrit argued.

The *denzit* stiffened. Three figures, two female and one male, wearing knee-length, light-brown tunics belted at the waist and soft boots had emerged from one of the structures below. They were approaching the table calmly but purposefully. It was clear they were not armed. Their hands swung freely at their sides, and there were no cloaks or jackets to conceal weapons.

"Let's meet them halfway," the admiral suggested. The group followed her down the hill. As they came closer to the natives, it was clear that they were from Sormana, but it was harder to distinguish the Rilnar from the Zahl. The young male and one female had similar, dark complexions. Both had the characteristic Zahl nasal ridge and some of the epidermal pitting. The other female was almost ancient, her hair thin and white, her pale face deeply wrinkled.

The *denzit* was struck by the realization that in all her years on Sormana, she had rarely seen a Rilnar that had lived so long, even at Felstar.

The two groups met each other just outside the grove of *jastin* trees. The natives looked them over, curious, but without any sign of fear or hostility. They focused a little longer on the *denzit* and the admiral, smiling placidly and sharing silent glances of surprise between them. Finally, the younger woman stepped forward and said, "On behalf of my fellow Keepers, permit me to welcome you to Batibeh. I am Irix. Normally pilgrims are brought here by shuttle from Jaxom. We apologize that we were not properly prepared to greet you."

The admiral stepped forward. "No apology is necessary. We didn't arrive here using conventional means."

The older woman spoke, her bright blue eyes twinkling. Her long white hair fell freely about her face. "You are time travelers."

The fact that this was stated with such simplicity seemed to both shock and relieve the admiral. The Temporal Prime Directive had been rendered moot by the Krenim's actions but she would not have chosen to reveal more information than was necessary to these strangers for fear of corrupting their timeline. It appeared that wasn't going to be a problem.

"You could call us that," the admiral replied. "How often do other *pilgrims* utilize the temporal displacement fields like the one up on that hill?"

"Never," the blue-eyed woman replied. Turning back to the rest of her group for confirmation she continued, "There are a few similar portals all over the planet. All have been appropriately marked and are not used by the Keepers. But we have often wondered if others from alternate realities might discover one in their own time and use them."

"They are naturally occurring?" the admiral asked.

"Yes. They began to appear about fifty years ago. We believe they are a by-product of the chroniton pools located on Rahalla. Scientists from far and wide often come to study them, but none of us have kept up on their research."

Cambridge was studying the group with a grin of unabashed delight. Finally he ventured, "Has your planet always been like this?"

"Always is a long time," the male Keeper replied. "Sadly, for many centuries, before the time of the brothers, Sormana was gripped by constant strife. This city, Batibeh, was destroyed in that conflict. Its destruction heralded a new era for our people. The Rilnar and Zahl agreed to abandon Sormana, to allow time and nature to heal the wounds they had inflicted on this world and one another. Most of the larger cities have fallen into disuse, although a few are still home to the Keepers. Batibeh was a special case. It was rebuilt as you see it now, as a reminder of our mutual beginnings and as a memorial to those who succeeded in bringing peace to Sormana."

"Do you know the identity of the brothers?" Cambridge asked.

The blue-eyed woman smiled shyly. "This way," she said, directing them toward the grove of trees.

The *denzit* felt a slight chill creep over her as they entered the grove and the voluminous *jastin* branches blocked the sun. Bright beams broke through in places, illuminating the monument that lay in the center of the grove, a series of small pools of water, clearly meant to represent the chroniton pools at Rahalla.

Above them, two figures stood carved in a beautiful cream, red-veined stone. They were a little taller than most men, but clearly meant to be larger than life, despite the realism with which the faces and fine details of their clothing and hands had been rendered.

Cambridge immediately moved closer to the statues, marveling at them.

The *denzit* was struck first by their pose. They stood perhaps a meter and a half apart, their arms outstretched, reaching for each other. Between them, suspended by some unknown method, a perfect sphere floated.

"Do you, by any chance, know their names?" Cambridge asked.

"Of course. This one," Irix said, indicating the taller of the two whose strongest feature was his chin and a tangle of dense, curly hair that fell almost to his shoulders, "was Obristian. And this," she continued, pointing to the other whose features, while handsome, were softer and whose hair had obviously been fine and straight, "was Danyaran."

The *denzit* felt the air around her begin to spin. Her feet suddenly seemed to have left solid ground. The admiral inhaled sharply beside her, and one of the Keepers placed firm hands on the *denzit*'s shoulders to steady her.

"Danyaran," Janeway said, turning abruptly to the *denzit*, who was now having trouble breathing.

"Dayne," she managed on a shallow breath.

Without another word, the *denzit* turned and rushed from the grove. She set a torturous pace for herself, climbing toward the stone table. Neither the burning in her chest nor the tears flowing freely from her eyes slowed her.

"Please, wait," a soft voice called behind her.

When she had finally reached the table, she placed both hands on its edge to steady herself. Her inhalations were heavy gasps. Her ears buzzed. Her limbs trembled with exertion and an overabundance of adrenaline.

A few moments later, the blue-eyed Keeper reached her. "Are

you all right?" she asked, placing a gentle hand on the *denzit's* back.

Kathryn turned, wiping her face and nose with her sleeve, and struggled valiantly to compose herself. Some deeply ingrained training took over, forcing her to display a sense of calm she did not feel. "I'm fine. I will be. I just need a few minutes."

"Your world is not like ours," the woman said kindly.

Kathryn shook her head. "*My world,*" she began, "the planet of my birth is actually very much like this. But I never dreamed I would see anything like it on Sormana."

"In your timeline the war still continues?"

Kathryn nodded.

"We have always known that the existence of the other time-lines meant that not all who have lived on Sormana knew the peace the brothers brought to us. It must be difficult for you to believe this is even possible."

"Where I come from, the brothers . . ."

Never existed, she started to say, but immediately realized her error. They *did* exist, at least Dayne did. But he had clearly done something to change the actions for which he was now memorialized in this timeline. Had he brought peace to Sormana before they met? If not, why would he have tried to change Sormana's past *after* they had fallen in love? Changing the past would alter the future. They would probably never have known each other. Was that his intention?

The woman's eyes were glistening as well. She seemed to be struggling with some deep emotion. Clearly she knew something of the other timelines and was moved to think she had encountered someone who was probably living during a time of strife and terror.

Kathryn attempted to smile, to reassure this kind soul that she would be fine. For the first time, she noticed subtle differences about her. The woman's age had been deceptive. The flesh of her cheeks was crisscrossed with deep wrinkles, but they were likely caused by years of exposure to the sun rather than inherited like the Rilnar's and Zahl's. The bones of her skull were structured a little differently. The nasal ridge was absent but her forehead seemed to be a little wider.

"Were you born on Sormana?" Kathryn asked.

"I was. I have lived one hundred and fifteen years on this planet, all of them in peace and prosperity. Most of the Keepers are children of the Wise Generation. It was our grandparents who came to this table and brought the war to an end. A handful chose to remain behind when Sormana was abandoned, both Rilnar and Zahl. They stayed so that they could witness Sormana's transformation. We are the Keepers of history. We remain so that no one will ever forget."

"What is your name?" Kathryn asked.

The woman smiled sadly. "I am Mollah."

"Kathryn."

Mollah's smile widened and warmed. "I—" she began, but turned at the sounds of the rest of the group approaching. It was a somber procession. Only the counselor and Silbrit were engaged in animated conversation with the male Keeper.

The admiral approached Kathryn warily. Mollah stepped back, rejoining the other Keepers.

"I'm sorry you had to find out this way," Janeway said softly.

"You knew?"

"Not this. I never imagined . . . but it fits, doesn't it? Dayne is Krenim. We know he has had a great deal of experience passing as a Rilnar. He was the one who sent me back to Sormana. He told me that his people had already executed a series of incursions. This had to be one of them."

"But *when*? If it happened after we met, *our* reality should no longer exist. That it still does means that at some point, he changed it again. I don't understand. If he was capable of creating this, why wouldn't he have let it be? Who could ever look at this and want to change it?"

"He might have been looking for a way to make your suffering unnecessary," Janeway suggested. "More likely, however, this was done and undone before you ever met."

"But *why*?"

"I wonder . . ." Janeway said, tuning back to the Keepers. "In whose space is Sormana currently located?"

"Our entire star system has been declared neutral territory. Our nearest borders are shared on one side with the Zahl colonists and the other by the Rilnar," Mollah replied.

"And the Krenim?" Janeway asked.

The Keepers exchanged curious glances. "I've never heard of them," Irix said.

"They are an alien species," the male Keeper said. "They control a single system very far from here and have a long history of conflict with the Mawasi and the Nihydron. I believe both the Rilnar and Zahl have tried to intercede. Offers of diplomatic and humanitarian aid have been made. But they do not welcome interference from outsiders."

"Forgive us," Mollah said. "Most of us are too busy with our other duties to follow interstellar politics with the same energy as Welfrek."

"Don't be so modest," Welfrek chided her good-naturedly. "Mollah here has written extensively on the way in which Sormana's past has informed the current political climate beyond Sormana. She is one of our most revered Keepers."

Janeway turned back to the *denzit*, who had begun to tremble violently. "This might have helped Sormana, but at a cost too great for the Krenim to abide."

"Admiral," Silbrit said, his tone clearly communicating his desire to end this diversion.

Janeway nodded. "Thank you all for sharing this with us. We have to go now."

"Will you send others here, now that you know we exist?"

"Perhaps," Silbrit replied.

The Keepers bid farewell to their pilgrims, noting that they would always be welcome at Batibeh. As they began to make their way back down the hill, Janeway addressed Silbrit and the *denzit*.

"I'm not sure I would risk bringing any of your contemporaries here."

"We shouldn't have to. Now that I know what we're looking at, I can use the portal displays to show our leaders everything they need to see," Silbrit said.

"Assuming we and the portals survive," Cambridge pointed out.

Janeway nodded. "It's time to talk to Dayne."

"He's *here*?" the *denzit* demanded.

"He's back there," Janeway said, pointing toward the shimmering air beside the stone pillar.

Without another word, the *denzit* rushed forward and vanished into the portal.

SORMANA

Dayne was about to lose consciousness. His mangled face was beet red and his gasps were desperate. A slight adjustment to the placement of Tuvok's thumbs would result in his immediate death. Much as Tuvok wished to crush his fragile windpipe and cervical spine, he could not until he heard the truth from this man's lips.

Bending low so that their faces were centimeters apart, Tuvok demanded vehemently, "Where is your daughter?"

Suddenly Tuvok's grip loosened. Chakotay had grabbed him under both shoulders from behind and was attempting to drag him off of his quarry. Dayne took the opening and bringing both hands up between Tuvok's in a frantic gesture, broke free. He rolled onto his side, choking and coughing violently. On one elbow he attempted to drag himself clear of Tuvok.

"Tuvok, stand down. That's an order," Chakotay shouted.

The Starfleet officer who had served with dedication and distinction for decades understood the seriousness of those words. Elieth's father ignored them. Jerking free of Chakotay's grasp, Tuvok kicked Dayne hard in the ribs. A faint, satisfying crack could be heard over his agonized shout.

"Where is she?" Tuvok roared.

That Dayne had lied to the *denzit*, tortured her, betrayed

her, and left her on Sormana to die, was unacceptable. He had strayed far beyond the bounds of civilized behavior and forfeited his right to mercy. But what turned him from a person to a *thing* in Tuvok's mind was his theft of Kathryn's child. For that, he must suffer, just as all those who embraced evil and wanton destruction of the lives of others should be made to suffer.

The torment of Elieth's senseless loss shook free of its shackles in Tuvok's mind. Over the last several months, he had sought to exert control over this most primal of emotions. But that control had been an illusion. His agony had waited patiently for a moment of free rein and Tuvok released it now, pouring it into Dayne with savage, righteous fury. Not long ago he had welcomed the thought of his imminent death. Now he wanted to live, if only long enough to destroy this monster.

Chakotay placed himself between Tuvok and Dayne, taking him firmly by the shoulders and locking eyes with him. "Tuvok, this isn't the way."

"This is all that evil comprehends. This is its native tongue," Tuvok raged. Grabbing Chakotay's upper arms in a brief embrace, he threw the captain clear and turned back to Dayne.

"Where—" Tuvok shouted again.

"She's dead," Dayne gasped. "I couldn't . . . save her. Too . . . great . . . a risk."

"Dayne!"

The anguished cry that brought Tuvok back to his senses was Kathryn's. Turning, he saw that the *denzit* had returned and was rushing toward him. Admiral Janeway followed on her heels, taking in the chaotic scene before her: Dayne curled into a fetal position, Tuvok's madness, and Chakotay picking himself up off the ground.

"What the hell is happening here?" Janeway demanded.

The *denzit* pushed Tuvok aside and knelt beside Dayne. As she did so, he spared a brief moment to meet her eyes with pity and a hint of disgust. He then grasped his right wrist with his left hand and vanished in a swirl of light.

"We're out of time," Chakotay announced. Tapping his combadge he shouted, "Chakotay to *Vesta*. *Now, Captain.*"

A massive explosion sounded. The cavern was suddenly alive again with flame. The scalding heat had barely kissed Tuvok's flesh when he felt the transporter beam take hold of him.

25

VESTA

Four hundred and twelve?" Captain Regina Farkas asked.

"Four hundred and eighteen if you count us," Kathryn Janeway replied.

The two women sat alone in Farkas's ready room, awaiting the arrival of the admiral. Kathryn, no longer the *denzit* and perhaps never again to be a Starfleet officer, had arrived ten minutes early for their meeting. Roach had escorted her to the bridge and Farkas had immediately ushered her into the ready room to spare her the understandable, curious glances of the bridge crew.

They'd managed small talk for a few painful minutes before accepting that silence was more comfortable. Farkas had broken it to ask how many had survived the destruction of the island base. *Vesta*'s transporter logs from those few desperate moments when they had struggled to retrieve as many as possible and move them to the nearest coastline could not provide an accurate count as they had not been based on discrete bio-signatures. The process had only begun after the successful transport of the full complement of chroniton torpedoes to *Vesta*'s hold and had been cut short by Chakotay's signal.

"Out of how many?" Farkas asked, steeling herself.

"Two thousand six hundred and nine."

"Damn."

"I'm amazed you saved as many as you did, given the time you had and the other pressing priorities."

The words were encouraging. Their tone was flat. Farkas didn't know half of what this woman had endured before the fleet had arrived at Sormana, let alone since then, but she knew post-traumatic stress when she saw it. There was a palpable distance between this version of Kathryn Janeway and the rest of the universe. She was retreating into herself. While performing all of the tasks required by her former positions with both the Rilnar and Starfleet, she seemed to be sleep-walking through the necessary motions.

Silence fell between them again. Farkas didn't bother trying to draw Kathryn out. Indeed, it would have been unkind to do so. It was going to take years of work by dedicated professionals to bring this woman back to anything resembling life. Quiet companionship was the only thing of value Farkas had to offer her, and she gave it most willingly.

A sudden spark of restlessness pulled Kathryn from her musings. She lifted her eyes to Farkas's face, keeping her own fiercely neutral. The two women stared at each other, not really communicating, simply waiting.

"How did that happen?"

Farkas was shocked by the question.

"What?"

Kathryn lifted her right hand and with her first finger, traced a line down the side of her face in the same location as a visible scar Farkas bore.

"Oh, this? Noncorporeal life-forms invaded my ship."

Kathryn nodded.

After another long moment Farkas ran her hand across the front of her neck where Kathryn's flesh was heavily scarred. "You?"

"Zahl—pardon me—*Krenim* shock collar."

Farkas nodded.

Finally, the door to the ready room slid open and the admiral entered with her aide, Decan, behind her. Farkas started to rise but the admiral gestured for her to keep her seat. She settled herself in the chair next to her doppelganger while Decan stood discreetly behind them.

The two Kathryn Janeways might have been difficult to tell apart were it not for the admiral's uniform and the other's plain brown tunic, pants, and jacket. *Until the admiral spoke.* Her energy, her *presence* was in sharp, vivid contrast to that of the woman who shared little with her beyond a physical resemblance.

"Day ten of formal negotiations between Sormana's leaders, the Rilnar Colonial commanders, and the Zahl Regnancy has ended. As best I can tell, they are still months away from finalizing a treaty."

"They're nine days closer to that goal than I thought they would ever get, Admiral," Farkas noted.

"The near destruction of Rahalla has changed everyone's calculations. At no time in the past was the leadership on either side concerned about a planet-killing event. The Rilnar didn't have access to weapons that could do it and the Zahl never had any intention of using theirs on Sormana. Knowledge of those chroniton torpedoes was classified to the highest levels of the Zahl military."

Turning to the former *denzit*, the admiral said, "You did very well yesterday."

Kathryn nodded almost imperceptibly.

"Your testimony and Silbrit's were exactly what the Regnancy and Colonial Command have been waiting to hear. It gave them the leverage they need to pressure Sormana's arbiters in a way they never could before. Now they have the military on both sides calling for peace. The politicians will fall in line."

"How long will it be until Rahalla is excavated?" Farkas asked.

"Silbrit thinks they will be able to access the pools within two weeks. They're already building the replacement portals and interfaces. Once everyone gets back down there and can see the future of continued conflict versus peace, things should start to move quickly toward resolution."

"How did they take your briefing about the Krenim?"

The admiral shrugged. "It scared the hell out of both sides. I hate to think that the thing that might ultimately unite the Rilnar and Zahl in common purpose is a new shared enemy, but . . ."

"You'll take it?" Farkas asked.

The admiral nodded. "I've agreed to share our temporal shield technology with the Rilnar and Zahl. The fact that our fleet has not observed any changes in the last week and a half with our temporal shields in continuous use is comforting, but I don't think anyone is going to sleep well here until they have rendered the Krenim's weapons obsolete. At the very least, the Krenim shouldn't be able to continue to alter time without the Rilnar's and Zahl's knowledge."

"The Krenim control more than twice as much territory as anybody else in this sector. Their fleet is strong. Their space is well defended. Maybe they'll just decide to leave well enough alone," Farkas suggested.

"Maybe," the admiral said without real enthusiasm. Turning again to Kathryn she said, "I've had temporary quarters prepared for you aboard *Vesta*. *Voyager* will be returning to the Beta Quadrant shortly to take Tuvok back to his ship. They'll return you to Earth at the same time, if you like. Starfleet Command is going to require a lengthy debriefing, but they will also do everything they can to make your transition as easy as possible. I'll see to it that you are assigned to work with Counselor Rori Austen. She was very helpful to me last year."

When Kathryn didn't respond the admiral added, "Of course, if you need more time, you're free to remain with the fleet a little longer. We have a number of fine counselors here as well, and they are at your disposal. I have no intention of forcing you to do anything with which you aren't completely comfortable."

"When do I have to decide?" Kathryn asked.

"We still have a few days."

Kathryn nodded.

Farkas hadn't noticed Decan moving from the doorway to her replicator but she was suddenly aware of him standing between the two Janeways, offering each a steaming mug of coffee. The admiral accepted hers gratefully, inhaled the steam, and took a generous swig. Kathryn nodded to Decan and after considering the beverage warily took a small sip. Everyone in the room watched her intently for a reaction.

Kathryn swallowed with a grimace, paused, and said, "That's disappointing."

The admiral appeared ready to argue the point. Farkas quickly interjected, "What about our cargo?"

"The Zahl want their torpedoes back. I don't really have a choice but to comply. At least the Rilnar know about them now and I have advised both sides of my belief that sharing the technology should be part of their final mutual defense pact."

Kathryn set her cup on the edge of Farkas's desk and rose from her chair. "Would it be possible for me to see Tuvok again before I make my final decision?"

"Of course," the admiral replied. "I'll take you to the transporter room myself."

"Thank you."

Farkas watched them depart, certain that the admiral was well on her way to putting this mess behind her and wondering if Kathryn would ever be able to do the same.

GALEN

Nancy Conlon didn't remember much of the last several days. They had passed in a blur of routine consisting largely of mornings spent in sickbay with Doctor Sharak, evenings in her quarters aboard *Voyager*, and once the fleet had regrouped, a transfer to *Galen*. Her new quarters on the specialized medical vessel were smaller than she was accustomed to. Most of her personal effects were still packed in storage crates piled beside her rack. Any day now she expected word to arrive indicating that she was about to be sent back to Starfleet Medical.

She knew this to be true because every time she spoke to B'Elanna, the commander had insisted that nothing of the sort was under discussion. Torres had visited briefly with her daily, usually with Michael and Miral in tow. Sometimes in their presence she forgot briefly that the life she'd built with the fleet was over. Torres had assumed command of *Voyager*'s engine room but kept promising Conlon that it was only temporary. *Nothing* had changed, nor would change. As soon as Conlon was well enough to return to duty, *Voyager* would be hers again.

Conlon would not allow herself to entertain the notion. She knew better.

It was getting harder to refuse Harry's daily requests to speak with her. Once the crisis on Sormana had passed he'd come to her quarters but she had still been confined to sickbay at the time. She had asked Doctor Sharak to refuse him access and Sharak had honored her request. Conlon knew she could trust Sharak and B'Elanna not to reveal her personal situation to Kim. She knew the absence of information and her transfer to *Galen* must be driving him to distraction, but she simply couldn't deal with him. She needed to know more about her condition before she decided how much to share with him. If in the meantime his understandable anger with her caused his feelings to change, that might be for the best for both of them.

Counselor Cambridge had also dropped by daily, but once she had come clean about her past lies their sessions had devolved into long bouts of silence on her part punctuated by his unsuccessful attempts to draw her out. Conlon wondered if he had already given up on her.

She had submitted to a number of new tests while aboard the *Galen*. Sharak had administered them with the Doctor always nearby. Both had assured her that they were working diligently to understand the nature of her current condition and would advise her as soon as they understood exactly what they were dealing with. Each day that passed further cemented her belief that whatever was wrong with her, the Full Circle Fleet's medical staff was not going to be able to resolve it.

She entered *Galen*'s sickbay that morning, as usual, expecting to find Sharak and the Doctor ready to describe the new day's tests. Instead, she found the two of them seated in the Doctor's office along with Doctor Sal and Counselor Cambridge.

She almost turned to go back to her quarters, suddenly queasy. Before she could, the Doctor noted her presence and nodded to Cambridge, who immediately rose and met her in the main bay.

"Good morning, Lieutenant," he greeted her.

"Counselor."

"Join us."

It didn't sound like an order, but it was.

Conlon entered the office and was given the chair between Sal and Cambridge. Sharak stood behind the Doctor, who sat at his desk, his monitor turned out so that all could see the data he was describing.

Sharak was the first to speak. "I apologize, Lieutenant Conlon, for the length of time it has taken us to brief you more fully on your condition. It is an extremely complicated case and it has taken us until now to determine the precise nature of the challenge before us."

"Before we could figure out what it was, we had to make sure we knew what it *wasn't*," Sal clarified.

"So what is it?" Conlon asked, wondering when and why Doctor Sal had been brought into the loop.

Sharak began the explanation. "Your previous panels and history suggested either a resurgence of the *appia veraba* organism you were exposed to while serving aboard the *da Vinci*, or a complication induced by the retrovirus that was developed to combat it. We have finally proven both of these hypotheses invalid."

Conlon released a full breath and her heart began to race in relief. "Really?"

Sharak nodded somberly. For a man who had just given her the best news she had ever heard, he didn't seem to share her relief.

"We then set about analyzing the alterations to your DNA that *are* present," the Doctor said, picking up the story. "We believe now that the changes we have detected in your immune system, the odd hormone levels, and noticeable absence of other infectious agents were the result of Xolani's attempt to assume control of your body."

"I don't understand. You said—" Conlon began.

The Doctor cut her off. "Xolani told you that you were slowly dying due to an old infection. That was a lie. *He* lied to you to convince you to stop fighting him. I, too, briefly encountered his essence when he tried to take over my holomatrix upon your death. Believe me when I tell you that there was *nothing* Xolani wouldn't have said or done to gain your compliance. He offered me . . . well, let's just say, the one thing I wanted most in the world."

"And you refused?" Conlon asked.

"Just as you did, until he made you believe that self-sacrifice was the best choice before you. But Xolani was the one who damaged your genetic material. We still don't understand the mode of transmission fully. I don't think we ever will. What we are left with, are the results, and they are undeniable.

"As Doctor Sharak first suspected, you have what we refer to as a DNA damage repair syndrome. The vast majority of your genetic material is unaltered. What Xolani's attack apparently did was eliminate your body's natural ability to repair corrupted DNA. Countless metabolic processes and environmental exposures damage human DNA on a daily basis. This would be a problem if your cells did not also have the ability to recognize this damage and fix it. If the damage is too significant, the affected cells are usually programmed to die, which is advantageous because they can no longer pass along their mutated genetic information.

"In your case, this essential process has been halted. Many

of the initial complications such as cancerous growths we can remove as they develop. But unless we can restore your body's ability to repair its own DNA, over time you will develop a number of degenerative conditions. You will lose mobility, your sight, auditory processing capabilities, and most of your higher brain functions. Unless we intervene, you will succumb to this condition within the next three years, perhaps less if an opportunistic infection takes hold and your immune system is no longer able to counter it."

"Eventually, a cold could kill you," Sal said simply.

Conlon's head was light. She hadn't begun to absorb all of what she had heard, but the broad strokes were pretty clear.

She'd been right. She was dying. *Of what* didn't really matter anymore.

"Yours is a unique case, with no proven treatment regimen," Sharak continued. "But that is going to change over the next several months. The Doctor, Sal, and I will be working together to develop the necessary protocols to restore what has been lost. Believe me when I tell you, we *will* succeed. Doctor Sal was personally responsible for the eradication of a DNA damage repair syndrome as complicated as yours. We are fortunate indeed to have access to her brilliance."

"It's true," Sal said, "not the brilliance part. The reason we are most likely to succeed is that you have something going for you that the victims of Vega Nine never did."

"What?"

"You're pregnant, Lieutenant," Sal said.

Cambridge shot her a stern look. "And people think I'm tactless," he muttered.

"No, I'm not," Conlon said automatically.

"Yes, you are," Sharak assured her. "You are three weeks along, still too soon for you to have noticed, but we detected it ten days ago."

Shock rendered Conlon incapable of doing the mental math required to confirm Sharak's statement, but she didn't really need to. She didn't know whether to laugh or cry, but tears began to stream down her face before she had consciously made up her mind.

"I don't want it," were the first words she could form.

"Hang on," Sal said, taking Conlon's left hand and squeezing it firmly. Staring Conlon directly in the eye, she continued, "I don't give a damn about your personal situation. You have to think about more than that right now. This baby is your salvation. The stem cells your body is creating are not affected by what Xolani did. They are perfect and we can use them to cure you. If you terminate your pregnancy before we have a chance to do that, the odds of us finding another solution in time to save you get a lot longer."

"I don't care," Conlon said. "I won't have a baby just to save myself."

"Most people have babies for significantly less compelling reasons," Cambridge said. "Listen to me. This is too much for anyone to take in and fully process in a few minutes. You need time. We need to talk. Everyone in this room appreciates how horrible this is and everyone in this room is committed to making it better. We are a team. We are going to work through this together. You will know everything we know as we go along. You don't have to decide anything right now, so don't even try."

"We have cross-checked the fetus's DNA. Are you inclined to consider telling Lieutenant Kim about your situation before you make a final determination?" the Doctor asked gently.

"You don't have to," Sal interjected. "It's your choice and your right to privacy in this matter is absolute."

"*Again*," Cambridge said, "a lot to process. For the moment, we will tell you how we intend to proceed."

Conlon nodded, wondering how many choices she really had anymore.

"You will be temporarily reassigned to *Galen*," the counselor said. "All of your treatments will be coordinated here because this medical marvel Starfleet was kind enough to construct has the ability to monitor your body's systems continuously in a way no other vessel can, no matter where you are on board. Initially, you will have access to your quarters, sickbay, the holodecks, and mess hall. You will not be expected to perform any of your regular duties until further notice. You and I will meet daily for several hours. You will report to sickbay as needed for further tests. You will be permitted to speak with any other fleet crew members you wish but they will have to transport here in order to do so. It is entirely up to you how much of your condition you wish to share with anyone."

"Am I a prisoner?" Conlon asked.

"For the next several weeks at least, your access will be restricted for your own good," the Doctor said

"Just tell her the damn truth," Sal said. "We don't want to see you hurt yourself, Nancy. A lot of people in your shoes might make that choice. That's the only course we're not going to allow you to take."

Conlon understood. They thought she might attempt suicide. To be honest, it seemed like a perfectly valid choice. That it might also be *murder* didn't really bother her right now. The baby growing inside her wasn't even real yet.

Harry's baby, she suddenly thought, and felt her gorge rise.

She considered the expectant faces surrounding her one at a time. They were as frightened as she was. When her eyes met the Doctor's a new thought crossed her mind. *You should never have brought me back.*

Perhaps sensing this, the Doctor said, "We're not going to pretend that this isn't a dark road ahead, Nancy. What we can promise you is that you're not going to walk it alone."

VOYAGER

After the Sormana crisis was resolved, Commander Torres had ordered Icheb back to *Voyager*. Apparently Lieutenant Conlon had been restored to active duty prematurely and had been ordered to take an extended period of recuperation. As a result, Torres was temporarily assuming command of *Voyager's* engineering while still functioning as the entire fleet's chief engineer.

There was no shortage of work to be done. Torres's hours in engineering were restricted, given the demands of her infant. Icheb was required to be present for every duty shift during which the fleet chief was unavailable. Initially, the staff had reacted to this unenthusiastically. Almost every time he approached one of the engineers, usually with a request from Commander Torres, he was met with wary silence and grudging compliance. Apparently his desire to take initiative in his early days as Torres's aide was going to haunt him for some time.

Icheb accepted this as cheerfully as possible. He understood that he had created the problem and believed it was his to resolve. Under no circumstances would he trouble Commander Torres with his personal concerns. He would earn the respect of *Voyager*'s engineers, just as he had begun to earn that of the *Vesta*'s. He had already discovered that he preferred to spend his off-hours with Phinn and his staff, and did so as frequently as duty and proximity permitted.

Vesta's engineers were engaged in a new and exciting project. They had been tasked with developing larger-scale applications for the temporal shielding Icheb and Bryce had implemented throughout the fleet. No one had told Icheb why this was necessary, but he assumed that it might be the Krenim's *existence*. This was a task that under normal circumstances Icheb might have been asked to be assigned to. As it was, *Voyager* could not spare him.

Icheb told himself he wasn't hiding in the chief's office on the second level of engineering. He was studying the morning's reports and prioritizing items for Commander Torres's review when much to his surprise, Lieutenant Bryce entered.

"Icheb, I hope I'm not bothering you."

"Never. I mean, of course you aren't."

Bryce grinned and tossed a padd on the desk. "Take a look at this when you have some time."

"What is it?"

"We'll call it a self-diagnostic."

"Huh?"

"I've done my own performance review. You and I never had a chance to complete yours but it's been bothering me. I want to do better. I know you can help me with that. Just don't try to tell me I'm being too hard on myself. I can take criticism."

"Do you have any idea how unique that makes you among our fleet's engineers?" Icheb asked.

Bryce seriously considered the question. "No."

Icheb's failure with Commander O'Donnell had never been far from his thoughts. As a rule, *failure* was not part of Icheb's routine. His reception by *Voyager*'s engineers was a constant reminder of all he had yet to learn and part of him was grateful that Commander Torres had ordered him to drop the *Demeter* issue. But he remained unsatisfied.

It was an unusual place in which to find himself and he wondered if Bryce could relate. Until now, Icheb might not have risked the question. Phinn's good opinion of him had become too important. But it was also possible that *Vesta*'s young chief engineer might have some insight into the matter. He had served with the fleet since launch more than a year earlier and already worked closely with each of the fleet's chief engineers.

"The first review I completed was for *Demeter*. I presented it to Commander O'Donnell and he refused to allow me to give it to Lieutenant Elkins."

Bryce stood uncharacteristically still. Icheb wondered at his apparent shock but forged ahead. "I found a significant number of violations, which I cited. I've gone back twice with modified versions of my review, each time highlighting fewer deficiencies, and I've still been met with complete disregard by O'Donnell. I don't understand it. Doesn't he want to know if his chief engineer is comporting himself according to Starfleet's standards?"

"I doubt it," Bryce replied.

"I understand O'Donnell's command style is quite unusual, but—"

"It's got nothing to do with O'Donnell, Icheb. Do you know who Lieutenant Elkins is?"

"He is *Demeter*'s chief engineer."

Bryce shook his head and perched himself on the side of the desk.

"Garvin Elkins created *Demeter*. He's actually the father of the whole *Theophrastus*-class. He's been one of the Federation's most innovative starship designers and advanced propulsion theorists since before we were born."

"Then he should be well acquainted with Starfleet regulations."

"I didn't say *Starfleet*'s. I said the *Federation*'s. Elkins washed out of the Academy as a plebe. I only know about him because I had to do a paper on Vulcan starship design in my third year at the Academy."

"Professor Grilim?"

"Professor Saspari."

"Saspari's course did not come highly recommended. My advisor suggested that Grilim would be more challenging."

"That depends on what you consider a challenge, Icheb. Not all of the Federation's brightest lights serve in Starfleet. Some of the most innovative thinkers just don't fit there. They're not good at following orders. They can't handle the bureaucracy. Change happens inside Starfleet at a glacial pace, which makes sense. We're out on the front lines exploring and defending the Federation. We go with what we know works.

"Guys like Elkins, and O'Donnell for that matter, can't help but think differently. It's how they're wired. Admiral Batiste had to drag O'Donnell back to active duty kicking and screaming and it's my understanding that O'Donnell used that leverage to get Elkins a field commission because he wasn't coming out here without him. They've worked together for years. Every time O'Donnell needed something Starfleet couldn't deliver in a timely manner, he got it from Elkins."

"Elkins is that good?"

Bryce replied with an exaggerated nod. "*Demeter* is a thing of beauty. Elkins originally created a number of vessels with her unique detachable ring-propulsion design based on a Vulcan/Andorian paradigm, but he's taken them to a whole new level. He brought their offensive and defensive capabilities up to Starfleet's specs, but *Demeter*'s primary purpose is transport of multiple exotic life-forms. The environmental systems on that ship are more complex than anything *Vesta* has. Every individual bay can be discretely optimized to handle even the most extreme configurations. That unique massive port integrated into the hull is basically an interstellar greenhouse, designed to collect radiant particles and then simulate precise light conditions on a variety of planets. I'd bet my life *Demeter* could safely carry a small singularity in one of her holds if she needed to. And that's not the half of it. Elkins has been tinkering with exotic propulsion designs his entire life. He was theorizing about intergalactic warp drives before Starfleet even started thinking about slipstream. He was the one who integrated the slipstream assembly for *Demeter* because Starfleet didn't have any other vessels on the drawing board at the time that could also accommodate the rest of *Demeter*'s mission profile. I'm telling you, the man is amazing."

"But he is not amazing enough to withstand a routine performance evaluation by an ensign?"

"You're missing the point. Elkins is never going to pass a Starfleet review because he's not trying to. He's running systems on that ship that O'Donnell's mission directives require but that we haven't even developed standard protocols for because Elkins just invented them. Starfleet trusts him to keep *Demeter*'s crew safe, but she is classified as an experimental vessel for a reason. You can't rate her based on our best practices. That's not her purpose. Elkins's job is to push the envelope. We're lucky to have the chance to watch him do it up close. Commander O'Donnell didn't deny you access to Elkins because he was offended by your review. He probably just didn't want you to embarrass yourself in front of somebody who has already forgotten more about how starships work than we've had time to learn yet."

"Then why did Commander Torres ask me to perform an efficiency evaluation on *Demeter*?"

Bryce shrugged. "I don't know how much time she's spent with Elkins yet. She tends to get involved when there are problems, and *Demeter* hasn't had any Elkins couldn't solve all by himself. Besides, she's never really struck me as a stickler for protocol. She's a bit of an outside-the-box thinker, isn't she?"

Icheb nodded.

"I wouldn't worry about it. Let it go. You've got enough on your plate as it is. Until I'm as good as Elkins, I'm relying on you to keep me in line."

"Thanks, Bryce."

Phinn extracted a promise from Icheb to join his staff for drinks at the end of beta shift before departing. As soon as he was gone, Icheb pulled up everything in *Voyager*'s database about Lieutenant Elkins and began to study it.

Kathryn Janeway hadn't witnessed the entirety of the conversation between Commander Tuvok and Dayne that had ended with the Krenim beaten to a bloody pulp. But she had heard his last words.

She's dead. I couldn't save her. Too great a risk.

And she had seen the look in Dayne's eyes before he escaped. The *pity*.

It had not been possible to speak alone with Tuvok since then. After spending a few hours in *Vesta*'s sickbay following her rescue from the cavern, she regrouped with the Rilnar officers that had survived the island attack and taken charge of identifying the handful of Rilnar prisoners that Farkas had transported to safety before the normal flow of time resumed. After testifying against Limlesh at Colonial Command's debriefing, his commission had been rescinded pending a tribunal for treason. She had resigned her position as *denzit*, ceding it to *Tilzitar* Cabriot. She had facilitated Cabriot's communications with Rilnar Colonial Command and been present for his first meetings with the Rilnar leadership on Sormana. She had been there when Admiral Janeway had met with all of the relevant parties and confirmed that Servitor Silbrit had been essential in preventing the destruction of Sormana. She had made certain that everyone who would have a hand in Sormana's future was moving forward with all of the relevant facts at their disposal and had spoken as passionately as she could about the need to end all hostilities and focus on the much greater Krenim threat that faced both the Rilnar and Zahl.

She had done everything she could possibly do to avoid confronting the fact that the life she had chosen for herself on Sormana had been based on a lie. The only hope that had sustained her over the years, reunion with Dayne and her daughter, was never going to happen.

She reached the doors of Tuvok's quarters and almost retraced her steps to the transporter room. She knew what he would tell her. She didn't really need to hear it.

Still . . .

Her hand shook as she raised it to activate the door chime. Before she could do so, the door slid open and Tuvok stood before her, staring at her with absolute serenity. "Please come in, Kathryn."

"How did you know . . . ?"

"I have been expecting you."

He stepped back to allow her to enter. She did so and turned back to face him as the door shut. Studying him briefly, she sensed a subtle change in him. He had always excelled at masking his emotions, but she had known him long enough to realize when they were first reunited on Sormana that something was troubling him. When he had finally opened up to her about the death of his son, the pieces of that puzzle had fallen into place.

Nothing had changed in the last few weeks. His son was still dead. Evil had been given a new face, a Krenim face. The future was as uncertain as ever.

But Tuvok was different.

"Do you require confirmation of the intelligence I received from Agent Dayne?" Tuvok asked as she stared at him curiously.

Kathryn's throat was suddenly dry. The words were there, hanging between them, but she could not bring herself to say them.

Tuvok waited patiently.

Finally she croaked, "She's dead."

A subtle nod ended her world.

Chakotay had ordered Tuvok to return to *Voyager*. Although he had been questioned repeatedly, along with Kim and Seven, about their mission on the island, the captain had not mentioned Tuvok's complete loss of control in the cavern, his assault on Dayne, nor had he asked about Kathryn's child. Tuvok expected an official reprimand on his record. Had Chakotay chosen to bring charges against him for conduct unbecoming, Tuvok would have accepted any disciplinary action deemed appropriate. The only thing Chakotay had done thus far was to limit Tuvok's duties to the required debriefing sessions. Otherwise, Tuvok had been left alone in his quarters.

Tuvok did not mind. He had a great deal to consider and the solitude Chakotay had granted him was exactly what he required. He had come to believe that his lapse in the cavern was a sign that the control he thought he had regained over the last several months had been an illusion. He had been unable to repress the primal emotion that had overtaken him when Dayne had appeared before him. Tuvok had witnessed atrocities in his years of service, but none—apart from his son's death—had so thoroughly shattered a lifetime of logic and emotional control. What Dayne had done had offended Tuvok's essential being. Even before he had confirmed the death of the *denzit*'s child, the sheer tonnage of Dayne's sins had demanded retribution.

Dayne might have deserved to suffer as he had made Kathryn suffer. He had been revealed as an agent of pure evil. Tuvok understood now that his true complaint had not been with

Dayne but with the Borg. He was seeking vengeance, and vengeance was not Vulcan.

The emotions Tuvok had failed to control required release. Tuvok wrongly believed that to lose his rage was to lose Elieth. Misplaced though the ultimate focal point was, the act of allowing the rage, torment, and deep sorrow to move through and out of him had been a cleansing act, a necessary purging.

Elieth was dead.

This thought, once the sword point that goaded him, had now lost its potency. All that was true and honorable in his son's life and death was clearer than it had been at any time. It was now possible to think of Elieth without simultaneously battling blinding rage. His son had lived a useful life. His death was not a pointless one, certainly *not to Elieth*.

For too long, the application of reason and logic to his unruly thoughts had been a painstaking process. Now, embracing Surak's teachings became a healing balm. It was far too soon to believe that he had accepted Elieth's death. But finally, he knew that it would be possible.

Kathryn's struggle was just beginning. He wanted to assist her as best he could. He had waited patiently for her to come to him, knowing that she would in her own time and that allowing her to make that choice was essential. Acceptance could not be forced upon her any more than those who loved Tuvok had been able to guide him toward it before he was ready.

Kathryn had fallen to the deck before him. He knelt beside her, allowing her wails of despair to echo throughout his quarters. The violence of them did not trouble his peace, nor did they awaken darker thoughts within him. They simply *were*.

Eventually, she reached for him. Despite his deeply ingrained reluctance to engage in physical expressions of emotions with non-Vulcans, he opened his arms to her and allowed her to draw from his strength what she required. He was a safe place, a fellow traveler on this road. The only comfort he could offer was his presence, his companionship.

Finally, she began to regain a modicum of control. She pulled herself free of him and settled herself on the deck, breathing deeply and allowing less powerful waves of anguish to wash over her.

"I didn't know . . ." she began.

Tuvok waited for her to continue.

"I didn't know he had so much evil in him. He was not the man I thought he was. But even if he could not love me, how could *she* have meant so little to him?"

As this reality was as alien to Tuvok as it was to Kathryn, he did not have an immediate answer beyond, "I do not know."

"I'm never going to see him again."

"I agree that it is unlikely."

"The way he looked at me . . ." She took a deep, ragged breath before continuing. ". . . I saw him then, for the first time . . . who he really is."

"It is alarming to witness our proficiency in hiding our true selves from one another. His motivation must have been incredibly powerful to have been able to convince you that he was worthy of your trust and regard when that was never the case."

"Whatever she did to him—*your Admiral Janeway*—he can't forgive it."

"There is nothing anyone could have done to him to warrant the depravity he displayed. His sociopathic need to avenge himself on her and you has nothing to do with your choices or the admiral's. They go much deeper and I doubt we will ever acquire sufficient data to understand them in all of their complexity."

A grimace traipsed across her face. "You almost killed him."

Tuvok nodded, unrepentant.

"Was that for me?"

"It was for me."

Kathryn smiled faintly.

"So what do we do now? How do we continue to live in a universe that is so cruel?"

"There are but two choices, both of them painful. We may

choose further conflict. We may seek vengeance on those who have wronged us and perpetuate the cycle of violence that creates men like Dayne.

"Or we may choose the harder road of learning to accept and forgive them."

Kathryn started as if he had slapped her.

"Forgive him? Never."

"That will be your decision to make, Kathryn. But bear in mind that what I am suggesting to you is no more than what is now required of the inhabitants of Sormana."

"Have you forgiven the Borg?"

Tuvok considered the question for a long time.

Finally, he said, "There is more to my life than their cruelty. There is service to my fellow beings. There is my family and friends. There is knowledge yet to be discovered. There are truths yet to be revealed. Forgiveness grants me access to those things."

Kathryn stared at him. He had never before seen her so empty.

"I have no idea what is mine."

Tuvok reached out to her and took her hands in his. "Start with this."

26

VOYAGER

When Counselor Hugh Cambridge had seen Lieutenant Conlon settled into her quarters aboard *Galen,* he returned to *Voyager* with the intention of spending the next few hours rearranging his schedule to accommodate the hours he would now be spending with Nancy and her medical team. He also wanted to review the notes from their previous sessions. It troubled him that she had so successfully concealed her inner turmoil from him. That others might have missed it was not alarming. That *he* had been blind to her deception suggested a lack of focus on his part that was unacceptable.

Seven was waiting for him in his quarters. A single glance at her beguiling form quickened his pulse. She was seated with her legs pulled to one side on his sofa, her elbow resting on its back supporting her slightly tilted head with her hand. As was often the case these days, her eyes were distant, focused on some internal landscape he could not access.

Perhaps his recent myopia wasn't that hard to understand after all. Seven seemed to have managed the task of separating the personal from her duty much better than he had. This might require further exploration. She had been his patient. Her task had been to learn from him. Their professional relationship had ended long ago, but since then he had clearly given too little thought to how much *she* might be able teach him.

"Good evening, my love," he greeted her. "Have you eaten?"

"I have."

"I won't be ready to turn in for a few more hours."

Seven brought her legs to the floor and placed her elbows on her knees, resting her chin in her hands. "I have violated Starfleet regulations several times since I first came to *Voyager*," she said dispassionately. "I did so again today and for the first time, regret that choice."

Intrigued, Cambridge moved to sit opposite her. "Go on."

"I have been assisting the officers of the Rilnar command center in their analysis of the readings they were able to take of Rahalla prior to its destruction. The admiral authorized me to give them access to the data we collected on our tricorders and what was discovered by *Voyager*'s sensors when in orbit. I have also been working with their engineers, explaining the modifications that will be required to add temporal shielding to their current defensive arsenal."

"None of that sounds like a crime to me."

"A point of data has troubled me since we first learned of the *denzit*'s existence. No one else has raised the issue in our subsequent briefings, but it has not been resolved to my satisfaction."

"What point, love?"

"The *denzit*'s survival."

Cambridge looked away briefly, attempting to recall the information the *denzit* had provided. "Didn't some doctor revive her after she died?"

Seven met his eyes, her disappointment clear.

"Kathryn Janeway's death was a fixed point in time. Every single version of her that ever existed died across all timelines at the same moment in a variety of manners. Our admiral was saved by the unprecedented intervention of an omnipotent lifeform. Do you honestly believe anything less could have saved the *denzit*?"

"Now that you mention it, I don't know. But does it matter? She lived. She's here now. Her survival has complicated this fleet's mission as only Kathryn Janeway can."

"During my review of the Rilnar's databases, I was able to access their medical files. I knew it was wrong, but I copied the *denzit*'s file."

"Ah, there it is. *Yes, that* is certainly frowned upon by Starfleet."

"If I tell you what I found, you will also be vulnerable to disciplinary action."

"I'll risk it."

"The circumstances of her death were not precisely what she described to Captain Chakotay."

"*She lied?* Imagine my surprise."

"She did not succumb to injuries sustained in an attack on her base. She died in childbirth."

Cambridge sat in stunned silence for a full minute. Seven waited patiently until he asked, "Did the child survive?"

"She was taken by her father from the medical center in the chaos that followed the *denzit*'s death. Her current whereabouts are unknown."

"*Merde.*"

"The doctor who revived the *denzit* made no formal report. No one even recorded his name. Her vital signs just prior to her death were such that no standard intervention could have reversed the process. Her blood loss was massive. The duty nurse reported that the doctor in question initiated mouth-to-mouth resuscitation and chest compressions to successfully revive her. Blood transfusions were immediately initiated and stabilized her condition."

"I grant you, it was a one-in-a-billion chance, but we're not talking about just any woman. Kathryn Janeway is a force of nature and it sounds to me like she had more than most to live for."

"Perhaps," Seven agreed.

"But you don't think so."

Seven shook her head.

"Are you going to tell the admiral?"

"Do you think I should?"

Cambridge shrugged. "It explains the *denzit*'s choice to stick with the war to the bitter end. I'd bet a year of shore leave that Commander Tuvok knew about it. When he spoke of the personal concerns that kept her tethered to that rock, he might have been talking about more than her husband."

"If Dayne took the child, she could still be alive."

Cambridge thought back to the chaotic moments following their return to the cavern after Batibeh. Tuvok had assaulted Dayne. The Krenim man had been saying something . . .

"*She's dead,*" Cambridge said. "That's what Dayne told Tuvok."

"Are you willing to take his word for it?"

Cambridge sighed. "Of course not."

Several hours after she had arrived, Tuvok escorted Kathryn back to her quarters on *Vesta* and requested a mild sedative for her, which Doctor Sal willingly provided. When he returned to *Voyager* a message was waiting for him from Captain Chakotay.

As requested, Tuvok reported immediately to the captain's ready room.

"Take a seat, Commander," Chakotay ordered upon his entrance.

Tuvok would have preferred to stand but saw no reason to add rudeness to the list of charges Chakotay was surely prepared to file against him.

"I'm in the process of completing my report on the incidents at Rahalla. I require a little clarification, if you have a few minutes."

"Of course, Captain."

"The child you asked Dayne about . . . that was Kathryn's child as well?"

"Yes, Captain."

"And you learned of the child's existence from . . . ?"

"The *denzit* shared that intelligence with me during my first visit to Sormana."

"I see. You, of course, chose to omit that information from your report because . . ."

"The *denzit* asked that I respect her privacy."

"You didn't think that our need to fully understand the *denzit*'s motivations took priority over respecting her privacy?"

"I did not."

Chakotay leaned forward in his chair, placing both hands on the desk. "One could argue that was dereliction of duty."

"I fully expect that *one will*."

Chakotay exhaled slowly, shaking his head. "I probably had that coming. When I accused you of failing us back in the cavern, I did so in the absence of significant data."

"Indeed?"

"It seems to me that you have been acting this entire time out of concern for the child's well-being. Knowledge of her existence could have compromised her safety. Despite Dayne's assurances to you that the child is dead, that intelligence was offered under extreme duress and can hardly be considered unequivocal proof."

"Kathryn believes it to be true."

Chakotay nodded somberly. "She might be right. If she has no intention of pursuing the matter further, that is her prerogative."

"I agree."

"My problem is this. At the moment, Admiral Janeway is inclined to continue monitoring the Krenim but we are not going to pursue further contact. None of us, *least of all the admiral*, are interested in provoking another protracted conflict with the Krenim. By providing technology to the Rilnar and Zahl that will permit them to defend themselves against future temporal incursions, we've done all we can reasonably be expected to do to secure this region against further alterations to the timeline."

"A logical and tactically sound course of action."

"But if I note in this report that the other Kathryn had a child and that we believe it is possible that the child is being held by the Krenim, the admiral is going to feel a sense of personal responsibility to investigate that claim. She's never going to take Dayne's word that the child has died. She's likely to demand proof."

"Any action this fleet takes with regard to that child will put her at risk, should she still be alive."

"I know."

"The only individual among us with legitimate cause to pursue the matter is the former *denzit*, and she would surely find a willing advocate in the admiral."

"Which would also compromise this fleet's safety," Chakotay noted.

"Agreed."

"So if you were me, what would you do, Tuvok?"

"I am not you, Captain."

"No."

"If you are requesting my opinion as a friend to the admiral, the former *denzit*, and you, I would suggest that no one's interests would be served by creating an issue that could provoke a greater conflict where none currently exists. Whether or not we believe Dayne's assertions to be grounded in fact, Kathryn does. To continue to pursue the matter will create greater anxiety for her than our suspicions warrant and may be detrimental to her healing process. More important, it might force Dayne to take action to prove the truth of his words, thus endangering an innocent life.

"I cannot weigh Starfleet's interest in this matter as greater than a child's interest in continuing to exist," Tuvok continued. "Indeed, the only solace I can find in this circumstance is to believe Dayne's assertion. If she is dead, there is nothing to be done. If she is alive, any attempt we might make to reunite Kathryn with her child could prove fatal, both to the child and us."

"My inclination is to leave well enough alone."

"And yet you feel that to do so is to personally betray the admiral?"

"I think she would see it the way should she ever learn about it."

"Are you willing to accept the consequences, given the magnitude of the alternatives?"

Chakotay paused for a long time. Finally he said, "I think I have to. I think the only thing worse than the child living the rest of her life as Dayne's daughter would be learning that something *we* did resulted in the child's death."

"Is it possible you aren't giving the admiral sufficient credit? Your reasoning is sound. Whatever her initial reaction to this information might be, you should be able to persuade her of the most appropriate course of action."

"I'd like to think you're right."

"But?"

"My heart tells me it's not going to be that simple."

"I would never advise you to ignore the demands of your heart."

"You wouldn't? Is that logical?"

"Logical or not, it is unwise."

"I've missed your counsel."

"Should you have further need of it, Captain, you have but to ask."

"Thank you, Tuvok."

GALEN

Lieutenant Nancy Conlon didn't want to talk to anyone. She *had* to talk to Cambridge and her doctors, but in the day that had passed since she had received their diagnosis and begun to enjoy their polite version of confinement to quarters, no one had pressed her to make any choices regarding her treatment or the fate of . . .

Conlon still had to force herself to think the words.

The baby.

The shock of the previous day had given way at first light to a visceral need to destroy something. As *she* was not an option, she'd chosen the next best thing. *Galen*'s holodeck was smaller than *Voyager*'s, but the range of programs available was substantially greater. To her dismay, all the hand-to-hand combat scenarios were denied her. The damned counselor was clearly getting back on top of his game to have thought of that. But the standard twenty-kilo punching bag that came with the gym program was better than nothing.

Conlon had been beating her fists against it and leveling vicious kicks at its midpoint for more than an hour when an unexpected voice sounded behind her.

"Hi, Nancy."

Conlon turned, flushed and spent from her physical exertion. "Harry."

For a split second she considered trading him for the bag. The next moment she was certain she was going to burst into violent tears. Finally that anger and pain morphed into a question in her mind.

"How did you get here?"

Kim shrugged. "I co-opted Waters's sensors for a few minutes at the end of her shift, and trained them on *Galen* to determine your location. I waited for the gamma shift crew rotation cycle for our shields and *Galen*'s to drop long enough for routine personnel and supply transports. I initiated a site-to-site transport to this holodeck."

Nancy smiled in spite of herself.

"That's a lot of trouble you went through."

"You didn't leave me any choice. No one will tell me anything about what's happening to you. The last time I saw you, you were ripping my clothes off in Chakotay's ready room. I've sent you ten messages a day. I honestly don't care anymore if you love me or if you ever did. I just need to know one thing."

"Okay."

"What did I do wrong?"

Tears threatened again. Nancy held them at bay.

"You did nothing wrong, Harry."

"That's not possible. I know you were angry with me, but this—"

"You did nothing wrong, Harry. *This*," she said, opening her hands to take in the room at large, "has nothing to do with you. I have a problem. It's a medical issue. It's taken this long for every doctor in this fleet to figure out what it is. I'm off duty for the foreseeable future."

Harry had been angry when he first arrived. He'd controlled it, but his fury had been real. It evaporated with the gut-punch of her admission.

He stepped closer to her and she immediately retreated, keeping her distance. Hurt, he said, "What's the issue?"

Nancy had heard the words. She understood them and could do a fair job of explaining. But she had not yet *said* them aloud, even to herself.

"I have a progressive degenerative disease."

Harry's face reddened. Now she wasn't the only one fighting back tears. Far from adding to her pain, his concern, coupled with the act of speaking the truth, lightened the load she was carrying an infinitesimal degree.

"It's curable, right?"

"We don't know yet. It might be."

Determination replaced fear. "It *will* be," Harry assured both of them. "The Doctor is the best there is. From what I've heard, Sharak and Sal are no lightweights either. If they say there's hope, there is. You're going to be fine."

So far, this had been easier than Nancy had anticipated. The rest was going to destroy everything they had built between them in the last year. She wasn't sure she had that in her.

"Why are you trying to do this alone?"

"I'm not alone," she insisted. "I've got a whole team of professionals, including Counselor Cambridge ready to talk with me all damn day."

"They're not . . ." He struggled to complete the sentence. "What about your friends?"

I don't deserve them, Nancy thought.

"I can't ask any of you to take this on," she said. "I understand why you'd want to. But we both know what it's like out here. One crisis after another. Everybody has too much to do. More, now that I'm off duty. You don't need this."

"That's stupid."

Nancy flinched, taken aback.

"That's the dumbest thing I've ever heard in my life, and I'm best friends with Tom Paris. Some artists work in oils, some in clay. *Dumb* is Tom's true medium. But right now, you're giving the master a run for his money."

"Harry, I—"

He closed the distance between them in four quick strides but stopped short of touching her.

"I love you. I am yours. You took my heart, and even though you seem to want to give it back, I'm not going to let you. Not over something like this. I get that this is awful, terrible, frightening-to-your-core news. You probably think letting me go is some ridiculous noble thing to do. It will hurt a little now, but less than if we go down this road together and it ends badly. Well, guess what? You don't get to make that choice for me. Live or die, we're doing this together. You try to shut me out again and I'll get myself transferred to *Galen* as your personal security detachment and become a frigging permanent fixture. You won't go to the 'fresher without my knowledge. This is not a game to me, Nancy. I've spent weeks now wondering what I did wrong, how I hurt you. It almost killed me. Walking away, it's just not possible. I can't and I won't. So say whatever you like. Kick my ass from one side of this room to the other. You're not getting rid of me."

Nancy had liked Harry since they'd first met. It was moments like this that had made her love him. When he got himself worked up, Harry Kim was a sight to behold. He would run headlong into an inferno for his friends. He'd suffer untold physical and emotional misery recovering from the burns. And the next day, he'd do it again. People like Harry, they never learned. That's why you wanted them beside you.

But he *couldn't be* for this. She had to make this choice for both of them. Either way, it was going to destroy his world, his hopes for the future, every dream he'd allowed himself to imagine since they'd met. This wasn't his fault. She'd used him to keep her terror at a distance. That was all. There had been times she'd imagined something more and even allowed herself to believe it could happen with Harry. But not like this. He deserved better. She had to make him see that.

"I'm pregnant," she said softly.

Righteous indignation fled from his face. Now it was his turn to experience shock.

"I don't want the baby," she continued, just in case there was any doubt in his mind. "I'm not ready and neither or you."

"I don't— Wait. Can you even . . . ?"

"There's nothing wrong with it. My condition won't affect it. They, the doctors, want me to keep it so that they can harvest cells from it to repair the damage to my DNA."

Harry stepped back.

That's right, she thought. *Run. I would if I were you.*

Harry didn't.

He looked around for a moment, as if he had suddenly been transported to the surface of an inhospitable alien world, then he dropped like a stone onto a nearby weight bench. She watched him process this minor detail. Every emotion, every thought he was having was plain on his face. He seemed to settle on overwhelmed.

"It's all right," she said. "You can go. This isn't your problem."

"You don't want the baby?"

"For God's sake, Harry, what do you think?"

"I don't know. I've had all of thirty seconds to process this."

"You don't want the baby either."

"You don't know that. Remember that time you got pissed at me for thinking I knew better than you what you needed? I stopped. You need to do the same."

Good point. "Sorry."

Harry rose abruptly and took a few unsteady steps. When he reached the punching bag he seemed to seriously consider taking a swing at it, but instead grabbed it for support and hugged it with both arms.

"If you weren't sick, would your choice be different?"

Nancy released a long, deep breath.

"I have no idea. And now I'm never going to know."

"Pretend, just for the sake of argument. Could you see it— you and me and a child, out here, doing what we do?"

"Not right now. A few years from now, maybe. Today, not really."

"But if you . . . " Harry swallowed hard, unable to bring himself to utter the words.

She did it for him. "Terminate it."

"Then you'll die?"

"My odds of survival go way down."

"Then you have to keep it."

"I don't *have* to do anything, Harry."

"You'd rather commit slow suicide than raise our child together?"

"I won't create a life for the sole purpose of saving my own."

"You didn't. Did you?"

"Of course not."

"Then why not keep it?"

"Look, I'm having a hard enough time sorting this out on my own. I understand why you think you have a stake in this, but you don't. I have to do what I can live with. I'm sorry, Harry, but your needs can't factor into this decision for me."

Harry rested his face against the bag. He began to slowly pound his forehead against its soft surface. After a few moments, he pulled back and nodded, more to himself than to her.

"Okay."

"Okay?"

"That's what I said."

"What does that mean?"

"It means you get to decide what you want to do about this. It means I'm not going to pressure you one way or the other. I want you to live. But I get that you need to do that on your terms. I'm not going to make this harder for you. Whatever you decide, you don't even have to tell me. Just . . . do it."

"Thank you."

She expected this to be the end. She wasn't okay with that, but it was necessary.

"So, what else is going on?"

Nancy was struck dumb. Insensate of this fact, Kim moved slowly back toward her, crossing his arms at his chest.

"What?"

"How are you doing otherwise?"

"You're not my counselor, Harry."

"No. I'm the man who loves you. Whatever you do, whatever you say, that's not going to change. If you'd rather, we could just take turns beating the hell out of that thing. Or . . . hang on . . . we're on a holodeck."

Harry moved to the controls and briefly scanned the menu. He tapped a few commands into the panel and the scene around them shifted. Nancy suddenly found herself in an alien land-scape. They were in a forest, surrounded by tall trees. Two large white suns hung on the horizon, bathing the grove in which they stood in beautiful pink and orange light. A gentle breeze blew. As it did so, the leaves around them rustled, *no*, trilled softly, creating an almost musical sound.

"What is this place?"

"It's a planet out here called Alastria. I visited it once, briefly. This is my version . . . it's how I remember it."

"It's beautiful."

"I know. I come here sometimes when I'm tired of thinking."

Harry seated himself on the ground and stared out at the sunsets. After a few moments, Nancy settled herself beside him.

"How come you never brought me here before?"

Harry shrugged. "I don't know. I've never shared it with anyone before."

"Don't you have to get back to *Voyager*?"

"Eventually. But with all the extra duty shifts I've pulled lately, I don't think Tom or Chakotay would mind if I took a little time for myself."

"Do you want me to leave?"

"Yes, Nancy. I just reprogrammed the holodeck to show you the most beautiful, deeply personal space I've created for myself because I wanted to be here alone."

Nancy smiled.

"Stupid," Harry muttered, lifting his arms and pulling her close until her head rested comfortably on his chest.

They sat like that, in silence, long after darkness had fallen around them.

DEMETER

"I don't believe it," Commander Liam O'Donnell said when Ensign Icheb entered his private lab.

"Good morning, sir. I hope I'm not disturbing you," Icheb said.

"That remains to be seen."

"That last time I came here to present my review of Lieutenant Elkins, you told me to come back when I understood. Now, I do."

O'Donnell sat back and crossed his arms over his chest.

"Really?"

"On stardate 42954, an unclassified Starfleet vessel, registered as NX-00771, was destroyed because of a malfunction in its warp drive assembly. She was an experimental ship, a test bed for a new type of core powered by a series of small singularities. Forty-one Starfleet officers and crewmen along with six civilian engineers were killed. She was built at Utopia Planitia as a joint venture between Starfleet and the Federation Science Institute. She had been designed by a team of civilian experts led by Garvin Elkins. After the disaster, Starfleet terminated their work with the Institute and since then has rarely engaged in similar initiatives. Starfleet's official investigation revealed that the explosion was caused by a breach in the containment field caused by unexpected stresses on the core during the formation of the warp bubble. Elkins was cleared of any responsibility for the accident. Still, he has not cooperated with anyone in Starfleet other than you since that time, until he decided to modify *Demeter* for use by the Full Circle Fleet. I am guessing he only agreed to do so because of the deep respect he has for you and in light of your close personal relationship."

"Those records were classified."

"It's possible that you have not been fully briefed on my capacity for inappropriate conduct at times when our regulations place unacceptable obstacles between me and the truth. It is a tendency Admiral Akaar hopes my service with this fleet will temper."

A ghost of a smile flickered across O'Donnell's face. "I wish your commanding officers good luck with that."

"As best I can tell, this incident is the only blemish on the otherwise extraordinary record of Lieutenant Elkins. Most of his peers believe him to be one of the most innovative engineers currently in the field. I know, from personal experience, how mistakes weigh on the minds of men like Elkins. They do not forget. They are haunted by thoughts of what they should have done differently."

"You're what, twenty-something, Ensign?" O'Donnell asked. "You haven't had time to make those kinds of mistakes yet."

"Of course not, sir. I understand now why you would not permit me to submit my original review to Lieutenant Elkins. I initially assumed you were being dismissive of my abilities. That was not the case. You were unwilling to risk the chief's reaction. My review would have been an unpleasant reminder to the lieutenant of his past failures and might have unduly shaken his confidence in his choice to once again risk working in conjunction with Starfleet."

O'Donnell nodded somberly.

"Which means we have a problem."

"It means *you* have a problem."

"No, sir. *We* have a problem. *Demeter*'s status as an experimental vessel allows for a certain amount of leeway in deviation from standard Starfleet protocols. I did not take that into account in my initial review. I would like your permission to repeat the evaluation, in light of this ship's unique status, and when it is done, to offer my assistance to the chief to bring any systems he believes can be safely modified closer to compliance with current standards. I would, of course, defer to his judgment, given his vast experience and deep knowledge of this vessel's capabilities. I would not presume to stand in judgment of his work. I believe I could learn a great deal, however, by observing him and offering any insights that might arise during that process. I trust the lieutenant to make this crew's safety his first priority. But for *Demeter* to become more than a test-vessel, for Starfleet to invest in other similar ships, her systems and procedures will have to be brought into full compliance. This is a task Lieutenant Elkins should delegate to a trusted subordinate. There's no reason to trouble him with these details. I am offering my assistance with this most mundane of duties. I am certain that even with my limited experience, with his assistance I can complete it to the lieuten-ant's satisfaction and in the process, fulfill my responsibilities to Commander Torres."

O'Donnell did not reply for several moments. Finally he extended his hand and Icheb passed him the padd he had been holding. The commander read it thoroughly and tapped the screen, adding his approval to it. When he handed it back to Icheb, his eyes held a new respect for the ensign.

"Works for me."

"Thank you, sir."

27

VESTA

Admiral Kathryn Janeway sat alone in her quarters staring out the port at the planet below. She was sorely tempted to remain in orbit of Sormana until the final peace negotiations had been concluded. But just as this had never been the *denzit's* war, this was not *her peace*. Nothing she or the fleet had done thus far ran too far afoul of their mission directives or the Prime Directive. She had succeeded in extricating a former Starfleet officer from a dubious situation. She had shared intelligence with two other warp-capable civilizations and was helping them to prepare to meet a greater threat, should her worst fears about the Krenim prove real.

It was time to move on.

This meant, among other things, that it was also time to send *Voyager* back to the Beta Quadrant and bid farewell to Tuvok. They hadn't spoken since the destruction of Rahalla. Her plate had been heaped high with diplomatic requirements and she was averaging three to four hours of sleep each night. She had hoped, perhaps naively, that once they had a chance to speak face-to-face the distance Tuvok had intentionally placed between them would have dissipated. She understood his position now. She knew that he, alone, would have to walk the path toward wholeness and peace. She wondered if his experiences with the *denzit* had helped or hurt his chances of finding his way back to Surak's teachings. Perhaps at some point, she might raise the issue with the other Kathryn. It would be interesting, to say the least, to hear her perspective.

At least now there would be time.

"Bridge to Admiral Janeway."

"Go ahead, Lieutenant Psilakis."

"The Truon has just appeared and her captain is asking to speak with you."

Janeway dropped her head into her hands. She had expected Dayne to seek her out again and sincerely hoped it was simply to allow her to fulfill the bargain they'd made. *If he was contemplating more aggressive actions . . .*

The admiral shook her head. *One moment at a time.*

"Order all fleet vessels to yellow alert and forward Agent Dayne's transmission to my quarters."

"Aye, Admiral."

When Dayne's face appeared on her monitor, he looked worse than she had anticipated. There hadn't been time for a close examination when she returned from Batibeh. All she had really seen was a great deal of blood covering his face. Now large purple and yellow bruises testified to the barbarity of Tuvok's attack. The admiral had chosen to allow Chakotay to mete out any disciplinary action. For her part, she couldn't fault Tuvok. He had done no more than she had wanted to, despite the fact that it was clearly conduct unbecoming. She chose to believe that Dayne had instigated their *disagreement* and remained mindful of the fact that the extent of his injuries might have made it impossible for him to intervene with *Vesta*'s rescue operations. Whatever the case, Dayne's current condition was better than he deserved.

"It seems you have succeeded once again, Admiral, in avoiding appropriate consequences for your actions," Dayne said.

She had no intention of rising to his bait.

"I have seen no evidence of further Krenim interference in Zahl or Rilnar territory. I hope this is a sign of things to come."

Dayne's gaze hardened. *"You owe me an answer."*

"I do," she agreed. "But before I satisfy your curiosity, there is one thing I'd really like to know."

Dayne shook his head in disbelief. *"Don't try my patience, Admiral."*

"Are you aware that while I was investigating the temporal portals at Rahalla, I briefly visited an alternate timeline, one in which you and a man the Rilnar believe to be your brother were responsible for bringing peace to Sormana two hundred years ago?"

"I am."

"Would you have to betray any closely guarded secrets to explain to me why you would have gone to all the trouble to secure a peace treaty on Sormana and then apparently *undone* it?"

"I know that you believe my people's understanding of time has given us an unearned sense of superiority. I am certain that you do not think us capable of acting from an altruistic sense of moral obligation and instead, paint all of our actions with the same broad, dangerous brush. I suspect you believe we are continuing to act with the same reckless selfishness Annorax displayed during your encounter with him.

"None of that is true. We understand time better than you possibly could. The fluid intersection of cause and effect is not a mystery to us. But we have learned the hard way that even with the best of intentions, we can err. When we do, we take responsibility and correct our mistakes. One of the most important lessons Annorax taught us was that trying to eliminate troubling variables from temporal equations was the surest road to disaster. The consequences of destruction are much easier to predict than those of creation but they are also much harder to reverse.

"We have known for a long time that Sormana's fate was

inextricably linked with our own. In an attempt to avert wider conflict and eliminate a number of troubling variables, we decided to try to end the war. The days after the battle of Batibeh were the most conducive to our purpose while at the same time presenting the fewest possible counter-indications. Another agent and I, posing as Rilnar and Zahl civilians, intervened. As that timeline has shown, we were right to believe that from the ashes of Batibeh peace could rise. What we did not accurately foresee was how the Rilnar and Zahl would continue to develop in the absence of that conflict.

"They were in the early stages of colonial expansion at that time. The Peace of Sormana filled both sides with a sense of self-righteous superiority. They decided that given their accomplishments, it was their right to dictate to other species the terms of interstellar relations. When we returned from Batibeh, our territories had been reduced by more than seventy percent. This had always been a negligible possibility according to our calculations, so small that we were willing to risk it. The much more probable outcome of our success had been stabilization of this entire sector.

"The only way to restore the Imperium was another small incursion."

"You went back and killed the Rilnar and Zahl leaders the night before their peace accord could be finalized."

"We did not. We made sure that several individuals who were less than pleased with the prospect of peace had access to those leaders. What they did with that access was their choice."

"At what point in the study of temporal mechanics are the Krenim taught to master the art of rationalization?"

"A course you could certainly teach better than I, Admiral."

Janeway nodded. "Fair enough."

"Your turn."

"Are your people familiar with a species known as the Q?"

"No."

"They are among a handful of incredibly powerful beings my people have encountered, and for many years they have taken a disquieting interest in the Federation. A number of Starfleet captains and officers have interacted with them on several occasions. They have mastered the manipulation of space and time to a degree even you would find humbling. To them, all of us are nothing more than children, barely taking our first steps toward a wider understanding of the possibilities of sentient existence."

"What is their planet of origin?"

"They have their own continuum. They exist outside of space and time and are not bound by any limits imposed on most corporeal and non-corporeal beings. Honestly, you should count yourself lucky that you've never had to deal with them. I would too were it not for the fact that I would not be here right now if it weren't for Q."

"They saved you?"

"More or less."

"Just you?"

"Yes. When I first learned of the *denzit*'s existence, the most troubling part was the fact that based on what I had learned from my experience with the Q, she should have died long ago."

"I see."

Janeway went on to explain in some detail the existence of an imbalance in the multiverse caused by the Anschlasom through their breach of the Omega Continuum and the lengths to which the multiverse had gone to correct it, including the creation of the Omega Continuum's avatar and the deaths of all versions of Kathryn Janeway across all timelines to ensure that avatar's presence at the critical moment.

Dayne listened intently, interrupting only occasionally for clarification. When the admiral had finished her tale, he appeared puzzled, but satisfied.

"Are we done here, Agent Dayne?"

"For now."

"Am I going to find it necessary to return to this sector any time soon?"

"Your actions here have not created sufficient counter-indications to warrant further incursions. You might want to advise the Rilnar and Zahl that the Krenim pose no threat to them and are content to

allow them to live in peace as long as they return the favor. Should they initiate conflict, I doubt even you would argue with our right to defend ourselves."

"Not with your right, but possibly with your methods."

"Again, I am appalled by your willingness to hold others to standards you clearly believe do not apply to you."

"This area of space is far beyond the Federation. We have no stake in its development beyond the hope that all sentient spacefaring races will find peaceful coexistence preferable to conflict. That said, a number of our scientists have dedicated their lives to the study and the preservation of the integrity of time. I had hoped when you first told me of the existence of your Temporal Defense Agency that this was a sign that your people had reached the same conclusion as ours about temporal manipulation. I am still willing to be convinced that this is the case."

"Time will tell."

"Indeed. I have one final request, Agent Dayne."

"Just one? How refreshing."

"The woman you captured, tortured, and betrayed is now my personal responsibility. I assume that by answering your questions, I have eliminated any possibility that your people will feel it necessary to interact with her again at any time in the future. If you once again find yourselves troubled by chaotic variables, I must insist that you take the matter up with *me*. Are we clear?"

"Yes, Admiral. In fact, on this point, we are in complete agreement."

"Farewell, Agent Dayne. It is my fondest hope that we will never meet again."

"A hope we share."

TRUON

Agent Dayne spared no attention for the quantum duplicate he had created or its current conversation with Admiral Janeway.

His double would exist only for the few minutes Dayne required. There had been no need to debrief him. He knew all that Dayne did, including this mission's objectives, and understood implicitly that his only task was to keep the admiral talking for as long as possible without arousing any suspicion on her part.

In the meantime, Dayne would use the wave on which the transmission was being carried to transport himself undetected to the *Vesta*. The temporal synch disruptor he had already attached to his arm would permit him to board the Federation vessel in a state of temporal flux that should prevent their sensors from detecting him.

Should was the operative word. No one must know what he was about to do. The duplicate would be destroyed as soon as Dayne returned. The *Truon*'s logs would be purged. A number of things could go wrong with this plan, but Dayne didn't care.

It was time to bring Kathryn home.

VESTA

Kathryn Janeway didn't know what had awakened her. She didn't even know where she was. Preferring oblivion to these questions, she tried to resettle herself on the pillow when a voice whispered in her ear.

"Kathryn, wake up."

This time, a sudden rush of adrenaline kicked in. She was alert and scampering as far from that voice as possible. She had reached the far side of the bed and narrowly avoided tumbling to the deck between it and the bulkhead. Her instinct was to grab a weapon but all she had at her disposal was a blanket.

"Don't be afraid."

Some half-remembered gesture was immediately resurrected. Lifting her hand to her heart, Kathryn tried to tap the combadge she had been issued when she came aboard. Her hand found only her shirt. The communicator was gone.

Dayne held it in his hand. Dropping it to the deck, he crushed it under his boot.

"You don't need to contact them. I'm not going to hurt you."

Panic was rising. *Of course he was going to hurt her. What else had he ever done?*

She couldn't think. She could barely breathe. She started to scream and in a flash, Dayne had flown over the bed and clamped his hand down firmly over her mouth.

It didn't help that he looked like hell. That evidence of his injuries still remained so many days after they had been inflicted testified to the damage Tuvok had done. That Dayne was obviously also Krenim was equally disturbing.

"Calm down, Kathryn. I need to affix this synch disruptor to your arm. You're coming with me."

She struggled against him. Her left elbow met his gut and though he gasped in pain, his hold remained true.

"*Listen to me.* I've come to help you. I can take you to our daughter, but you have to stop fighting me."

A new wave of fury rose within her. With strength unsuspected, she pulled her arms free, sending an elbow flying toward his face. He staggered back and she stepped forward, throwing both her hands into his chest, pummeling him to the deck. She tried to step past him but got tangled in his hands. He grabbed her right foot, tripping her as her momentum carried her forward.

She crawled, desperate to reach an open space and run.

He found his feet first and jumped over her, stopping at the doorway that separated her bedroom from the rest of her quarters. As she was pulling herself to her feet, she saw him reach inside his jacket. A scream of terror died in her throat.

He was reaching for his weapon. She was going to die.

What did it matter?

Spent, she stood before him, completely vulnerable.

"Do it," she said softly. "End it. *Please.*"

He seemed shocked by her words. His hand cleared his jacket and she realized he wasn't holding a disruptor. He had removed a sheet of heavy brown paper. Wordlessly, he unfolded it and turned it out so she could see it.

Etched onto the surface of what appeared to be parchment was a face, an agonizingly beautiful face.

She was young, maybe two years old. Her brown hair was short and fine, curled at the ends. Her eyes were the same clear blue that stared out at Kathryn from her own baby pictures. What stopped Kathryn's heart, however, was her smile. She had been captured in a moment of arrested delight, innocent joy suffusing her entire face.

"Look at her, Kathryn. Isn't she gorgeous?"

Tears were streaming down Kathryn's face. Ripping her eyes away from the image, she dropped her head into her hands, choking on her sobs. Through them she babbled, "You said she was dead. Why are you doing this? You said . . . she is dead. My daughter is dead."

Dayne knelt before her, taking both her hands in his and pulling them from her face. "*Of course I said that*. You didn't expect me to tell *them* the truth. I've kept her safe. She's hidden in a place where no one will ever be able to hurt her. Come with me now."

"I don't believe you. I *can't* believe you. Nothing you have told me from the moment we first met was the truth."

"Some of it was. When you and I were alone together, almost all of it was. It's taken me a long time to figure out how to do this. But it's finally possible. I won't ask for your forgiveness. I don't deserve it. I just need you to know that what *we* had was real, and what *we* created is the only thing in this universe I cherish."

Kathryn stared at him, into the eyes where she had once discovered the will to go on living. She had dreamed of their reunion for so long. It had been poisoned by lies, but looking at him now, she felt only confusion. Her heart had become a lead weight.

A soft alarm sounded. Dayne tapped his wrist and silenced it.

"We're out of time," he said. "Come with me now, or lose her forever."

Kathryn was already lost. Resigned, she nodded faintly.

Admiral Janeway stood outside Kathryn's quarters, hesitating. It was too soon to conclude that neither Dayne nor the rest of the Krenim would ever trouble them again. But their exchange had been promising. She hoped it might comfort Kathryn a little. She had also made copies of a few recent family photos. She had no idea how her mother and sister would react to the knowledge of *this* Kathryn's existence. Once the shock wore off, she expected both of them to offer whatever support they could. Kathryn was, after all, family. Her mother and sister had always longed to spend more time with her. During the trials that were to come as Kathryn struggled to begin a new life and leave the past behind, the admiral believed Kathryn would find the same solace and peace that had recently been so essential in helping her find her own new perspective.

She was surprised when she requested entrance and received no response. When several subsequent requests were met with silence, the admiral asked the computer to locate Kathryn. She did not allow her concern to morph into panic until the computer advised her that Kathryn was not on board the *Vesta* or any other fleet vessel.

Using her security override, the admiral unlocked the door to Kathryn's quarters and entered. The living area was silent and in perfect order. Scanning the room, her eyes fell on the entrance to the bedroom. Through the doorway she could see that the bed had been slept in. The sheet was askew and the blanket hung haphazardly over the far side of the bed.

Cautiously she moved forward. When she stepped over the threshold into the bedroom, she heard a dull crunch beneath her boot. Lifting it, she noted the crushed combadge.

A large piece of paper rested on the edge of the bed. The image it contained filled her with wonder and dread.

Nine hours later, an exhaustive search of every ship in the fleet and thorough sensor sweep of Sormana had revealed nothing apart from the fact that the woman Admiral Janeway had risked so much to save had vanished.

Those assembled in *Vesta*'s briefing room shared the same confusion. Captain Farkas sat to one side of Janeway, Decan on the other. Captain Chakotay, Tuvok, Seven, and Counselor Cambridge rounded out the small group.

In the center of the table, the image of a young female child who could have been Kathryn's twin at the same age sat face-up. For several minutes, everyone at the table seemed unable to focus on anything else.

Captain Farkas was the first to break the silence. "How did he do it? How did he take her? Did our shields malfunction?"

"Lieutenant Bryce is analyzing the carrier wave used during Dayne's transmission to me. He doesn't have anything definitive yet, but it was the only link between our ship and the *Truon*."

"Why didn't internal sensors detect his presence?" Chakotay asked.

"Are we even sure he transported aboard?" Cambridge wondered aloud.

The admiral shrugged, her eyes still glued to the image on the table. "The logs show some unusual energy readings and fluctuations in her quarters just after the *Truon* hailed us. I was speaking to him for almost ten minutes. He might have had an accomplice with him. I didn't see anyone else on the bridge but that doesn't mean anything."

"I still can't believe that she would have willingly gone anywhere with him," Farkas insisted.

Several pairs of eyes looked toward Farkas with doubt.

"If this child is hers, she might have." Admiral Janeway redirected her gaze toward Tuvok. "Is it possible, Commander, that she mentioned this to you and you didn't think to report it?"

"I weighed her right to privacy in this matter as greater than yours to that piece of intelligence."

Janeway's shoulders drooped visibly.

"I see." The admiral lifted her forefinger to the middle of her forehead and began to massage it, her expression pained.

"For what it's worth, Admiral, I understand Tuvok's position," Chakotay said.

Janeway dropped her hand in surprise.

"When he first learned of the child's existence, he shared the *denzit*'s concerns that if we did anything to attempt to locate her, it might compromise her safety. At the first opportunity he had, Tuvok tried to force Dayne to tell him where the child was. Dayne reported that she was dead."

"You knew about this as well?" Janeway asked softly.

Chakotay nodded.

"Anybody else?" Janeway asked.

After a moment, Seven raised her hand. Cambridge stared at her for a moment, aghast, then lifted his as well.

The admiral pushed back from the table and rose to her feet. She started toward the door, but thought better of it, turning back to face her senior officers with restrained fury.

"What am I supposed to . . ." she began, but trailed off, planting her hands defiantly on her hips. "Captain Farkas, begin long-range sensor scans for any signs of the *Truon*. Alert all fleet vessels to prepare to break orbit and begin a coordinated search."

"You want to go back to Krenim space?" Farkas asked.

"Not unless it becomes absolutely necessary, but I'm not ruling it out either."

"Admiral," Cambridge began, rising from his chair and approaching her warily, "are you sure that's warranted?"

"Dayne was responsible for creating her, capturing her, torturing her, manipulating her emotions to secure her trust, leaving her to die in the middle of a war zone, and apparently *stealing their child from her*. Yes, I believe a little follow-up might be in order."

"But Admiral—" Seven began.

"I'm not leaving her at his mercy."

"You don't know that she is," Chakotay offered. "I think you need to ask yourself why Dayne left this picture behind."

"It is no longer possible to distinguish between lies and truth in the case of Agent Dayne, so I'm afraid attempting to discern his motives strikes me as an exercise in futility."

"Let's make the attempt anyway," Farkas suggested.

Janeway turned on her, stunned.

"He didn't have to leave this," *Vesta*'s captain said, picking up the parchment. "Clearly he was capable of getting her off this ship with us none the wiser. He would have assumed that once we searched our ships and the planet and didn't find any evidence of her that we'd go looking for him. Maybe he left this *so we wouldn't.*"

Decan reached forward and Farkas handed him the image. He began to study it intently as the conversation continued.

"I agree," Seven offered. "Furthermore, this Kathryn Janeway is no longer our concern. We have identified her and removed her from the middle of the conflict on Sormana. We are not responsible for her subsequent choices."

"If she was taken against her will, we damn sure are," Janeway countered.

"And if she wasn't, we could be setting ourselves up for another round with the Krenim for no reason," Chakotay argued. "Think about it, Admiral. Take a minute and separate your fears from the evidence at hand. She loved him enough to marry him and bear his child. He might have been lying about a lot of things, but there had to be something between them that was real or I don't think she could have done that. If the two of them have managed to escape us and the Krenim, we wouldn't be doing her any favors by pursuing this."

Cambridge moved closer to the admiral. "You know, much as I hate to admit it, it's possible that most of what Dayne told us about his history with Kathryn is true, apart from his attempt to frame the Zahl for her original capture."

"I was there too, Counselor. His story changed every time he opened his mouth."

"To a degree," Cambridge allowed, "but why? What was his agenda? Before he came aboard he knew that the situation on Sormana had deteriorated and that the planet was about to be destroyed. Why not just lead with that? Why bother telling us anything else at all?"

"He went to great lengths to dissuade us from challenging the Krenim in any way," Farkas said. "He assured us that despite the Year of Hell, the Krenim really aren't our enemy anymore."

"Those assurances became meaningless when he admitted to Kathryn's capture," the admiral noted.

"Yes, but he did indicate that those were the orders of his *superiors*," Cambridge retorted. "If *he* truly loved her and had been planning to rescue her from Sormana on his own, our interference could have destroyed his perfect equations.

"Put yourself in his position for a moment," the counselor continued. "His agency is ordered to capture you and they end up with a temporally displaced woman who was of no use to them. Along the way, she claims his respect and perhaps his heart. He convinces his superiors to have her placed on Sormana and goes to incredible lengths to do so and then stays with her for what he believes will be the rest of her life. He never mentioned the child to us because *that* was the one variable still in play. He took the child and hid her away somewhere and as soon as he learned that Kathryn had survived, began planning to rescue her."

"Could Sormana's destruction have been part of his plan?" Farkas asked.

"When Dayne first appeared in the cavern, what did he say?" Cambridge asked of Chakotay.

"He said we were violating your agreement by transporting the torpedoes out," Chakotay replied.

"He wanted the planet destroyed. He *wanted* those chroniton pools and transporters destroyed. Not damaged, not buried under a few tons of rock, but obliterated. He could still have saved her and by eliminating Sormana made sure that wherever he planned to go, none of us would be able to follow," Cambridge insisted.

Reason broke through simmering rage. "Even *you* mocked his professions of love for her to his face," Janeway said.

Cambridge shrugged. "It was clear enough he was lying about *something*. The issue was *what*? *This*," he continued, gesturing toward the image Decan was still studying, "changes everything."

"*You* were the original problem, Admiral," Farkas said. "But all he had to do to make sure you and the *denzit* died was *nothing*. Sormana was about to go boom and we were staring down six Krenim warships. I'm not sure he cared one way or the other if *we* survived, but by allowing us to intervene when and how he did, he ensured *Kathryn's* survival."

Janeway shook her head slowly. "It's a nice thought. It's tempting to believe it because if it's true, our work here is done." She studied the faces of each of her senior officer in turn and landed on Farkas. "You honestly believe we should just let this go?"

"I think we should consider the possibility," Farkas said. "We could chase down the Krenim and demand satisfactory answers, but they might not have them. It's tough not knowing, and yes, I'm going to lose some sleep wondering if she's still being victimized by those bastards. But I don't believe it's in our best interests to go off half-cocked against a species that can predict all of our potential next moves. If we're going to take this on, we're going to need better intelligence than we have right now."

"What if we never find that intelligence?" Janeway asked.

"Why don't we give it a little more time?" Farkas suggested.

Janeway's head buzzed and a deep weariness settled itself in her bones. She had been here before, certain she knew what to do and unafraid to do it over the objections of her crew. Some deeper wisdom counseled patience, but that guidance was hard to trust when her fears were so powerful.

"Admiral, did you notice this?" Decan asked, pointing to the image.

Slowly she moved back toward the table. Settling herself

beside her aide, she stared at the picture and was struck again by the stark realism of the face. Decan's fingers grazed the bottom edge of the image, the collar and sleeves of a pale blue dress the child wore. Its edges faded out below her shoulders, but fine, dark blue lines suggested motion in the fabric. He then pointed to a distinctly heavier series of lines.

Janeway squinted at the area where Decan's fingers rested. They weren't just more intricate detail. There was a word, almost impossible to discern in their arrangement, but there if you looked hard enough.

"Mollah," Janeway whispered.

Cambridge was suddenly at her side, peering over her shoulder. "Where?"

Janeway traced her fingers over the name. Looking into Cambridge's eyes, she felt tears forming.

A slow, mystified smile spread over his lips. "I don't think that can possibly be a coincidence, do you?"

BATIBEH

Until the moment they returned to Batibeh, Kathryn Janeway had believed she was experiencing some odd, grief-induced fever dream. The clear skies above, the tall grass, the fragrances of wildflowers, the stone table, brought her back to her senses.

If this was a dream, she no longer cared.

Dayne stood beside her, his face betraying a complicated mix of emotions. Paramount among them was relief.

The village at the base of the hill was not as large as she remembered it. There were fewer structures, but more people. It was still under construction. Men, women, and children roamed about, strolling, talking, working, *living* as no one on Sormana had lived in any other version of its history.

"*When is this?*" Kathryn asked.

"Ninety-seven years after the ratification of the Peace of Sormana at this table. One hundred thirteen years, six months, and eleven days prior to your arrival with the admiral's team."

"You brought her here?"

Dayne nodded. "Moments after she was born. It was the only place I knew she would be safe."

"There's a temporal portal right there," Kathryn said, turning toward the stone pillar.

"This timeline is a temporal tangent, which means it is inaccessible from any timeline other than yours and only after the transporters are built over the chroniton pools, which won't happen for another sixty-three years. And we both know now that you were the first to use it. You were the first to look for evidence of a timeline where the war had ended. No one else on Sormana bothered. No one else thought it possible."

"You created this, and then you changed it?"

Dayne bowed his head. "Long before I met you. Then, I was only thinking of my people."

"The Krenim."

"Yes."

"Was anything you told me about yourself true?"

"I lied to you about my species and the identity of those who captured you. Nothing else."

"Have you been with her this whole time?"

"I couldn't. My people could never know she had survived. Even if they had discovered it, they wouldn't have come here to retrieve her. This is a mistake they have already corrected. They can't risk further interference here without jeopardizing the entire Imperium."

"Did you leave her to be raised by wolves?"

"Of course not. When I learned you were going to die, I came here and began to make discreet inquiries. I was looking for a couple who might be willing to take in an orphaned child. Quinn and his wife had just arrived. Apparently they had lost a child of their own. They were more than willing to raise ours. They have told the other residents that she is their niece.

"I assumed at the time that would be the end of it. Then I returned to our timeline and learned you had been brought back from the dead. You can imagine, I am sure, my relief and devastation. My Krenim superiors believed that my work with the Rilnar had ended. I couldn't convince them otherwise, nor could I return to Sormana. Since that day, my life's only purpose has been to find a way to bring you home."

"Thank you," Kathryn said sincerely. "Does this Quinn know we're coming?"

"I've kept in touch with him, even visited once a few days ago. I needed evidence that would convince you to come with me. He and his wife have understood for a long time that I intended to bring you here. They are prepared to turn over our child to your custody."

Kathryn nodded somberly.

They began to make their way down the hill. They attracted a few curious stares, but most of the inhabitants paid them no mind. Dayne directed her past the small main street toward a long row of trees where several large dwellings had been erected.

The last house on the end had a blue door. It hung open. Faint scuffling sounds could be heard within.

Kathryn paused at the low stone wall that surrounded the house's generous grounds. It was almost too much to believe that any of this was real.

A toddler stepped into the doorway on unsteady legs. She laughed in delight as a woman's voice called after her, "*I'm coming to get you.*"

With a squeal the child took a few more steps before tripping over her feet and landing in the soft grass. A woman stepped into the doorway. She was tall with a mane of flowing red hair. She wore the same rough homespun clothing as the rest of the villagers. It seemed out of place on her. She carried herself like royalty.

"Mollah," the woman chided playfully.

Kathryn's breath caught in her throat as she remembered the old woman with the bright blue eyes who had shown such concern for her the last time she'd been here. Turning a questioning gaze toward Dayne she asked, "Mollah?"

"You said you wanted to name her for your sister."

"*Phoebe* is my sister. *Molly* was my dog."

Dayne's face broke into a wide, somewhat chagrined smile. "Are you sure?"

"Were you ever listening to anything I said?"

Dayne reached for her, but stopped short when she instinctively retreated a few steps.

"I'm sorry," he said.

"No, it's just . . ."

"I understand."

Mollah was engaged in a game of tag with the woman. Kathryn watched her play as a wave of warmth washed over her, setting her extremities tingling.

The child was finally caught and lifted from the ground, laughing in her captor's face. They turned in a brief dance until the woman caught sight of Dayne and Kathryn. "Hello," she greeted them.

Her face fell as soon as she recognized them. Kathryn did not know when she had been expected to return, but the mingled sadness and resignation on the woman's face told her that *never* might have been soon enough. "Kathryn Janeway," she said, walking toward them. For her part, Mollah buried her face in the woman's neck, peeking out shyly between locks of her long, red hair.

"Hello," Kathryn said.

"Darling?" the woman said in a raised voice.

A man appeared in the doorway. Like her, he was tall. His hair was short and black, his features fine and chiseled. For the first time Kathryn was struck by the fact that both of them appeared to be human.

"There you are," he said congenially. "Took your own sweet time, didn't you, Dayne?"

"My apologies, Mister Quinn."

Quinn waved him off. "It doesn't matter. You're here now." Shifting his gaze and staring at Kathryn inscrutably he said, "Welcome home, Kathryn."

Turning to the woman, Quinn nodded. Reluctantly she said, "Mollah, it's time for you to meet your mother."

With a little effort, she pried the child from her arms and handed her to Kathryn. Mollah didn't struggle. She simply stared in wonder at Kathryn's face.

"Hello, Mollah," Kathryn whispered.

Several weeks later, in the middle of the night, Dayne accompanied Quinn and his wife back up the hill toward the stone table. He had met them here the day Mollah was born. It seemed appropriate to bid one another farewell here as well.

After a few days it had become clear to all that Kathryn was adjusting quickly to her new life. She threw herself completely into this existence, refusing to dwell on the darkness of the last several years. Mollah couldn't make her forget the pain. Kathryn spoke often with Quinn and his wife late into the evening about all she had endured. She feared that her past trauma might have broken her, that for all her love, she might not be the best influence on her daughter. She seemed to envy the simple love that existed between Mollah and her aunt and uncle.

They had counseled patience. In time she would see that her past did not have to define this present. They encouraged her to nurture the tenderness in her heart that Mollah effortlessly evoked. Its opposite lived there too, well fed and watered by circumstance and fear. But in time, those dark shadows could be banished by the light of her new life. In time, she would learn to forgive those who had wronged her, if not for her own sake, for Mollah's.

The other Keepers accepted Kathryn as eagerly as they had accepted Quinn and his wife. The couple had always introduced themselves as Mollah's aunt and uncle and had spoken freely about her mother, Kathryn, who would soon join them. The people of *this* Sormana lived to help one another. Their generous spirits sustained Kathryn as she acclimated and she soon began to find many ways to contribute to the society they were building. From time to time, Dayne, Kathryn, and Mollah journeyed to the grove where the statues of the brothers stood and once, Kathryn had asked Dayne to tell their daughter the whole story of the brothers and all they had achieved. Of necessity, Dayne had eliminated a number of details, but Kathryn had seemed satisfied.

While Dayne had visited daily and gorged himself on the many details of Mollah's first years as Quinn recounted them to Kathryn and showed her the masterful drawings he had done chronicling Mollah's development, each night Dayne returned to the *Truon,* stationed in a temporal fold just outside Sormana's orbit. There, he could perform the necessary sensor sweeps to assure himself that he had not been discovered and create the false logs that would be necessary to cover his tracks in the future.

Revealed as both Kathryn's tormentor and savior, Dayne refused to ask anything more of her than a seat at their small table for meals and the opportunity to get to know his daughter. The previous evening, Kathryn had escorted him from her new home, walking with him as far as the low wall that lined the property. She had thanked him again for making all of this possible. For the first time since they had arrived, she had permitted him to embrace her gently and hold her in his arms for a few healing moments.

He had known then that the time had come for him to go. Quinn had agreed.

Dayne had left his wife and daughter sleeping in Kathryn's bedroom, Mollah nestled in her mother's arms. A long letter explaining everything else Kathryn needed to know sat on the table by their bed, including the fact that Mollah must be instructed in the basics of temporal mechanics to avoid creating a paradox when Kathryn and the admiral visited Batibeh in a hundred and thirteen years. When she woke in the morning, Kathryn would read it. She would suffer her last betrayal at Dayne's hands. She would proceed to live the rest of her life in peace among the Keepers.

When they reached the stone table, Quinn paused. His good cheer throughout the evening had been a little forced, as had his wife's. All three had agreed upon their imminent departure. None anticipated it with any eagerness. Dayne had offered to transport them back to his ship and ferry them wherever they intended to go next. They had refused, indicating that it was unnecessary.

Placing a heavy hand on Dayne's shoulder, Quinn said, "You don't have to do this, you know."

"I do. He'll never come after her here, but he would hunt me through eternity. I can't allow that."

"You've done better than I expected."

"Thank you. *For everything.*"

Dayne turned back toward the village and took his last look at Batibeh, filled with regrets, but no doubts.

When Dayne had gone, Q turned to her husband. "It went faster than I thought it would."

"I know."

"Couldn't we stay a little longer?"

He turned to her with a kind smile and, placing an arm around her shoulder, pulled her close. "Why make it harder than it has to be? This is Kathryn's life, not ours."

"Only because *you* decided it should be so."

"I couldn't help it. Countless Kathryn Janeway's have inhabited the multiverse and only *one* chose to create a child. I couldn't let her die, any more than our son could allow his godmother to die."

"You could save all of them and it would never be enough."

"I don't need to save all of them, just this one. *She* deserved better."

"I seem to remember our son making the same argument about his godmother once and you disagreeing strenuously."

"He also asked me to forgive them. I promised I would. She is the fulfillment of that promise. She is my redemption."

"He would have loved Mollah."

Q nodded. As he inhaled deeply, a smile crept over his lips.

As he exhaled, his wife sensed the shift and stared up at him in surprise.

"Did you just. . ."

". . . Sever this timeline from the rest of the multiverse for the rest of Kathryn's life? Yes, I did. I know it has to be restored eventually, but this is one happy ending no one is going to take away from me."

"That's cheating."

"I don't care. He would have approved."

"Now you're playing God?"

Q's gentle smile turned wicked.

"Who's playing?"

Epilogue

VESTA

Good morning, Admiral Janeway."

"Captain Chakotay," Janeway said, pulling on her uniform jacket as she checked herself in the mirror and put a few errant strands of hair back in place.

He hadn't shared her quarters for the last week. He had hoped she would reach out to him and had been disappointed. He would be departing with *Voyager* for the Beta Quadrant in a few hours and despite the fact that he knew that eventually they would again make peace, he didn't like leaving with so much unsettled between them.

"How much are you planning to share with the Nihydron?" Chakotay asked.

"The truth, the whole truth, and nothing but the truth," she replied.

The response stung, as she had, no doubt, intended. "Are you ever going to forgive me?"

Kathryn exhaled slowly, crossed to her replicator, and ordered a cup of coffee. After a few sips she said, "I already have. I had to for my own peace of mind. We've been down this road before, Chakotay. We're intelligent, powerful, compassionate people. When we believe we are right, we are rarely compelled by the arguments of others to abandon our position. There is nothing either of us would not sacrifice to secure the safety of those we command. We ask a great deal of each other, sometimes because duty demands it, and sometimes because we know we can. Loving each other means accepting all of it, even the worst we have to offer each other.

"Much as I might have wanted to at first, I cannot lay the blame for this one entirely at your feet. We teach others how to treat us. If you honestly believed me incapable of choosing the right course had I known of the child's existence, it's because I have yet to show you otherwise."

"That's not true."

"No?"

"You and I haven't enjoyed any length of time together uncomplicated by the needs of the fleet or this mission. You've made choices since you returned that I found disturbing. In the fullness of time, however, I've come to see that usually when that happens it's because you're thinking a few steps ahead of me. It's unnerving. I'm supposed to know you better than anyone and when I start to lose my bearings, I tend to look at the past for guidance. It occurs to me now how great a mistake that is. Neither of us is operating from our old technical manuals. We're in new, uncharted territory."

"You weren't wrong about my first instincts. Neither was Tuvok, Seven, or Hugh. When I believed it necessary, I *would* have done anything in my power to save her. Where you all erred was in your assumptions about my willingness to consider other points of view. It's hard to accept that those you trust can't return the favor. It's harder to accept that there's good reason for that. I don't blame any of you for fearing that I would do exactly what I've always done in the past. What troubles me is that you all seem to doubt my ability to learn from old mistakes."

"If I do, it's only because I have the same problem."

Janeway nodded thoughtfully. "Something we both need to work on then."

"I think so."

"I want to say good-bye to Tuvok. Walk with me?"

"Of course."

VOYAGER

Much to her surprise, Admiral Janeway found Tuvok in the Paris family quarters, holding young Michael Paris in his arms. Tom and B'Elanna hovered nearby. Lieutenant Kim was also present and divided his time between helping Miral construct a tall tower of magnetic blocks and joining in the others' conversations. The remains of a large breakfast littered the dining table.

As Janeway watched Tuvok share a few stories of his own children when they were infants, she marveled at the transformation she was seeing in him. She didn't know precisely how to account for it. Most of the choices Tuvok had made during this extended mission seemed to indicate a distinct desire to keep his distance from his old friends. He had kept his own counsel, to a fault. Given what he had shared with her of his ongoing struggle to accept his son's death, it was extraordinary to see him holding Tom's with such obvious tranquility.

The group was forced to disperse a few minutes before the beginning of alpha shift. Tuvok offered to accompany the admiral back to the transporter room to see her off.

As they walked, they chatted about the baby, the utter transformation of Tom and B'Elanna, Lieutenant Kim's ease in his new role as chief of security and ongoing command training, and how small the galaxy was becoming with the advent of Starfleet's use of slipstream technology.

They reached the transporter room much too quickly for the admiral's taste. Turning to face him for what she assumed would be the last time for at least a few years she said, "I want you to know how much I appreciate your willingness to assist us with this mission."

"It is I who owe you a debt of gratitude, Admiral."

"Oh?"

"For more than a year, the majority of my time spent in personal reflection has been dedicated to restoring my mental discipline. My wife, T'Pel, has been a constant source of support, but she was not present for most of the years I served Starfleet and as a result, cannot fully appreciate the depth of the relationships I have formed. She has attempted to protect me from distractions. What we both overlooked was the fact that insight is not only gained by personal reflection, often it is acquired by unexpected experiences that bring new perspectives to our analysis. This mission has been most unexpected and extremely helpful in that regard."

Janeway wished there was time for him to elaborate. She wanted desperately to understand exactly how he had come to this realization. She could only trust his words and be grateful that he had found something of use in the time he'd spent with her fleet.

"You should know, Admiral, that I counseled Captain Chakotay to withhold his knowledge of Kathryn's child from you."

"Somehow that doesn't surprise me. It seems both of the men I consider my closest friends share a certain amount of pessimism when it comes to my ability to evaluate the ratio between risk and reward."

"Do you believe that fear to be well grounded?"

"Not anymore. I do wonder how long it will take for both of you to stop judging me by the sins of my past and simply walk beside me into the future. Before this mission, if anyone had asked me to name the two people I trust most in the universe, it would have been you and Chakotay. That's still true, but it's odd to think that the feeling isn't mutual. The Krenim classified me as a *chaotic variable*. I guess they're not the only ones."

"Did they not classify all Federation contacts as such?"

"I suppose."

"Then you are in excellent company, Admiral. For my part, I can only apologize for any actions I have taken that have caused you to doubt my personal regard for you. Please forgive me."

Janeway nodded.

"Captain Chakotay is in a difficult position. His primary concern is the safety of his crew, as it should be. When that conflicts with his sense of obligation to you—"

Janeway raised a hand to silence him. "Chakotay and I are still struggling to find an appropriate balance between our duties and our personal relationship. We are a work in progress."

"Permit me to wish you success in finding that balance. Despite these setbacks, the choice you have made seems to agree with both of you."

"It does."

"As someone who has been married for several decades, I can tell you that eventually, misunderstandings such as this will prove comforting given their frequency and familiarity."

"So, I've got that to look forward to?"

"I arrived during what seems to me to have been a period of transition for you. I am sorry that the requirements of this mission did not give us the opportunity to discuss your recent experiences in more detail. I would appreciate the opportunity to hear more about them and the corresponding insights that have arisen from them."

"I'd be willing to keep in touch when time permits."

"As would I."

Janeway offered Tuvok her hand. He accepted it, holding it in both of his for a long moment. "Take care, my friend."

"Live long and prosper, Kathryn."

KRENIM TEMPORAL DEFENSE AGENCY VESSEL *ARCANA*

Almost as soon as the *Truon* had emerged from hiding, Dayne received the signal he had been dreading. He lowered his vessel's shields as ordered and was transported aboard the Krenim Temporal Defense Agency's commanding vessel, the *Arcana*.

Dayne materialized in a holding cell. His brother was waiting for him.

"Obrist."

"Brother. I would ask when and where you have been, but I fear I know the answer. What I do not understand is why you have chosen to betray us."

"Did you not receive my last report? Nothing of note has transpired since then, or I would have made contact."

"Yes, your report. *Admiral Kathryn Janeway was restored to life by an omnipotent species known as the Q.*" Obrist's fury began to seep through the cracks of his stoic façade. "You didn't believe that nonsense, nor did you think for one minute that *I* would accept it, did you?"

"While outside the realm of our experience, what she said is not impossible. It explains a great deal, including our inability to appropriately calculate her ongoing impact on the Imperium."

"If it was true. *But it isn't, is it, brother?*"

"We should incorporate that data into our equations and examine the results together, just as we always have."

Obrist's face turned cold, suddenly devoid of emotion. Simultaneously, Dayne felt the heavy embrace of the collar being secured around his neck by one of Obrist's interrogation specialists.

"We have been of one mind for so long, brother. It never occurred to me that we would ever reach a parting of the ways. It saddens me more than I can tell you to have arrived at this day. But the security of the Imperium we have built depends upon our ability to distinguish the possible from the probable, the truth from the lies. Tell me the truth, Dayne. *When* have you been?"

Dayne brought the image of Kathryn and Mollah sleeping peacefully in each other's arms to the forefront of his mind and held it there, one last time. Then, he locked it away in the compartment in his mind reserved for truths he could never tell.

Abruptly, a searing beam of white-hot energy shot through his body. He had watched the interrogators inflict similar suffering on others, including Kathryn. Until now, he had never truly appreciated her strength. The pain gripping him was exquisite. As long as it continued, it banished all other thoughts and feelings. It enveloped him in agony so complete it seemed he *must* cease to exist. In none of her interrogation sessions had Kathryn ever betrayed the total despair the sensation provoked.

He would die before sacrificing the safety of his wife and daughter. After the second wave of fire took him, he could smell the charred flesh where the collar rested. He knew better but clung to the hope that death would take him quickly.

He had already tasted all he would ever know of paradise at Batibeh. It was enough.

ACKNOWLEDGMENTS

I've had the story of the *other* Kathryn Janeway living in my mind for so many years, pestering me without cease, I simply had to get it out. I'm grateful to Margaret for allowing me to do so, for her patience, and for always guiding me through the rough spots. Also to Ed, who always makes me look way better than I am.

Massive thanks, as always, to my fellow authors Chris Bennett, David Mack, and David R. George III. Chris's work continues to challenge me to explore concepts I find terrifying. If Mack would just write one less-than-fantastic novel, I'd sleep better at night rather than constantly worrying about how far I have to go. I ran this story by DRG before I even started to outline the proposal. His first comment: "You're going to solve that in 100,000 words?" I hate how much smarter he is than I am.

Mark Rademaker deserves yet another nod for his quick and brilliant responses to my questions.

Maura's faith in me is unsurpassed. One day, I'll prove worthy of it.

This one is for Lynne. Everyone should know a woman like her, someone defined by their generosity of spirit. I am blessed beyond reason by her presence in my life.

My family and friends are still standing by me. I'll never know why, but I'll take it.

What little I know of truth lives in every breath of my daughter, Anorah. The strength of my husband, David, stuns me at every unexpected turn in the road. Their love is carrying me through this life. I wouldn't be here without them.

ABOUT THE AUTHOR

Kirsten Beyer is the author of nine of the last *Star Trek: Voyager* novels released by Pocket Books. Between the first and second, she wrote an *Alias* novel and the final novel ever written for *Buffy the Vampire Slayer*. She has also written a few short stories and articles, most about *Star Trek*, and a few original screenplays, not about *Trek*.

She does not have a website, a blog, a Facebook page, nor does she tweet. Those wishing to find her online should check out the literature section on the TrekBBS. She looks forward to establishing a more robust presence on the internet—just as soon as she figures out how to write faster or discovers more than twenty-four hours in each day.

Kirsten received undergraduate degrees in English Literature and Theater Arts. She also received a master's degree from UCLA. She never intended to use her education to pursue a career as a novelist. But apparently, somebody up there had different plans.

When she's not writing, she tries to extract every last drop of happiness she can from her life as a wife, a mother, a daughter, and a friend.

For now, she has no complaints.